GUARDIAN
OF THE CORE

GUARDIAN
OF THE CORE

THE TRIALS OF THE CORE

MICHAEL E. THIES

Writer's Block Press

Slinger, Wisconsin

Guardian of the Core
The Trials of the Core
©2014 Michael E. Thies

For information, please contact:

 Writer's Block Press

Writer's Block Press, P.O. Box 438, Slinger WI, 53086
info@writersblockpress.net

The Trials of the Core is a work of fiction. Names, characters, places and incidents originate from the author's imagination and are used fictitiously. Any resemblance to actual persons, living or dead, events, or locales is entirely coincidental.

Cover Design by Angela Schmitt
Family Crests and Badges by Melissa Thies
Map by Melissa Thies

ISBN: 978-0-9895668-0-3
eBook ISBN: 978-0-9895668-2-7
Library of Congress Control Number: 2013952444

www.guardianofthecore.com

TABLE OF CONTENTS

Thank you to my family who helped fund this dream.

*A special thank you to Eichy and Jon
who have been with this story from the beginning.*

*And, finally, to all my fans who have supported me
throughout its creation.*

I hope you enjoy the adventure as much as I enjoyed writing it.

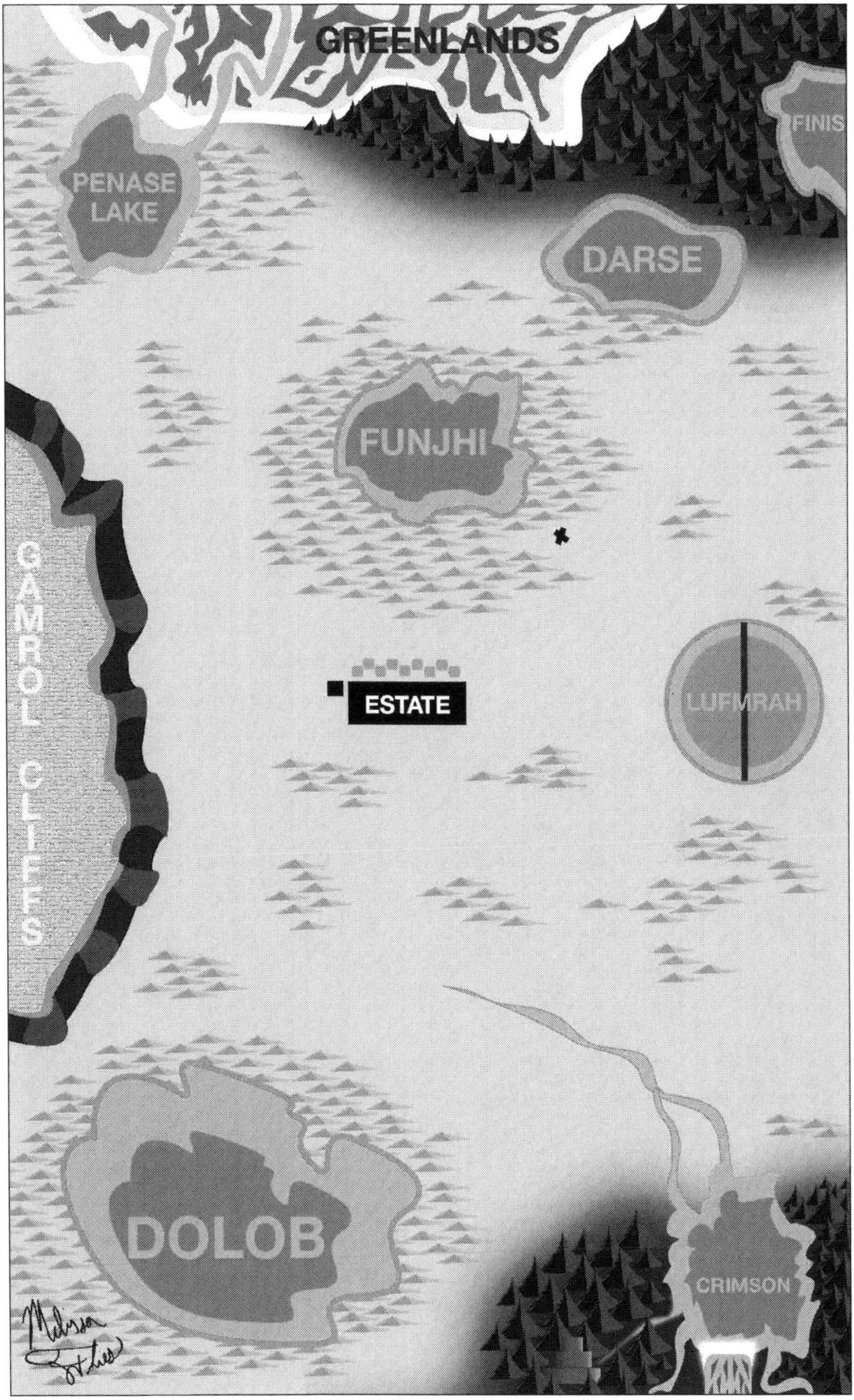
GREENLANDS
FINIS
PENASE LAKE
DARSE
FUNJHI
GAMROL CLIFFS
ESTATE
LUFMRAH
DOLOB
CRIMSON

✤ PROLOGUE ✤

Greetings,

I take this pen in hand today as you have taken your life in your own hands. It is my greatest honor to congratulate you in your acceptance of the application sent two years past. Tens of thousands applied, but only you and select others will have the chance to participate in the event of a lifetime. My trusted conseleigh have been examining you and have recommended individuals of the highest tier, excelling in strength of self, mind, and body.

If you accept this offer, the Trials you face will be extremely difficult, designed to push you past your maximum potential. The winner will be titled as my apprentice and will have the honor of training under my staff and I until my two hundredth year as Guardian of the Core arrives. Further details will be explained upon your arrival. Good luck.

> *Sincerely,*
> *Guardian Edwyrd Eska*

• • •

The pen flitted across each letter in rhythmic repetition as Guardian Eska signed the last of eight invitations. Cards of thicker stock had previously been laid on his desk by two of his conseleigh. Eska waved his gloved hand over all eight sets. The cards hovered, defying wind and gravity both. The letters slid into the crimson envelopes and then fell to an onyx desk thick with emerald veins.

Eska removed his ring, given to him during a Coronation long past. Golden wax coated the obsidian band, hiding Eska's sigil—a dragon, with wings outstretched, spewing fire. He pushed the ring down and sealed the first envelope. Footsteps echoed in the hallways across the midsize cavity of moss-green aventurine floors and jade pillars, stopping before the stairs that led to where Eska sat. Though they echoed, Eska wouldn't have needed the sound to sense the man's presence. He continued sealing the rest of the envelopes. "Is the ship ready, Luvan?"

"Lady Tundra is readying it now. The air here is short. How long will it be?"

For Eska, the air in the room was fine. But the others were sure to be having difficulties. "We will have leave soon enough."

"Thank you, my guardian."

While his conseleigh's footsteps retreated, Eska waved his hand over the finished envelopes. He stood from his chiseled and polished seat of shakti—a rock of celadon color corded in black. As his hand passed over each envelope, it rose and floated above him, following him through another hallway that led deeper into a cavernous floating isle—to a place he had not been for one hundred and fifty years. Only he and his conseleigh knew of this place, but only he knew of the woman waiting for him at path's end.

Lighted moss clung to the pale-blue walls, serving as torches. A dominance carried with Eska, the sort no other man or woman in the universe wielded. His eyes were narrowed like the pathway. His glove was stitched of the same darknether material as his jerkin, black like the shadow that lingered behind his silken cape of gold and crimson.

At the corridor's end, the narrow path opened to a large cove with blue walls that spun like the wind in five separate places—one portal for each planet. A woman waited in the center of the room, and Guardian Eska took his spot next to her. Her lips, lush and blue like the hair that bounded past her shoulders, gave false testimony to her age. Through her transparent gown, her skin shone like a moon during the grave of night.

This wasn't his first time in the cove, but it was his first time using the portals on the wall. The halo of letters that had been floating above him separated to three spots on the wall, ignoring two. Here, the air was even thinner. From a strand of gossamer around Eska's neck, a gray orb moved toward the woman; her power attracted it, a desire to return to its creator.

Eska nodded at her. "All of the letters will be delivered, yes?"

"As sure as the wind blows," she said.

"Then let the Trials commence."

❧ CHAPTER 1 ❧

PRINCE HYDRO

Even past midday, Freyr didn't have much bearing on the stone court. Lord's Keep was too tall, and the sun was not even at its zenith yet. In its current position, the two sparring figures managed to produce two slender shadows dancing in rhythmic beats of one another.

Hydro Paen's younger brother, Aiton, looked on closely from the shaded portion of the castle walls. Aiton sat in a longchair, held tight by his mother. His mother's friends were there too—marchionesses from different provinces of Acquava. Elias Ward, his father's adored, had also taken a spot amongst the crowd, waiting to tend to any injury. Hydro tried not to focus on them, but every so often he caught himself stealing a gaze, watching for his mother's eye, which never seemed to look. Mostly Hydro focused on the man in front of him: Korth.

Korth swung his sword upward, forcing Hydro into a backflip. Upon landing, he ducked to avoid another stroke. Using his momentum, Hydro propelled his body forward, lance in front, attempting to pierce Korth's seachrome armor—the front and back pieces attached by strong fishing lines, and instead of chainmail covering any openings on his side, rows upon rows of tightened clam shells protected him. Upon the breast was a droplet of water pierced and shattered by a sword. It was the Paen insignia, the pride of Hydro's house.

Hydro missed. Now his back was exposed. He tugged on the golden chain attached to his sapphire lance and spun around, ready to block an incoming attack.

"Good reflexes, Prince," said Korth. His thick moustache bobbed up and down beneath the gap of his seachrome helm.

"I do not need your praise, Korth."

Hydro jabbed his lance forward, but it was batted away. A heavy boot struck his stomach, causing his chest to heave inward. Defeat rang thrice as the lance clattered on the court.

"You may not need my praise, but you certainly need my help. Your lance skills are still only mediocre." Korth grinned, extending his sea-leather glove, dotted in brine, down to Hydro.

Hydro looked toward the crowd and saw his mother smirking at him.

I will show you I am not a failure. Hydro ignored the hand and returned to his feet by himself. "I do not need my lance when I can best you with a sword. Shall we practice that?"

Hydro crouched down and pushed aside the golden chain on his lance, exposing a small slit. Slightly above the slit was a silver band, colored different from the rest of the sapphire lance. A black button rose outwards from the lance a quarter-inch above the silver. Hydro gripped the band and pushed the black button with his thumb. He concentrated on forming a sword, and within seconds, the malleable liquid steel—zircha—started to transfer. In no longer than five seconds, he held it ready.

"No. You will practice power now. A prince must be trained in both."

"Humph. Very well." Hydro stowed away his sword and waited for the court to be set.

From the shadows of East Wall, a water basin was brought forth by guards Hydro didn't bother taking note of. Lamps—one of gas and fire, the other of electricity—were placed alongside the basin. Elemental power could only be cast if it already existed in its natural form and only if visible—thus it was labeled the lowest of the three tiers of power. Now, with the addition of the lamps, all four elements could be drawn from. (Earth was the easiest of them all due to its overwhelming majority and proximity. In fact, it would always be the easiest element to conquer, unless one was falling through the air or at sea.)

Hydro allayed his mind by breathing and closing his eyes, letting some of his untapped senses investigate the surrounding. Seagulls chirped, and the sound of water splashing against the rocks soon became obvious, as did the smell of salt and brine. Power flowed, tingling the tips of his fingers. The cool warmth calmed him as nothing else could. Hydro opened his eyes and saw Korth pace around the individual elements, then flick his hand and move his lips.

"*Maa*," Hydro said. Parts of the stone court shot up to deflect the incoming lightning bolt. Hydro soon saw flames dance over the top of the earthen shield, so he jumped back and let the spell die—the stone court returning to normal. "*Vesi*," Hydro said. Water from the basin overflowed and slid to the fire, quickly drowning it.

The session continued like this for another five rounds. Korth constantly tested Hydro's speed and knowledge of power's hierarchy: earth for thunder, thunder for water, water for fire, fire for earth. The ferocity of the spell and its speed was linked to emotion and confidence. Because of this, Hydro constantly readjusted and prioritized which spell needed attention. As fatigue replaced his strength, sweat slid down his body beneath his tunic. Then, the spells stopped.

"Practice endurance now. Start with earth," Korth commanded.

"*Maa*." A spire cracked from the middle of the stone court and shot upwards, increasing in girth all the while.

"Raise it higher."

Hydro let the power seize him, and he pushed the spire up, soon nearing the height of the parapets.

"Hold."

Hydro closed his eyes and focused, thinking of nothing else but the spire of earth in front of him. His brow started to sweat, but he continued holding the spell. His heart throbbed and his fingers twitched as he dug deeper into himself. He wanted to open his eyes, but that would cause him to lose focus.

"Release."

Hydro opened his eyes and gasped. The spire fell back to the stone court, returning it to normal.

"Impressive, Prince Hydro. You are quite the sorcerer," said Korth.

Korth's praise was empty flattery. The earth could have risen like Mount Klaff—to the very heavens of Axiumé itself—instead of only reaching the height of East Tower.

Still panting, Hydro looked up and noticed a man—completely bald—hobbling his way from the shade of East Tower with the help of a golden cane inlaid with sapphire vines. Gray spots on his head resembled the islands of Acquava. Hydro recognized the Paen insignia on his overflowing white robe before the man started speaking.

A hand extended a sealed bag of cerise leaves. "Would my prince care for some ard leaves to replenish his strength?" The man's voice shook just as much as the large bracelets on his wrist. The bracelets represented his knowledge in unique elements and compounds created and given by Ancient Lyoen, the alchemist—ard leaves being one of them.

"No, Elias. I will call you over if I need your assistance."

"But you must."

"I must not do anything—unless my father commands it of me. Do well to remember that."

"Elias," Korth said, "it's fine. Prince Hydro will regain his strength as he watches Aiton's training."

"Very well."

To Hydro's dismay, this would be one of his shorter sessions; usually he went through all the spells at least once, but holding a spire of that height for so long was more taxing than Hydro had anticipated. He ran a hand through his jet-black hair and watched as Aiton was released from his mother's clutch. His brother of eight years had the same hair as Hydro, which was attributed to them by their father. Like his mother, though, Aiton had green eyes, whereas Hydro had hazel—a mixture of his parents.

From the longchair near his mother's location, Hydro glanced at her. She exchanged quick words with Marchioness Luuise Tityle of Katarh and flicked her brown hair, exposing the pearls pierced to her ear and her fingers fit with rings—all things made available to her through marriage. Then she returned her gaze to Aiton and took a sip of red wine.

Hydro watched the light session of sword play with dilapidated interest, remembering the times when he was forced to spar and train with power so that upon going to the privileged school, Finesse, he would be completely competent. Since graduating there, Hydro was required to sit in at his father's council sessions and study languages and customs with the family's receiver, Darien Dornell, and the family's advisor, Len Posair. Hydro found all of it rather droll.

At certain points during the light sparring session, Hydro glanced at his mother, who never seemed to take her eyes off of Aiton. *Mother has never watched me the whole time.* Before he looked away, he noticed his father walking toward them from the entrance to the castle's open interior. He held something in his hand, but from a distance Hydro couldn't tell what it was.

He returned his gaze to Aiton, who focused on moving his hips in sync with his strokes. The real lesson Korth was trying to teach, though, was to not be stationary. "Warriors still standing do not stand still" is what he preached in an accent that befit a true native of West Hart, an island in the Broken Sea. It was that accent and Korth's superb skill in melee fighting that charmed the crowd during the tourney celebrating Hydro's birth. With age, he grew in rank and now was commander of Lord Paen's acqua guards.

For fourteen years younger than Hydro, Aiton showed true promise with the blade—he already stabbed and sliced with combinations he had most likely gleaned from Hydro's sessions with Korth.

Heavy footsteps pulled Hydro's attention away from his brother. A hand squeezed his shoulder, and Hydro looked up to see his father staring down at him.

His father let a crimson envelope fall to Hydro's lap. "Open this."

He picked it up and turned it around, instantly recognizing the golden wax seal. *Guardian Eska!* He looked up and noticed that the sparring had stopped, and now Hydro's mother looked at him with curiosity. Behind her, the marchionesses stood, wanting to get a glimpse of what was occurring.

Prying apart the seal, Hydro took out the letter and read its contents aloud. Upon the word *accepted* he stood up and looked at his father and then at all the others. "I have been accepted to partake in Guardian Eska's Trials."

Hydro heard clapping and for a faint moment saw a smile form on his mother's lips, but quickly it faded into conversations with her guests: Lyane Puwl, Marchioness of the northeastern province, Rhemu; Luuise Tityle, Marchioness of the northern province, Katarh; and finally, Enya Periwinkle, Marchioness of East Hart isle. Here, where the sea breeze kept the warm air in check, each female noble wore a loose-flowing gown of a different color of silk patched with her province's sigil—the seahorse of Rhemu trotting over a sea, the frozen flower of Katarh, and the coral reef of East Hart isle.

"Hydro, follow me. We have much to discuss."

Without hesitation, Hydro obeyed. As he was led away from the stone court, he noticed his mother's glare. *Do you despise that you will have to answer to me when I win the Trials?* After blaming him for his sister's death six years prior, his mother had never taken note of any of his accomplishments. He didn't exist to her, unless he failed.

Inside the mansion, which stood inside the castle walls guarding their home, a butler stood ready with refreshments on a tray. Hydro took one and continued following his father through the first floor hallways.

Pictures of his family's lineage embellished the light-colored walls. Guest rooms were located here for the families of power who decided to visit the keep or engage in business with his father.

The second floor is where Hydro's room was, adjacent to his younger brother's room. His sister's room was also located on the second floor, but it had never been opened since her death. All three rooms were stationed on one side of the floor. The study and the communication and information processing chamber were on the other side.

The third floor was patrolled by suited guards armed with poleaxes. Seachrome half-helms exposed only jaws and noses, and a visor was placed over their eyes. From each veranda to the right and left of the royal chambers one had the perfect spot to see the Amughd Forest and, rising from the very heart of it, Mount Tyld—a starseer's dream to watch the night sky. Also from the veranda, one could get a marvelous look at the labyrinth of hedges located beyond the stone court. In the center of the labyrinth was a water fountain shaped like a dolphin, in recognition of the bonded animal of Acquava's first Paen ruler, Lyonell Paen.

Once inside, Hydro took note of the renowned chamber. It hosted a king-size bed with delft-blue sheets tucked beneath golden-silk pillows resting against a polished and petrified black walnut board. A walk-in closet—extended ten paces to the left—stood next to the bathroom, which included faucet handles made of gold against ivory.

Brushing a wrinkle out of the sheets, Hydro asked, "Why did you want to talk with me?"

"Not anyone can just go to the Core. There must be some sort of transportation. From where does the letter say you need to be picked up?"

Hydro reread the letter. "It does not say." He looked inside the envelope and noticed a little card he had not seen before. "Wait." There was a black button on the center of it; underneath it was a timer counting downward. The ink that created the numbers changed continuously—but by power or technology, Hydro couldn't tell.

"That is a telecard. Play it."

Hydro pushed the button, and a green light cascaded from the card, stopping directly in front of his face. A hologram played before him.

"Hydro Paen II, my name is Tundra Iycel, one of Guardian Eska's four conseleigh. Listen closely, for this letter will only play once. A ship will pick you up from Encenro Falls once the timer on this card reaches zero. If you are

not there within the allotted time, you will not be allowed to attend the Trials. Guardian Eska looks forward to meeting all of the contestants in person. Good luck."

Hydro glanced at the timer. Slightly more than forty hours remained. "Do you know where Encenro Falls is?"

"It is on Dotted Isle, near Roil, across from Crake." Hydro's father leaned forward with his hands on top of a dresser as he looked into the large mirror directly across from their bed. He straightened his posture and walked over to Hydro. "Although there is easily enough time to get you there, an event like this needs to be treated in proper fashion. I will begin making proper arrangements."

Hydro felt the squeeze of his father's hand on his left shoulder. "What will you do?"

"Do not worry about that. Go prepare for departure. We leave by midday tomorrow."

Hydro left the room and descended the staircase. *What does Father have planned for me?* Possibilities spun in his mind as he packed. It wasn't long after he started that he heard a pattering of feet on the marble flooring. "Aiton," he called. The patters stopped. His door creaked open.

"How did you know it was me?"

"Power," Hydro teased. In truth, it was their blood that connected them. *Blood brothers*, as some called it. But Aiton would learn about that soon enough. "How were the rest of lessons today?"

"Short. When you left, everyone wanted to know what you and Father were doing."

"Planning, Aiton."

"You are going to become the next Guardian of the Core?"

"When I win the Trials, I will be apprentice. And then guardian."

"What does apprentice do?"

Hydro folded another piece of clothing and put it in his bag. "I assume learn everything the guardian does . . ."

"As guardian are you going to fight monsters like Guardian Eska does? Are you going to climb Mount Klaff like Guardian Eska?"

"If monsters need to be fought and if climbing Mount Klaff is a requirement, I will. But the guardian also protects something very valuable."

"What is it? From whom?" Aiton's eyes widened.

"No one knows what it is. Father does not even know."

"Will you tell me what it is when you become guardian?"

"Yes."

"I know you will win. You are so powerful with your magic. . . . I cannot even cast yet."

Hydro lifted his brother's head by taking his chin. "I promise, Aiton, that I will do everything in my power to help you cast."

"You promise?"

"Yes."

"Thank you, Hydro."

Hydro got the hug he had been waiting for.

"Aiton, here!" His mother's voice cut short Hydro's moment of relaxation. "If you hug your brother while he still wears those filthy clothes, you will ruin yours. We have company tonight."

Aiton bobbed his head. "Yes, Mother."

"Go along to your room now."

"Yes, Mother."

"What is it your father wanted to talk with you about?"

Hydro looked at his mom, who stood at the threshold of his door. "Ask him." Hydro stood.

"He is gone."

Already? What does he have planned? "He and I leave tomorrow midday. I am sure you are glad about that." He walked over to her and looked down into her green eyes, the same eyes Aiton had acquired.

"I only hope you do not make a fool of this family and lose."

You would hate that even more than I would. Before Father, you were nothing. And now you're blood is our family's greatest secret. "What makes you think I will lose?"

"You cannot even best Korth."

"You missaw, then."

"I saw the first part of your training perfectly."

"Well, then you missed the second."

"In war, you do not get a second chance. If you are bested the first time, you die. Please, tell me if it is different."

Hydro roiled inside. *Father never should have married you. I could have been born by another. How dare you. Ever since—*

She spoke again, "Be down to supper at the proper time. And bring your letter. I, along with the other families here, want to read it." She turned and left, her heels clacking all the way.

Why does she continue to hate me? Hydro hung his head and stopped the slight wetness in his eyes. If either of them could just forget the mutual wrongdoings they had incurred—not conversing unless necessary, forgetting the past pain of Anya's death—maybe then they could stomach each other. That would never happen though. Their Paen pride wouldn't allow it.

❧CHAPTER 2❧

EIREK

"Ena, you need to resurface that dirt. It needs to be level and not clumpy." Mara Surg hadn't looked at the saddle in her hands for ten minutes. "Osker, retrim the hedges. Daphne, bring water here for the flowers."

Eirek tapped his fingers on the side of his hip. *How much longer is she going to order them around before she finally approves of the last saddle?* He looked around to the open expanse of yard with multiple flower gardens and pine trees, tall and strong.

"Kywin, bring the tarp to the back; there will need to be shade once the guests arrive."

"Lady Surg, the saddle, if you will," Eirek said, hoping to draw her attention away from her servants so he could leave her battalion.

Mara Surg twisted her lips and clicked her tongue. After glaring at Eirek for a moment, she twisted her hands and examined every inch of the saddle. They ran over the leather three times. "It will have to do."

Thank you.

"Payment?"

"Both saddles come to a silver spell and six copper cures."

"Wait here. Do not come inside; I do not want the dirt on your shoes to affect our floors. They are being done." Mara Surg turned around, opened the door, and walked into a lobby with a checkerboard floor of white and black. "Ella, you missed a spot before the stairs. And do not forget to polish the stairs either." She walked up the staircase, constantly looking at the unlit chandelier. "And the chandelier needs to be lit—still. I suppose I will have to do that."

How does Angal treat with these people?

Ever since abandoning Eirek twelve years previous, Angal had spent his time traveling to various families of power and telling tales. He was good with words, but never good with family. But Eirek wasn't his own, so what did it matter? He was only the uncle.

When Mara Surg came back down the staircase, she held a candle in her hand. Eirek saw her lips move with her hand as she flung multiple separate fires to the candles on the chandelier. *Power!* Eirek stole a quick glance at his hands. It was not quick enough.

"Do not worry about being able to cast. You probably cannot. Here is payment. Also, here is a golden bond. It is the birthday of my twin daughters, so I am feeling generous." Mara Surg extended a golden coin.

How does she know I can't cast? Eirek avoided looking at her, not wanting to chance ruining the opportunity to get additional money. He held out his hand and let her drop the coppers and silvers and gold coin into it. "Thank you, Lady Surg."

"Yes, well, safe travels." She reentered the lobby and closed the door behind her.

Eirek turned around and walked back to his caravan located on the gravel path that led to the estate. He climbed up and sat down on the bench, setting the golden bond next to him—it was the only pleasant thing about the appointment.

As he drove the caravan away, he saw all the workers under the watch of the open suns: Freyr, the great red sun, and Lugh, the small blue wanderer. *How can they stand this?* At the end of the path, he steered the horses left, to a road that would eventually lead through the Amon Forest and back to Creim. *Is she always this demanding or is it because it's her daughters' birthdays?* Still, Eirek was impressed with how she was able to cast power.

A slight bump due to a strewn tree branch signaled that they had reached the skirts of the forest. Eirek let go of the rein with one hand and held his other to eye level. "*Palo.*"

Nothing.

Looking toward the suns, Eirek held his hand up high. "*Palo.*"

Still nothing.

He then looked toward the ground and lowered his arm in that direction. "*Maa.*"

And still nothing.

Eirek slouched a little more, picked up the golden bond, and returned to gripping the reins with both hands. *Why can't I cast?*

To avoid answering the question he posed himself, he looked at the surroundings. Trees, tall and thin, stood stationery to the path of fallen brush and dirt that helped guide Eirek. Squirrels scattered to and fro, and birds chirped.

Eirek listened, but eventually the sounds of nature fell and were replaced by raucous noises of drunken activity in Creim's Square, located five miles from the skirts of the forest. Instead of trees, hip-high crude metal fencing soon became his companion as he traveled another three miles to the place he called home. He hadn't started hearing it until a mile and a half out of the forest, but here at the burgundy house he called home, it was quite the distraction, and a broken screen door wouldn't alleviate the problem any time soon.

This was the Mourses' house, and he had been left here by his uncle, Angal, twelve years ago when Eirek was only seven. Although the Mourses weren't blood family, they were complete, and that's what mattered. Unlike Angal, they saw him more than once every year; unlike Angal, they had a steady profession of blacksmithing instead of a wandering minstrel; and unlike Angal, they cared about him.

Eirek walked up the steps and didn't bother opening the front door, just pulled back the screen, hoping to keep quiet. To his dismay, the wooden door creaked, betraying his presence.

"Jerald . . . Jahn, is that you?"

"No."

"Eirek?"

"Yes."

"Help set the table."

In the kitchen, Eirek found Sheryin preparing a meal. Upon his entering, she turned around and smiled at him through portly lips and eyes the color of the salad greens that had already found their way onto the table. They were the kind of eyes that obliged him to do anything he was asked.

As he set the plates, Sheryin laid a bowl of ham and another of skinned potatoes in the center of a table too large for the kitchen. Or perhaps it was Sheryin who was larger than expected compared to the lean and muscled men she lived with. Eirek was lean, but not as muscled as the blacksmiths who pounded iron and steel daily.

Jahn and Jerald came in fifteen minutes after the last of the plates was set. Their clothes, covered in sweat and charcoal, signified a hard day. Both had lean faces with eyes the like of the steel they forged. Jahn was near

Eirek's height. Jerald was shorter, with a stockier frame and a belly hard and round from good eating. His hands were thicker than his son's and made the silverware look small. Neither bothered changing clothes but simply washed his hands in a bucket of water on the kitchen counter and sat. Jahn took a spot next to Eirek.

"Eirek, would you like to lead us in prayer?" Sheryin asked.

"Goddess Trema, thank you for your seeds of fertility to which we owe ourselves and our livestock. We offer thanks to you and the Twelve for continuing to watch over us long after the Ancients of Gladima vanished. The Twelve, to this we pray. . . ."

"Well said, Eirek." Jerald's deep voice resonated.

Eirek had learned the prayer in his twelve years of living there, and to his knowledge, it was the one uttered by most people who believed in the Twelve. Old-Way Believers, like Angal, clung to the beliefs of Gladonity, only worshiping Ancients Lyoen and Bane. Eirek was caught in between the two: a Dual Believer, as he saw it. He believed that the Ancients created everything in the universe of Gladonus, but lost their power during the Great War, so the Twelve picked up their reins to govern all planets except the Central Core. Those who believed in only the Twelve thought that each god held a separate responsibility but only five were responsible for the creation of Gladonus—Trema created the planets; Pearl, the oceans and lakes; Anemie, the sky; Myethos, the suns; and Luenar, the moons.

Sheryin finished swallowing a forkful of potatoes. "Anything interesting happen today?"

"Drunks upon drunks came into the shop today—'ad to run 'em off with a 'ot iron," Jahn said between mouthfuls of food. "Stumbled in thinkin' it was an inn or a pub most like."

"Jahn, did you really have to use a hot iron?" Sheryin asked.

"Pops told me to."

"Jerald!"

"I 'ad orders to get in today! You know 'ow busy this time of year is."

Sheryin rolled her eyes and exhaled. "Anything else?"

Eirek looked outside and then back down toward his lap—the golden bond matched the waning light perfectly. *Should I show it?* Eirek let it play between his fingers for a bit before releasing it onto the checkerboard tablecloth.

"Is that a golden bond?" Sheryin asked.

"Where'd you get sometin' like that?" Jahn said.

Jerald picked it up and bit on it. "It's real. Eirek, 'ow'd you get this?"

"Marchioness Surg gave it to me today for pay. She was pleased with the craftsmanship Lagon did on her saddles." Eirek watched as the coin got passed back and forth between the family. "I want you to have it."

Sheryin took the coin, admiring it between her index finger and thumb. "Eirek, what makes you think we would want something like this?"

"For raising me ever since Angal let me off . . ."

"Now listen 'ere, son," Jerald chimed in. "Your uncle ain't no fool; 'e left you off for a good reason. You're bein' too 'ard on 'im. Sheryin, give the boy 'is coin back."

"I'm just admiring it. . . . They say all bonds come in two. Perhaps—"

"Who says 'at?" Jahn butted in.

"It's a saying! I don't know who actually said it. . . . But, here, Eirek." She slid the coin back over to him. "An envelope came for you today. Or, I found it today anyways. I didn't bother looking who it was from." She stood and moved around the edge of the table to a desk with envelopes. "Here it is."

Eirek looked at the crimson envelope. In golden lettering on the front was *Eirek Mourse.* Living with Sheryin's family made it as good a name as any to take. The Mourses didn't seem to have any quarrels about it. On the back of the envelope was a golden seal about half the size of the bond he received. Embossed was a dragon, wings outstretched, breathing fire.

It couldn't be. In shock, Eirek dropped the letter. "I don't want to open it."

"Is something wrong?" Sheryin grabbed the envelope and put the wax seal close to her spectacles. "My Twelve—" She dropped it too. "That . . . that . . ."

Jahn snatched it before his father could grab it and examined the seal himself. "From Guardian Eska!" Without a moment's warning, Jahn was already prying apart the seal.

"No, Jahn. Don't."

"Someone 'as to." Jahn pulled out a letter and started reading. "Greetings . . ." Jahn mouthed the words until he found something of note. "It is my greatest honor to congratulate you in your acceptance of the application sent two years past—" Jahn stopped.

"What did you just say?" Eirek asked.

"Eirek, you're in. I don't know what you're in, but you are. What is this?"

Eirek snatched the letter away from him and read it himself. He let it fall to the table as he slouched in his chair. *Surely this must be a mistake . . . . What would his conseleigh have even observed?*

"Eirek, does this mean you'll be the next guardian?" Sheryin asked.

"It doesn't mean that. Look it 'ere." Jerald's fingers pointed out a sentence. "'e's a participant to attend."

"You're goin' to do it right, Eirek?" Jahn asked. "I 'ear the guardian gets to meet with the Twelve face-to-face."

"The guardian is more than treating with gods, Jahn. It's about protecting. My great-great-great-grandmother, Ahna, said that when Deimos came here to Agrost and started pulling the islands of Mistral out of the sky, Guardian Eska levitated them all so that they wouldn't crash. He saved a whole nation. Lucky, too, the man she later married lived on one of those islands."

"'e doesn't usually do that, Sheryin. I 'ear for the most part 'e just stays on the Core protectin' what's there."

"What's there, Pa?" Jahn asked.

"Beats me to death. I 'aven't ever been tere."

"But why did he choose me?"

Each of them avoided his gaze. The room was silent as everyone tried to find an answer to his question. Eirek tried too, but he couldn't.

"I don't know why. But 'e did. Isn't that sometin'?" Jahn said. "You could be guardian."

"This is a once in a lifetime event, Eirek. *You* were chosen . . . the boy I've raised since seven . . ." Sheryin was trying to hold back tears. "If . . . if . . . I've seen anything in you from these past twelve years, it's been your thirst for knowledge and joy."

"But I can't save people; I can't even cast power. I tried again today—"

"Eirek!" Sheryin took two of her fingers and lifted up Eirek's chin. "That doesn't mean you can't. You just may not know how. There is always time."

When a hand gripped his shoulder, he arched his neck to see Jerald looking down at him. "You need to do this, Eirek. If Angal were 'ere, 'e'd tell you no different."

"Well, he isn't. He never is. . . . I . . . I . . . need to leave." Eirek got up, keeping the golden bond clenched in his hand.

As he walked over the broken screen threshold, he thought about what would make him feel reality. Surely he wasn't living it now. There was only one place that would allow him to collect his thoughts. It was in the forest, by the mouth of the river that flowed from Spera Mountains. He had found it one day when he was eight. He was playing with Jahn and some other village kids until he got lost and found a spot next to a stream. He remembered staring at the flowing water from that mouth for hours—wondering where it came from and where it went—until the Mourses found him.

The once-bright world was slowly turning shades of gray and blue. Ahead of him, Eirek saw Syf soldiers donned in leather padding and with greatwood shields strapped to their backs. The group was lighting torches that were spaced every few feet along paths called fireways.

Gazing at the fire, Eirek walked at their pace for a bit. He held out his hand. *"Palo."*

Nothing.

If Guardian Eska wanted him to compete, surely it was for a good reason, but he had yet to find it. He hoped that such an invitation meant he was capable to use power, but so far that hope had gone unfulfilled.

The walk to the outskirts of the forest took no longer than an hour. The guards stopped lighting torches twenty paces before the forest for fear of starting a wildfire. When they boarded their hovercraft and drove off to start the other side of the forest, Eirek took the opportunity to steal one of the torches from the pricket. Even though he had traveled the forest a myriad of times, he didn't know it in absolute dark. Songs of chirps and squeaks and twigs cracking underneath his weight played for him as he walked silent and reserved. Foxes and wolves lived in this area, but none would attack. Not so long as he had fire.

Within another hour, Eirek found himself with limited light sitting on a patch of grass that could easily observe Spera's mouth during daylight. He spent minutes there in contemplation, gazing at the stars. When he was tired of looking at the gold and bronze he could never hope to touch, Eirek reexamined his coin. An embossed serpent swallowing its tail ran along the outside of it. The coin's middle resembled a barren field with words in raised gold lettering: *Ajid Volintasey Fuan.*

"Ajeed . . . Volan . . . Volintas . . . hey . . . Fuy . . . an."

"May we find each other again is what it means."

Angal? Eirek spun around. He hadn't heard anyone approach.

His uncle stood there, a torch in one of his scarred hands. A spun shirt of gold and white with ornate patterns stitched down the sleeves covered him. Black breeches covered his lower half.

"What are you doing here?"

"I am here to make sure that you are not, come this time tomorrow."

Eirek looked away from him and stared off into the river. "How did you find me?"

"I was passing by Creim on my way to Syf for their New Day parade. I figured I would stop here for a spell and see you. The Mourses said you were not there though. . . ."

"But, here, how did you find me?"

"The Mourses told me you would be in the forest. And the fire you have makes you quite noticeable."

"What do you want?" Eirek continued to look at the flowing river.

"You have an opportunity in front of you, Eirek. One that people would kill for. Why can you not see that?"

The Mourses would tell you about my acceptance. Eirek stood up and walked toward Angal. "Because *I* was picked. *Me!* I have no special talents. I can't cast power. I've never been trained with a weapon—"

"Eirek, strength does not solely come from that. It comes from under-standing. . . . It comes from courage and vindication. . . . It is not something that can be taught. . . . It has to be realized. . . ."

Angal reached out for Eirek's shoulders, but Eirek pulled away. "You show up in my life again and expect me to forgive you? How long will it be this time until I see you next? A whole eight seasons have passed since I last saw you."

"Eirek, I've neglected you. Any fool or beggar could see that. Even the trees can see it. You have the potential to be more than some Creim vil-lager. You have potential not even the stars in the sky could measure or all the bonds that spells and cures could buy. I'd be a fool to neglect you even more by not helping you realize it."

Eirek let those words sink in. Despite his best efforts at denying Angal anything, his uncle had a way with words, a way with motivation. That is what caused Eirek to fill out the application two years ago when last they met. Eirek had spent seven days in Syf with him completing it. How was it that Angal reentered his life now, when Eirek thought his past was behind him?

"Where were you for the past two years?" Eirek choked back tears.

"Traveling. I go wherever the wind takes me, Eirek; you know that. It's led me all over the universe during my life. I've seen every nation. I've lived on every planet. But I have never maintained a solid relationship . . . with anyone. . . . I was separated from the love of my life in traveling." Angal showed the copper and silver band on his ring finger. "I missed the most important adventure of my life, and because of it, the woman I love I will never get to see again in this lifetime."

Eirek had never felt this close with his uncle before; he had always remained distant—literally and emotionally. Now Eirek wanted to learn more about this woman, but he knew Angal wouldn't tell. When Eirek was old enough to know what marriage was, he had asked Angal once who the copper and silver band on his finger was for. But Angal never told. And never would. Looking at the stars, Eirek searched for a reason to hate him. They were few and dim.

"I don't even know where I'm supposed to go . . ." Eirek sighed and looked down, listening to the flowing of the stream and the blowing of the wind.

"It does not matter where you need to go; I will get you there. But before that, there is an important item you need in Syf."

"What is that?"

"You will find it tomorrow. We leave from The Spell at nine in the morning. Do you understand me?"

Eirek nodded, acknowledging that he heard, not that he would go.

"We will need to walk through the forest, but from there I can transfer you back in my caracraft. Are you ready to leave?"

The wind blew again. It was cold here, even with the fire. Eirek wouldn't want to stay much longer anyways. He nodded and picked up the torch from its holder and followed Angal through the forest. As he walked, his mind wandered like the profession of his uncle.

☙CHAPTER 3☙

ZAIN

"Two years ago I sent in this application, and I finally got something back. Guardian Eska must have seen my skills at the tournaments."

Zain Berrese sat on the leather couch of the apartment listening (half with a piqued interest and half with mild annoyance) to his friend Zakk Shiren. Their apartment had a huge main room with a kitchen located on the left side and carpeted rugs and even a fireplace. More importantly though, there was wall space. When they first moved in with each other five years prior, the walls had been white and bare. Now the walls were still white, but the space was anything but bare, and Zain couldn't help but notice all of Zakk's trophies as his best friend continued on.

"Guardian of the Core can do anything. Eska has his own power. Through Gazo's, I already know we're denied, but there I could gain a different power."

Could do anything? Could have power? Zain flexed his fingers, thinking of the possibilities. How Zain dreamed of having power, but he knew he couldn't cast. At the age of eighteen, he and Zakk were tested for power, as was every other Gazo's student. Neither had been found to be blessed, but both remained eligible to continue their standard training.

"I would constantly train. I would be able to protect people . . . people who need protecting. So that no one would need to go through what I went through," Zakk said.

"We have all lost someone . . ." Zain looked down at his right hand and flexed it.

"You didn't lose your family at the age of six though."

Doesn't mean that my loss was any less important. But Zain didn't say that; he figured that growing up without parents meant Zakk was never taught to be as respectful to people as he should. Or as modest. Zain looked to his collection that surmounted to nearly three-quarters of Zakk's accomplishments, accomplishments that would never have been possible without Zain and his family. He kept his gaze there, reminiscing about how their training at Gazo's started.

When he met Zakk eighteen years ago, it was at a park in Konmer, Zain's hometown. From what Zain could remember, Zakk had seemed normal. But for six years, they only continued to stay in touch by picking a place to meet or Zakk saying he had been dropped off by his parents, who always seemed really busy. Little did Zain know at that point that it was all a lie.

In fact, Zain never found out until he mentioned his enrollment in Gazo's Premier Fighting Academy on his thirteenth birthday. Zakk had come over, along with Jarson and Lyle (both of whom joined a few years later, but Jarson was the only one to still continue in the program). Zain received one sword made of steel and had a leather grip. It was the ruby pommel that was most important to Zain though, because it was a symbol of his father's craftsmanship.

Zain's father had brought wooden swords for all the boys to play with, and during their friendly melee, Zakk pushed Zain down a hill and pounced on top of him, hitting him three times with the wooden sword. "Why do you have everything?" One stroke. "Why can't I have what you have?" Second hit. Harder this time. There was a shift from horseplay to outright hostility. "Why do you have family?" Zakk hit him the third time, then he collapsed and started crying.

Zain wasn't hurt; he had learned roughhousing with his older brother, Jamaal, but he was confused. "What are you talking about?"

And that is when the truth spilled—how Zakk's parents had been murdered in the Konmer Killings, where a group of five men killed over twenty people with swords and axes and fists, how Zakk had been living at his home until people came and kicked him off the vacant property, taking him into child custody. His foster parents cared nothing for him; they simply took him for a tax advantage. They hardly gave him food, but they gave him a roof and water in exchange for an occasional hit or chore. Zakk confessed to even stealing food from Zain's family when he could so that he wouldn't starve.

All of it made Zain cry. "Why didn't you ask to stay here?"

"I didn't want your family to know what happened. I didn't want their pity."

"Well, what do you want, then?"

"I want to train at this school with you. Gazo's, is it? I want to be able to protect people before it's too late. . . ."

"I . . . I—"

"Zain! Zakk! Where are you?" Jarson called.

"We have to go. I'll talk to my parents about it."

"Don't tell them about my family."

"But, why? You told me."

"You're the only one I've ever told. Don't tell them. Lie if you have to. Please."

"Okay . . ."

Zain didn't keep it a secret though. He couldn't. He knew Zakk didn't want to continue living like that. They agreed to enroll Zakk into the program under their sponsorship only if he allowed himself to stay with them. Zakk agreed and, in time, came to forgive Zain for telling, but ever since then, they had been advancing together through the program. Originally Zain wanted to do it just as a way to stay in shape and to learn to defend himself, but after Zakk's confession, he championed his friend's vision to protect people, no matter the cost.

The five large trophies, as tall as Zain's forearm, stood as testament to his triumph over Zakk during the years. Fifteen other trophies of similar height stood on Zakk's side of the wall. Zain would have never known Zakk was a natural fighter from the way he hit with the wooden sword, but there was a passion that ignited when Zain told him that his parents were enrolling him. He wondered if it was because he had betrayed Zakk's secret. Now Zakk was going to compete at the Trials hosted by Guardian Edwyrd Eska, if the letter was correct. *Great . . .*

"Zain, what's wrong?"

"It's nothing."

"There must be something. Are you not happy for me?"

"I am. . . . It's just that . . . Kendel couldn't complete his training session today. I can't advance yet."

"We don't always need to advance together."

Yes, we do, is what Zain would have liked to say, but instead he said, "I guess not."

"It doesn't matter anyways though."

"What do you mean by that?" Zain looked at his friend, who stood the same height, with the same dark-skinned complexion, and the same dirt-brown eyes. Where Zain had cropped hair like his brother though, Zakk had long braids that extended past the shoulders. Zakk also had a tattoo of Viper, the sword he used to win his first tournament—a sword he'd had made using the money from Zain's family.

"Guardian Eska is arranging my transport to be at Lake Kilmer tomorrow."

"It didn't say that in the letter."

"A separate telecard told me that."

An awkward silence crept into the apartment. Zakk stepped from the kitchen to the main living space and picked up the letter that Zain had left on the small glass coffee table in front of him. Zain looked at Zakk and sighed. "Are you coming to eat with me and my mom tonight?"

"I can't. I have packing to do. You'll be okay here, by yourself?"

"I'll figure something out. Take care." Zain threw on a wind jacket specially stitched with Gazo's logo and headed to the door. At the threshold, he paused and turned back. "Hey, Zakk?"

"Yeah?"

"Congrats." Zain waited for a little bit, but he heard nothing. *Is it that hard to say thanks?*

Zakk had never been the one to give praise, or if he did, it came off as condescending; at least, that is how Zain interpreted it. He accredited it to Zakk's loss of family, but how many times would that become an excuse?

Their apartment was located only a few blocks from the academy and was where most of the people who attended stayed if they came from other nations or planets. It was located in Stel, in remembrance of Gazo Sabore's hometown. He founded the academy in the times before the Great War. Zain's hometown of Konmer was located an hour's drive east near the Anga Mountains, a small range that overlooked the Krine Sea.

In the parking structure, Zain found his hovercraft's stall and got inside. The hovercraft was a sleek red with a black stripe down the side and sat on its rectangular belly with rounded edges. Each hovercraft required a stall because of how it was fueled. Anitron rock made it possible to defy gravity; it was smoky gray in color and harvested only in the last half-century from the floating lands of Mistral. But it was only in the last thirty years that hovercrafts were actually engineered. Once activated, the anitron emitted a shockwave around the perimeter of the hovercraft to jolt it and keep it afloat. If an individual was near a hovercraft while it was activated, one would be catapulted into the air and likely die on the fall down. The larger the vehicle, the larger the rock—and the larger the stall as well. Guardian Eska mandated that every planet have large cargo-transport ships; those, Zain heard, contained rocks as large as hovercrafts themselves. His father bought him a hovercraft when Zain decided to move out of the house, and since then, he had only needed to replace the anitron once, two years back.

Outside of the small city of Stel, the drive was traffic-free. Ahead of him Zain noticed Freyr start to descend behind the bands that circled the planet. Lugh was already in front of its larger counterpart, nearing the horizon. It would still be hours before both disappeared completely, losing authority to the two moons: Tovia and Hoffnung. Myoli was the only planet that had suns set in the east and rise in the west. It gave him something to focus on when he drove to his mom's house after Gazo's finished. It let him see the nation of Empora all the way across the Krine Sea from his special spot halfway up the mountain. Zain's gaze drifted to the Anga Mountains and then lower to his hands once again as he thought, I need to go there. There would be plenty of time for that though; first he needed to eat with his mom, Brisine.

• • •

The door opened.

It wasn't his mom who answered; it was his brother.

"Jamaal? What are you doing here?"

"It's nice to see you too, Zain." Jamaal chuckled. He readjusted the black-rimmed glasses and stepped aside so Zain could enter.

"I . . . I . . . was just . . ." Zain's face flushed red. "How did you get here? Why are you here?"

"There's a lull in senate activity, so I decided to visit for a few days. And you should know that Dad gave me my own ship as a wedding gift. Didn't you see it in the backyard? Now, what's with all the questions? Come here and give me a hug."

Zain hadn't noticed his ship. He was too preoccupied. The hug felt good and strong, just as Zain remembered it from more than half a year ago. Even though time had passed, Jamaal still managed to keep thin and trim his beard.

"I didn't know you were coming," Zain said once their hug ended.

"That's the idea of a surprise visit, dummy."

Zain smiled awkwardly.

"You okay, Zain? You seem . . . preoccupied."

Am I really that obvious? "I'm fine."

"Supper is ready!" Zain's mom called from the kitchen.

Zain followed his older brother of five years to the kitchen and sat down on the opposite side of the cherry table from his brother and his mom. His mom had dark-brown hair streaked with blonde that flowed past her neck. She wore a long-sleeved shirt that was the color of snow. Zain wanted to eat quickly and leave; he wanted to visit the Anga Mountains, to clear his head.

As soon as he reached for the food though, his mom swatted away his hand. "We have to pray first," she said.

"Oh yeah." Zain forgot. He didn't bother closing his eyes like the others. While everyone else moved their lips, Zain stared at his hands. His side began to ache—like it always did whenever he stared. It was the only reminder he had of her, and it was a constant one at that. *Why did she have to die?*

"Ava," Zain said. He usually didn't let her name escape. Did anyone else hear?

He looked up to see his family eating. His mom gave him a suspicious look, but she dug deep into her plate of field greens. Did she hear?

"So, Zain, where are you at in Gazo's now?" Jamaal asked.

"Still just a trainer," Zain said dismally. "Kendel didn't pass today."

"Who's Kendel?"

"The trainee assigned to me about a year ago. Kendel Gensen. Scrawny kid with no muscle. I'm not sure how I'm ever going to get him through an hour session."

"You'll get there," his mom said.

"Is that why you're so out of it today?"

No, Jamaal, if only you knew. "Yeah," Zain lied.

"Jamaal, how are things going on Mistral?" His mom changed topics.

"Good. Talks of how to neutralize the wormhole traffic have stalled. And with the rate of increase in interuniversal commerce, I don't think a solution will be constructed anytime soon. New taxes on interuniversal shipping rates are being sent back to the lords and ladies of the planets for acceptance or veto. Even if it does get accepted though, Guardian Eska will still need to approve it, and I'm sure he will have no time for that due to the fact that his Trials are about to take place soon."

"How did you hear about that?" Zain asked.

"News has spread like the wind on Mistral that Senator Nyom Numos will be attending the event as an honored guest."

"Why him?"

"Well, every senator from every nation had the opportunity—from what I hear. All you needed to do was fill out a simple card of information. If you were lucky enough to get picked, well . . ."

"Did you fill one out?" His mom asked.

"You should know that a family keeps one busy enough." Jamaal chuckled. "I don't have time for a month's reprieve, even if it is the opportunity of a lifetime."

"Now you know what I dealt with for eighteen years. I might as well have had three boys to take care of with Zakk over here all the time."

"Where is he anyways, Zain? Mom told me he was supposed to come."

"Something came up . . ." Zain looked down at his chicken. It was almost done. Quickly he put the rest of it in his mouth. "I need to go. I have a long day tomorrow too."

"Don't be a stranger. I'll be here tomorrow if you want to catch up more after Gazo's."

Zain nodded and left. *Perhaps I will. If I even go to Gazo's tomorrow. . . .*

An hour and a half later, after an easy hike, Zain sat on a ledge that jutted out on the eastern side of the Anga Mountains. The cliff looked out toward the murky-gray Krine Sea. Seven years ago, from this position, he had been with Ava, Zain's only serious relationship, and they saw Rhayna, the golden bird of legend, flying across it. In this spot of phantom remembrance, he felt Ava burying her head on his shoulder, crying the struggles of her grandmother's death onto him. *Why couldn't I hold onto you?*

Zain flexed his hand and watched Freyr touch the horizon. It would disappear soon. He reached into the pocket of his windjacket and pulled out an envelope. It was crimson with a golden-wax seal. He twirled the envelope between his index finger and his thumb. *Zakk would get accepted.*

Zain broke the golden seal and took out the telecard. Underneath the indent, numbers counted down continuously from twenty-four hours. He pushed the center button, and a hologram of a small figure appeared just in front of his face.

"Zain Berrese, my name is Ethen Rorum, one of Guardian Eska's four respected aides. I am conseleigh to Myoli and liaison for te nations of Ka'Che, Empora, and Chaon. Listen closely, for tis letter will only play once. A ship will pick you up from Lake Kilmer, at te edge of Trent's Forest once te timer on tis card reaches zero. If you are not tere witin te allotted time, you will miss tis great opportunity. Good luck. Guardian Eska looks forward to meeting all of te contestants in person."

Zain didn't know how long he continued looking out past the Krine Sea to the nation of Empora. His father was there on business with Victor Zigarda. He had been there for two months, already longer than usual. His father and his mother had been there for him when Ava fell to her death while out on a date with Zain on this very same mountain range. But not here. Zain only went back to that spot once a year. Even Zakk had been there for him through his loss, and who better to comfort him than someone who had lost his own family?

As guardian, I could do anything. Zakk's words stuck in his head. The possibilities were supposedly endless. But only one person could become guardian. . . . Only one person could do anything. Zain flexed his right hand once again, feeling phantom fingers slip through. His side ached, then a tear came to his eye and slowly slid down his cheek.

CHAPTER 4

FORGOTTEN CAUSE

Eirek awoke as trumpets blared a song of festivity into the heated air. Freyr still shone greatly in the sky, making its way west toward the horizon. He had fallen asleep in order to deal with Angal's stubbornness. The telecard he had found in his envelope told them to go to Domnux Plains, not Syf, but Angal insisted that he needed to go to Cresica's capital to find something he forgot. What that was, Eirek still wasn't sure.

"You're awake. We just entered Syf."

"I heard," Eirek said. He looked around. Syf was separated in four sections, each connected to one another hill upon hill. They passed the first, a squalid section of town. Brothels and ruthless taverns lay there. The main square was located in the second section with the majority of the population. Three maidens carved of copper, silver, and gold stood center in the three separate fountains of water—a symbol to Cresica's matriarchy. People stood in storefronts along the cobblestone road that lined the city streets. Roofs were packed with straw or wood, both as copious on Cresica as the farms and food.

To Eirek's left, the procession had started. It would open with a storyteller accompanied by harps, lyres, and other strings. Drums would soon follow as the story grew more intense. He had only seen the parade once, when his uncle was chosen to lead it five years prior.

Eirek watched as Angal mouthed every word of the story by heart:

> *"The men bred from fire emerged one day.*
> *With a sense of entitlement, claims were made*
> *For throne and blood. They laid only assault*
> *On our lands, 'cause their land proved false.*

The horses came with rein in their mouths and fire in their manes.
The riders from the land of Kane,
The riders from the land of Kane
Came on horses with rein in their mouths and fire in their manes."

The song would go on to tell of the hero who rose up against the riders from Kane with help from the god of war, Tomahawke, and the god of fire, Fueoco. But they left the road, maneuvering past hoards of people through the main square. Eirek could see the storyteller and strummers garbed in brown with white sashes underneath their cloaks. They passed the alleys intersecting with small houses to the third tier. Private gateways of steel protected the houses made of block and brick and stone. Above the rich part of Syf was another hill and, there, Lady Clayse's mansion.

Following cobblestone to the left, they passed a variety of large estates. Angal's house was stationed half a mile in, between two white mansions. After punching in a few numbers on a keypad on the gate, Angal guided his caracraft past the electronic gate and down a paved driveway until stopping at a turnabout.

"What did I leave here?" Eirek asked, exiting from the passenger side.

"I left something here. You left something there." Angal pointed to the castle on the fourth tier.

Eirek couldn't help but notice the gray clouds rolling in. "How do you suppose I left something there?" He had only ever been to the mansion once, when he was fourteen. He and Angal were invited after his uncle finished leading the parade. Even Jahn had come along for such an event.

Before Eirek could receive an answer, Angal disappeared into his estate. Eirek gently kicked the ground, annoyed. He never received answers from Angal.

Two granite statues of hawks, wings expanded, eyed him as he made his way up the steps to the roan-colored wooden doors, large enough for an army of soldiers to enter. Once inside, rows upon rows of books filled the shelves against the walls. These texts were Angal's pride—to remain untouched by even a butler or maid. Eirek figured this because most were riddled with dust and cobwebs.

He wandered aimlessly, his hands stroking the hard wood of tables littered with maps and books. Many of their pages described the nation of Nova on the planet Pyre. Eirek hunched over and started flipping through one of the books until a map of Nova caught his eye. The nation was certainly small, about half the size of Cresica. Eirek's gaze lingered on the map until Angal called his name as he reentered the room with a large knapsack hanging over his back.

Angal descended a short set of stairs that led to a different hallway. "Are you ready?"

"Yeah," Eirek exhaled.

Outside, rain drizzled. Freyr struggled for attention. Eirek sprinted to the caracraft and entered. Like the drums in the parade, rain beat on the caracraft's steel siding and window.

"How are we going to get into the castle?"

"I have a performance. With this rain, I'm sure Lady Clayse will be even more pleased."

"But we need to get to Domnux Plains. We don't have time for a performance."

Silence.

Eirek exhaled and slouched in his seat. Angal activated the caracraft and started out toward the fourth section of Syf, enclosed by a stone wall and a barred gate. Its grandeur was guarded by men in hard-boiled leather and helms and shields made of greatwood. Their lances were taller than them. Angal was granted passage by a man of soft jaw who filled his leather armor as full as food-filled bellies.

Driving another half mile up the hill, they arrived at an enclosed dome made of metal. A portion of the egg-shaped dome folded open, spraying an orange glow on the damp ground outside. Angal was directed by guards into the enclosure, parking alongside similar hover-type vehicles near the front of the area past ships and warwagons.

A man waited for them, his neck thick with a metal brooch that fastened the silk cape trailing behind him. A metal pin, shaped to the likeness of a clock, on his doublet fashioned in celadon and brown threads, symbolized his position—receiver. Only his prominent mustache seemed unkempt, curved upwards with even thicker sideburns.

"Embry Knossol, dreadful day for a parade and a story, don't you think?"

"Angal the Bard, hopefully it is not too dreadful; I would hate to hear an awful story."

"I have never told one of those yet."

Embry let out a light laugh and then said, "Does the title still please you, or do you finally have a last name for me to say?"

"The stars are the only ones that know my last name. And I haven't managed to track mine down yet."

"That is an old folklore from before the Great War."

"Aye, and I am old." Angal laughed.

The man joined in Angal's chortle, squinting and covering the shades of brown. "It is nice of you to come again."

"It is good to see you as well." Angal stepped forward and hugged the man, patting him on his back.

"Do you remember Eirek?" Angal gestured toward his nephew.

"Vaguely . . . it has been years since I have seen you." Embry extended his hand.

Eirek accepted it. "Yes, it has been awhile." What else could he say?

The receiver led them through the palace's courtyards. The recent rain necessitated the ejection of a dome, forming a gray ceiling over the outdoor gathering place. Servants in suits of celadon and maids in dresses of brown bustled in and out of the stone walls. When the dome wasn't in place, only libraries, repositories, and individual living quarters were domed; otherwise all other places were open to sky and sun alike. Rows of green lined the cobblestone paths, dividing the traffic of those entering and leaving the palace grounds. Trees stood in grassy plots reserved for their growth. Birds, now trapped beneath the metal sky, squawked from the trees.

Eirek and Angal followed Embry through corridors upon corridors of grandiose columns tapered toward the top. Most rooms were orthogonal, consisting of many right angles. The throne room, however, was oval shaped, domed, and covered with a large portrait of a man in earthy armor staring down horses with manes of fire and riders with fiery hair.

Atop a dais sat three greatwood thrones with golden leaves that extended down their frames. The royal family sat on them atop plush celadon cushions. Below the dais were two guards at either side donning golden armor. A celadon flag hung from one wall, depicting a lonely white mansion that sat atop a steep mountain. When the Clayses assumed power, they utilized this new design. The previous flag showed only a forest of greatwood trees; this one symbolized their palace, a new beginning for Cresica.

Eirek noticed the receiver halt before the throne and bow. "Lady Clayse, it is my pleasure to introduce to you Angal the Bard and his accompanist, Eirek."

"Angal, I am pleased you contacted me earlier today, considering how dreadful of a day it turned out to be. I need a riveting tale; do you have one?"

Earlier today? When did he call? It must have been while I slept.

"I have many tales the family in power has not heard yet." Angal bowed.

Eirek followed suit. He couldn't help but notice the woman to the lord's left, the lady's daughter, Linn Clayse. Since last he had seen her, she had filled into her mother's beauty. A scarf—spun from brown thread—covered part of her silk dress that was colored in celadon. Her ears held tourmalines, and her eyes were blue as sapphires.

"So, what tale will we hear today?"

"A tale of origin."

"Deriving from the Twelve? I have heard it already."

"No, from the Ancients, if it pleases you."

The lady turned her upper lip and looked at her husband and then to her daughter. "I suppose it will have to do. Commence."

"Eirek, here you go." Angal pulled a flute form his bag and handed it over.

Eirek took it with reluctance. He hadn't played flute since leaving school six seasons ago. He used to teach flute to other interested kids, but whenever he did play it, it reminded him of his connection with Angal, a connection he had grown to hate after Angal exploited his trust during the week Eirek spent in Syf filling out the application. That whole week, Angal had made Eirek feel important. If only he was.

The lights seemed to dim, most likely at Lady Clayse's doing. A soft spotlight shined on Angal, Eirek barely in its breadth. Aligning his posture upon a wooden stool, he tried to find a comfortable position from which to play. He didn't really know what melody to play, but he tried keeping cadence with Angal's voice.

> *"This is a tale, telling of three powers:*
> *The mysterious Other, Lyoen, and Bane,*
> *Blood ran pure, their ambitions ran sour,*
> *Fueling the war that lost their homeland and reign.*
>
> *Lyoen, the creator of all humans born,*
> *Known as the Alchemist, followers adored.*
> *He gives us strength when our bodies lose form.*
>
> *Bane, source of authority, power's true test,*
> *Known as the Warrior, followers blessed.*
> *His brother gave us life, so he gave us death.*

The Other, his real name has never been known,
Never been seen, so never has he been shown,
But murmurs tell that he still freely roams.

Their jealousy brought war; their war was called Great.
The survivors took power, claiming First Blood.
The Twelve that you know, but yet you don't know eight
Waiting to go home once the prophecy's sung."

The lights returned to normal. Angal bowed and so did Eirek. As he looked to the carpet, he couldn't help but wonder about this Other Ancient. Who was he? Why hadn't Angal ever mentioned it to him whenever they talked about religion? Did the Mourses know anything about it?

"You may stand straight," Lady Lynda Clayse said.

"Thank you, my lady." Angal returned to his normal posture, and Eirek did as well, handing the flute over to his uncle.

"You said there were three Ancients. Explain yourself."

"My lady, it is a story. I do not have any such idea." Angal fidgeted with his fingers.

"Well, then, how can you tell it?"

"I assume there is. How else could both Ancient Lyoen and Ancient Bane take leave of this universe at the same time?"

"Angal," Linn spoke. "What is this prophecy that the Twelve wait on?"

Angal cleared his throat and said:

"Chosen will be blood from all five domains.
Hope they will bring through chaos, anger, and pain.
Twelve will lose favor, four will regain form.
Bringing with them more death than the Great War."

"And who came up with such a prophecy?" Linn asked.

"The Four Smiths, if legends are true."

"And are they the Four that will regain form?"

"My lady's daughter, if you truly wish to learn about lore and prophecy and the olden days, I suggest you study under one of your starseers or lorels."

Eirek looked toward the dais. Lady Clayse seemed taken aback by Angal's shortness with her daughter.

"Angal, that kind of shortness is not appreciated, but I understand the truth of what you say, so I will not berate you further. You are skilled with your tongue; make sure you do not lose it."

"Mother, I took no offense." Linn blushed.

"Lynda, Angal is right."

"I know, Rybert. Let us have no more discussion of this. Now, Angal, about your payment?"

"Yes, I hoped to talk with you in more detail about that. Perhaps over a meal? The airroads to Syf today were nearly as busy as the land roads. We had no chance to eat during our ride here."

"Food will serve well enough for conversation. Cathreene, please ready something."

"Yes, my lady." A maid with silvery hair and a narrow face retreated into a chamber attached to the thrones room's rear.

• • •

Eirek and Angal were led through stone entrances to the dining room. A large carved granite table stood erected around stumps of stone. A chandelier lit the table from above. Windows stood open with beaded curtains down either side. The scent of either pork or chicken held Eirek's senses in the heavens of Axiumé—or was it the sweet acorn paste for the bread? Eirek swore by Trema's garden there was another smell—pine needles, ever so delicate and faint.

"So, Lady Lynda," said Angal, "before talks of business, let us first talk pleasure."

"And what kind of pleasure would Angal the Bard like to hear?" She buttered her bread with the acorn paste.

"Any new tidings, the likes of which might call for a song someday?"

"Linn. Share your news with Angal; it would surely make a great song."

"My twenty-fifth birthday is coming soon in four months. If what our starseers say can be believed, it will be near the time when the two suns eclipse."

"Pirini Lilapa," Angal muttered. "Are you certain, my lady's daughter?"

"If that is what it is called, then, yes."

Eirek saw distaste on Angal's face. "Aye, then I am sorry for you."

Linn's smile quickly faded. "Why is that? It is supposed to be beautiful."

"Beautiful it is, but bad things have happened when the suns eclipse."

"Are you referring to Deimos?" Lord Clayse asked.

"I am."

"Guardian Eska locked him away, and there has not been trouble since."

"There has not been Pirini Lilapa since," Angal said.

"You will need to be here then to tell a tale and make good things happen," Linn said.

"Yes, Angal, your stories are rather great. Will you come back to tell a story for her?" Lady Clayse plucked a carrot from her tray.

"If it pleases you both, I may."

"It does. And her especially. The next few months will be quite dry for Linn. She will start courting other families of power. Upon her twenty-fifth, she can take the ladyship if I should die, as I am sure you are aware."

"I am."

"She has a courting with Marchioness Albony Evengale's younger son, Ezra, tomorrow."

"Why not Oswyn?" Angal asked.

"That one is denied. I would never let Linn marry someone who cannot cast; that is like marrying a cripple."

So I am a cripple? Eirek couldn't help but glare a little at Lady Clayse. Perhaps if Marchioness Surg had been more receptive to his delivery, it wouldn't have stung as much. How they clung to their status and authority as basis for mannerisms. How would someone like her react to him being guardian?

"It's only a courting, Mother. He still needs to win my favor. And my favor is not so easily won." Linn looked at Eirek and smiled.

Did she smile to taunt him? She was nicer than her mother, yes, but did she think of him as a cripple the same way her mother surely would if she knew?

"I have a feeling it will turn out well. But enough of pleasures and favor. Let us speak of business. Angal, if you will," Lady Clayse said.

"My business comes with a sort of favor. But before that, let me extend my gratitude to both you and your husband for your recommendations of Eirek."

"Recommendations for what? Angal, please refresh our minds."

"Two years ago, applications for apprentice to Guardian of the Core were being accepted and you helped write a recommendation for Eirek. Well, just yesterday, Eirek received a letter declaring his acceptance."

Gasps of astonishment escaped from throats. Eirek's face grew hot. Eyes beamed at him, for better or worse.

"May I see the acceptance letter?" Lady Clayse asked.

Do they assume I'm illiterate? In truth, Eirek hadn't believed so either, but Angal had made a convincing argument for why he should attend. *Strength comes from understanding; it has to be realized. . . .* What made the Mourses any different than the Clayses? Both endured strife, both were human. But one had finer clothing. Was this what he was supposed to find?

Eirek retrieved the letter and held it out. A butler emerged from along a pair of beaded curtains, snatching the letter from his hand and handing it to Lady Clayse.

After reading it, the lady passed it to her husband.

"Congratulations indeed are in order for you, Eirek." Lord Clayse gave a faint clap.

"Yes, they are. Now, what is it you need for the favor, Angal?"

Eirek shivered as Lady Clayse stared him down like a guard eyeing a prisoner.

"A telecard accompanied the letter. Conseleigh Luvan Katore instructed Eirek to arrive at Domnux Plains in the allotted time."

Lord Clayse picked up the letter and searched for any sort of number.

Angal took notice. "No, it was a separate card altogether. Eirek, will you please read how much time is left."

The thick-stocked card had not creased in Eirek's pocket. "Only fifteen hours."

"We were hoping perhaps you could transport us there. Time is our enemy," Angal said.

"This is certainly no small request." Lynda had put away her utensils and started to fan herself again. "Tell me, Eirek, why do you want to become guardian?"

She stared at him then—with Linn's eyes, just older. Judgment waited for his answer. And as matriarch of the family in power, she would be quick to do so.

"He wishes to—"

"Angal, you made your case for the boy years ago. I want to hear Eirek's reasoning."

Eirek tilted his head and looked toward the chandelier. Time seemed to crawl and flicker like the candles above. He remembered the way Mara

Surg tossed flame to the candles, how she controlled everyone below her because of her title and her power.

"I am sorry, Angal. If Eirek has no ambition to become guardian, then—"

"I want to be able to support those who have never been supported," Eirek cut in.

The lady seemed taken aback. "Like the beggars, whores, and drunkards?"

Tread carefully. "Perhaps. . . . In stories, you hear about great men and women doing extraordinary things . . . but . . . it is only great people who receive the opportunities. Not anyone from my cloth. . . . By helping me get there, a story might eventually be told of an ordinary man doing extraordinary things."

Lady Clayse looked around the room. Her husband nodded, as did her advisor and receiver. And, finally, Linn. "Very well. I offer you my support wholeheartedly. Aeryn . . ."

"Yes, my lady?"

"You will transport these two to Domnux Plains. They must leave twelve hours from now at the very latest if they wish to make it there on time."

"Aye, I will ready the ship for tomorrow morning." The advisor got up and exited down the hallway from whence he had come.

While Lady Clayse was busy exchanging private words with her receiver and her family, Angal grabbed hold of Eirek's shoulder. "Did you figure out what you left here?"

"Yes."

"And what is that?"

Eirek turned his head to look at Angal's blue eyes. There was a glint of purple in them, Eirek had failed to realize, sort of like his own eyes. "Strength and purpose."

CHAPTER 5

LAKE KILMER

From the cockpit of his brother's ship, Zain saw the deluge of raindrops beat like ratamacue, but no bolts of lightning accompanied it. With each splash, Zain's anxiety grew. Would Zakk make it? Zain already knew the answer—yes. Each tournament's top prize wasn't solely a trophy. There was a monetary value as well, and Zakk had used the silver spells and golden bonds from his winnings to buy a hovercraft two years after Zain moved in. Before then, he had relied on Zain for transportation, and Zain obliged because of their friendship.

"This storm certainly brewed up out of nowhere," said Jamaal. "I wish I could get you closer."

Zain wished so as well, but he didn't want to push his brother too far. It had taken a lot of convincing to even get him to agree to take him. Jamaal was too analytical; Zain couldn't blame him. Jamaal needed to be in order to analyze every angle of senate policies and bills, but that kind of thinking wouldn't take Zain to Lake Kilmer. It was only when Zain pried apart Jamaal's past that he had found a connection.

"What is the one thing you regret in your life the most?"

Jamaal exhaled. "Zain, don't go there. Don't bring her up."

"How can I not? Guardian of the Core can do anything—"

"No one can bring back the dead, Zain. No one can reverse the past. You need to move on, and stop continuing to live in your dreams."

"The problem is when you don't live your dreams. What if there is a way to bring her back? What if I can finally get this . . . this . . . guilt off of me?"

"It was an accident."

"And one that I still live with every single day. Sometimes I can still feel her fingers slipping through mine. . . ." Zain turned around. He needed to convince his brother. In deep contemplation, Zain exhaled.

"It was the middle of summer seven years back when Reine and I were strolling through a park with curved wooden bridges over a small stream. We were headed back from sitting on a plain and overlooking the arcs of rainbows. The arcs! It went up and over Boras, if you can imagine. Anyways, with the rainbow still in the air and the water sparkling more than ever, I thought it was the perfect moment to propose to her. The only problem was that I didn't have a ring. After that, after that date, I knew I wanted to be with her, so I called Dad, and he said he would make one. And he did. I carried it around with me all the time after that, waiting for the perfect moment, but it never came. The winds were especially brutal one cold day, so I let her put on my jacket, and she found the ring in there, ruining any chance I had at surprising her."

"Why are you telling me this?" Zain asked.

"You asked what my largest regret was. . . . We all have them, Zain . . . but we learn to live with them."

"But if you had a chance to make up for that, you wouldn't take it?"

His brother didn't have a comment after that besides, "Go get your things." And now, here they were, combating the elements as they tried to land. The alcove that his brother found was double the size of his ship, but in a storm like this, it still made it hard to land.

When the ship touched down, Zain was bounced around in his chair. He was thankful to be strapped into his seat. Jamaal opened the cargo ramp, and Zain proceeded to struggle to gather his things without falling backwards.

"How much longer do you have?"

"Half an hour. Should be enough time to get there."

"I hope you find whatever you're looking for."

I hope so too. "Thanks. . . ." Zain turned around but was stopped by his brother placing a hand on his shoulder.

"Mom has a right to know where you are."

He hadn't told Mom about his acceptance. She had been with him all through Ava's death, the hearings, the trials, and Zain never forgot the longest and hardest hug he received once the judge found him not guilty, but if his mom knew he was going to become apprentice to atone for her, she wouldn't have let him leave. She would have been even more stubborn than

Jamaal saying that he already paid for his accident and shouldn't open up old wounds.

"Then tell her. . . ." Zain looked into his brother's hazel eyes.

"I will. . . . Make sure you answer your telecommunicator if she calls."

Zain searched for any signs of lenience but found none. Jamaal had shifted to acting like a father figure instead of a brother. "Bye."

"Good luck, Little Bear."

Zain grinned and gave his brother a hug. "Bye, Big Bear."

He turned around and exited the ship, facing the onslaught of rain and wind. The rain obscured most sound, but there was the faint sound of birds squawking their protest of the storm. Branches thrown aside and acorns and pine needles ripped from trees littered the floor. Even the thick canopy of trees failed to keep him dry. The smell of worms and fish stuck to his senses like sweat after a sparring lesson. Zain had always been told that when one sense fades, the others strengthen in order to compensate. With his vision reduced, he felt as if he could hear more. A faint crack in the air popped like knuckles on a hand. Zain looked around. No fallen branches.

As Zain reached the last set of trees that enclosed the small area of land before a white pier, he noticed Zakk standing halfway out onto that pier amongst the wind and rain, bags over each shoulder. The soft mud and the loud cracking of thunder covered the sound of his advance. Skiffs tied to the pier kept Zakk occupied as Zain continued to walk farther. *Any minute now, the ship will be here.*

As Zain's footsteps transitioned from mud to the whitewood boards, Zakk turned around.

"Zain."

Zain's neck tightened.

"What are you doing here?"

Zain reached into the inside pocket of his Gazo's uniform and pulled out a red envelope. "You weren't the only one who was accepted."

"Two warriors from the same school. What are the odds of that?"

Do you not think I am capable? Zain tried ignoring the comment as best he could. He looked out onto the lake, watching the ripples roar with intensity.

"Did you know when I was telling you?"

Zain nodded.

"Why didn't you say anything?"

"What was I supposed to say? That I was accepted too? I hadn't even opened the letter; I picked it up from my mailbox at Gazo's after my training session with Kendel and put it in my pocket. When I saw yours, I knew."

"Zain, you don't have to be jealous of me. . . ."

"My family *gave* you everything you have! Without me, you would be nothing!" Zain looked at Zakk, who had reserved himself to looking down at the dock.

"I . . . I . . . think you're wrong," Zakk said. He looked up and held Zain's glare. "Without me, *you'd* be nothing."

"How so?"

"I was the one who helped you pass your continuance exam when you couldn't figure out the order of combinations you had to block while blindfolded. I was the one who gave you purpose to even continue through Gazo's. I have always been the one pushing you. I'm not going to say, 'Sorry that I'm better than you.' I'm not—"

A low reverberating noise cut the air, the sound of continuous thunder. Except it wasn't thunder; it was the ship.

The ship's coming. Zain watched it descend. His fingers started to flex. His side started to ache as the scenario of Zakk beating him crossed his mind. Such a victory would ruin any hope he had of atoning Ava's death. Of finding some way to see her again.

"Why can't you ever just let me win? Always you have been there by my side, shoving the victories in my face."

Lower and lower the ship descended. It was almost at touchdown now.

"Zain, you're like a brother to me; of course I'm going to be by your side. We advance together. That's always how it has been."

Zain closed his eyes and shielded his face as water splashed up from the ship's landing. The deluge crashed upon them like a tidal wave on an island. Zain maintained his balance throughout and looked over at his friend who was doing the same.

"Not this time," Zain muttered. He heaved his shoulder into Zakk, forcing his friend to fall—with bags and sword—into the lake.

The pier shook as the ramp landed harshly on the rotted surface. Zain spun around and sprinted up as fast as his wet clothes would let him. Once inside, he threw his bags to the ground and tried to walk to the pilot's area to demand its departure. The area was blocked with glass, so Zain pounded, but the pilot would not acknowledge him.

From inside his pocket, Zain pulled out the soaked telecard to see how much time remained. Less than a minute. *Come on. Come on. Take off.*

"Strap in and prepare for takeoff," a man's voice boomed through the cargo area's speakers.

Zain didn't listen. He turned around, withdrew his sword, and watched as Zakk pulled himself up out of the water. *Come on. Come on.* Zakk sprinted toward the ramp. The ship started to take off, causing Zain's knees to buckle and lose a moment's readiness. The ship was in the air, the ramp slowly closing, and that is when he saw the last of Zakk.

Zain sheathed his sword and took a moment's breath. He looked up and saw a forearm make its way over the top of the ramp. Did Zakk make the jump? Zain crawled on his knees to the cusp of the cargo area; his body felt as if it would be sucked out. A set of fingertips struggled to gain traction. The ramp apparently sensed Zakk hanging from it and stopped. When at the cusp, Zain poked his head out. Zakk now dangled fifty feet above the lake's blue exterior. And that distance was increasing.

"Zain, help me up!"

Zain wanted to help. He knew he should help. Scenarios started reeling in his mind: Zakk coming on board and killing him for his near betrayal, Zakk showing off his skills during the Trials, Zakk winning and leaving Zain once again—behind and inferior. Zain extended his torso forward and gripped Zakk's wet forearm. Although Zain couldn't hear it from the roaring engine, he could see his friend's teeth chatter from the blowing wind and the cool water that soaked him. He looked down into the dirt-brown eyes of Zakk. They were soaked, sullen as the earth below. Zain couldn't see the helplessness in those eyes, only the choler that rose like hills and mountains from Zakk's pupils. Zain's hands shoveled under Zakk's forearms.

"I'm sorry. I can't." He couldn't say it. He mouthed it instead. But the intention was clear. His hands pried apart Zakk's grip; his eyes watched as Zakk plummeted through the air. Zain had never seen such a look before . . . except once. Awhile ago. The look of pain, betrayal, fear—it was all there.

The ship's ramp proceeded to close. Chilled air vanished. Its absence, though, did little to soothe him.

Vapid breathing conveyed his sorrow. His side ached—enough for two this time. Daggers of guilt sliced through his intestines, forcing him to limp across the ship's interior over to a bench on the right side. *What have I done?* Water mixed with tears slid down his face, keeping him cool and vulnerable. *What have I done?* Zain sat like The Thinker of Pelopon, watching droplets crash on the floor below. Then as he looked up, he saw another body—a woman—seated upon another bench across the cargo area.

Three-inch black heels pecked the floor. Crossed legs subtly revealed a fuchsia garter, a dagger attached to it. The slit purple dress covered her body tightly, and her crossed arms accentuated her breasts. Her lips, pierced on the lower left side, smirked at him. A hand, weighed down by bracelets of varying colors, brushed black bangs out of her familiar blue eyes.

"Well, Zain, zat was razer unbecoming."

CHAPTER 6

BLESSING

Hydro could not believe how many people managed to crowd into the castle walls. With his father, Hydro progressed slowly, all eyes on him, all knowing the task he was about to accomplish. Roy Tityle of Katarh and his wife, Luuise; Marqiss Puwl of Rhemu and his wife, Lyane; Hekter Sigurd, the young Marquis of Roil; the dark-skinned Alyn Bloctor of the Summer Isles and his wife, Ayanna; Cadell Periwinkle of the Hart Isles and his wife, Enya; and even the old hermit Seth Axyel, Maquis of Talyn, stood before him in front of their respective families and thousands of others to pay Hydro homage. *How did Father arrange this?*

He had seen them from the veranda when his father made a speech about his new adventure. "Families of Power, and those of Acquava lucky enough to catch wind of this momentous occasion, I received word yesterday that my son is to compete in Guardian Eska's Trials. . . ." His father had let the announcement sink in before continuing, "It means a great deal to my family that you could come on such short notice to our castle to see him off. Once he leaves here today, he will not return a prince; he will return an apprentice and a soon-to-be guardian. Even once the Trials complete, though, there will still need to be approval from the lords and ladies of each nation. So I encourage you to make contact with the families in power in other nations and start rekindling any connections you may have. Tell them why my son is competent to become apprentice. . . ."

Hydro stated sweating at this point and tapping his leg as he waited for his father to continue and hopefully finish.

"He will become apprentice because of his determination, because of his perseverance, because of his skill, and, finally, because he has the blood of an Acquavan!"

Roars and cheers burst out at this point.

"He has seablood in his veins!" More cheers. "And because of this, he will have the ability to adapt to each trial, whatever it may be, just as water changes its form. We have lasted as a nation because of this ability, and it has given us confidence, and this confidence will be used to win the Trials. So, my son does not leave to attend these Trials for his own gain; he attends for the sake of Acquava."

Hydro had never heard such applause before. It sounded as strong as thunder. As discreetly as he could, he wiped his hands on his tunic, glad that the speech was done.

The feeling he had while up on the veranda, of being an idol for everyone to worship, continued through the progression. Eyes upon eyes upon eyes watched him progress, his father at his side and his mother and brother behind him. The acqua guards were close, as well as Darien and Len of his father's council. Hydro walked at his father's gait—a slow pace that allowed for all the more admiration.

"Thank you, Father," Hydro said. They were almost to the castle gates now, where a hovercraft waited for his father and him. The gates were open to allow for an overflow of people, and Hydro saw all the spaceships and hovercrafts parked on the flat plains outside the castle walls.

"You deserve a parting that befits your rank. I am glad you approve."

Hydro did. It was a nice gesture, but now there was no choice but success. (Like there ever had been anyway?) "It seems like everyone in Acquava is here to see me off."

"No. Not everyone. One wishes to see you off personally."

Hydro stopped. The hovercraft was less than fifty paces away. *There is still more. . . .* "Who?"

"Pearl." His father smiled, put his arm around Hydro, and walked the rest of the way to the ship.

Hydro had a feeling his father was going to say that name. *The goddess herself wishes to see me off.*

As Hydro walked the remaining paces, he thought about the weight this visit would hold compared to the three other times he had been brought before her. His father told him that upon his birth, he had been brought before Pearl. After Hydro cast his first spell of power and officially became a blessed at the age of nine, his father brought him to her as well. But the time that Hydro remembered most prominently was when he killed his first man and ascended into manhood. A man with no promise besides that of thievery was brought before his father, and Hydro could still feel the hilt of his father's coveted ether blade, Purge, in his hand when he commanded Hydro to swing the sword. That was at the age of thirteen, and Hydro had needed both hands to wield his father's longsword. The splatter of blood that caused Hydro to look away, the head rolling on the floor of the stone court, had been worth it then to hear his father say, "Congratulations, Son."

Hydro entered the passenger side of the hovercraft and waited as the trailing servants piled the baggage in the back. Though he never looked back, he could feel the eyes still upon him.

"Bye, Brother." Aiton was at the side of the vehicle.

Hydro smiled. "Bye, Aiton." He looked up and locked eyes with his mother. "Bye, Mother."

"Bye . . . may the Twelve be with you."

The comment seemed rather forced, but so was Hydro's. His mother walked away, pulling her son backwards with her so that the hovercraft could be started.

As his father pushed the start button underneath the container of ani-tron, Hydro asked, "How do you know she wants to see me?"

"She bid me. You cannot deny a goddess's bidding."

"No. You cannot. . . ." The hovercraft jolted off the ground. "Why does she wish to see me?"

"You will see."

The hovercraft drove off, and as it did so, Hydro took one last look at the people he had known, the people he would never see again.

• • •

Greedy eyes took in the sights like a newborn. Checkerboard-blue-and-white mosaic tiles stretched the length of the hallway. Between ivory columns sat white-washed statues carved in the likeness of the past rulers of Acquava. The Hall of the Lords.

"Do you remember these halls, Hydro?" asked Lord Paen.

Hydro nodded and said, "They always seem more magnificent than the time before."

"They always are."

Hydro walked with his father, passing the statues. Their soles shattered silence with brisk steps of anticipation. He bypassed earlier lords—such as Graynon Paquar, the first ruler of Acquava, and Symian Symer, founder of the city Symeria. And he also saw lords who ruled after the Great War—such as Karl Katarh, who froze to death in his own kingdom and had his lineage pass to Louis Hammersfall, the husband of his daughter, Karla. Their reign was short, and it was then that Hydro's family started rule under Lyonell Paen. History lived here, untainted by the salty air or unwanted eyes.

Hydro's grandfather, Áylan Paen, from whom Hydro received his middle name, was the last statue added, shortly before Hydro's last visit. Frail and old and suffering from mindloss were the last things Hydro remembered of him. Whenever he would talk to Hydro, he called him Hymin; it had become a nickname for Hydro, but Hydro wished he could see the man his father talked about—a man who stood as a symbol of their continued reign through three uprisings. One thousand feet from where his grandfather stood, the hall started to decline.

"Are you nervous, Hydro?"

"Never," Hydro lied.

"Your voice quivers. What is wrong?" Lord Paen stopped and looked at his son.

"Father, why are we here? The ship leaves from Encenro Falls, not here. We will never make it."

"You will see, Hydro. Be patient. Before you leave here today, you will see the true power of a goddess."

Hydro exhaled and tapped the side of his body but continued walking with his father. The last time he met Pearl, her deformity had left Hydro speechless. Gods were supposed to be flawless, not some creature in the form of a mermaid with seaweed hair and scaly arms that were as shiny as pearls. Hydro saw no magnificence so far, only those cruel yellow eyes. Did that make him wicked?

Minutes passed, and only their soles spoke. Down and down they went until the air became cold and he could taste the brine of the nearby ocean water. As the earthy path leveled out, the sconces that had lit the way earlier stopped. Hydro did as well.

Before him and his father stood a wall of water, fifteen feet in height and held in place as if encased in a glass box. The dark path hid from most of the suns' rays. It shone a little—enough to see that before them lay an

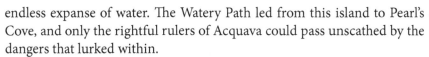

endless expanse of water. The Watery Path led from this island to Pearl's Cove, and only the rightful rulers of Acquava could pass unscathed by the dangers that lurked within.

"Before we enter, we must pray. Would you like to lead?"

"Pearl, navigate me through your waters, steer me to land, and drench me in your power."

Hydro trailed after his father as they passed through an invisible threshold; the glass-like material rippled up and down, sending out a low hum that reverberated throughout the hallway.

Power is how places like this existed—how Hydro and his father were able to breathe underwater, how their clothes did not get wet even in a chamber filled with water and sharks, and how they were able to stand on a surface while that same area rippled with the ocean's traffic. It was wondrous and rare, like the leviathan that roamed Leviathan's Bay near Talyn Island. That is how power would stay, too—in the hands of the powerful, until the Ancients came again.

Books and schooling taught Hydro that ever since the Great War and the disappearance of the Ancients, power stopped surging through the veins of just anyone. Those who had it before the Great War kept it in their lineage, but even that wasn't a guarantee. Children could still become denied instead of blessed, and families in power might have no power at all after centuries. Rulers on other planets had lost their reign due to their child's ineptness to cast. *A good change too*, Hydro had thought at the time. *Everyone having power seems too fair.*

After rounding a few bends in the path, a school of sharks circled them. Red eyes examined Hydro's worth. He did his best to ignore his heavy breathing. The sharks circled for awhile longer until some became bored and swam away from the Watery Path.

"You do not have to be afraid, Hydro."

"Who says I was?"

"Your breathing, your hand on your hilt, and your tone. Control your actions; you will need to if you wish to win the Trials. Otherwise you may become too predictable."

"That is only a small advantage."

"An advantage all the same, and one that might cause you to roam these watery halls one day instead of the proper place of a guardian."

Since the first ruler of Acquava, the deceased lords became guards to their god, even in the afterlife. Whether it was true or not, Hydro could not help but admit that he sometimes wondered if his grandfather lurked about.

After a few more turns, they ascended to a cove above land. The water sloshed against the granite steps. White-washed walls held the salty scent of the departing sea, and once the steps ended, the room opened up to a large, circular alcove supported by cobalt columns. After the columns, a mound of circular steps rose to support a pool of water with a golden fountain that misted the room. Open-mouthed clams—large enough to devour Hydro whole—lay waiting by each cobalt column. Mermen and mermaids inside of them carried various musical instruments. Above, the dome was painted with a ripple of waves that constantly changed to different views of Acquava.

Water rushed over the pool's edge and dripped down the circular steps, wetting the soles of both Hydro and his father. Hydro relieved the slight trembling in his leg by kneeling. Even after he rose, he tried not to acknowledge it. His pride, if nothing else, would keep him standing.

"I hear you are to attend Eska's Trials?" Pearl said. The goddess bathed in the pool of water. Hydro could only see her head and scaly, sleek arms. The moisture and mist made her seaweed hair cling to her face.

"Yes."

"And will you win?"

"If you see fit, my goddess."

"I do." Pearl shifted her gaze. "Lord Paen, what is it you wish of me?"

"I want you to show Hydro the power of a goddess. One-twelfth of the power that he will obtain by becoming guardian."

Pearl smiled. "Prince Paen. Come."

Hydro gulped and walked forward. As he climbed the steps, he passed two mermaids strumming harps. The female creatures were of fair skin and covered in nothing but necklaces of pearls and shells. Seaweed hair fell past their shoulders. Hydro looked at them; they looked back with daffodil eyes that made his groin tighten. The sweet music they plucked from the air enthralled him. Too much so. He looked away to regain Pearl's dark-blue eyes, but soon he regretted that decision.

To break the gaze, Hydro knelt at the top of the stairs. Pearl hoisted herself out of her pool and slid on her tail like a serpent around Hydro. The scales dissipated near her midriff. Bare skin lurked beneath her shirt of clams and shells—they rattled while she circled him. Hydro winced as Pearl dragged her long nails across the back of his shoulders. He closed his eyes.

A soft chant started. It wasn't power's language—it was older, more guttural, a language privy to gods and forgotten by years. At the end of it, Hydro expected to feel something, but he didn't. *Did it work?*

"Your destination is Encenro Falls." Pearl's voice was soft. Helpful. Seductive as the sea was to pirates. "I will transport you there now."

Pearl moved past Hydro to the pair of mermaids. A claw from each hand stole perfection away from their faces. As she dug into their skin, creating a trail of cerulean blood, they whimpered but remained stationary until their eyes glowed a dark yellow. In some unwritten code, the mermaids smeared their cheeks, covering their hands in the blood, and then they played again. *Did Pearl control them?*

The song strung was soft at first. Slowly it intensified. Each of their cheeks healed and they began to sing. It was a song Hydro had never heard.

> *The sea sways us.*
> *The sea guides us.*
> *The sea steers us.*
> *The sea! The sea! The sea!*
> *The sea listens to us.*
> *The sea demands from us.*
> *The sea allows us*
> *To see! To see! To see!*

From above, a swish echoed like waves on a beach. To his surprise, the watery dome shifted to one large image of Encenro Falls. Pearl said nothing; she only slid to the back of the room, circling around the throne. Hydro waited for his father, then followed. He stole a glance at the mermaids before he left. Their eyes pleaded for liberation.

On the wall behind the throne a large body-length mirror hung, its frame decorated in true gold. The glass shifted and reflected the image that rippled above them on the watery dome. The once-solid glass changed, as if it was liquid. It reminded Hydro of the Watery Path.

"This will take you to where you need to go."

Pearl didn't enter. Her blue eyes continued to look at them with slight satisfaction. His father stepped through. The act stupefied Hydro, but then, there were many things about a goddess's power that left answers to be desired. Pearl's gaze fell on him like a lone animal. "Do not abuse the power given to you, Hydro Áylan Paen."

Hydro paused. *What does she mean by that? Does she sense my doubts?* But he crossed the threshold, and a slap of wind jolted his senses. Pine trees lingered in the air, and rushing freshwater filled his ears. A dozen paces ahead, his father stood on a jutting rock that overlooked a forest below. A flock of morning birds cawed. "They are migrating. Is it that time of season already?"

Hydro didn't respond. He extended his arms, looking them over. "Father, I do not feel any different."

A sharp slap stung his cheek. "Hydro, you question a god's gift? Did you see that dome? She can see anything at any time—hear anyone at any time. Do you think Pearl would be pleased to hear disapproval?"

Hydro's flared temper subsided. "No . . ." He understood that he over-stepped his place. It was not his right to question the authority of a goddess.

A low rumbling like thunder pierced Hydro's ears. From the cloudy sky, a ship descended. It was a massive black-and-green army cargo trans-port. The roaring engines hushed the rushing water. "This is what Guard-ian Eska decides to send to pick us up?"

Lord Paen did not comment until it descended a few hundred more feet and hovered in clear sight of the jutted rock. "At least there will be no question of your safety." Lord Paen took Hydro by the shoulders and looked into his eyes. "I may not know when I will see you next, but I have no doubt that you will do our family proud. You have Pearl's blessing, the strength and sigil of the House of Paen, and also my praise and tidings—not as Lord Hydro Paen, but as your father. Atesia and Aiton will miss you. If you do return, I hope that it is for the better."

Hydro couldn't escape the hug that followed. During that embrace, he thought of Aiton, of his mother. When a tear slid down his cheek, he turned his head, leaving it to dry on his father's shoulder. For the first time, he realized how many duties would fall upon Aiton's lap at his departure. A heavy thud jolted him, and the embrace ended. "I know my departure will leave Aiton more responsibility to the family. But please let him main-tain his youth for as long as possible. I do not want to see him grow too old too fast."

"I will keep that in mind. Now go. Make Acquava proud."

Hydro walked up the ramp and entered the empty cargo hold. He claimed his spot on the far right wall, just underneath an audio box.

"Please strap on your harnesses and prepare for takeoff. Next stop, Gar."

Hydro chuckled to himself. *Garians? They don't know how to fight. Not truly. Even their precious elites are nowhere near the caliber of Father's acqua guards.*

Hydro didn't worry. He tilted his head back on a hard red neckrest, which comforted soldiers traveling long distances for war. He closed his eyes, but even there he couldn't escape the thousands of people who saw him off today. Even there he couldn't escape Pearl's gaze and the amount of confidence she put in him by her blessing. Even there he couldn't escape the duty he owed his family to win and uphold their pride.

CHAPTER 7

DOMNUX PLAINS

"One hour until Domnux Plains is reached."

The voice was gritty and mechanical, causing Eirek to tilt his head away from the holographic chess game. The message finished, he returned his focus to the game. In front of him was his opponent, Angal, examining each possible outcome while Eirek scanned for the opportunities. The onlooker of their game was Lady Clayse's advisor, Aeryn Shirewood, who sat on a blue bench to their left. Behind him a silver metal wall curved upwards to a glass ceiling. Shirewood was a man of missing teeth and large bifocals, which clung to a nose that sagged with the rest of his skin. On the man's doublet was a badge of an ear—the symbol of an advisor. On each of the man's fingers was a different ring, and on some fingers, two rings.

"Your move."

Eirek entered a few numbers on the keypad located on a stand attached to the table and watched a scene play out for him: The bishop advanced on the horse from behind, slit the horse's neck, and shoved it down on the holographic board, where it shattered into pieces of data. Eirek had never seen anything like it and looked on in amazement as it happened.

"Entertaining, is it not?" Aeryn asked while playing with the bands on his fingers.

"It's . . ." Eirek stumbled for words, "unusual."

"Unusual? Well, what is usual, then, for Eirek Mourse?"

He looked toward his uncle, still in contemplation. "Mystery."

Eirek watched as Angal mouthed scenarios to himself, drawing hypothetical lines of where he thought Eirek might move after he moved.

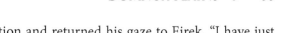

Finally he entered his option and returned his gaze to Eirek. "I have just the perfect mystery."

What riddle is it this time? No visit was ever complete without a riddle of some sort. Angal usually asked them the first day and let Eirek ponder the possibilities for the next few days until finally solving it or forfeiting.

"What's that?" Aeryn arched his eyebrows and scratched the scruff on his chin.

"What is it that the Ancients never saw, that the Twelve seldom see, but what we see every day?"

"A very interesting riddle you pose, Angal," Aeryn said.

Eirek scanned the battlefield while in contemplation of the riddle. Once satisfied with the battle plan drawn in his head, he entered his move. "How about—"

"A shackle?"

You might as well have said a tree. "No," Eirek said, in place of his uncle. "Eirek, you know?"

"No, but I know it cannot be a shackle. I was going to say humans."

Aeryn laughed. "And you think your answer is better? It is too plain. Now, why cannot mine be a shackle? People see the environment they are in as a shackle constraining them."

Only because the Clayses are not as receptive as you would attest. Even before Eirek was dropped off twelve years ago, the Clayses had been in power. Growing up in the impoverished city of Creim, needing to walk ten miles to Lisyn for schooling because Creim was too small to have its own, and the constant highwinds that roamed their area during the summer months, constantly tearing down homes and dreams just so they could be rebuilt without any aid from the family in power gave testament to their lack of receptiveness. Aeryn could never see that though; he came from a different cloth; so did Angal.

"Likewise, the Twelve are confined to their homes or their mountains of Volan and Klaff."

Eirek scanned the board again; Angal had just moved. His uncle's mischievous grin told him that he enjoyed their bickering. "And the Ancients were shackled. Although they might not have seen it," Eirek finished. "Everyone knows they didn't disappear; they were locked away."

"That tale is child's speak. And I thought you were older," Aeryn shot back. "Why is your answer better?"

"Well, you and I see others like us every day. The Twelve are not solely confined to Mount Volan or Klaff, so families in power see them occasionally—"

"And the Ancients?"

I was getting to them. "Our blood is what makes us human, you and I age the same way. The Ancients never saw anyone without First Blood." Eirek entered in numbers on the keypad for his last move. "Checkmate!"

The lord and lady and bishop all advanced Angal's lonely and unarmed lord and slaughtered it to the likeness of *One Thousand Soldiers' Steel*—a book from the Mourses that Eirek had read once; it told of a Marquis's rise to power and lordship, a great war that ensued, and finally betrayal when the thousand soldiers who fought for him stabbed him for his reluctance to acknowledge their part in his rule.

The speakerbox cut short the advisor's chortle. "We have arrived."

"Your idea is foolish, Eirek. But I will attest to your skill at that game. Angal never beat you in all four times you played."

"Well, you both are foolish. Neither one is right," Angal said.

"Pray tell, what is it?" Aeryn asked.

"A wordsmith who explains his answers is like a magician who shows his tricks."

Aeryn's smile turned to a flat line.

Past the second half of the lounge, the steel door with Cresica's crest slid open, and the pilot strode out. Using the three fingers that remained on his left hand, he pushed a few buttons, opening a side near the throat of the ship. Light crept in along with the noises of nature and streams. Angal picked up an object hidden underneath a red cloth and led Eirek and Aeryn out the door.

What in Trema's Garden is he carrying? Eirek had wanted to ask even before they boarded the small Aral unit; but since Angal had told him nothing up until then, why should he change now?

Domnux Plains was a long lay of land. A river flowed through it, separating two land masses if not for three stone bridges. The height of the bridges easily allowed biremes or large budgerows underneath, and the width of the river allowed two ships to travel side-by-side.

Eirek looked at the scenery in awe. To the west lay a stretch of rising flat hillsides, and to the east Eirek saw a large expanse of blue. *It seems too big to be a lake.*

"Dear boy, you seem confused," Aeryn said.

"I have never been this far north."

"Well, those bridges are called the Three Maidens. They were Trema's most devoted worshipers, and everywhere they stepped, they created land. To divide the two continents, however, they walked on air over the water to form bridges."

"What is that called?" Eirek pointed to the blue expanse.

"An ocean. The Open Ocean, to be precise. Now, how much time do we have?"

Eirek watched Angal, who had his back turned, carrying the red-clothed object in his arms like a mother watching her child. "You know, Aeryn, instead of tearing the boy down for not knowing his geography, you should be encouraging him to succeed. He is representing the Clayses, after all." Angal turned around, showing the present in his arms—it had the distinctive shape of a sword, but Eirek didn't want to get his hopes up. His uncle had been known to let them fall.

Eirek looked at Aeryn, who crossed his arms and tilted his chin up but said nothing. *That was amazing.* Eirek smiled at Angal and then set his bags of clothes given to him by the Clayses on the ground. *I wish I could say something like that.* Eirek took the card he kept in his pants pocket and looked at it. "Half an hour," Eirek replied.

"Half an hour, you say? What are we going to do in such a boring place?" Aeryn scratched his chest through his wool doublet, which was dyed in the celadon and brown of House Clayse.

"Here is something that may pass the time." Like a magician, Angal yanked the cloth off the object. In his hand was a smoky-colored scabbard outlined with amethyst.

"A sword!"

"You will need this in the upcoming Trials. Here." Angal handed over the gift.

Eirek's fingers traced the amethyst lines over the scabbard. The case was worn but appeared regal in its antiquity. The leather grip fit perfectly to Eirek's hand. *This is what a blade feels like.* He had felt one before at Jerald's shop, but never his own. His hand lingered on the hilt.

"Pull it out, already," Aeryn said.

Eirek obliged. Different hues of gray composed the steel's blade and moved with the suns' gazes. It reminded Eirek of storm clouds. At the tip, the blade was pure white. Its guard was a deep amethyst color, extending like bull horns a hand's length from where the steel started.

"Quite the blade, Angal. Where did you find that treasure?"

Eirek looked up and saw Aeryn's eyes evaluating it closely.

"I received it a long time ago. It was a . . . a . . . wedding present."

Angal never spoke about her, and hardly about the wedding or separation. Eirek wondered if Angal even knew the tale anymore.

"This is magnificent. Thank you, Angal." Eirek lost himself in the sword.

"Better to suit you than me."

Eirek approached Angal and wrapped his arms around him. *What am I doing?* Eirek let go and tried to pull away, but Angal's arms wouldn't budge, as if he had been waiting for the embrace all his life. *He still abandoned me.*

Shade and a gust of wind afforded his body a reprieve from the torn torment. The ship was here, hovering above the ground as it prepared for landing. As it descended, Eirek stole a glance at Angal, who had ended the embrace. A certain sadness Eirek had never seen betrayed Angal's look of pride. *Has he had this look every time he's left me?*

The ship was an ugly army-green. It looked like a large cargo ship, comparable to a tank. Its behemoth size dwarfed the Aral ship Eirek arrived in. Multiple black flaps jutted outward from one side in order to slow its descent. Eirek caught just a glimpse of large cannons that could slide through those gaps if attacked. *Well, I'll definitely arrive there safely.*

When the ship hovered only a few feet above the ground, it let itself drop, creating a violent tremor. The shockwave would have knocked Eirek over, but Angal caught him. A thick steam escaped the ships exterior, and from out of it, a steep ramp extended.

Eirek turned back to Angal. "I can't do this. . . ."

"You most certainly will!" Aeryn called out. "I woke at dawn's breath to get you here."

"You can do this. Eirek, everyone there, regardless of status, is just another person like you. They are your equals. You all have an equal chance of winning. Why else would Guardian Eska pick you?" Angal asked.

Why was I picked? The thought had wandered in and out of his mind since receiving the letter.

"Listen, Eirek," Angal said, "each person completed the same application; each person received the same acceptance letter. There it is. There is your equal. Will you remember that?"

Eirek didn't understand Angal's logic. But he did get accepted. That must mean something. Eirek looked into his eyes and nodded. "Yeah. I will."

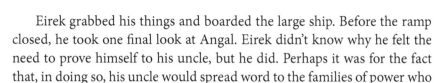

Eirek grabbed his things and boarded the large ship. Before the ramp closed, he took one final look at Angal. Eirek didn't know why he felt the need to prove himself to his uncle, but he did. Perhaps it was for the fact that, in doing so, his uncle would spread word to the families of power who he treated with.

The ramp closed. Eirek sighed, turned around, and sat on a bench to the left, laying his things on the floor. Electric lights casted a dim glow in the cargo hold—apparently bright enough for reading, for another young man garbed in silks that Eirek could never hope to own had his head down and a book in his lap. Stitched to his green shirt was a badge of purple and gray that depicted an owl perched on a branch of a tree. *Whose sigil is that?* The fiery hair reminded him of the riders of Kane. Glasses without rims sat on top of his long aquiline nose and protected green eyes. The man glanced from the book to look at him a second, but then he continued reading.

Eirek was about to ask what book he was reading, but before he could, a voice from the speakerboxes in the corners of the cargo room cut him off. "Next stop, Mistral. Please adjust yourselves for takeoff."

Mistral. I have never been to the nation in the sky. Eirek looked to the other man; it seemed the announcement had no affect on him. *Is the book that engrossing?* Eirek noticed the emeralds and topazes on the man's fingers and realized how stupid he was. The man was royalty; he had probably traveled everywhere there was to travel. And just like Angal, he engrossed himself in texts. For not being a major part of his life for twelve years, Eirek wondered how his uncle continued to cross his mind. *Were the times we spent together really that memorable?*

Not wanting to continue in silence, Eirek said, "My name is Eirek. What's yours?"

The man looked at him, then back to his book. "Prince Cain Evber from Epoch."

Silence again.

"What book are you reading?"

The man ignored him, but he held up the book so Eirek could see. *A Hundred Tales* was stitched into the cover with gold threads. Eirek hadn't read it; there weren't many books at the Mourses. "What's it about?"

"Tales. There are one hundred in here, if you were paying attention to the title." The man never looked up from his book.

"What kinds of tales?"

"The kind that require silence to read. Thank you."

I will just not to talk to royalty anymore. But the silence felt foreign to him. As he tapped his fingers on his crossed arms, he contemplated the possibility that maybe royalty didn't understand him, just as he didn't understand royalty. *I need to change that.* By winning these Trials, he hoped to prove to royalty that success isn't just measured by blood or power; it's measured by determination.

❧ CHAPTER 8 ❧

THE CENTRAL CORE

What did I do? Zain looked at his hands. *What did I do?* He put his palms into his eyes and cried. Even after an hour of riding in the ship, guilt still clung tight to him as if it were the rain that still soaked his body. "Zakk . . ."

"I zought he looked familiar."

What? Zain looked up and noticed the woman still staring at him. He had forgotten about her. Her name was Gabrielle Ravwey, and she was the star student at Gracie's Academy—the sister school for Gazo's, one only for girls. *She knows. She knows I killed Zakk. She knows Zakk.* Zain had caught glimpses of her tournament bouts and a few times taken to the winner's ring with her when the winners of all different divisions were pooled together for a photo and celebration.

"You don't understand. . . ." *No one does. I don't even understand.* He looked at his hands and tried to figure out why they let go.

"I suppose I don't. But I do know zat we ladies over at Gracie's are much more decent zan you brutes at Gazo's. We actually look our enemy in za face before using our daggers. We actually do not kill others from our own academy. We actually—"

"Enough!" Zain yelled. "Please. . . . Stop it. . . . Don't say that. . . . He's alive. . . . He has to be. . . ." His mind reeled as he imagined the fall: how time must have slowed, how Zakk's life must have flashed, the mixture of emotions he was sure to have. Why? Zain cried again and closed his eyes. Even in the darkness, he still saw Zakk's confusion as Zain let go. Even as silence settled, he could still hear Zakk's plead for help. His fingers felt heavy. He flexed them, trying to wake them and revive their use, but all he felt was Zakk slipping from his grasp.

• • •

Zain opened his eyes to a mechanical voice filtering through the speakers. "An hour to the Central Core."

Zain gazed out of one of the windows near his seat. Another identical ship approached, one wingspan away. The ship floated through space as seamlessly as a boat on ocean waters. Gazo's taught Zain that the wormholes in Gladonus were like the veins and arteries of a body. They led to vital parts of the universe—aurorae, magnetic fields, and planets. Many different wormholes led to the Central Core, the heart of the system. All wormholes stopped, however, parsecs from the Core, near the militia base of Hown, led by General Soren Satorus. From there, only one wormhole led to the Central Core.

The ship hummed and moved again. On the monitor in the cargo room, a large asteroid, large enough to be a moon and suspended amongst stars, came into view.

"Is that Hown?"

"Yes," Gabrielle replied. "Zey are shutting off za guard beams so we can enter."

"And the other ships?"

"You didn't zink it would be just you and me competing, did you?" She smiled at him, bent her hand toward herself, and laughed.

Zain blushed. *Stupid. Stupid. Stupid.* He looked at her smile. It caught him off-guard. It was the same smile. . . . But Ava was gone. She fell to her death, just like. . . . Zain caught his hand trembling again.

For the next half hour, Zain kept his gaze steady on Gabrielle. She saw. She knew what happened. Would she let others know? If she did, what would it mean for Zain? Would he still be allowed to compete? There were several times she caught his gaze and appeared to be disinterested. Finally she asked, "Why do you keep staring at me?"

"Are you going to tell what happened?"

"No. It isn't my business to tell."

The knot that had been tightening in his stomach loosened a little. He let his shoulders relax. He tried not moving his hands, because that caused him to think of it. In fact, he tried to do as little physically as possible. Now that he was guaranteed a chance to compete, he needed to use it. For him, for Zakk, and for Ava. For the sole purpose of pushing Zakk out of his mind, he tried to fill it with as much about whom these contestants could possibly be or where they could have come from.

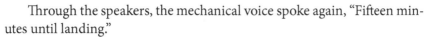

Through the speakers, the mechanical voice spoke again, "Fifteen minutes until landing."

How are we supposed to land? There is no planet here. Zain only saw empty space with two silver rings crossing one another. Past the rings was the red sun, Freyr, as large as a fist, and Lugh, as small as a thumb.

"Where are we—" Zain never finished his sentence, for at that point, as the ship glided underneath one of the silver bands, a large mass of brown, specked with dots of blue, and a mass of green to the north appeared instantaneously. "How did that happen?"

"Za Ancients Lyoen and Bane said a prayer before zey disappeared during za Great War. Zey wished zat zeir homelands wouldn't be discovered by zose not of first blood."

"Prayers don't work."

"It did. Zey always do. Gazo's wouldn't know about prayer zough. . ."

"Please fasten safety belts; touchdown in a minute's time."

Zain's was already secured. Dirt and dust made the other ships invisible, but he assumed they were in hovering mode as well.

The humming below stopped, and the ship dropped to the ground. They were here. Zain unbuckled and looked at the monitor displaying the view outside. Dust still held the air captive.

He turned toward Gabrielle and then back to the monitor above the door to the rest of the ship. The dust settled, and beyond it stood a mansion painted in sepia. Twelve columns of gold held up the second-floor balcony. Six columns of gold on the balcony held a third-level veranda, which overlooked a vast area of dirt and sand and emptiness. Behind the estate was a sky of purple. *This is the Central Core?*

"Unlocking door hatch."

The back of the ship opened, and a ramp extended down to the dirt below. Zain looked toward Gabrielle, who stared back at him. She gave a whimsical smirk and continued staring. *Why does she have to smile?* Zakk infiltrated his thoughts soon enough, and he could only look down at his bags. He tried not to cry, but he did. *Everyone else deserves to be here. I don't.*

A hand squeezed his shoulder. "Good luck."

Zain looked up, mopped up his tears with his forearm, and asked, "Why'd you wish me that?"

"Because I'm decent, and," Gabrielle picked up her things, "since you don't pray, you'll need it." She flounced down the ramp and out of sight, leaving Zain as confused as the dust that still wandered in the grave of night.

❦ CHAPTER 9 ❧

RIVALRIES

A picture-painted cupola depicted two warriors who were donned in a thick armor of gold. Swords brandished in silver pointed toward the land. Below that, a crystal chandelier hung. Even the spiral staircase—extending to the second floor and made of veiny marble—almost bewitched Eirek enough to make him forget about the competitors around him: Prince Evber, a large man, a black-skinned man, a woman, and a man with black hair and rich clothes. Besides the black-skinned man, all ignored the estate's beauty, busying themselves with eyeing each other instead; he merely stood with his hand over his head as if he was experiencing a headache.

When a man with a receding hairline and glasses spoke, Eirek pulled his attention from the surroundings and focused on him and the row of people behind him.

"Contestants, my name is Colin, Guardian Eska's chief servant. It is a pleasure to be at your—"

"When will we get to see Guardian Eska?" The voice was deep and low, so Eirek assumed it belonged to the large man with russet hair.

If Colin was annoyed about the man's interruption, he did not show it. "I am sure you are all anxious to meet Guardian Eska. However, each of you has had a long day. Introductions will happen tomorrow, once you have had ample time to prepare your manners and your attire." Colin analyzed each of them. "When I call your name, please step forward, and one of us will carry your bags and show you to your room. Now, Zain Berrese?"

Nothing.

"Zain Berrese?" Colin waited.

Eirek turned back and forth, trying to see who it might be. But no one stepped forward. He noticed the girl shaking the shoulders of the black-skinned man who was still in deep contemplation.

"Okay, if Zain Berrese, is not present, then—"

"Wait. Wait. Sorry."

The man strode forward with blush on his face and a squish in his step, as though he had been soaked in water before boarding the ship. Greeted by a slender woman who probably weighed more in bones than skin, he gave one of his large bags to her, and she buckled underneath the weight. This produced an enormous roar of laughter from the onlookers. Although he felt guilty, Eirek chuckled as well.

"Avery, take the bags for her," Colin said.

A different servant of a stockier frame but just as bald as the old man managed to carry both bags as he led Zain out of the lobby.

Once they were gone, Colin continued, "Cadmar Briggs?"

Eirek couldn't help but stare at the man who came forward. He was as tall as Prince Evber but with another one hundred pounds of muscle and bone, Eirek was sure—a giant. A shield was strapped to his back, but it did little to hide the man's girth. A male servant of dark hair and a heavy beard took both bags with no difficulty and led Cadmar out of the room.

"Cain Evber?"

"Prince Evber, please." The man stood at least a foot taller than Eirek, but compared to Cadmar, he was a twig to his trunk. Fiery hair bounced as the man approached.

"My apologies, Prince Evber."

"Apology accepted. Now, my room?"

"Yes, Geoffrey will show you the way."

An older man of gray hair and drooping back hunched over even more to pick up the bags and then led the prince out of the lobby. Eirek took that opportunity to look at the other two—a female and a male both graced with black hair and fine clothes. Neither looked at him but, rather, kept their arms crossed over their chests and glanced at one another every so often.

"Peter Koluma?"

Eirek looked toward the man with black hair. He didn't move.

"Peter Koluma?" The butler swept his head from Eirek back to the other man.

He must not have made it. Was he the man we were supposed to pick up in Mistral?

"Okay, if Peter Koluma is not present, then Eirek Mourse?"

Eirek stepped forward and was greeted by a woman shortened by age. Gray curls didn't extend past her neck; she had bushy eyebrows, thick bifocals, and a squished face pressed together by numerous wrinkles. Her eyes reminded him of Sheryin—the same ones that obliged Eirek to do anything she asked. The only thing she asked, however, was for his bags. Eirek followed her to the left and into a hallway but glanced back at the two competitors who still remained nameless to him. *I wonder who they are?*

Paintings of various strange places adorned the walls. Halfway into the hallway, near a small crevice, stood a statue of a man plated in gold armor—similar to the cupola painting in the lobby.

"Is that a statue of Ancient Lyoen?"

The woman didn't hear him, or ignored him, for she kept walking.

"Excuse me, miss?" he spoke up.

The woman turned around. "Yes, dear?"

"Is that a statue of Ancient Lyoen?"

The woman seemed taken aback, as though it was unheard of to receive such a question. "Yes, dear, it is. He created—"

A man cut her off, "The worlds, the elements, and humans. His brother, Ancient Bane, grew jealous that Lyoen created life, so he established death and equipped us with swords, words of power, and emotions—according to the Old-Way Believers, if you believe such a thing." Eirek turned and saw that it was the man with black hair and fine clothes, who followed a dark-skinned man.

A peculiar scent wafted in the air. It smelled like the sea—an aroma Eirek only experienced faintly as he waited for the transport to pick him up from Domnux Plains. But this scent was overpowering, as if the man who had interrupted came from a place where there was more sea than land.

"Thank you. What's your name?"

"Prince Paen. Do well to remember it."

The dark-skinned man opened a door and stood to the side as the black-haired man picked up his belongings.

"Aren't you going to ask mine?" Eirek stopped at the threshold of Prince Paen's door.

"No."

"Why not? Common manners says that—"

"Commoners use common manners, but my common sense tells me that in a month your name will not matter to me." Prince Paen closed the door.

Eirek rolled his eyes. *Why is royalty always rude?* He turned back to the old woman, who remained expressionless.

"Here is your room, Sir Mourse." She unlocked the door and handed the key to Eirek.

"It's Eirek."

"I will do my best to remember, dear. If you need anything, don't be hesitant to ask." She set his bags on the floor and hobbled past him down the hallway.

Before she got too far, Eirek called out, "And for whom do I ask?"

She stopped and turned, a smile on her face. "Dina, dear." She turned back and continued walking.

Eirek smiled, facing his room. The scent of freshly-cooked food drifted through the air, which was filtered by an open window. A rumble occurred in his stomach then—whether from his hunger or his nervousness, Eirek didn't want to know. He gathered his bags and crossed the threshold into the place that would be his new home for the coming month—or longer.

CHAPTER 10

IN THE LOBBY

It was the day after they arrived, the day when Hydro would finally meet Guardian Eska. Hydro made sure he was properly dressed, adorning himself in garbs of rich royal-blue silk buttoned up with polished anthracite buttons and his family's sigil stitched on a field of black.

Hydro was the third contestant to arrive in the lobby patrolled by the old servant. The other prince had already arrived and was chatting with the woman whose name still escaped him. Prince Evber wore a shirt of light yellow with his sigil of a purple owl perched on the branch stitched on a field of gray. His fingers were adorned in emeralds and topazes. The woman wore a blouse as black as her hair (cut slightly past the shoulders) that extended to her skirt of red. A poppy red scarf hung to the breasts near the frilling of her blouse. Stitched in purple and white to the upper right of her blouse was a badge with the word Gracie's next to a circle with a dagger protruding from its bottom. Rather than earrings, she had a pierced lip—its ring ebony black. Bracelets of many colors reminded him of Elias Ward. *Is she skilled in the practices of healing?*

"The broken tear of House Paen," Cain called to him. "You are Hydro Paen, then, correct?"

Hydro would have corrected any other contestant by demanding to be called *Prince Hydro Paen*—but he and Cain Evber were equals. He did correct him on one article though. "The second. I am not my father."

Cain chuckled. "My apologies. How was the voyage here?"

"I shared time with a Garian; a huge brute at that."

"Cadmar was his name. . . . I wondered where he was from."

That wasn't interesting. Hydro knew his name. Instead he wanted to learn about the woman next to Cain. He had yet to hear her name. The woman's eyes wandered between the two of them. Was she studying them? *Clever lady.* Hydro couldn't imagine her to be too large of a threat though. As far as Hydro knew, there were no female fighters on Acquava—only men bred of the sea and salt. Instead many preferred to study adored arts and confront the battle that happened behind the lines—the battle to save lives.

"And how was your travel?" Hydro asked.

"I traveled with the poorer fellow."

"To a prince, isn't everyone poor?" The woman spoke with a slight variant of Common Tongue.

Cain chuckled. "I suppose you are correct, there, Gabrielle. I traveled with the brown-haired fellow."

Hydro eyed her with intrigue before returning his gaze to Cain. "The commoner?" Hydro looked up at the ceiling. He hadn't noticed the painted cupola before.

"I cannot tell you his name. All he did was ask questions."

"And is zat a bad zing?"

"Do you like the man?" Cain raised his eyebrow.

Gabrielle chuckled. "Of course not. But he seems decent, like me. . . ."

Footsteps came from the other side of the lobby. Hydro took his eyes off the cupola and saw Zain enter. He wore a black vest with gold buttons and a crimson, long-sleeved undershirt. On the left side of his chest, there was a red circle with a sword pointing diagonally through it. Embroidered in red stitching was the word *Gazo's. Gazo's Academy?* That meant something. Compared to Symmetry Academy in Symeria, Gazo's was far above it in caliber.

"Zere are too many unbecoming people out zere." Gabrielle looked at Zain and then back to Cain.

"Your accent tells you are from Empora, yes?" Hydro asked.

Gabrielle furrowed her sleek eyebrows at him and nodded. "What of it?"

"Nothing. I hear people there have taken to prayer quite much."

"We need to. Victor Zigarda is a horrible ruler. Prayer is za only zing zat works for hope to stay alive. . . ."

Hydro looked around and noticed Zain with his head down as he flexed his hand. He had remained silent this whole time; Hydro wondered why. When he heard heavy thuds coming from the staircase, Hydro turned to see a large man in silk. *I did not know Eska kept pig pens in his estate too.*

"Girl, he is not a *horrible* ruler. He has just ruled a *horribly* long time. I find people get restless when one person's reign continues for so long."

"It is Senator Numos, correct?" Cain asked.

"Why, yes, Prince Evber. I am glad you recognize me."

"Well, rumors spread to Epoch that you were the one selected for witnessing this event."

Hydro eyed him in disgust. *I'm sure it wasn't by choice.*

"Rumors spread as fast as wind." The senator's goatee couldn't cover the three levels of chin that bobbed as he spoke.

Or as wide as your girth. Hydro studied the wooden cane that the man used for support, and he wondered why it hadn't broken yet. Opal jewels adorned the man's right hand; his left hand, gloved in white, held a small glass eyepiece. A white gown with ornate designs—laced in various golds and silvers—tried to cover the man's obesity. It only succeeded in making him look more handsome than any other garment could.

"Senator Numos, if you will join the others in the lobby's circle. It is nearly time for introductions," the old servant directed.

Hydro had not noticed the sapphire circle amongst the tiles of marble. "When can we begin?" He stepped forward, positioning himself beside Cain on the sapphire circle.

"When the other contestants arrive. There is still time," the old servant said.

No less than a few seconds after the butler spoke, the Garian and the commoner emerged out of the hallway talking to one another. *Finally.* The Garian wore a skin-tight muscle shirt as dark brown as his hair. On his shoulders, extending down to his elbows, were steel armor plates, and strapped to his back was a shield. He carried an axe by his hip. He wore dirty-white breeches on his lower half. The commoner wore a white shirt, which seemed to be large enough for the Garian; upon it was the sigil of Lady Clayse in celadon and brown.

"Please take a spot on the sapphire circle at the lobby's center." Once they took spots near Gabrielle and Senator Numos, the old servant continued, "Please remain on the circle. This is the only way up to Guardian Eska's floor."

After pushing a small button on a device in the man's hand, a low rumbling noise purred from the bowels of the palace. A sudden jolt upwards

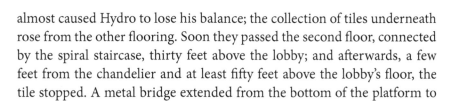

almost caused Hydro to lose his balance; the collection of tiles underneath rose from the other flooring. Soon they passed the second floor, connected by the spiral staircase, thirty feet above the lobby; and afterwards, a few feet from the chandelier and at least fifty feet above the lobby's floor, the tile stopped. A metal bridge extended from the bottom of the platform to a gap in the third floor that was otherwise barricaded by a marble railing.

Hydro was the first to step over the bridge and onto the circular floor carpeted in a dark amaranthine. Two men waited before aurulent double doors. *Are they two of his conseleigh?*

Hydro walked closer toward them but stopped as he noticed a portrait of a lady hanging on the wall; next to her was a portrait of a man. He glanced around the walls and noticed that twelve individual portraits were spaced throughout. It wasn't the portrait, though, that got his attention, it was the name—Pearl. Hydro glanced from the nameplate to the portrait of a woman with fair skin and dark hair and the same dark-blue eyes. *How is that possible? What happened to her scales and her seaweed hair?*

Is Eska how I imagined him to be? His father told him that although Eska was more than two hundred years old, he looked no older than himself. That he was a tall man, half a foot taller than himself. That he was a man who answered to no one besides the Twelve. And that he, too, had an ether blade called Adonis—given to him by the Twelve.

With a hint of doubt, Hydro rejoined the group outside the double doors. A man of normal height with hair as red as fire stood next to a shorter man who displayed more hair on his face than his thick forearms.

The man who hid behind a thicket of hair stepped forward. "Contestants, my name is Ethen Rorum, conseleigh of te planet Myoli. Congratulations on coming tis far. As Guardian Eska will point out, tese next monts will be tough. Good luck to you all."

The shorter man, with hair as red as fire, stepped forward and spoke, "My name is Riagan Inferno, conseleigh of the planet Pyre. Behind these doors Guardian Eska waits to meet you personally. Enter and declare yourselves fully dedicated to these Trials and the events about to take place."

His eyes were a shade of orange Hydro had never seen before, and his skin was the red of Freyr's sunlight. He appeared young though, no older than forty-five—much younger than Hydro would have expected for a conseleigh. A badge of a red circle with a golden C in the center sat pinned to his vest of black, which was layered over a red dress shirt with ornate lines of orange silk.

"Contestants, line up one by one in te order by which you wish to introduce yourselves. Senator Numos, you will be at te end, saving introductions until te rest 'ave finished." Conseleigh Rorum strummed his conical beard, smiling and surveying the contestants. He readjusted his own conseleigh badge, and the smile turned to a grim line. "Line up!"

No one moved. The inaction enabled Hydro to make his way to the front of the line. He would be the first to introduce himself, setting the bar; and the others would fail to grab hold.

CHAPTER 11

INTRODUCTIONS

The door opened.

Nine individuals marched inside. Guardian Eska knew two of them intimately—they were his youngest conseleigh. Still, they gave council as well as any. The oldest member of his council, Tundra Iycel, was sixteen to thirty-one years their senior. She stood by his side now, just as she had stood by his side and behind his decisions for thirty-five years when she replaced Neil Marmod at the age of thirty-eight. She had been widowed by that point after her husband died in a mammoth hunt. He hoped each would remain until he passed his duties in his two hundredth year.

Guardian Eska focused his mind toward Tundra. He didn't want to speak aloud to all of them. Not yet at least. *Is that Prince Paen of Acquava leading, Tundra?*

Yes. He resembles his father greatly, doesn't he?

Indeed. Any others you recognize?

The large man, third in line. Cadmar Briggs. His father is an elite in service to Lady Aprah.

Father and status doesn't matter. Not here. Competence does. Those here are equals until the Trials conclude. If Guardian of the Core was based merely on a family's lineage, I may not be here right now; Victor Zigarda may be in my stead.

Yes, I was merely telling, Edwyrd.

Guardian Eska moved his eyes to each of them. Only six of the eight candidates showed. *So, the sorting begins.* He took note of the owl of Epoch, the badges of both Gazo's and Gracie's Academy, and the mansion of the Clayses.

I did not know the Clayses had a son.
They do not, Edwyrd.
Then who is that? He is wearing their sigil.
Luvan would know better than I, but he is not here.
I suppose it matters not.

Guardian Eska studied them all equally. His mentor, Guardian Matthau Crevon, told him to not let sigils, badges, or prestige bias the choosing of apprentice. The Trials would sort the strong from the weak. Nothing else mattered.

By the time he finished his examinations, the other Conseleigh were by his side. Like the conseleigh before them, they made Eska feel complete. They had been his family since time took his. He raised one hand, gloved in darknether, the only material strong enough to contain the different powers given to him by the Twelve. It was the same material that made up the reimaje on his head, but that was dipped in a pool of ether from Gladima itself. Although it looked like a black bandana, its function was much greater than that. It stored memories as he willed it to, and because of that, he was able to see everything that Guardian Matthau Crevon saw and Guardian Jorey Raule saw before him. When removed from his head, it had even greater power.

"Contestants, state your name, where you are from, and who you are here for." Eska remained stern.

Prince Paen stepped forward and laid his sword on the ground. "My guardian, I am Prince Hydro Aylán Paen II, son to Lord Hydro Paen from the nation of Acquava. I am here for my family and my nation." Afterwards, the prince bowed and knelt.

Most princes are. The woman from Gracie's stepped forward next. "My guardian, my name is Gabrielle Ravwey from za nation Empora. I am here on behalf of Gracie's Academy, which taught me to be zankful for our minds, free to think." Gabrielle placed the palm of her left hand to her forehead. "For our bodies, free to fight." Her right hand clenched into a fist and was placed over her heart. "And for our souls, free to bind." She then combined her two hands at her lips and kissed them. She curtsied alongside Prince Paen.

Eska resisted the urge to raise his eyebrows. He needed to remain stoic. It wasn't her Emporian accent or her answers that stood out to him; it was the prayer she performed. Few knew all three steps to the Old Prayer. *Does she understand its significance?* Chances were unlikely.

The man with dark-brown hair and a body larger and stronger than most stepped forward. He bowed and took the shield off his back with his left arm and grabbed the axe attached to his hip with his right hand. When he rose, he banged both together three times and set them to the floor before his introduction. "My name be Cadmar Briggs, sir. From the nation of Gar be where I'm from. I fight for my lady's honor, Lady Olivia Aprah." He bowed and knelt, resting his forehead on the knob of his axe.

The banging didn't bother Eska; that was merely custom in Gar. *He fights for his lady.* The answer was decent; it showed he valued someone other than himself. But it wasn't original. The next contestant stepped forward. Compared to the man before him, this man was half Cadmar's size and wearing a shirt of gold and white meant for the person before him. The mismatched sigil stitched to his shirt stuck out to Eska, begging a second look. Upon obliging his curiosity, Eska noticed faint-purple eyes. How *intriguing...*

"My . . . my . . . guardian, my name is Eirek Mourse from the nation of Cresica. I am here on behalf of the Clayses . . . and also . . . those like me . . . those of the same cloth. . . ."

Guardian Eska kept his gaze on him a little while longer. *No unsheathing of a weapon. No prayer. Nothing else. The man lacks confidence, but his answer is strong.*

Next, the dark-skinned man from Gazo's stepped forward. *Which one is this now?* Eska recalled inviting two from that academy.

"Guardian Eska, I am Zain Berrese from the nation of Ka'Che. I am here . . ." The man paused as he looked at the sword in his hands. "I am here on behalf of those who are unable to be." Zain took his sword and raised it up to the sky. He balanced the pommel on his palm for a moment and flipped it to the floor with grace and speed. The man knelt and rested his forehead on the pommel.

How am I supposed to take that answer? Rather vague. There are many who are not able to be here. At least his performance with the blade was good. Eska switched his focus to the last candidate—Prince Cain Evber of Epoch.

"My guardian, my full name is Prince Cain Emery Evber from the great nation of Epoch. I travel here on behalf of those yet to be born." From behind his back, he pulled out a silver lance and twirled it like a mad oarsmen; at the end of his routine, he broke the staff in two, held both pieces in the air in an X-formation, and laid the pieces on the ground as he knelt.

A good display, but you did not need it to pad your answer. He didn't let his gaze linger too long on Cain but instead scanned the kneeling contestants once more. Guardian Eska clapped, and the conseleigh soon followed.

"Congratulations, all were fair and truthful answers. Senator Numos, what do you think?"

The large man stroked his chins and readjusted his cane. "They were fair and true, I agree."

"Contestants, please rise." Eska raised his arms, waiting to lower them until everyone stood. "Please turn to face our honored guest for these Trials. Out of all the names entered to be my sole spectator of this historic event, Senator Numos was picked. He has been here since late last week. Senator, if you would please tell them about yourself."

"Guardian Eska." The Senator bowed once. "Conseleigh." He bowed again. "And Contestants." The man extended his arm to all six contestants. "My name is Senator Nyom Numos, politician under the fairest lady, Lady Liliana. I am owner of several estates on Mistral and author of a few books. I have proposed and passed laws benefitting Mistral."

"Very well received, Senator Numos. Contestants, please turn back to face me," Guardian Eska said. "Outside, you all met both Ethen and Riagan of my conseleigh. To my left is Tundra Iycel, conseleigh of Onkh. My last conseleigh, Luvan Katore, is away finishing preparations for the first Trial. In the months to come, it is they who will be responsible for designing and determining the Trials. Before they are underway, let me lay out some clear guidelines.

"Although there is a possibility of death, no death will occur at the hands of another contestant. If one dies, it will be due to the trial or the environment. . . ." Eska paused and evaluated all of them. He noticed a slight movement from Zain, and Eirek tapped the sides of his legs. "Secondly, any contestant caught in gratuitous acts of violence outside of the scope of the Trials may face dismissal. Thirdly, there will be a total of four Trials, but not all of you will participate in all four. Your performance in each trial will ultimately decide who gets to advance and who will eventually become my apprentice. After my apprentice is chosen, you will need to earn the majority of favors from the families in power. Are there any questions?" Guardian Eska looked around and noticed estranged looks from all but the two princes.

"Good. Further details will be given when necessary. You have the next days, until Luvan returns, to explore outside or in the estate. Colin is waiting downstairs to take you to a brief lunch. Feel free to use any of our facilities and amenities while here. Finally, may the Twelve and Ancients be with you all. Ethen, Riagan, please lead them out."

"Contestants," Ethen said. With Riagan by his side, he walked around the contestants. "Follow us." They walked forward then, shuffling everyone out of the door, leaving Eska alone with Tundra.

Eska looked at her, wondering if she saw what he did. *Tundra . . .* Although they were alone, he talked with her through telepathy—preferring the intimacy it added to their conversation.

She looked back with chilling blue eyes that glowed, representing her use of telekinetic power. Strands of blue were still present in her mostly gray hair. *Did you find the answers you were looking for, Edwyrd?*

Some of them were interesting. But words are water, rarely ice. You should know that better than most.

I do. The Trials will be their ice, then?

Yes, they will.

🕷CHAPTER 12🕷

A LOOK AROUND

Zain looked from the glass window with scarlet drapes on the other side of the dining hall to the chicken broth that sat before him on a table that could seat fifty and no more. The mountains were in the distance, and Freyr and Lugh were an arm's length apart from each other in the sky. What was here for him? Was there really power that could bring Ava back?

He steadied his hand by scooping a spoonful of chicken broth and swallowing it. Across the table, Gabrielle conversed with Cain, and Hydro conversed with the senator. Beside him, he heard Eirek and Cadmar talk. But there was no one for him to talk to. Not anymore. *Dammit, Zakk.*

His stomach roiled, dissolving his appetite. Abruptly he left the table. Only one entity could know what Zain was going through—his sword. It was a Gazo's-issued sword provided to him once he had outgrown the one his father gave him when he first enrolled. It had been there through the tournaments; it had seen why he needed to do what he did to Zakk. His friend would have won, again, but Zain needed to. For Ava. But now . . . now it was complicated. Who was he really fighting for now?

Zain strolled down the hallway from the dining room and took note of a variety of rooms. He assumed they were servant rooms. One corridor led to a stained-glass door that prevented anyone from seeing inside. *I wonder where that leads?* He still hardly knew the place; he needed to find someone who could help him locate any training facilities.

In the lobby, Zain found a servant sweeping out dust and dirt that had rolled in from outside. The servant's skin was dark, although lighter than Zain's. "Excuse me, sir."

The man stopped and looked up. "Yes?" He smiled.

"Does Guardian Eska have any training facilities here?"

"Go down this hall . . ." The man pointed back in the direction that Zain had come. "At the end of it, take a left. Keep to the left when the hallway splits, and you will find a circular room. There will be a steel door that leads to the facility."

"Thanks." Zain went to his room to assemble his training gear.

Easily enough he found the room, and upon entering, he saw the steel door the man talked about. He tugged on the handle, but it was locked. *Great.*

"Do you have an appointment?"

Zain looked to his right to see an old man with liver spots and receding gray hair hunched over a microphone behind a glass window.

"No." Zain walked toward the man, confused.

"I will get you set up then, sir. May I have your name?"

"Zain Berrese."

"Barase, Barase . . . there is no Barase who's supposed to be here."

"No. Bur-eh-say"

"Could you spell that?"

"B-E-R-R—"

"Ah, Berrese. Found it. I will meet you in the next room. The steel door is open now."

The old man waddled to a door located on the side wall. Zain retreated to the steel door and gawked as he entered the large space. *This is a habitat arena, just like Gazo's.* It was empty now, but Zain knew that environments could be uploaded and then trained in. It provided experience in different terrains. Safe, efficient training against opponents took the form of holograms that thought and acted on their own accord. At Gazo's, graduates from the academy were asked permission to upload their data so that future students may train like a graduate. When Zain made it to the point of fighting more than standard enemy holograms, he challenged Baron Gaul, his trainer at Gazo's, when he was no older than Kendel's age.

From a control booth to the right, the old man spoke through another microphone. "How would you like to train?"

Zain did not want to try communicating with the man any longer, so he walked over to the control booth and entered through a sliding glass door. Large servers lined the back of the wall; at waist height around the booth was a control panel with many screens and buttons. "I can handle it from here."

"If you insist."

The man didn't leave, which rather annoyed Zain. He looked at the panels and adjusted it to his needs.

Time limit: No.
End on first fatal contact: Yes.
Holographic enemy: On.
Upload holographic enemy data: Yes.

Zain wondered what kind of data this habitat arena had, so he scrolled through the electronic menu. Among the choices to battle that were listed in alphabetical order were holograms of Guardian Eska's conseleigh and numerous strangers who might have been trainers. There was no data uploaded, however, for Eska, nor the guardians who preceded him. Probably to protect their secrecy.

Zain eyed the last option suspiciously: Yourself. Did it already have data on him? He pushed the button, and a mechanical voice spoke, "You have chosen to battle . . . yourself. Please identify who you are by placing your hand on the screen next to you."

A black screen retracted to reveal a glass box with red lasers skimming underneath it like a scanner. Zain cautiously lowered his hand. Once it touched glass, the voice came back on again.

"Scanning in progress. Please keep hand in place . . . Zain Berrese."

Zain's eyes bulged when he realized that data had actually been collected on him. *Too many tournaments*, he thought. *Bound to be information on me somewhere.*

"Data will be uploaded momentarily. Please continue to choose your type of terrain."

At Gazo's they had offered forest, desert, shallow water, and caves. Here, all of the previous options existed, with the addition of others: City Streets. Mountainous Terrain, or even the Cargo Hold of a Flying Ship. *I wonder how that last one would work?* Zain chose City Streets, and the voice resumed, "You have selected to spar yourself, Zain Berrese, in the City Streets Arena. Is this correct? Please respond with YES or NO."

"Yes!" Zain shouted, not knowing how apt the machine was of distinguishing his voice.

"Please wait while your battlefield is arranged."

Zain waited. After the usual fifteen minutes, the empty space that was once the arena had been turned into a cramped city dwelling with upper and lower levels. A flowing water fountain claimed the middle level. Hous-

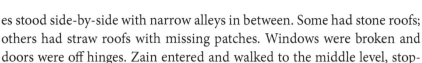

es stood side-by-side with narrow alleys in between. Some had stone roofs; others had straw roofs with missing patches. Windows were broken and doors were off hinges. Zain entered and walked to the middle level, stopping next to the flowing fountain.

Inside the control booth, the old man was hunched over into the microphone. "Are you ready?"

Zain nodded, giving a thumbs-up.

From the top, a tile slid open and spit out a black ball. It hummed through the air and stopped five paces in front of him. Rotating continuously, it shot out a beam of green light. Strands of data molded to take the shape of Zain's own likeness. Zain moved closer and felt as though he looked into a mirror—except he was green. The hologram withdrew his sword, took the blunt end, and hit the side of his foot—a habit of Zain's before every battle. *It's really me.*

"Three . . ."

Zain shook his head and jumped back.

"Two . . ."

He pulled out his sword, tapped his right foot, and raised it to the hologram.

"One. . . . Begin."

His counterpart wasted no time in attacking. Zain was almost thrown off balance—did he really charge into battles so abruptly? Zain sidestepped a vertical swing, then he swung his sword horizontally, parried a lunge, and punched with his left hand, which connected with the hologram's cheek. His fist tingled as the hologram stumbled backward. Zain swung while it was staggered, but the hologram blocked it.

The hologram swung horizontally, but Zain blocked it. The hologram drove its shoulder into Zain and then elbowed him in the face, causing Zain to stumble back near the water fountain. *Is it mimicking me?*

When Zain regained his composure, he noticed the hologram had darted into the water fountain and proceeded to kick up water at Zain. When the splash hit his face, a sudden chill came over him. As he blinked, he saw the hologram take on the face of Zakk. He gasped and fell, toppling backwards and landing on the cobblestone. His sword dropped from his hand upon contact. Then Zakk's sword came down upon him.

He had lost to Zakk. That face. It seemed so real. *No. I lost to myself. Not to Zakk.* The dimmed lights turned on again, and Zain proceeded out of the arena so it could reset to the original settings. Past the steel door, he found Hydro waiting in the circular room. He moved past, failing to acknowledge the prince, but that did not shield him from the prince's jeer.

Hydro snorted and chortled. "I thought Gazo's students were decent at sparring!"

He doesn't know what happened. Zain shook his head and continued walking. "What makes you believe I'm not?"

"The old man told me to wait my turn. A whole seven minutes have passed. Congratulations," Hydro jested.

Zain clenched his fists but continued walking. *He doesn't know what happened. I am good. I am better than Zakk. That is why I am here.*

"I cannot believe you represent such a prestigious academy." Hydro snickered.

Zain's ears perked. He halted and looked to his left to check if the old man was behind the glass window. He wasn't. Zain turned around and walked, chest outward, toward Hydro. Hydro didn't back away. Zain swung an uppercut right into his abs, causing Hydro to double over. "Congratulations," Zain whispered.

"For what?" Hydro huffed.

"For giving me a reason to hit you."

Zain walked away. Before he took five paces, there was a tap on his shoulder. He spun around. It was Hydro, smiling.

The next thing Zain knew, he was on the ground—the left side of his face throbbing. And then a foot kicked his stomach; he growled in pain.

"Hit harder next time. Now, I have a real sparring session to attend. Excuse me."

Zain lay there until Hydro went to the next room. Had his punch affected Hydro? He stood up and faced the steel door. His shoulders slumped a little more, and he looked down at his sword. He needed to win. It wasn't about Ava anymore; it was about showing his worth—it was about showing why Gazo's had two students selected; it was about showing why he was better than Zakk.

But Zain could do nothing now. Only blade would hush nobles.

CHAPTER 13

THE FIRST LETTER

It was the morning of the fourth day after introductions. Just like each day before, Cadmar returned from his run exhausted. Both suns had risen, sand had invaded his shoes, and his joints still ached from the hour-long sparring session the night before. He barely got six hours of sleep, but he needed to run—he ran four days a week. His father, Corrigan, ran six, but he was an elite like his father, Caerul, before him and second in command in service to Lady Aprah of Gar. Cadmar looked up to him like a bird would the sky—because it was the only thing that made sense to him.

In fact, his father was the only person Cadmar had left. His mother left when he was nineteen, after he killed his first man and almost made his family lose everything. Now Cadmar wasn't anything. Not yet.

Cadmar noticed the estate bustling now, more so than last night and this morning; he wondered how long Eirek had trained after him. He found it odd that the culchie trained during the grave of night. But who was he to judge?

Cadmar walked past Eirek, who was oblivious to his presence, engrossed in a piece of paper in his hand. On his own door was a crimson envelope with his name in golden lettering. *Another letter. It wasn't there when I left.* Cadmar plucked it off the door and turned it around to see a dragon, with wings outstretched, breathing fire.

"What be this?" Cadmar broke the seal.

Just as he read the first word, Eirek's voice made him stop. "The first trial."

That made Cadmar read it all the faster.

Dear Contestants,

    This morning Luwan Katore completed the last preparations of the first trial. This trial aims to test your partnership. As guardian, you will need to work with your conseleigh and will need to interact with the lords and ladies of Gladonus. Information for this trial will be given tonight at supper at seven. Luwan Katore will be in attendance to answer questions you may have.

                  Sincerely,
                  Guardian Edwyrd Eska

"Did you just get done with the sparring arena?"

Cadmar's ears perked, and he stopped reading momentarily as Eirek walked over to him. "No, I ran." Cadmar sized the culchie up and down. "How be your session last night?"

"Okay." Eirek shrugged. "The one I use back home is nowhere near as sophisticated as this one."

"My aul man has one for him and me back home. Which model you use?"

Cadmar noticed Eirek's frantic search for an answer. He didn't expect the culchie to actually have a habitat arena—country boys could hardly afford it. Eirek was trying to fit in; Cadmar couldn't blame him. Everyone needed someone to identify with. Cadmar had been trying to fit in his whole life.

To help Eirek out, Cadmar expanded on his question. "The HA One Hundred, Two Hundred, Three Hundred, Four Hundred, or Five Hundred?"

"Oh, yes," Eirek said. "The HA One Hundred."

"No wonder. You still be using the first model. Every two years, a new model be on the market. No doubt this one here is the newest. At home, we got a HA Three Hundred. Works fine."

"What are you doing for the rest of the day?"

Cadmar's stomach growled. "Going to lunch."

"I'll walk with you."

"Naw. I'll meet you there. After I shower." Cadmar could sense a glimmer of hope dying within Eirek, who skulked away to his room. He thought the request odd. Did the culchie really need someone to walk with him? Why? Cadmar remembered how he waited for him before introductions. Had he ever been a part of something? Cadmar furrowed his eyebrows and entered his room.

At lunch, the talk at the table was of the trial. The food was croissants, tossed greens, and mixed meats, including pork, snake, and frog legs. Guardian Eska and his conseleigh were nowhere to be seen, but they never had lunch with the contestants, only supper. Cadmar sat between the dark-skinned man, Zain, and Eirek. Both were scrawny. In fact, everyone at the table was smaller than Cadmar, with the exception of Senator Numos. And Numos had no muscles to show. Cadmar had seen plenty of people like that on Gar in the inner city of Visis, named after the leader of their revolt against Sereya. Ever since freedom from Sereyan rule, Gar excelled in technology. Unfortunately that technology now made them lazier than the frostbitten Sereyans or the water-washed Acquavans.

"So what do you think this partnership trial will be?" Eirek asked him.

Cadmar considered the possibilities. Only one thing came to mind—a part of the test done to become an elite. "To help each other climb a mountain without rope."

"I hope so, Garian. I am quite good at that. I would not need a partner."

Cadmar narrowed his eyes on Hydro. Since the trip to the Core, he had refused to call Cadmar by name, only by the nationality of his people. *That man be a caffler. If he represents all Acquavans, it ruins my taste for visiting the waterlands.*

"What mountain have you climbed, Hydro?"

Cadmar smirked at the question the other prince posed. Acquava was waterlands; there weren't any mountains there.

"Mount Tyld, the second largest mountain in Acquava."

"That mountain be more like a hill compared to ours. Mount Volan be the second tallest in all of Gladonus," Cadmar commented.

"What's the tallest?" Eirek asked.

"Mount Klaff, Commoner. But I hardly think we will be climbing that."

Does he refer to anyone by name? The man he killed had been one of the prince's type, one whose arrogance overrode his confidence.

"Why is that?"

The gingernut prince spoke, "Because it is suicidal. No one has ever finished the climb."

"Guardian Eska holds the record though. I heard that after he climbed the first level of the mountain and saw yet another ahead of him, he turned back."

Cadmar looked at the paunchy man who sat to the caffler's right. A glass piece sat in his eye and attached to a device that clamped onto his ear. A cane of black wood leaned against his spot, the top carved to resemble the head of a mockingbird. It must have been his favorite bird, because he also saw the mockingbird as the sigil on his garb of white silk. The man looked like an obese ghost with his milky skin.

"What if it's a riddle and we have to find something?" asked Eirek.

The culchie had an imagination on him. That was for sure. He was the only one ever suggesting anything—perhaps the others thought if they talked it might give information away. He noticed Gabrielle and Zain still had not said anything. Zain didn't even appear to be aware of the conversation, constantly playing with his food, but Cadmar noticed Gabrielle's eyes dart back and forth between speakers.

"Then I hope I'm not paired with you, Commoner."

Cadmar glared at the caffler. He was the type of person who caused Cadmar's mother to leave, who almost cost his father his rank. Being Acquavan only added ice capping to the mountain. "And I sure hope my partner not be you."

"Why is that, Garian?"

"Because Acquavans be slimy. They be from the sea."

"And Garians were carved from the earth and mountains."

"So our stories go."

"Water erodes mountains, Garian."

"Fire topples mountains. Not water. How much fire can an Acquavan produce?"

"*Palo,*" Hydro said.

Before the word was even finished, Cadmar saw the glare given by Hydro. When his lips started to move, he knew what the caffler was doing. "*Vesi.*"

Water from the glass in front of him and fire from the candelabra near the middle of the table collided, cancelling each other out. Everyone was now riveted in their chairs and looking at the two of them glare at each other.

"Enough. Both of you," Senator Numos said.

"Save it for the Trials, Hydro," Cain advised. He had stood up and tried to lower Hydro back into his seat.

"Why are all men so barbaric?" Gabrielle asked, her arms folded across her chest.

Only princes are barbaric, Cadmar wanted to correct, but he didn't want to lose the duel of glares that continued for a few more intense seconds. Throughout it all, Cadmar remained seated, but Zain and Eirek had gotten up from their chairs.

Hydro didn't sit down; instead he threw the golden linen he held onto the table and stalked away—the first and only one to leave. It was a small victory for Cadmar, but he had learned to accept them when he could. The greater triumph would be becoming something greater than an elite or an apprentice—it would be becoming Guardian of the Core.

CHAPTER 14

TALES

Even hours after the small display of power in the dining hall, Hydro fumed. When he left, he wandered outside and went to the training court he had noticed when he was exploring the library in the days before. There he cast power. He wanted to cast every element, but he reserved to casting earth, due to its proximity and overwhelming majority. As he did so, he thought about the Garian. *So the Garian knows power; he is still probably as horrible with the axe as Zain is with that sword.* A spire erupted out of the ground. *He is lucky Cain stopped me.* The spire expanded from waist-height to the mansion's height. *The worst thing I can do is let that Garian win.* He then increased it to nearly double the estate's size before releasing the terrain back to normal due to exhaustion. He dropped to the ground then and pounded his fist on the hot stone court. *If fire wasn't so far away, I would have been able to cast it. . . .*

Now the first contestant to arrive in the dining hall, he had cleaned up from his makeshift training session, dressing himself in worsted wool pants and a royal purple vest. When the guardian entered, he tried his best to ignore the Garian. He did this by focusing on the head of the table where Guardian Eska sat with his conseleigh. Compared to previous dinners, Guardian Eska seemed to be noticing him more, for Hydro caught his glance thrice during the course of the meal. *Did Senator Numos tell him of the dispute?*

To Eska's left was a man with blond hair streaked with silver, who Hydro had never seen before. Lightning-bolt studs clung to his earlobes and no-frame glasses exuded a certain intelligence about the man. *He must be the one who will talk about the trial.* But Hydro found the interactions between Guardian Eska and his conseleigh more interesting than knowing what they cared about. He found it odd that Eska never smiled. Or talked. *When do I get to dine with you and learn your secrets?*

A hand on his shoulder tore Hydro from his observations. "Is the prince better?"

Hydro looked up to see Senator Numos above him. A faint stubble was starting to grow from his neck. "Much," Hydro lied. There was no reason to alert anyone of his annoyance.

"I am sorry about intruding earlier . . . it was not my place to . . ." Senator Numos leaned in so close to Hydro that he smelt the man's breath. It wasn't as bad as Hydro thought it might be.

"We all have a part to play," Hydro said. He looked toward the Garian, who talked with Zain, but when the Garian did look at Hydro, his eyes were daggers.

"That we do. That we do." Senator Numos laughed, slapped Hydro's back, and took his spot a few seats down from him near Conseleigh Rorum.

That was queer. What purpose do you serve, Senator? The beautiful silk was wasted on Numos. It was stretched too thin for someone so thick. Sweat poured from the senator's forehead. How hard was it to walk? To Hydro, it seemed the cane served more purpose than Numos himself. Over the past five years, as he sat with his father during political meetings, Hydro found politicians to be people who talked much but said very little. They did have some power though: If two-thirds of the active politicians agreed, they could usurp his father's throne. His father had even told him once, "I do not come to these meetings for my enjoyment but, rather, for the safety of my family."

When Guardian Eska stood, he commanded the room. "Contestants, I would like to take this moment to introduce to you Luvan Katore, back from business on Agrost. He is responsible for your first trial. At this moment, I will let him speak."

The man dabbed his lips with a golden cloth and then stood up. "Thank you. Contestants, I am sorry for my absence, but from this point forward, I will be here. Because of my absence, however, I will ask you to tell me your name when you stand, if you are not from Agrost. Understood?" Luvan paused and then continued, "As guardian, you would be responsible for contact with all planets of Gladonus and must learn to cooperate with others in difficult situations. For this trial, you will be paired at random with a teammate to test cooperation. The three groups of two will be announced in the moments before the trial begins. At this moment are there any questions?"

No one raised a hand.

"Your first task will take place in the Zas Labyrinth." Luvan snapped his fingers, and the lights dimmed. In the middle of the table, between the sets of contestants, a hologram of a foreign place appeared.

From his peripherals, Hydro noticed Cain, two spots to his left, shift in posture, lick his lips, and breathe heavier than normal. *That's strange.*

"The labyrinth is found in the territory of Epoch," Luvan continued. "Inside I have placed a scroll. The team that retrieves the scroll and maintains acquisition over it until leaving the labyrinth will win the task." A hologram of a scroll tied with a ribbon replaced the spinning labyrinth. "Now are there any questions?" Luvan looked around. "Ah, Prince Evber, of course. What shall it be?"

"Have you not heard the rumors surrounding the labyrinth?"

"You did not come to the Core because you thought the Trials might be safe. Guardian Eska outlined in his letter that they were designed to push you to your maximum potential. You were all chosen for your skill by blade or tongue or mind." Luvan turned his head toward the commoner, who'd raised his hand. "Mr. Mourse, go ahead."

"What if one person on the team retrieves the item? Both still receive credit?"

"Precisely. Are there any more questions?" Only one hand fluttered in the air. "Your name, please?"

"Zain Berrese. Is there anything about the labyrinth we should know before we enter?"

"If you knew everything, it would not be much of a trial now, would it?"

Guardian Eska and his conseleigh chuckled. Luvan beamed. He snapped his fingers, and the rotating hologram slowly disappeared. Lights returned from overhead.

Hydro's eyes closed. He reopened them to see Guardian Eska standing and Luvan sitting. Guardian Eska raised his gloved hand and said, "Good luck, Contestants. It is a trial I most look forward to." He snapped his fingers then, and servants carried in trays of food from the hallway: steak, pork, venison, greens, fruits—anything anyone could ask for.

As he ate, Hydro observed everyone, but he conversed little. He struck up a few sentences with Gabrielle in which he discussed the training and life in Empora, and to his surprise, she was rather critical of the fact that

Acquava had established such a strong relationship with Victor Zigarda. When the conversation turned sour, Hydro spoke over her to Cain and found areas of subject between their mansions, trainers, and their beliefs on Epoch.

Before long, everyone finished eating, and Guardian Eska stood once again, halting all conversations. "The rest of the night is yours to do as you wish, as is tomorrow. Remember, though, that two days from now your first trial will start at noon. The ships leave for Agrost at dawn. Make sure you are awake and have your equipment ready. If you are not in the lobby, you will not be participating." Eska settled down in the chair again and continued listening and observing, but never talking.

Next to Hydro, Gabrielle left shortly after Eska sat down. On the other side, he noticed the Garian and the commoner leave together. Zain had already left. Had he even stayed to hear Eska? Although Hydro could not care less about his competitors, a curiosity about Cain nagged at him. *Why did he act so peculiar?* Cain stared down at the golden linen on the table, and then after taking a sip of water, he stood and left. Hydro followed.

Cain noticed his presence behind him in the hallway. "Is there something I can help you with, Hydro?"

"There is."

Cain stopped before the statue of Ancient Bane. From a corner pocket in his brown dress shirt, he removed a set of keys. "And that might be?"

"Can we discuss in your room?"

If Cain was annoyed, he didn't show it. "Certainly." Cain unlocked his door and went in.

Hydro entered Cain's room, taking in its similarity to his own—a bed large enough for two people, a closet that could hang all the clothes he brought and store his armor and gear on the floor, a dresser that stood about five and a half feet off the ground, a mirror attached to it that extended another two feet, and a desk to write on. Hydro strolled over to the window beside a nightstand and looked up to a night full of stars and wishes.

"Why do I receive your presence tonight?" Cain shut the door.

"I need information." Hydro tore his gaze from the stars and looked Cain in the eye.

"What kind of information?"

"The kind dealing with the Zas Labyrinth. It seems you know something about it."

"I do, but what makes you think I will tell? You probably assume knowledge is power, since your family is such good friends with Victor Zigarda."

"Knowledge is power. And that is why we powerful people should have as much of it as possible. Is someone who is denied really capable of handling apprenticeship?"

"To me, knowledge is feeling. And I feel that Guardian Eska had his motives for not limiting this contest to those just with power. And even now, how would you know whether or not they do?"

"I do not . . ." Hydro looked away. *He is too analytical. Just tell me what I need to know.*

"Sit."

Hydro looked back toward Cain, who had extended the chair from his desk to him. His thin eyebrows were arched. Hydro sat on the chair while Cain sat on the hardwood desk.

"I will tell you a folktale I heard from a bard who used to entertain at the castle. Whether you believe it to be myth or truth is your decision." Cain cleared his throat, and then began, "A wife to a Lord Pavos long before my family took reign bore two sons for her husband. Now, ruling states that if a lord or lady shall die, a son or daughter can take over the throne upon his or her twenty-fifth birthday, as long as they can wield power. When time came of age for each of the sons to be tested, both were found to be denied. Because of this, their father turned his back on them—this family had only been ruling since before the Great War, from the beginning of Epoch. The knowledge that their rule would end with him, quite understandably, weighted him. One of the sons grew the same resentment for his father that had been placed upon him being labeled denied. The other son, though, wanted to come into his father's good graces again, so he devised a plan. . . ."

How does the labyrinth play into any of this? Hydro tapped his arms. He got up and moved his chair closer to the window.

"He had heard about an object that could bring a denied the ability to use power. His searching took him to the Zas Labyrinth. For days the son didn't return, but when he did, he showed his father that he could cast fire. His father couldn't believe it; neither could the other families of power who were getting ready to inherit the throne. To make sure it wasn't some hoax, the sages were called in again to test his power. True enough, he could cast—"

"What of it? Why did you react so poorly to it?"

"One night, the brother who had stayed denied killed his father because of the support his father showed the other son. A battle waged between both sons, and the whole family was massacred, but neither son's body was discovered. Some say they killed each other, then the prize swallowed them both, and they only escaped the labyrinth by selling their souls. They believe that the brothers live there and eat others who try to steal the prize the younger son stole."

"That is foolish."

"Others say that they could see fire coming from inside the labyrinth, as if someone lived there even still."

"And have you seen it?" Hydro looked at the stars. He tried to find Agrost, but he never had much luck finding planets other than his own.

"Yes. One night when I was young, I went there with my father. He told me to stay away from the place whatever I do. I have not returned since."

"Why does anyone even venture there?"

"For greed. And because a voice calls you there. It calls anyone who wants power and tempts them to grab its prize—a prize that can give power to a denied, to a source who cannot even cast. But perhaps its true function is to grant the ability to cast power without a natural source present. That would explain the fires being constantly lit, even during nighttime. Have you ever thought about times when you wished you could cast a certain spell, but you could not because it was not present in nature?"

Hydro looked from the stars to Cain. He noticed freckles on the man's face. The fiery hair allured him. He looked back to the stars to try and find Acquava. It was taking him longer than normal this night. Hydro didn't say anything, just looked and pondered.

"Are you okay?"

"I . . . I . . ." Hydro looked across the room to a candle that flickered in a lamp attached to his wall. "I . . . know exactly what you mean. There was a winter, a terribly cold winter, where I wanted to cast fire, where I needed to cast fire, but I could not. . . ."

"Is that why you were mad at what Cadmar said today?"

"Yes. . . . When I was fourteen, my mother insisted that my sister and I go skating with her on a lake near the castle walls. Father was busy treating guests, and Aiton, my younger brother, was only two. . . ." Hydro looked at Cain, who waited on his words as if Hydro was reading aloud some sort of book.

"My sister, only eight winters to her name, fell into the water once the ice cracked. I pulled her up, and within minutes, she was shivering. 'Cast fire. Make her warm,' my mother said to me. And I tried. I knew I could; I cast my first spell at the age of nine, and here I was struggling to cast a simple spell. 'Are you denied?' she asked me, while holding tight onto Anya. I tried. I did . . . I said, '*palo*' . . ." Fire rushed over to his hand from the candle flickering inside the lamp. It circled his hand and then lay in his palm. Hydro clenched his fist, putting it out.

"My mother left me there then as she took the hovercraft back to the castle, more than two leagues away. I walked back in the cold that night, wet and shivering, and dusk was setting, so the warmth of Freyr and Lugh left me soon enough. Korth, one of our guards, searched for me, but by the time we got back to the castle, she had passed. . . . Her room has not been opened since; neither have my mother's eyes toward me. . . ."

Hydro looked toward Cain, who seemed to be deep in thought. "My mother, only years into her marriage, before I was born, ran away from Castle Thoth. She was a woman of power, yes, but she still found it strange to be married to my father, whose family had been in power for over five hundred years. I suppose she was scared about carrying on his legacy, or at least that is what she told me. A month later, she came back to my father with renewed love, and she has never been afraid since. . . ." Cain looked down underneath his dress shirt. "She gave me this on my seventh birthday when I was afraid that since I had not cast yet, I was denied. . . ." Cain showed a warm-colored feather that dangled from a red-stranded necklace. "She told me, 'You should never be afraid. About anything.' But she . . . she was afraid at one point in her life, and then that fear was gone. . . . To me it seems that everyone has events in their lives that change them. It is only a matter of how they let those events change them. I do not think that event has come yet—for me anyways."

Hydro thought back to Anya and the pale-blue arms he saw as he looked at her cold, dead body in the apothecary. He thought back to his father, who had stayed strong, catching any tears in his thick hands. A wetness came to Hydro's eyes. He needed to go. He stood up and left without saying anything to Cain as he departed.

As soon as he closed the door to his own room, Hydro hunched over his desk and held his hand up to his face, catching the tears that had started to form in Cain's room. He thought about his mother's wails and her screams to the Twelve and her heaving sobs. Hydro's mother had not been as careful about where her tears fell. Perhaps it was then that she was no longer a Paen; a true Paen would never let tears fall to the ground.

☙CHAPTER 15❧

PARTNERSHIP

As soon as Guardian Eska dismissed them, Zain left. He went back to his room and leaned against the headboard of his bed. He focused on nothing particular, perhaps his sword leaning against the closet doors, but while he focused aimlessly, he spun the crimson envelope between his index finger and thumb. *A trial on partnership. Are the Twelve mocking me so soon?* It seemed like he had always been a puppet of irony—from Ava and him sharing a moment considered rare and beautiful and lucky by many (that of seeing Rhayna flying) to her dying on that very same mountain to this, a trial testing partnership when he had just killed his best friend.

Looking toward his sword, he remembered all the times he had fought Zakk. The times he won were slim. *I had to do it. I had to.* Zain let the card fall in between his legs, and he reached beside him for a pillow. He put it to his face and screamed. As he screamed, he cried. The screams tapered off, the tears soaked into the pillow, and then only heavy breathing remained. His wrist vibrated, and soon a lofty beeping filtered through the air. *Who's calling?* Zain removed his face from the pillow and checked the telecommunicator on his wrist. *Jamaal?*

Zain activated the call by pushing the device's crown. A miniature hologram of his brother's face, no larger than the size of his fist, hovered above the clock reading. A green laser scanned Zain's face, transmitting it to Jamaal.

"Jamaal? Why are you calling?"

Jamaal looked away, and then refocused on him. "Zain, I . . . I have some bad news for you."

A knife jabbed Zain's stomach. "Is it Dad? What happened to him?"

"No. No. No. It's not Dad. We received a letter yesterday from him. It seemed rushed, but he seems to be fine."

Zain breathed. "What is it then?"

"I'm . . . I'm . . . not sure how to tell you this . . . but . . . Zakk's dead . . . at least . . . that's what reports claim."

Zain wanted to break down in tears again, but he kept it together. "How . . . how do you know?"

"Someone from Gazo's called us today. Zakk is listed under our sponsorship, and they asked us why he hadn't been in this past week. . . .We didn't know, so we checked with the owner of the apartment you two have together. . . . They examined the room and found it cleaned for the most part . . . like . . . like he was leaving for somewhere." Jamaal looked down and then returned his gaze to Zain. "Zain . . . did you see him while waiting at Lake Kilmer?"

Zain tightened his neck. "No." He shook his head as well, as if even he needed to convince himself. "Why do you ask?"

"Well, every applicant for apprenticeship needs a sponsor; you know that. It seems that Zakk applied as well. And Klum Barrata sponsored him . . . if I remember correctly. . . ."

The headmaster sponsored him? Zain had been too timid to ask him for sponsorship, instead receiving it from his trainer, who had since become an aerial guard for Lady Liliana Voux on Mistral—Baron Gaul.

"How do you know he is dead though? And not just missing? You know he's lived on his own before."

"A body hasn't been found, but . . ."

That's because it's at the bottom of Lake Kilmer. Zain looked down toward his hands, and his side ached. "But what?" He wiped a tear from his eye as he looked at his brother.

"There is no response from his telecommunicator. . . . It's been turned off or broken . . . or something. It can't even be traced. Zain, I . . . I don't know what to tell you. It . . . isn't looking good. I know you two were close. . . ."

We were more than close . . . we were family. Zain put his hand to his eyes and wiped the tears away.

"Zain, keep your head up. How are the Trials going so far?"

"They aren't. Our first one is the day after tomorrow."

"Oh, I'm sorry. Use this as strength. . . . Listen, before I go, I have one more thing I need to talk with you about."

"What's that?"

"Mom thought that with this news, you could receive an early present; your birthday is only a month and a half away now, you know. Dad had something in the process of being made for you before he left on business. Mom says he was going to give it to you when he returned, and even though he isn't back yet, it might cheer you up."

"What is it?"

"A secret. Make sure I have proper permission to arrive; I plan on delivering it while I am en route for Agrost."

Zain nodded but remained silent.

"Listen, Zain . . . I know it's not what you wanted to hear, but . . . keep your head up. *I'm Possible,* isn't that your corny Gazo's saying?"

Zain smiled a little bit. It was corny, but it was meant to show that even when things seemed impossible you just had to believe in yourself and say, *I'm Possible.* "Yeah . . . it is."

"Is everything all right now?"

"No . . . nothing is right. But I'm going to try and make things better. And I won't stop 'til they are."

"Take care, Little Bear."

Zain smiled and plugged a loose tear with his thumb. "You too, Big Bear."

The communication ended, and Zain tilted his head back against the headboard. He turned his face to the right and looked out to the night sky. Through the purple sky, stars resembled the jewels his father worked with. Zain felt closer to home.

When he was younger, his father had told him that he built the sky himself, and it was really a giant's cape laden with jewels. The giant hadn't paid him yet, because he wasn't finished, but the payment would be great— he would be rewarded in the rays of Axiumé. Upon death, his father would live in Axiumé, making jewels for the lost Ancients and creating stars everyone could see.

A star fell. A bad omen.

Zain turned his head to his hands and flexed his fingers. His side ached.

CHAPTER 16

INTO THE LABYRINTH

Hydro wouldn't have known it was noon if Guardian Eska hadn't told them. Dark clouds eclipsed both Freyr and Lugh—faces holding back tears. For the moment. Ten-foot sandstone slabs were located on top of a barren hill with sparse grass. Tree branches from a forest to the west swayed in a light, cool breeze that carried the scent of oak and mud and worms. It rained here recently. Hydro looked past Guardian Eska and the four conseleigh who stood behind him, to the slabs of sandstone, hoping to see a fire coming from inside. But there wasn't any glow.

Hydro was first in line. He looked toward the man next to him: Cain. His breathing was staggered, and his eyes searched past Guardian Eska as well, even Hydro could see that. Cain was adorned in a steel helm shaped like an owl. A green linen gambeson padded and protected him behind chainmail that hung from his shoulder pads. His leather gloves were sewn with iron knuckles. *Is this place really that deadly?* Compared to Cain, Hydro was under protected in his rhinoskin armor and a silver helm with a nose guard. Vambraces guarded his forearms, but Hydro wore only leather padding for his knuckles, no iron.

"Contestants, before you is the Zas Labyrinth. I will now begin the process of forming teams. When I finish, speak your full name, starting with Prince Paen and continuing to the right, ending with Cadmar."

Hydro could not read Eska's lips but a hologram of a jeweled box hovered in front of the guardian. With his gloved hand Eska, directed it to stop before Hydro.

"Hydro Paen." Something tugged at the back of his throat. Hydro opened his mouth and yawned to assist the spell in the process. A green line encoded with his name floated toward the box and went inside.

Besides telepathy and the occasional strengthening spell, Hydro rarely used the tier of telekinetic power. Out of the three types, it drained the most energy, for it relied on the spellcaster's energy to use it, not another outside source. One could easily tell when someone was using that type of power because the eyes glowed. That was normal. Eska's hand glowing behind his glove, though, was unusual. *What type of power is that?*

After receiving all the names, the jeweled box returned to Eska. As it started shaking, a low-pitched hum reverberated in Hydro's ear. The box shook in rhythm to the humming, which reached its crescendo as the box disappeared in a violent spasm. The noise stopped. Eska's eyes stopped glowing. Before him, in green lettering, Hydro looked at his partner's name: Cadmar Briggs. His brows furrowed and his tongue clicked. "Assemble into your teams and follow me," Guardian Eska said.

Hydro didn't bother waiting for his partner to walk up the slight incline. As he stood outside one of the labyrinth's entrances, he noticed that Cain had been paired with the commoner and that Zain was paired with Gabrielle.

When the Garian finally took his place next to Hydro, his arms were crossed and his chest puffed. Staggered metal padding slid down his arms, connecting with vambraces on his forearms. His chest was only covered in leather, though, and his head had no helm.

"You may enter the labyrinth now. Good luck to you all," Guardian Eska said.

Hydro walked forward, his arms no longer crossed. Instead his right hand constantly stayed on his hilt. If this labyrinth was as dangerous as Cain made it seem, he would need to stay ready. As Hydro walked, he made no effort to talk to the Garian, and besides looking back occasionally to see if he followed, he kept his gaze forward and focused.

For the first couple paths, everything was normal—dirt floor and an open sky. There were no flames though—sconces, but no flames. *What are you afraid of, Cain?* It was only after turning left at a split did Hydro see rats scurrying to and fro—some out from forgotten clothing, others from cleaned ribcages of humans. Maggots laid claim to the skulls, but fetor overpowered them all, holding the air hostage. Hydro pulled up his rhinoskin padding and tried tucking his nose into it the best he could. *What is that?* The stench hadn't been present when they entered, but it increased with every turn.

A raindrop. Hydro looked past the blue moss that clung to the higher parts of the labyrinth to the gray clouds that had been harboring over the

labyrinth and were now more black than gray. *It's going to storm soon.*
"Garian, we need to move faster."

"You be the one setting the pace, Caffler."

Normally Hydro would follow his adversaries, not be followed—but the Garian was a different breed. Without Hydro's help, he probably couldn't distinguish his left from his right. The oaf needed him, and as much as Hydro didn't like to admit it, he needed the Garian too—if only for an extra pair of eyes. *Finding a scroll in this labyrinth? I didn't know Guardian Eska's Trials would consist of hide and find.*

Even when Hydro heard a distant scream, he wouldn't talk any more to the Garian than required. He did quicken his pace though. He did not want to be here when the rain was; it created too many disadvantages in battle, especially with unfamiliar terrain.

Bones littered the floor, and faint blood stains painted the walls. Rounding another bend, Hydro saw a black puddle on the floor. He vaguely recalled two other ones earlier, when the path had started smelling. *What are those things?* Hydro was going to put his hand on it and use power to trace it, but the Garian stopped him.

"I'll trace it."

"How do you plan on doing that?"

"With this. Power has its perks, but technology be more thorough." Unexpectedly, the Garian pulled something from one of the holders on his belt.

"What is that?" Hydro asked. In the middle of the device, three rotatable digits resembled a lock; extending to the top, a metal box displayed numbers like a digital watch, while the bottom contained a long, pointy needle.

"It be called SeeSu."

The word meant nothing to Hydro. He stood, shocked and appalled. How did he not have this trinket, and how did the oaf have the knowhow to use, whatever it was? "What does it do?"

"The prince be asking for my knowledge?" The Garian shook with laughter.

"Shut up and tell me what it does."

"It be a substance tracker. Every known substance in the universe has a number allocated to it. This device tracks that number. And this device . . ." the Garian pulled another tiny screen from a pocket attached to his belt, plugging it into a cable port near the top of the device, "will tell us what that number means." The Garian laughed again.

Hydro clenched his fists and sneered. He watched the Garian dip the needle into the pool of black. Seconds passed, and the lock dials turned to form three numbers: 9-7-2. Hydro then leaned over him when an image—captioned with blurbs of text—appeared on the device.

"Well?" Hydro asked. Even though his silver helm and noseguard didn't obscure his line of vision, the typeface was much too small for him to see.

"It be peenatar, a black acid that boils the skin. If not handled immediately, it can burn through even bone. Be the thick density that makes it so dangerous." The Garian cleaned the needle with a transparent cloth and stuffed the parts back inside their proper compartments.

Hydro looked at the substance. *So the Garian can read—so what? He might have fancy gadgets, but not skill; I have never even seen him swing that axe.* Hydro continued forward before glancing back the Garian's way. The smell from the puddle traveled with Hydro, and only worsened as they walked more. Soon they came to a three-way split.

The Garian moved to Hydro's side. "What now?"

Hydro scanned each pathway. *Something isn't right.* He sniffed the air; the fetor surrounded them. It burned his tongue. *It should have died with the puddle.* A faint patter accompanied the smell.

"Grab your weapon, Garian." Hydro unsheathed his sword, now regretting the protection of his leather-padded gloves, as it would make switching the weapon impossible. "We are trapped."

From each new split, a creature approached. They were twice the size of the chimpanzees they mimicked in their gait but looked like dogs with large talons clicking behind their front two legs. The peenatar, as it was called, slid down their vertebrae of braided dark hair and dripped from a stubbed tail. Yellow teeth matched their slit eyes and hung in a slab of tar. Two columns—made of the same elastic and tarry material as the body—connected the upper and lower portions of their faces. The stench rising from the creatures made Hydro's eyes water. Quickly he plugged his tears and regained composure. He wouldn't allow himself to vomit.

"What are those things?"

While back-to-back with the Garian, Hydro felt the Garian's shoulders heave up and down. "You are not afraid, are you?" Hydro chuckled. "I did not know elites surrendered to fear. Your father needs to teach you to suppress it. A good father would." Hydro saw the creature in front of him dig its nails into the dirt. "Duck!"

"What?"

Hydro kicked the back of his partner's legs, causing them to buckle. The creature soared overhead, leaving a trail of black tar that dissolved on their clothes. There wasn't enough to cause more than a tingle to the skin.

"What the . . ."

"You can thank me later, Garian." Hydro snatched his partner's chain-mail and pulled, dragging him backwards.

Both side creatures leaped into the vacated space, howling at the loss of their prey. Now the two contestants weren't surrounded, just outnumbered. The Garian rebounded to his feet. Hydro swung and slashed, keeping his body close to the Garian's, but his offensive only consisted of a handful of misses—the creatures were fast, bobbing and clawing like cats. One slice did manage to connect with a monster's cheek and sent it skidding to the labyrinth wall. The creature howled and glared at Hydro. The line of tar that connected the upper and lower jaw had been sliced open, but it re-formed as they stared one another down.

The other two creatures sat on their hind legs and opened their mouths. A harsh coughing followed and then shrieks of high-pitched calls. *What are they doing?* Hydro couldn't observe their movements, for the angered creature pounced and slashed at Hydro and the Garian both—rebounding off labyrinth walls to constantly keep them on their toes and twisting their bodies. Because of this, Hydro lost focus on the shrieking pair. When the shrieking stopped, the creature that had been occupying Hydro and Cadmar ducked. Black tar flew past it.

Hydro rolled to the side and heard the Garian curse as it hit his ear. He immediately wiped his ear on his shoulder pads. The attacks of all three continued—mostly jumps and slashes, but they came in such quick succes-sions that Hydro had little time to think, just do.

He rolled onto his back as a creature soared over him, then he stabbed his sword into the creature's stomach. A roar came then, but it was not from any of the creatures. It seemed to shake the foundations of the labyrinth, as though a god had been angered. The creatures stopped. Their yellow eyes glowed as they stood still, clueless to the world around them.

"What just happened?" Hydro asked.

"Our chance to win."

Hydro watched as the Garian slashed through the three creatures one by one. It seemed too easy. None struck back. None howled in agony. At every blow, each beast crumbled to the ground like rocks crumbling to the force of picks and the miners who wielded them.

Hydro didn't partake. His father told him that if a man should die, he should die with honor, with a sword in his hand. Hydro's second kill had taught him that when another wrongdoer was forced to face Hydro in a sparring duel. Hydro remembered dodging his attacks with ease and feeling as powerful as a god as he controlled this man's fate; it was just a matter of when he wanted to slash. He ended it rather quickly, with only two stabs, but the look of desperation on the man's face stayed with Hydro for months afterwards.

"This was too easy." Hydro hesitated, reluctant to sheath his sword.

The creatures dissolved to pools of black. Seconds passed. Nothing. Now that there was no danger present, he looked at his armor, which had tiny holes in it from when the creatures pounced over him. He fingered the holes and noticed that some of them went through to the skin, but no further. *Did they affect me? What would cause them not to?*

"Are you coming?"

Hydro snapped out of his trance. The Garian had chosen the north path. "Yes."

The slight patter on his helm alerted Hydro. *It's starting to rain.* He looked to the ground and saw droplets dotting the brown surface. And then he noticed that the pool of black was gone. A noise caught his ear; sconces on the wall had caught fire, even in the rain. Hydro felt a chill crawl down his body. It prickled his hair and perked his ears. *What in Pearl's name is going on?*

CHAPTER 17

A LOST SOUL

Two creatures with braided hair down their vertebrae, noses up in the air, and tar that slid off their bodies crept in a hallway perpendicular to theirs Eirek tightened his grip on his sword and followed Cain's lead by brushing up against the wall. He didn't care about dirtying his white crushed-leather tailcoat with rows of braided fastenings that extended down his chest; it was already dirty from their encounter with an identical creature earlier in the labyrinth. Eirek had done nothing besides get in the way then.

"We won't be able to take on both of them. We barely managed one," Eirek whispered.

"Now that I know power cannot be used, I will not get distracted," Cain said. "Even if you cannot kill, you can distract one of them while I manage mine."

Eirek sighed. The most he had done in the first battle was slice the creature's vertebrae, but it congealed only seconds later. Cain had finished it then with a single swipe through the neck, clean and thorough.

Eirek peeked around Cain; the two creatures were not visible anymore. "Where did the creatures go?"

"Down the path I believe." Cain tilted his head against the sandstone slab. In front of him was a picked carcass—scraps of clothing, dirty and uneaten, still clung to the ribs. Cain exhaled and gripped his dual-bladed halberd. "Ready your weapon."

Eirek was ready; he had been ever since entering the labyrinth. But his readiness only consisted of a shaking arm and slow reactions. When Cain moved from the wall to the next hallway, Eirek followed him.

Nothing.

A roar occurred—a powerful roar, as if the planet itself was cracking.

A single raindrop hit his nose. And then another on his cheek. A sconce on the wall that had been unlit like all the others now glowed with fire. *What kind of power is that?* "How is that possible? It's raining."

"It is this labyrinth. Let us quicken our pace."

Eirek followed Cain around the next bend. "Did the roar make it happen?"

"Potentially. My father told me that an item lives here that gives the ability to cast power without any natural source present. Like this." Cain pointed to another flaming sconce. A little farther down the path, Cain paused. "Did you hear that?"

Eirek hadn't. He shook his head as he perked his ears to try and catch what Cain heard. A light patter of sporadic raindrops hitting the dirt barely reached his ears.

"We need to move faster." Cain's pace quickened, and Eirek found that he needed to keep a light jog to stay with the man's long strides. His partner took a left and then a right. A dead end. Eirek looked at the slab of sandstone and wondered how the others were doing. That was their sixth dead end so far. A rustle of footsteps echoed behind them.

"Did you hear that?" Cain said.

Eirek gulped and nodded. He put his forehead to his arm and wiped his face clean. He noticed Cain touch the side of his glasses. A red film slid down the lenses from the frames.

"What's that?"

"A heat sensor. We are being followed. To the left."

Eirek saw only sandstone.

An eerie, tenebrous laugh echoed throughout the maze. "Lost, are you?"

Eirek kept close to Cain as he walked back the way he came. Whenever Cain tilted his neck, he did the same. Rain started to patter more frequently now. Eirek looked up and noticed the clouds no longer contained any hint of gray.

After returning to the split and going the other way, Eirek saw a man step out from the labyrinth walls. He was of Eirek's height, with dark-brown hair. He smiled and went through the opposite labyrinth wall, which opened up for him and closed immediately after.

"How did he do that?" Eirek asked. His neck tightened, and his shoulders became rigid. He gripped his sword tighter. "Cain, did you see that?"

Cain only nodded and walked forward, keeping his head to the right. At the end of the path, Cain went right for a few paces.

"You are going the wrong way." A sick laugh followed.

"Show yourself!" Cain moved his head slightly.

"As you wish."

From the path where they had just come, a man with trimmed brown hair and dark black eyes emerged. Bags had formed underneath his eyes, as if he hadn't slept for centuries. A circle with an equilateral triangle inside was etched into his left cheek. Tattoos covered the length of his arms.

"Tr . . . Troy Pavos. . . .How is this possible?" Cain slid his hand down the middle of his dual-sided halberd and pushed a button. He broke the long piece of steel in half, carrying one axe in each hand.

"How do you know my name?"

"I have been acquainted with the myths of this labyrinth for some time now." Cain twirled each axe in his hand. "My family inherited what was once yours."

Eirek took a place by Cain's side. He saw the man contemplate Cain's words, his dark eyes never leaving him.

"A prince from Epoch, this ought to be fun." The man cackled and withdrew his sword. "Let us test powers." The man smirked. *"Palo."*

Fire roared toward them. Eirek hugged the labyrinth wall and felt the heat crash behind him. When he looked back, he saw that Cain had rushed the man.

Water tried to swallow Cain, but he sidestepped the spell; the labyrinth floor tried to trip him, but he jumped. Eirek ran after him, propelled by his courage. *I need to show my worth.*

Steel on steel echoed as Eirek watched Cain exchange blows with Troy. Cain was agile and managed to keep Troy engaged. Eirek slowly approached, then he stopped and watched the steel blades protest one another in rings and chimes. *This isn't just some fight. They are fighting for life and death.* Eirek cringed at the thought and stepped backwards, not wanting to interrupt his partner's cadence. Cain elbowed Troy and then proceeded to punch him with his iron knuckles. The man skidded to the labyrinth floor. As Cain was about to bring down both axes on him, he rolled toward the labyrinth wall, disappearing for the time being.

"Eirek, we need to move."

Eirek nodded and ran to catch up to Cain's position. A right and then another left. And another left. Thunder and lightning now accompanied the rain. The ground was becoming muddy. Cain was ten paces ahead of Eirek and gaining distance. Before he knew what was happening, Eirek was thrown against the labyrinth wall. His side erupted in pain. Troy was standing over him, a sly grin on his face.

"Cain!"

The man raised his sword and brought it down. Eirek managed to put up his sword in time. He darted his eyes toward the right and saw Cain running back to him.

"I do not think so." A mound of earth shot up from the labyrinth floor, separating him from his partner. Eirek took the time to slash at the man's leg and roll out of the way. The man cursed, and Eirek noticed the mound of earth release. Cain continued to run toward them.

"You will pay for that." The man threw his arm down, and a bolt of yellow hit Eirek.

Shocks swirled throughout Eirek's body, shaking him in a violent throe. His eyes became dizzy as he floated in and out of coherency. Steel scratches kept him awake. It accompanied talk, but Eirek couldn't understand what was being said. Fire soared over the top of him, nearly scathing his face. Eirek twitched his fingers. A deluge of water, as if a waterfall had just been placed on top of him, made him gasp for air. He jolted up and noticed Cain sidestepping Troy. He only had one weapon now.

Steel argued for dominance. Eirek massaged his head and looked for his sword—it had fallen out of his hand and was an arm's length away from him. He rolled over in the mud and grabbed it. When he returned his gaze, Cain was kneeling on the ground, mud-splattered freckles on his face. *No!* The man slashed downward at Cain, but Cain managed to raise his weapon. He couldn't hold onto it, though, and it went skidding to the floor.

I need to help him. Eirek got to his feet and started to inch toward his partner. The continuous stream of raindrops muffled his steps. Another swipe. Cain put his arms up to where a sword would be and roared in agony. Blood dripped down his arms, joining the mud on the ground soon after.

Getting within range, Eirek jumped and lunged at the man, sword first. Despite the weak jab, there was only slight resistance. It wasn't like stabbing a piece of cooked meat with a fork or pounding a shovel into the earth; it was smooth, like a spoon dipping into a piece of creamcake with a nut-like base. When the blood splattered Eirek's face and clothes, he let go of the sword, shocked at what he had just done.

I . . . I . . .

Troy fell to his knees. Then to all fours. Then to his back. Blood wet his lips. Rain pounded his face. Eirek looked toward Cain, who lay on his back. Eirek inched closer and hovered over Troy's still-breathing body; the blade Eirek used protruded from the man's chest, drenched in dark red. Eirek turned his head and vomited. Dizziness plagued him, shaking overtook his hand, and heavy breathing controlled his mouth. Only after he heard noise did he look. The man was talking.

Eirek tried ignoring the sword sticking up from his stomach. The black eyes had faded into brown. "Take . . . take . . . this path . . ." He raised his arm and pointed it the way they had been going. "At the split . . . go left . . . it . . . it will take you to . . . to our prize. . . ." His body collapsed. "Brother . . . I am coming. . . ." Troy closed his eyes for the last time and got the rest his eyes were searching for.

"Eirek!" Cain coughed.

Eirek stepped over Troy's dead body and noticed Cain. Red and brown freckles dirtied his face, but his glasses remained clean. Forest-green eyes darted back and forth between Eirek's.

"Are you okay?" Eirek asked.

"Nothing is fatal. We . . . we are close. You need to complete the trial."

"Together."

"No . . . I . . . I . . . will get there, but I will be of no use. I cannot hold anything; Troy slashed my arms open."

Eirek looked down to the cuts in Cain's biceps. The rest of his body remained unscathed due to the chainmail and gambeson. His silver steel helm was now a dirty brown with a splash of red throughout.

"But . . . but . . ."

"Eirek . . . my story is ending here. Your chapter continues and . . . and when you win the trial, it will mean another chapter written in our success. Do your duty as a partner. . . . Win this trial for both of us."

"What about . . . my . . . my . . . sword?" Eirek looked at his sword, still lodged in the man. To retrieve it he would need to roll the man over and pull. He had never killed before. How was he supposed to just retrieve his sword?

"Imagine you are pulling a book from a shelf. . . . That is what I did until I became accustomed to it."

Eirek gulped and knelt by the dead man. He stuck his hands under the man's arms, raised them, and pushed. With his left hand, he held the man on his side, and with his right, he grabbed the swords hilt, which was covered in blood. Since receiving the sword, he had found the pommel fascinating, as it was never attached to the sword, but it floated next to it—a dark sphere with two silver rings. *Like I'm pulling out a book.* Eirek closed his eyes and started pulling. There was more resistance this time. He continued pulling, not thinking about the rain or the warmth he felt draining from the man's body. Then a release. Blood soaked the ground, managing to grab hold of Eirek's pants. Instantly Eirek stood up and covered his nose, trying to avoid the metallic stench that the bloodbath gave off. Without his touch, the man slumped onto his face, drowning in mud.

"Go. Hurry . . ."

He was pulled back to reality by Cain's voice. Not able to look at the blood, he sheathed the sword. His gait started at a walk, but before he could advance to a run, Cain called out to him, "Eirek . . . you did well."

Eirek smiled and looked back. "Thank you, Cain."

Turning around, he continued on the path. He followed Troy's directions but was fueled by Cain's words. He ran, hoping that by doing so he would have no time to think about what he had just done.

✺CHAPTER 18✺

LETTING GO

"Tell me, pretty lady, are you afraid of death?" The man clutched her tresses even tighter and pulled back, exposing her delicate neck.

Shortly after the roar that had caused an arising in Zain's skin, the man appeared out of nowhere, seemingly traveling through the labyrinth walls. Dirty pants were the only bit of clothing the man wore; otherwise his feet were bare and his chest full of tattoos. On his right cheek was a symbol branded into his skin—a circle with an equilateral triangle inside.

Is another person going to die because of me? Zain approached, inch by inch. Gabrielle had lost her rapier sometime during the battle that ensued after he appeared. He dragged his left hand up along his Gazo's uniform to the knife pocket strapped to his chest.

"It has been years since a woman has entered this labyrinth. I am going to slit your throat, then savor every crevice while you die, and then eat you. I can tell you will taste good." A long, blood-red tongue licked Gabrielle's neck as if she was food. "Your boyfriend there will watch it all." The man laughed and looked at Zain with those inhuman black eyes—eyes that had become as black as the clouds above them.

The man brought his sword to Gabrielle's throat. It was no normal blade though; it had teeth like a chainsaw—not meant for slashing, but for digging and dragging. Zain's eyes darted back and forth between the sword and Gabrielle's eyes. She was panting, but she didn't struggle. He unbuttoned the pocket where his knife was. He would only have one chance. He grabbed the hilt and was pulling it out when he caught sight of Gabrielle moving her right hand down her ballistic nylon one-piece. There was a flash of silver behind a fuchsia garter. Lower. And lower her hand slid.

It happened fast. Zain couldn't process it until its aftermath. From underneath her garter, Gabrielle whisked out a dagger and drove it into the man's leg. Then she tossed her head back, connecting her scalp with his jaw. Swiveling, she swept the man's legs out and pounced on him. While on the ground, Gabrielle yanked the steel from his leg and stabbed it into his chest.

The man didn't cry in agony. Instead, he laughed. She held the dagger with both hands above her head. He continued to laugh. So Gabrielle stabbed him again. The harder and more raucously he laughed, the greater and more intense were her stabs. A fountain of blood spewed up onto her face and clothes.

What is going on? Zain ran to her.

The laughing slowly ceased, as did his smile, now just a grim line. "I can finally see . . . my family . . . again. . . . Brother, I will wait for you. . . ." His arms went limp.

Gabrielle stopped stabbing. The black eyes turned dark blue. She let go of the dagger and collapsed to her hands and knees. Zain heard her pants. He knelt beside her. She grabbed her dagger again and used her arm to wipe her face. His arm slid over her shoulder; at his touch, she pushed him back and held the steel up to his throat.

"Gabrielle, it's me. Just me."

She dropped the weapon and slunk back. Her shoulders heaved up and down for only a little while, then she regained composure. "Why didn't you do anyzing?"

"I . . . I was going to . . ."

"To wait 'til he slit my throat?"

No. Zain dropped his sword and clenched both fists. He shook his head. "Zen what?"

Zain looked at Gabrielle. Her blue eyes searched his for an answer. "I was afraid I was going to kill you too."

"Better you zan him." Gabrielle stood, tucked a strand of hair behind her ear, and crossed her arms.

Zain buried his face into his hands.

"I'm going to find my sword. It's somewhere back zere."

The subsiding sound of her squishing steps is how Zain knew she left. He looked to the sky and let the rain mask his tears. It couldn't hide his guilt though. *Why? I couldn't even save her. Am I even meant to be here?* He slammed his left fist onto the muddy ground and looked at the lifeless man.

Blood ran from underneath him. Zain found it strange that this is what death looked like. (Even though he had caused two. Now, nearly three.)

He noticed Gabrielle come around the bend again, sword in hand. "Let's leave."

How is she able to stay strong? Zain picked up his sword and got to his feet, following Gabrielle. Torches lit their way, since the suns still refused to show. Zain had a slight limp, but he wouldn't let it slow him. If he could do anything for their team, it would be to continue going.

She has never killed anyone before. She just did. But not someone close to her. Zain's psyche battled within itself. The once navy-blue ballistic nylon armor was now brown with mud and wet with rain. If she had been affected in any way, she didn't show it.

"Listen, Gabrielle . . . I'm . . . I'm sorry."

"Sorry? Is zat all? Would you still be apologizing to me if I was lying on za ground, raped and killed?"

"I . . . I . . ." Zain couldn't finish his thought. "What do you want from me?"

"I want you to stop feeling sorry for yourself, and start acting, not reacting."

Before he knew what was happening, Zain was pushed up against the sandstone wall. Gabrielle forced her dagger to his throat, letting the blunt side tickle his skin.

"How do you feel right now?" Gabrielle looked into his eyes. "You're scared. Well, stop being scared. Zere are zings worse zan deaz."

Zain gulped. He became cross-eyed as he tried to keep focus on the blade. "Like what?" He looked back into her dark-blue eyes filled with lost agony.

"Like pain . . . and hopelessness . . . and futility . . ." She took the dagger away from his throat and put it back underneath her garter. Her face held drops of red, unaffected by the rain or her tears. A warrior's mark.

Zain thought about what just happened. *She's hiding something.* Zain could sense some hidden pain within her.

She turned away from him. "Now where do you zink zis scroll is?"

He pushed himself off the wall and stood beside her. "It has to be in the center chamber. Accessible to every contestant."

"Do you zink zis chamber is close?"

"With any fortune, it will be."

"We should hurry. Or zey will beat us." She sounded strong—the type of woman who was independent.

Zain nodded, and for the first time, he led the way. Ever since the awful roar, torches held by sconces had continued to light their way through the maze, even through the rain. Minutes of navigating countless winding paths led them to a long, singular hallway. In the distance, Zain saw two figures—a large man with a shaved pate and Hydro.

"Gabrielle, look." Zain pointed, and they crept closer.

The prince flailed in midair, as the man had picked him up with only one arm—there was no other arm. In front of Hydro was a strange, unfamiliar device. It served as a surrogate for the left limb, resembling a giant metal pincher with a smaller one in between its claws. A black orb hovered within the inferior pincher like a piece of anitron.

Zain kept his back to the wall but continued forward. Gabrielle slid against the wall in front of him. The stealth tactic didn't work, for ten paces from the chamber, the large man turned his head and snickered. He held the same cruel black eyes of the man before.

The distraction, however slight, allowed Hydro an opportunity to withdraw his sword and slice at the man's exposed chest. The bald man reeled back as blood spurted from his body, branding him with a sick hiss. Out of instinct, the bald man swung his pincher, knocking Hydro clear across the chamber with superior force. The giant regained his composure. "None of you may have our prize."

Was he talking about the scroll? Zain spotted a white tomb in the back of the labyrinth. It was partially opened. Had Hydro already seen its contents?

"All we want is the scroll!" Zain yelled.

"Lies! Everyone who enters covets our necklace."

Gabrielle tapped Zain's shoulder and pointed toward the giant's midsection. "Look at his chest; it's zat symbol ze ozer man carried."

Zain recognized it now. What did it mean?

The man followed their curious gazes. "You like? It's very special. It grants me the ability to do this." He aimed his pincer device toward them. The black ball grew in size. The man's lips twisted upwards, exposing a row of yellow-stained teeth.

Zain froze. The ball of black sped toward them. His heartbeat quickened. Life didn't flash before him . . . only Gabrielle's words: pain, hopelessness, and futility. He looked at her and charged, hoping to avoid the blast. He grabbed her waist just when his own was shot with pain. Warm, electric, and powerful pain. A deafening crack sounded as they hit the slab of sandstone behind them. Zain blinked. Dust scattered his vision. Pain shattered his thoughts. *Where is Gabrielle?* He looked back to see her lying sideways in the muddle, entombed by pieces of rubble.

The ballistic nylon had done its job in protecting her body, but blood marred her hands, neck, and face. Blood crept from Zain's side and from cuts on his face where sandstone debris hit him. Adrenaline told him to ignore it though. So he listened. And he focused on her.

"Gabrielle . . ." Zain shook her. "Gabrielle . . ." She didn't stir. Her blue eyes never fluttered. He put his fingers to her throat. She was alive, just unconscious.

Rage boiled amid his watery eyes. *Stop reacting and act. . . .* Zain punched the floor and unsheathed his sword. He turned around and saw Hydro in combat with the bald man; he was barely holding his own. Zain stormed ahead.

When knocked onto his back, Hydro rolled gracefully to stand again. He turned his gaze toward Zain. "I hope you can last more than seven minutes this time."

"The battle won't even take that long," Zain spat. He charged his adversary; the man raised his hand and muttered a foreign word. A pillar of earth shot up from the ground, but Zain sidestepped it and swung his sword, meeting the man's pincer. Slash. Strike. Duck. Lunge. It was a constant sway of defensive and offensive maneuvers that only succeeded in a stalemate. Normally Zain would have thrown punches too, but the man's extremity forced him to keep his distance.

At one point, the man jumped back and put his fist to the ground, creating a large pillar of earth that blocked both Hydro and Zain. It collapsed soon after, and a large, black orb sped their way. Zain felt Hydro's hand tug him back by the shirt, pulling him out of the orb's trajectory. The blast's residual impact still managed to send them back toward one of the chamber walls.

His ribs throbbed, but his pride had never hurt more. *The prince even has to save me.* Rubble coated his body, and through dust and confusion, the man's voice taunted them. "You cannot handle the power of the necklace. No one can."

Closer. The man strode closer. The orb grew larger. This was it. Zain kept his eyes open; he always would in the face of death. That's how one's soul found its way to Axiumé.

Abruptly the man stopped and turned his attention to the other passageway. Eirek stood there. Alone. *This is my chance.* Zain tossed the rubble off his body and rose to his feet. Hydro followed suit. Zain ran the opposite direction as Hydro charged the man. When a sick hiss—like the branding of skin—resounded throughout the chamber, Zain knew Hydro had wounded the man.

Zain was close now. Just a few more feet. *What is so special about this necklace?* Zain recalled the man before mentioning it when he was taunting and stalking them in the labyrinth. The tomb creaked as Zain pushed the bone-white top farther open. There was no corpse inside—only a pedestal, and on it, a necklace of three golden triangles sat. The outer perimeter was a circle of black, thick scales—like dragon scales. They shined like one of his father's jewels. A female voice called to him. *Don't you want to see Ava again? Wear me and I'll show you how.* Zain stepped back and shook his head but then stepped forward. *No one should be denied.* Her voice enthralled Zain, causing all of his other thoughts and concerns to vanish.

"Zain, look out!" Eirek yelled.

A faint hum followed. Zain turned around and threw himself to the ground and covered his head and neck. The tomb shattered into slabs and shards, raining over the chamber in a white cloud. The necklace appeared to be gone. He pivoted on his belly, scanning the floor. *How can I see Ava?*

The man advanced toward Zain, who began to crawl away, ignoring his new foe. *Where is Hydro?* But by the time Zain got to his feet, the pincer connected with his body and threw him back against a wall. Pain thundered against every one of his nerves. He scrambled, but a kick came to his stomach, adding to his injuries. He thought he felt ribs crack, even behind the steel plate in his side—the one he had received after Ava's death when a boulder nearly crushed him, forcing him to lose his grip and let go of the only thing he had been certain of.

Zain turned around on his elbows; he had lost control of his sword in the blast. Hopelessness entered him with each exasperated gasp for air. Even though he noticed movement across the chamber, there was nothing for him now. Eirek was approaching the man slowly, not fast enough to save Zain. And Hydro scrambled for the necklace that had landed near the chamber's center.

Zain was unable to stand. Hydro grabbed the necklace. Zain spat out blood and reached with his hand. *That's mine . . .* All he could do was look at the man's inhuman black eyes—the orb in the pincer grew even larger— a futility crept into him then, so very cold.

CHAPTER 19

THE TOMB'S PRIZE

Wear me. I will give you victory. Hydro ignored the necklace; he didn't have time to put it on. This man needed to die. As he clutched it in his hand, the dragon scales bit into his skin, sharp as teeth. If what Cain told was true, this necklace would be able to grant him power here.

"*Maa*," Hydro said. He focused his mind to raise the earth between Zain and the bald man. With ease, a slab of earth rose and separated them.

The commoner, who had been inching closer to the man in hopes of saving Zain, stopped.

The man with the bald head looked back toward Hydro.

"Let me make good on my promise. I told you by the end of this you would die." The rain had stopped, but wetness was still in the air. "*Palo.*" Fire circled his hand.

The man smirked. "Well, a prince who can use power. How quaint!"

The black orb flew toward Hydro. He released his spell. The energies sped toward each other. Time seemed to slow. They collided, erupting in a flash of light. Blindness overtook Hydro. He was lifted and sent back onto the muddy ground. Pushing up his body, he looked around. Everything was a blur for the most part. It came back into focus in seconds though, and he saw that the bald man had been thrown against a sandstone wall.

The commoner and Zain limped over to the man. They bent down over him as he began to shake his head. *They're holding him.*

"Hydro, finish this!" The commoner yelled.

Hydro shook his head and looked around. His sword was a few paces away. After crawling and picking it up, he got to his feet and staggered over to the man. As he approached, he could see the man's muscles surge from underneath their hands. Zain shifted more of his weight. *Hold him a little longer.*

Five paces.

Hydro readied his sword.

After a loud grunt of defiance, Zain and the commoner were thrown off. The sandstone slab slid. The man stood. Before he could escape, Hydro used his left arm to hold onto him while he shoved the sword through his tattoo-ridden chest. Blood splattered.

The moment seemed to linger. Hydro stared into the man's inhuman black eyes. Neither of them blinked. The tattooed man grabbed Hydro's shoulder and walked toward him, plunging the sword deeper into his own body. Hydro's eyes grew. Closer he came. Hydro trembled.

The man leaned in toward Hydro's ear and whispered to him; lips moved, and broken teeth dangled amid the coughing of blood on choked gasps. "You cannot handle the power. Only one can. . . . Beware of the girl with black hair. . . ."

It was barely audible to him; Hydro doubted the others heard. The man pushed himself off of the sword, collapsing with a thud upon a slab of sandstone. Hydro looked at the man and then down to the necklace in his hand. It felt like it pulsed, but it was probably just his hand, weary from battle.

Zain grabbed his shoulder. "What did he say to you?"

"What does it matter?"

"It matters because the necklace should be mine."

"Well, it is not yours. I grabbed it." Hydro's eyes reverted back to the man. *The girl with black hair . . . . Is this girl the one who can handle the necklace?*

"You lie."

"What I do is none of your—"

"Eir . . . Eir . . . ek."

The voice barely made its way through the chamber. Hydro looked around. From the slab of sandstone that had fallen in the aftermath of the explosion, Cain crawled toward them. A trail of blood oozed behind him. *What happened to him?*

Hydro sheathed his sword and ignored Zain. He couldn't have the necklace; it was as simple as that. He and the commoner went over to Cain. It took both of them to bring Cain to his feet.

"Do you believe the stories now?"

Hydro nodded. He looked to the necklace in his hand. *Wear me.* He put it in his pocket and looked around. Zain had disappeared to tend to Gabrielle.

"Eirek . . . did . . . did you win?"

The commoner's mouth opened, but Hydro spoke for him. "No. He did not. I did."

Hydro saw Cain's hopes sink. *You should have been paired with me.*

Cain took his gaze off the ground. His eyes furrowed. "Oh no, my beautiful flower. What happened?"

Hydro turned back around to see Zain carrying Gabrielle. He collapsed underneath her weight. He tried to stand, but collapsed again. "She was hit by . . . by . . . We have to help her."

"My chance to prove my undying care for her, and I can't," Prince Evber lamented. "My arms will not allow it."

"I'll help," the commoner said.

"You both will need my help too," Hydro added. With everyone there, Hydro remembered his own partner. "I suppose we should find the Garian before we leave. He is down this way." Hydro pointed down a path and then went to grab one of Gabrielle's legs.

The commoner carried the other leg while Zain took hold beneath her shoulders. Her arms hung lifeless. Her purple lip ring was no longer purple, but dirt brown.

Going through the labyrinth was slow for a little while. Cain followed them, his hands massaging Gabrielle's lifeless ones. After a short time though, her eyes fluttered awake.

"What happened?" she asked.

"You were knocked unconscious," Cain told her.

Hydro released Gabrielle's leg, and the others followed suit. Once on the ground, she leaned against Cain for support. "What happened? Did he hurt you too?" She ran her fingers up his slit arms, streaked with blood.

"No. This was done by another. . . ."

"Who?"

"There is enough time for talk later. Let us leave," Hydro commanded. He turned his back from the group and started walking. *Now where did I leave the Garian?* After a huge tarlike creature that looked like a praying mantis had attacked them, the monster had rendered the Garian crippled. Hydro had to deal with the monster by himself. *It's a shame he will still get a point because of me.* After a few wrong turns, Hydro managed to lead them back to the Garian.

"I see you extracted your axe," Hydro chirped.

"You left me. You left my axe in that thing." The Garian lay on the ground. Blood seeped out of his shoulders, and his axe lay in his hands.

"You should be thankful, Garian. Because of me, you now have one point in the Trials."

"You found the scroll?" Zain asked.

"Of course I did."

"Where is it?" Zain asked.

"So that you can snatch it from me?" Hydro snorted

Hydro brushed aside Zain and extended a hand toward the Garian. *I suppose I'll help. If only we can leave faster.* The Garian eyed his hand for a few seconds before taking it. Hydro said nothing to him, only turned on his heels and led them out of the labyrinth walls.

The wind was a welcome feeling to Hydro. As was the oak smell and the dirt and the worms that came with the forest to the west. Anything instead of the fetor smell of those creatures. The black clouds had returned to a normal gray, but they still hovered above the labyrinth. *I won.*

Guardian Eska, his council, and Senator Numos greeted them.

Guardian Eska stared at them expectedly. "Who has the scroll?"

Hydro reached inside his pants pocket and felt the parchment. And the necklace. His hand lingered there, tempted to pull it out as well. *Beware of the girl with black hair.*

"Zat is what you ask? Zain and Eirek and Hydro needed to carry me zrough half of za labyrinz and each of us come out of zere bleeding, and zat is what you care about? Zere were men in zere. Zey tried to—"

Gabrielle's rebuke pulled Hydro from his thoughts about the necklace. She had hair as black as his. *Is she who I need to fear?*

"Ms. Ravwey, do not raise your voice to Guardian Eska. If you have problems with the trial, address them to—"

"Luvan, enough." Guardian Eska put his hand on the blond man's shoulder and stepped forward, his eyes darted between Hydro, Eirek, and Zain before returning to Gabrielle. "Ms. Ravwey, I outlined how difficult the Trials were before you set foot on my ship. The legends surrounding this particular labyrinth are exactly the reason I approved of this trial. To some, it is dangerous; but as guardian, you may encounter danger. To some, it is scary; but as guardian, you cannot forfeit to fear. To some, it means death and life; as guardian, your hands alone control the balance of that scale for those of Gladonus. Ms. Ravwey, if you cannot adapt to your surroundings, if you cannot tolerate working with others, then I highly suggest you continue no further in the Trials. There are more ahead; some may make you change who you think you are. The question becomes—how willing are you to accept such change?" Guardian Eska turned, heading for his ship. "Conseleigh, find out who won and rejoin me. The others will ride with Senator Numos."

Was Guardian Eska angry? Hydro stole a glance at Gabrielle, who blushed deep scarlet. Even after Eska's departure, no one said anything.

"Who retrieved the scroll?" Luvan asked.

"I did." Hydro put his hand back in his pocket and grabbed the scroll, ignoring the necklace.

"Congratulations are in order, then, for you and Mr. Briggs."

"He had nothing to do with it," Hydro said.

The comment went ignored as Tundra spoke up, "Contestants, I advise all of you to check into our apothecary, where the adored shall examine any injuries you may have sustained. They will administer medicine and herbs. The next trial continues as scheduled, regardless of whether you go or not." There was a slight crack like a whip in her voice. "You will all be escorted back to the Core in the vehicle you arrived in. We will see you there."

Throughout it all, the senator had been very silent. Hydro noticed him glancing to and fro and tapping his cane. *There are not many sights here to admire.* Once Hydro reached him though, he stopped tapping his cane and turned to have a word with him.

"So, it is official. You have won the trial. You and Mr. Briggs will need to schedule an interview with me."

"Whenever is fine. What is its purpose?"

"To report on the trials, of course. How does tomorrow evening sound?"

"Fine, tell the Garian."

Hydro walked faster to escape Senator Numos's company. In the cargo hold of the ship, he took a seat and leaned his head against the leather neckrest. Only three trials remained until he took his spot by Guardian Eska's side. He would have no problem securing the votes from the families in power after the trials were finished.

Each person filtered in after him—Zain the last amongst them. But even after Zain sat down, Hydro swore he heard footsteps. Perhaps it was just the tapping of his feet—impatient to get the Trials over with.

CHAPTER 20

GUILT

Eirek looked down to the bottle of pills in his hands. Adored Isaac Amiti, dressed in a golden shirt that had a crimson-heart-shaped pocket, had given it to him and told him to take one a day with water for a week to relieve the ache in his ribs. *But what about the tremble in my hands?* When Eirek told him of what he had done in the labyrinth, the old man tried to relate it to a story about his time studying the adored arts, but it helped Eirek little. He wondered if anyone else was going through what he was.

Before Eirek left the apothecary, he took time to visit Cain. While walking from the back of the apothecary to his bedside, Eirek noticed female clerics wearing gold visors and crimson dresses with golden hearts around the sleeves checking Zain and Gabrielle. Both of them were asleep already. Cadmar and Hydro had already been checked and cleared to leave.

Once at Cain's beside, Eirek whispered, "How are your wounds?"

"They are healing. I can flex my arm again." Cain clenched his fist and moved it toward his body. "It hurts though when I do it."

"I'm . . . I'm sorry we didn't win. I let you down."

"We survived to see another trial. That is a success in itself. I owe my life twice to you."

Eirek nodded, lost in deep thought. "What does Adored Amiti have you on?"

"A mixture of Angelica Root with a dose of isolated protein. Rebuilds the tissues that were sliced open when . . ."

The blood splattering onto his face. How easy the sword slid through the man. And retrieving his sword. *Pretend it's a book on a shelf. . . .* If only it had been. Then Eirek's hands wouldn't be shaking even now, nor would they have through the whole ride back from Agrost.

Cain placed his hand on top of Eirek's shaking one, steadying his but also causing Eirek to look into his forest-green eyes. "Guilt is only natural. My father would tell me that a guilty man is his own executioner."

"What did he mean by that?"

Cain took his hands off Eirek's and placed them on his lap. "If you let the past dictate your future, you end up killing your future." Cain glanced toward Zain and Gabrielle and then back at Eirek. "There is a city called Lorian on the outskirts of Epoch, near the land of Kane. For seasons, it was pillaged by savages from Kane, and my father one day sent guards to safely secure the village. When I was twelve, he received word that they captured some five savages, so my father brought me and three of his own royal guards, and we rode out to Lorian. We took the captives, who each had ginger hair and red skin, to a bluff that overlooked the firelands of Kane. On the bluff, there was a massive stump of what used to be a yggdrasil tree, where we all took a turn slicing off each one of the captive's heads.

"When . . . when it came time for me to do it, my father placed his axe in my hand and had his guards hold the man's head. That man looked at me . . . he said something to me. . . . 'You cannot kill me, Brother.' I . . . I still remember it. . . . But he was no kin of mine, and my father urged me. He said, 'Come on, Cain, swing the axe. Help the villagers.' I did. It took me three swings to completely sever his head, and when he was dead, one of the guards threw his head over the bluff with the others while the other two guards tied rope to their legs and then around the stump. We let them hang there for all of Kane to see so that no one else would pillage that city anymore. . . ."

To help villagers, he had to kill. Is the guardian any different? Am I even cut out to be guardian? Eirek's gaze wandered to his hands. "Did it work?"

"Yes . . . I am not sure if they still hang there. . . . I have never been back to Lorian since, but my point is . . . is that if . . . if I continued to live with the guilt of that day . . . well, I would be one of those hanging captives, never seeing the morrow's sun. My mother did not speak with my father for months after the incident. Why? I do not know—probably because of the gruesome act of violence it was . . . but so was the pillage the savages did. . . . It helped to justify what I did, but there were times then after that too. And that is when I started finding other ways to deal with killing until I eventually became numb to it."

"You mean the book idea?"

Cain smiled and then yawned. "Yes. This medicine is affecting me. I need to sleep. Take care, Eirek."

"Bye, Cain." On his way back to his room, Eirek's eyes kept being pulled to his scabbard. His hand gripped the hilt; he was tempted to see if blood still lingered on the blade. After withdrawing it a little, he shoved it back and looked ahead. He was nearly there. *Don't look at it. Not before you go to bed. It'll just make you sick.*

As soon as he entered his room, he unhooked his scabbard, opened his closet, and put it inside, shutting the closet door afterwards. Eirek was too tired to look at the stars that night, even though Angal always told him he should. Each person in the universe had a star, and if he ever found his and said his name, it would whisper back his enlightened name—a single name that told who he was meant to be. It would also grant him a single wish—for anything. But stargazing wouldn't ward his feelings, so he let sleep take him to a place no amount of stargazing could. Away from guilt. But desires only traveled so far.

• • •

One moment, he held a pen and was writing a letter to Angal, and the next moment, he stood over Angal's dying body, the pen dabbed in the ink of his blood. Transformed into a sword, the pen had scrawled three letters in red upon a note atop the floor. Eirek never got a chance to make out the letters though, for a knock at his door whisked him from his slumber.

He awoke to a beating heart and cold hands.

Another knock.

His side hurt. *I'll deal with that later.* Eirek climbed out of bed and, with a slight limp, made his way to his door, pausing to look at his closed closet next to his dresser. He was tempted to look inside.

Another knock. "Eirek, you be there?"

In his state, he barely recognized Cadmar's voice. "Come in."

Cadmar entered. "How come you weren't at supper?"

"I felt . . . sick." Eirek turned away. How many people found him stupid for being sick about killing? Especially when protecting all of Gladonus was a responsibility of the guardian. That meant killing.

"Well, I be sick too. I'll be in an interview tonight with that caffler and Senator Numos."

That was news. "For what?"

"For our win during the first trial." Cadmar crossed his arms.

"That should be enjoyable."

"Don't know what you be sayin'. I hate that caffler. I pray to the Twelve it doesn't last long. The whole dinner last night he stared at me but never spoke. He talked with the senator though; that's what he be doin' tonight, I reckon."

Eirek couldn't bring himself to chuckle at the scenario. His eyes wandered back and forth from Cadmar to his closet. No matter how many times he tried to remove himself from the scene, it was a part of him. He needed help. Would Cadmar judge him? His mouth started moving before he could stop it. "Cadmar . . ."

The giant turned around at the threshold of Eirek's door.

"I, uh, ummm, do you have a minute?"

"Yah, what be it?" Cadmar closed the door and sat backwards on a chair, leaning his chest on the chair's back.

Eirek sat on the corner of his bed, which was large enough for two. "Have you ever . . ." Eirek looked Cadmar in the eyes, nervous, "killed someone before?"

"Why do you ask?"

"Because . . ." Eirek's hand started trembling.

"You did?"

"Yes," Eirek whispered, nodding his head.

"Was it your first?"

Eirek nodded again, averting his eyes.

"Did he intend to hurt you?"

Eirek found the question strange. Why else would he have? Did anyone kill out of want? Eirek supposed that was a stupid question; that man in the labyrinth wanted to kill them. Eirek could tell by the cackle in his voice and his inhuman black eyes.

"Yes."

"There be a saying by us Garians: A man bent on conquering the mountain tall is a man meant to eventually fall."

Eirek squinted.

"We Garians were made from the earth; we are the mountains that should never break. When a man drives his picks and spikes into us, we know he hopes to conquer us. Mountains can only take so many picks in them before they crack; after they crack, they break—and when earth breaks, men fall."

Cadmar looked to him with russet eyes. A muted moment, where Cadmar clenched his fists, followed. A necklace caught Eirek's eye; it had shifted underneath Cadmar's shirt as he sat down. It was silver-stranded with a steel eye and a red ruby in its pupil. Steel eyelashes, extending to the sides, guarded the eye. The ends of the eyelashes appeared to be little mechanical hands. "That's a nice necklace."

Cadmar's hands went straight to his neck, and he stuffed it back inside his shirt, almost as if he was ashamed Eirek saw it.

"Where did you get it?"

"A present from my mom . . . before she . . . before she left my aul man and me." Cadmar stood up to leave.

"I'm sorry, I shouldn't have asked. . . ."

"You didn't know." Cadmar paused at the threshold. "All mountains break, Eirek. Sometimes, when they do, it be more than just the people climbing that break."

Cadmar departed before Eirek could ask more. He appreciated the giant's efforts, but he still didn't want to be reminded of his decision—regardless of how it was self-defense and how the man, in Cadmar's words, intended to climb his mountain.

Eirek went over to his closet and grabbed his sword from within. His arm quivered. There was only one way to erase some of the guilt.

He left his room and turned right, walking until he came to the door at the path's end. He knocked on it, and a butler with stubble on his chin and a faint black mustache answered with a bewildered expression on his face. Eirek knew his name was Dominic.

"Sir Mourse, how may I be of assistance?"

"Can you clean this?" Eirek held out his sword.

"Your sword, sir?"

"Yes."

Dominic seemed hesitant at first, but he grabbed it nonetheless. "Of course. You will have it before you retire for the night."

"Thank you."

Eirek left quickly. Before reentering his room, he went to the bathroom and grabbed a glass from the yellow counter streaked with white. He filled it with water and went back to his room, slamming the door shut and collapsing onto his bed. Reaching over to his nightstand, he grabbed the bottle of pills Adored Amiti had given him. After popping the cap, he took one out and put it on the back of his tongue, then he washed it down with water. If he couldn't make the guilt go away, he would at least try to make the pain leave. Even after taking one though, Eirek couldn't stop from crying into the palms of his hands—a stream of tears eroding the strength of his mountain.

CHAPTER 21

INTERVIEW

Hydro trailed the Garian to the lobby. The oaf had said nothing to him since the last trial. Hydro didn't blame him; he knew the Garian hated owing their advantage in the Trials to him. Likewise, Hydro hated earning a point for him.

When the hallway spilled out into the circular lobby, Hydro noticed the senile servant, Colin, bracing himself against one of the two marble columns that stood at the base of the staircase.

Upon seeing them, Colin readjusted his posture. "Are you both ready?"

He is always leading everyone anywhere. He must be Guardian Eska's favorite. The man yawned and used his white-gloved hand to cover a mouth with missing teeth. *Probably past his bed time.* Hydro clicked his tongue.

"Yes," the Garian replied.

Was the Garian ready though? How many interviews had he ever done? During his schooling at Finesse Academy, Hydro had won five tournaments of power against other schools on Onkh. Each time he was interviewed, Hydro never lacked anything to say. *The Acquavan Attribute,* Hydro had named it. He knew words were water, taking form to whatever situation was current. That is why he never stumbled on a question.

Hydro and the Garian followed the butler up the winding marble steps to the second floor. The expansive library greeted them as they stepped onto the dark-blue carpet with red and white intersecting lines and black borders. Colin maneuvered them to the left. Two silver statues stood at the front of the hallway. Long, loose-fitting cloaks covered the idolized men. Stars and sentences Hydro could not read patterned those cloaks.

Farther down the hall, they arrived at a closed oak door. Inside was a room, as Colin explained, where Eska met with lords and ladies and his

council if urgent matters ever arose. Had Hydro's own father spent any time on the Core?

To the right was another door. When Hydro had explored the estate earlier in the week before, he was told that the room was especially for visiting sages of Gladonus—the beings who helped Guardian Eska banish Deimos to the Chains of Chaon; they were tasked by the Twelve to regulate the flux of power amongst all the people in the universe. When Hydro had cast his first spell, his father told him he would need to cast in front of the sages to be declared blessed. That was the only time he had seen them. There were four of them, but only one talked—an old man with one blue and one amber eye. Hydro could never forget eyes like that.

At the end of the corridor, they turned right. Soon after, Hydro saw Senator Numos waddle out of his room, leaving the door open upon seeing them.

"Senator Numos, your guests," Colin announced.

"Ah, excellent. I was just going to come and find you."

The butler left, and Hydro strode past the senator, who was adorned in a white silk robe. A red sash held up his breeches just under his large girth; however, the robe did little to conceal it. Gray breeches—the color of the mockingbird sigil located on a badge to the upper left of the overflowing robe—expanded fully around his legs.

"Please, come in and have a seat on the couch."

Hydro still smelled the food on the senator's breath. Although the man showed the mockingbird sigil of Lady Liliana, Hydro thought such a sigil was too regal for him. Instead Numos should use a lesser sigil—like the curly-tailed pig showered in mud used by the Talhend family of the Crunx province for Cresica.

He entered the room, and the first thing that he noticed was that there were no windows. *How strange.* Instead, ivory walls surrounded them. The walls were portraits of great sand dunes and Ancient golden temples and pyramids. The room had its own bathroom, like his father's. A glass table, large enough for a family of four, stood to the right of the black couches. Hydro took his spot on one of these couches, sinking into the leather.

After the Garian took the seat next to him, Hydro reached for the stemmed glass full of water, which sat upon an ivory table veined with blue and red. Atop the table was a metallic two-handed device. In between the handles was a speaker and an indent large enough for a finger. Senator Numos took a spot on the couch in front of Hydro.

Wasting no time, Numos grabbed the device and turned it on. "Quite the device, this is. It will record, write, and save this interview so I can transcribe it later. No doubt you will see these events in writings and reenactments after the Trials are concluded. In order for it to recognize you, however, each of you will need to insert your thumb or finger here." The senator pointed to the groove by the handles. "And state your name clearly into the speaker located here." Numos fidgeted with a gold band on his pudgy finger.

The Garian took the device without question; he inserted his thumb and spoke his name. "Ouch, that thing bit me." The Garian retracted his thumbs.

Sure enough, two slight indentations had appeared on the side of his thumb.

"You didn't say that thing be biting me."

"I forgot to mention that; in order to fully recognize who you are, it will extract a small blood sample and store it in a tube located inside the device," Senator Numos explained.

Hydro reexamined the device. He had never seen one before. The acquisition of his blood and fingerprint worried him. "Is not our voice the only thing you wish to be tracking?"

Senator Numos didn't respond at first. Sweat populated the folds of skin as he gripped his goblet of dark-purple and sipped, dabbing his lips before answering. "It is. But with events such as these, there has to be undeniable authentication. Anyone can alter his voice or use someone else's fingerprint; but blood, that is unique to each of us. Why I recall a story from one of my friends in the senate from Kuyan in Chaon. He told me the lord there, Zalos Kapache, is bonded with a chameleon. Do you have any idea what kind of power it gives him?"

Hydro shook his head. From his studies at Finesse he knew bonded power was rare and only useable by those who formed a bond between something essential in their life, something they couldn't live without. Because of that, it was also the most dangerous; typically if one entity dies, the other will shortly after. But, together, they are able to draw on each other's strengths and attributes, allowing it to be the greatest of the three powers, depending on the animal bonded with. There was an animal out there for every person, but it was not guaranteed you would ever cross paths. Even if you did, you still needed to decide whether or not you wanted to bond.

"It gives the lord the ability to shift his body to his surroundings. Imagine that. It is because of that, that I now, and most senators along with me, require blood sampling as part of the interview process."

Hydro put his thumb onto the screen, uttered his name, and waited for the prick. Once it occurred, he set it down on the table. Immediately Senator Numos pushed a small red button on the screen and reclined, settling back into his couch. Hydro glanced at his thumbs and saw little traces of blood. *How does this affect me but not the peenetar? What kind of blessing did Pearl give me?*

He didn't have time to ponder more, for Senator Numos asked his first question. "I wish to provide the future audience with some background. So, before the Trials, what was your training like?"

Hydro delved into his training before the Garian could open his mouth. . . .

"Quite impressive. You manage to train with three acqua guards at once?"

"Hardly impressive. My father fights all five of them at the same time."

"Your father's acqua guards are unlike Lady Aprah's elites," interjected Cadmar. "Each individual elite could rival three of your acqua guards."

"And how would you know?" Hydro rebutted.

"My father is second in command for the elites. He be acquainted with one of the guards."

"Who?" Hydro asked.

"Cassius Frauster. He tried being an elite with my father, but he couldn't handle it. He packed his pride and set sail for Acquava."

That was news to Hydro. Everyone knew Frauster to be from Gar—but to be denied becoming an elite and then come to be an acqua guard? Such a disgrace to the Paen estate. *I wonder if Father knows.*

"Tell me of your training, then, Cadmar," Senator Numos said.

"I've trained hard with my aul man ever since I could hold an axe. I've always wanted to become an elite, but have failed twice. I've climbed mountains, worked mines, and studied power with one of my aul man's friends."

"If you cannot even become an elite, what says you can become guardian?" Hydro asked.

"I . . . Certain instances . . . prohibited me from becoming an elite. . . . Surely I would be though . . . and now . . . now this is the only thing left to keep my family's honor. . . . 'When a man is pushed against a mountain, he climbs it.' That is what my father used to tell me."

"What instances were those?" Numos pried.

"I do not wish to say, if that be all right," the Garian said.

Hydro looked at him with more interest. *What is the oaf hiding?* The knowledge that he fought for his family's honor spoke a little to Hydro. But, they weren't equals. Nor would they ever be. Hydro was royalty and carried more skill than the Garian ever dreamed of.

"Well, let us change subjects, then." Senator Numos scrolled through his list of questions. "Now, tell me what you thought of the trial."

"The trial be interesting," Cadmar continued. "Slabs of earthen sandstone surrounded us, and creatures coated in the acidic peenetar attacked. All of which I cut down."

"The Garian may have cut them down, but when he did, they stood still like trees. You were no better than a lumberjack, in my opinion."

Senator Numos chuckled. The Garian tensed and turned his neck, glaring at Hydro.

Hydro locked gazes with the Garian. "Well I only speak the truth." Hydro turned his gaze back to Numos. "After he cut them down, I faced a two-headed creature entirely alone. That one fought back."

"Where were you at this point, Cadmar?"

"The Garian was incapacitated." Hydro stole the words from his partner's mouth. "He did have enough sense to throw me his axe so I could finish the job though."

"And you left it in the creature while it dissolved!" the Garian shouted.

"It was not much of an axe. I am surprised you managed to retrieve it."

"Go on. About the scroll?" Senator Numos leaned in.

"I found it in a central chamber. I was the first one there and took it and stowed it away so the others could not have it. Then a man appeared."

"And what did the man want?"

"To kill us and protect his prize."

"The scroll?"

"No."

"What was it then?" Numos leaned forward in his chair.

Hydro looked into the gray eyes of Senator Numos. There was a long moment of silence. "I do not know. . . . He never told us. . . ." Hydro said. "The man would not let us leave though. So I killed him."

"You say us. Who else was with you?"

"Zain and the commoner. Gabrielle was there for a short while."

"The commoner. Who is that?"

"The poor fellow."

"Eirek Mourse is his name," the Garian said.

"Are you two man lovers now?" Hydro turned away from the Garian, observing a grin forming across the senator's lips. "Yes, it was us three."

"Interesting. . . ." Senator Numos scanned his question. "Did either of you find fear present?"

"I'll be the first one to admit my fear," the Garian said. "There is a motto on fear my people have: Fear is only natural; those who do not fear are ignorant to weakness and, thus, are their own enemy. My father acknowledges his fears as an elite; by doing so, he knows he is only mortal, which therefore makes him less reckless in battle."

Hydro snickered. "If you were not reckless, you would have been able to face that two-headed creature with me instead of being incapacitated."

The Garian's fists clenched. He always had to have the last say. Always.

"So, you did not fear, then?" Numos asked.

"No, I did not," Hydro quickly said. "I knew my steel would shield me, and it did. It plunged straight through the man's heart. There is a saying by my family—who have ruled Acquava for more than three hundred years, since Lyonell Paen: Fear not what blade can slice or what magic can touch."

Senator Numos grinned. "So you are telling me that not even these acidic creatures, or this nameless monstrosity, struck an ounce of fear into you?"

Hydro eyed the senator cautiously. *What is he trying to get at?* "No."

"Most interesting. . . ." Senator Numos pushed the red button in the center of the device. The screen shut off with a beep. "Those are all the questions I have for tonight. I would ask you how your partnership faired during the trial, but I see it already in your answers. You both may leave now. Thank you for your time."

Even after the senator's dismissal, Hydro stayed. He refused to walk down to the lobby with the Garian. The senator stared at him through circular glasses, fiddling with the golden band on his finger. Hydro squirmed, waiting for the swine to say something. When he didn't, Hydro stood. He had allowed enough time since the Garian's absence. As he exited the chamber, the senator's voice stopped him at the door's threshold.

"Do not worry what he says about fear. My father told me when I was attending Fleetist Academy: Fear the powerful, because the powerful do not fear. Power only perpetuates itself. Because he fears, he is weak and will stay weak. That is how it has always been. That is how it always will be."

Hydro did not answer. He left the senator to himself and his wine.

✤CHAPTER 22✤

NEWS

In order to get better reception with his telecommunicator, Zain went outside and sat on the stoop. Clouds blocked an otherwise silver sky, and there was a light patter of rain mingling with a thunder that shook the air. To the left, a hovercraft was coming toward the estate, making its way through the empty plain of dirt. Zain couldn't make out the driver before it disappeared beside the estate. Zain went back to talking with his brother.

"There are still three more trials though, right?"

"Yeah . . . but . . . I need to win one of these next two to advance to the fourth."

"I take the blame for the first trial. I shouldn't have said anything until they were finished. I'm sorry."

It's not your fault. It's mine. Zain saw movement up ahead. It was Tundra. Her usually bouncy, blue hair was moist with rain. Instead of her usual dress, she wore a black uniform with a blue lapel and a golden C badge pinned to her left breast pocket.

"Have you notified Eska of my upcoming arrival?" Jamaal asked.

"Not yet."

"Smart of you to stay under cover, Mr. Berrese." Tundra walked up the side steps, smiling at him all the while.

Zain nodded and smiled back. What was he supposed to say to that?

"If you plan on having someone visit the Core, you must make your case to Edwyrd himself. The Trials are supposed to be free of interference. Make sure you do it soon."

Could she hear through the rain patter? "Thank you, Conseleigh Iycel."

"You are welcome. I will see you at supper."

Zain nodded and watched until Tundra entered the estate. Once she did, he turned his head back toward his brother. "I will talk with Eska tonight."

"Do so, and let me know his decision."

Zain nodded. "I will."

Rain fell harder. Lightning ripped through the sky. The signal died. *Shit. I didn't even get to say goodbye.* That was always a problem for him.

Zain stood up and entered the estate again to retire to his room. Attached to his door was a crimson envelope with a golden seal, a silhouette of a dragon embossed on it. *The next trial. Was Conseleigh Iycel preparing for it?*

He ripped open the letter.

Dear Contestants,

The next trial, conceived by Tundra Iycel, is ready for your participation. As guardian, you will need to be able to assess situations critically. This trial will test the strength of your mind and your ability to analyze situations. More information will be given by Conseleigh Iycel herself at tonight's dinner, which will be served at seven. Make sure you are present.

Sincerely,
Guardian Edwyrd Eska

He looked toward Gabrielle's and Cain's doors. The envelopes had already been taken off of them. Now he heard faint voices coming from Gabrielle's room next to his. It was Cain's voice. Zain crept over and listened.

"A trial of intellect . . . I wonder what Conseleigh Iycel has planned."

"Whatever it is, it will be easier zan za last trial."

"What makes you say that?"

"Because I will only need to rely on myself."

"Zain was not a good partner?"

"I don't want to talk about it. . . ."

Zain's breathing grew heavy. He leaned in closer.

"You can tell me, my flower."

"He just stood zere . . . while I was held hostage. . . . He didn't even try and save me."

"By whom?"

"Zis deranged man wiz black eyes. . . . He held a sword to . . . to my zroat . . . and told me . . ." Zain could hear Gabrielle start to cry. "He told me . . . he was going to slit my . . ." Gabrielle sobbed. "Zen . . . zen he was going to savor every . . . every crevice while I died."

"It's okay. It's okay. . . . If I was your partner, I would have protected you."

"Zank you, Cain."

Zain clenched his hands. *He can talk all he wants. But it's different when you are there.*

"To Zain's credit though, he did help carry you from the labyrinth," Cain said.

"Zat was only after I told him what was worse zan deaz. But . . . yes . . . zat was decent at least."

"What do you think is worse than death?"

Even after all of the hurt she showed, Zain couldn't pull away. He needed to hear more. He pinned his ear against the door.

"Pain . . . hopelessness . . . futility."

"What makes you say that?"

"I . . . I . . . I . . ." Silence.

"You can tell me," Cain consoled.

"My mozer was abused when I was young. . . . My fazer was horrible to her . . . to me too. . . . Imagine . . . imagine coming home from school and wondering . . . will my fazer only touch me today . . . or . . . or will he beat me too?"

"Your father did that?" Cain's voice rose.

"When I was eight, my mozer sent me away to Gracie's to not be around him anymore. By za time I was zirteen, he finally got taken away. . . .Now he is held by Victor Zigarda. . . . I don't even care to know if he's still alive."

"If Zigarda took him away, then why did you say he's an awful ruler?"

"He didn't take him away. Carla Sonatta, my teacher at Gracie's, knew someone in za senate. I . . . I told her everyzing one day . . . and she agreed to help me. It was only zen zat Zigarda incarcerated him."

Zain slunk away. Were his problems even bad? They weren't. *Get over yourself and just win this trial.* Zain decided to go train in order to sort out his emotions. It had always worked for him in the past, and hopefully it would continue to work for him now.

• • •

Zain took his spot next to Cadmar and Eirek. He glanced at Gabrielle, who showed no signs of crying previously. Hydro spent time talking with Cain—but about what, Zain couldn't hear. The tall prince's arms were still streaked with red, but it seemed like he could move them normally.

Guardian Eska stood, letting the crimson-and-gold cape behind him unfurl. Mythril scales on his body jingled lightly with the movement. "Contestants, congratulations for enduring the first trial. A special congratulations for Prince Hydro Paen and Cadmar Briggs." Guardian Eska extended his hand to each of them in turn. He raised a stemmed glass with purple wine and drank.

Zain felt obligated to do the same, seeing as all of Eska's conseleigh toasted Cadmar and Hydro too. His was a red wine though—a taste he had never fully acquired.

Guardian Eska's brows furrowed. "This next trial will require you to partner with your mind to think critically about situations. As Guardian of the Core you have the last say when it comes to matters of peace, justice, or even laws. Because all of these things have variables you cannot account for, you need the ability to analyze every angle." Guardian Eska looked at the contestants, taking a second and third glance at each one. "Conseleigh Tundra Iycel will have the floor now." With his ungloved hand, he snapped the air—killing light and creating darkness.

Tundra stood up and walked behind Guardian Eska, putting her hands on his shoulders for just a second. She walked away, her eyes glowing a light blue in the dimness.

"Contestants, two days from now you will meet in the lobby at noon. It is there where you will receive a riddle that reveals the location of one of three orbs I placed on the Core."

In the middle of the dining table a hologram of the Core appeared out of nowhere and rotated, the orbs circling around it like moons. Zain watched Tundra stroll behind Hydro, Gabrielle, and Cain.

"There are two sets of each riddle, so you will be competing with one other person for your orb." Tundra rounded the table. "Be careful how you gather your information, for time is of the essence." She lingered past Zain, Eirek, and Cadmar. "The first contestant who returns to the lobby with the orb in his or her hand wins the trial. Any questions?" She was back at the head of the table, behind Guardian Eska.

The room lightened, Zain saw Hydro raise his hand. When called upon, he asked, "Will this trial prohibit us from using power as well?"

"No and yes." Tundra paused. "Up to obtaining the orb, you will be able to use power. However, upon touching the orb, you will not be able to use power for the remainder of the trial. Nor will you be able to use power to locate them."

Zain noticed a twist in Hydro's face. Zain had never been able to use power, so the stipulation affected him little. He had his own question to ask.

"Yes, Mr. Berrese?"

"How long will we have to complete this trial?"

"Five hours," Tundra replied.

"And if no one finds the orbs in that time?" Zain pressed.

Tundra chuckled. "Although unlikely, if no orbs are brought before us within the timeslot, then the trial will be counted as a tie. That would leave Hydro and Cadmar still tied for first place. Mr. Briggs, go ahead."

"How will we navigate ourselves to the locations where the orbs are hidden?"

"By foot, Mr. Briggs. Unless you can fly." Tundra chortled a little.

Zain noticed Guardian Eska grin a little as well. Zain couldn't bring himself to laugh, although he did find Cadmar's question odd.

Tundra continued, "Any form of navigation is accepted, and to aid you in your quest, maps of the planet will be provided for each contestant on the day of the trial. Are there any more questions?"

Zain couldn't think of any. No one else could either. When Tundra reclaimed her seat, Guardian Eska stood again and snapped his fingers. Accordingly, Colin signaled for the trays of food to be carried out.

• • •

During supper, Zain picked at his food. Not because he felt sick, but because he was biding his time until the others left the room. He needed to talk to Guardian Eska, and he didn't want the others to question what he was doing. Half a breast of chicken marinated in a reddish-brown paste lay on his plate along with a few stalks of steamed asparagus. Gabrielle sat in front of him even after Cain and Hydro left. She massaged her neck with her hand, her bracelets dangling against her arm.

I was going to save you. I was. Zain looked down at his chicken and cut another piece. Cadmar and Eirek got up and left, so it was just he and her now. It took another minute, but she left, casting a glance at him before doing so.

When Zain heard the double doors close, he looked down at his meal, finished the rest of his chicken, and then stood. He wiped his mouth on the golden linen and proceeded over to Guardian Eska. Riagan was in conversation with Senator Numos. Otherwise it seemed like all of them waited his presence.

"Guardian Eska, I have a question."

"Tundra told me you would come."

Zain looked at Tundra and then realized why it seemed they all expected him.

Guardian Eska continued, "Let us do this in my room, where it is more private, shall we?"

Zain nodded.

"Riagan, we must leave." Guardian Eska then turned his head toward Senator Numos. "I am sorry, Senator, you can continue your conversation another night."

"Certainly, Guardian Eska. Take care, Riagan." The senator nodded and left.

Zain followed Guardian Eska out of the dining room and to the lobby. Soon enough they were ascending past the second floor on the sapphire circle in the lobby's center and were reaching the third floor.

In his room, Guardian Eska sat down in a plush velvet throne on a small dais in the living room. Guardian Eska's conseleigh sat by his side— Tundra and Ethen to his left, and Luvan and Riagan to his right. Zain stood while all of them sat. His hands were cusped behind his back.

"So, what do you ask of me?" Eska asked.

"My brother wishes to stop at the Core when he leaves Myoli later this week."

"To where is your brother headed?"

"Agrost. He is a politician on Mistral."

"So he knows Nyom Numos?" Riagan added.

"He does."

"How does the man manage to breathe up in the altitude of the Floating Isles?" Riagan chuckled.

Guardian Eska also chuckled at the comment. Zain couldn't help but smile a little too. He had been to Mistral a few times to visit his brother and always felt out of breath even just walking around.

"Enough, Riagan—although, you make a decent observation." Eska turned to Zain. "What does your brother intend to do here?"

"Jamaal says he has a gift for me."

"A gift? Do you know what it is?" This time it was Luvan who asked the question.

"No, he wouldn't say. It was from my father, before he left for Empora to work for Lord Zigarda."

Guardian Eska grimaced and looked to his left and right. He placed his finger underneath his lip and stared at Zain. "You realize the Trials are supposed to be free from interference of any sort, do you not?"

Zain nodded. "Yes, Guardian Eska, I do."

"Then tell me, why should I make an exception for you when all are supposed to be treated equally?"

Zain was silent. *What can I say to convince him?* Zain searched Guardian Eska's brown eyes. He tried to recall something that Guardian Eska mentioned. He needed to speak soon, though, in order to not look like a mute, or unprepared. So Zain started, "The Trials, you say . . . I mean . . . you said the Trials are supposed to test something in us. Conseleigh Iycel's trial will test our intelligence . . . and Conseleigh Katore's trial meant to test partnership. . . ." *Get to the point. He doesn't have all day.* Zain looked at Eska's council who all looked at him, eyes unwavering. "But . . . but you also said that the Trials were meant to test our adaptability. That's why each one tests something different . . . so . . ." Zain lingered here as he tried to think of how to phrase the request. "So it's not that you wouldn't allow another to visit a contestant here during the Trials; it is that I am the only one asking for your assistance. . . ."

Zain wondered how to end it. Something came to him, although he didn't know why. Perhaps it's because he saw her alone at supper, without the prince by her side. "I . . . I learned that you need to act, not react, to things. So that is what I'm doing. I'm acting and taking the initiative to ask you for your assistance."

Eska didn't answer for a minute. He leaned back in his chair, continuing to stare at Zain all the while. "And what of the gift? Should I allow you to use anything given to you during these trials?"

"If it pleases you, Guardian Eska, I would be willing to let you examine whatever item it is, so I may have your permission of its use."

"It does please me. I will let General Satorus know that your brother is allowed entrance. Be sure to let your brother know."

"I will; thank you."

Guardian Eska nodded. "Riagan, lead him out."

"Yes, my guardian."

Zain boarded the sapphire platform to transfer him down to the main level and noticed Riagan give an inquisitive look, followed by a quick and subtle smile. The gears hummed below him as the platform descended, and slowly the third level went out of view. He straightened his shoulders and exhaled. It still didn't amount to a trial win, but it was a step closer in atoning his past.

❧ CHAPTER 23 ❧

BOOKWORMS

A day had passed since explanation of the next trial. Unlike the first trial, Eirek felt as though he could contribute something to this one. He still could not figure out Angal's last riddle, but not just anyone could solve the others he had posed. Not just anyone could manage to learn to play the flute or strum a lyre—and teach others to do the same. Not just anyone read for fun when time allowed; even here on the Core, he found that most of his time was spent in the library, preferring to only practice his sword training in the grave of night, so no one else could observe him.

If he was to win this trial, he needed to do research. And he would do that after the chess match he had started with Cadmar. It was their third match, and Eirek was used to Cadmar's tactics. It wouldn't be much longer now; Eirek was already getting himself in position to win. Whether Cadmar knew it or not, he had four moves left.

Eirek typed his move into the electronic stand attached to the desk in the lounge. "Are your shoulders healed yet?" Eirek watched his bishop advance three spaces diagonally, then withdraw his sword and plunge it through the top of the rook. The violence still shocked him, and sometimes he found himself clutching the table to steady his hand.

Cadmar scanned the field. "They be better. I be able to lift my axe again."

Eirek looked at the man's shoulders and then his whole figure, never truly seeing how stocky the man was. He lowered his gaze to the field and saw a knight trample one of his pawns.

Without too much deliberation, Eirek typed in his next move. "How was the interview?" Eirek watched his rook slide down the board. "Check."

"Horrible. That one be a caffler through and through. Now that he won the first trial for us, he be even more entitled." Cadmar typed his move into the keypad.

"Invalid move. Try again."

"Damn that bishop." Cadmar scanned the field and reentered another number. "There we be. . . . How you be feeling? How be the other prince during the trial?"

Eirek scanned the field. "Better . . . but I . . . I sometimes have dreams that . . . that people die because of me. . . ." Entering in the coordinates, he watched the other rook slide down the other side, ramming a pawn out of the way. *One move left.* "Check. . . . And Cain was no caffler, I think . . . but he didn't refer to me by name until I saved him from one of those tar creatures. I've tried to make contact with him since . . . but he . . . he is always short with me."

"I haven't met royalty that not be a caffler. Well, that not be true. Lady Aprah not be a caffler; neither be a lot of Garians. . . . We learned that everything not be just given to us; we have to fight for it, even if that be a rebellion." Cadmar scanned the field, and after only a few seconds of scanning, his shoulders slunk. "How be your lady always alive at the end?"

"Because I prefer to save her until she is needed."

"But she can do anything. Why you not bring her out earlier?"

"She can do anything only because of the other pieces on the board."

Cadmar entered his coordinates. "This be the only move I can make." The lord moved one space up and to the left, avoiding the pawn.

Quickly Eirek entered his coordinates. "Checkmate." The final scene played out, where the two rooks, the bishop, and the lady all approached the lone lord and killed him.

"You be too good at this game. You know, there be a saying by my people for chess. . . ."

"What isn't there a saying for?" Eirek teased.

Cadmar looked at Eirek and smiled faintly. "Those who are good at chess lead the best. Lady Aprah could certainly give you a dash for your coin though."

"Well, perhaps I will need to challenge her if I ever make it to Gar." Eirek doubted that would happen though; this was his first time off of Agrost. He didn't have enough coin to take an interplanetary shuttle, nor did he have the means of getting to the port even if he did have the coin. Eirek got up from his chair and stretched. "I am going to get some reading done in the library before supper yet."

"I'll be training in the habitat arena. Take care."

Eirek nodded and left the lounge area that he had found during one of his first days in Eska's estate. It was located to the right of the staircase and featured bookshelves, desks, and couches for relaxation. When needing to pass the time, he would do so here.

In the lobby, he had started to climb the staircase when he saw Prince Paen coming from the second floor. There was a book in his hand. When they passed with only a glance at each other, Eirek was rather surprised. *No snappy dialogue from the prince? Is he feeling all right?*

He didn't know what he was particularly looking for in the library, but he figured he would try to find something on navigating the Core. Since the trial would take place on the Core, he thought it might give him an advantage. He wondered if others were doing the same.

While browsing through the stacks and columns of books, he noticed Prince Evber reading in a red longchair. The window overlooked the sparring court outside and the dirt that eventually tapered into sand.

"Hey, Cain."

The prince turned in his chair and picked up his glasses, which he had set down on the small wooden table next to him. "Eirek, how interesting seeing you here." He turned back around and flipped a page in his book.

"Are the arms feeling better?"

"They have regained functionality."

Eirek maneuvered to another column, but he took a quick peek over Cain's shoulders before doing so. "Researching for the next trial?"

"No. Not much I can research before I receive the riddle. Instead I prefer to keep my mind sharp with books and stories."

"Like what kind of stories?"

"Ones of Knight Barristan Corbello and his feats before the Great War. Or Lukas Kaplurn and the group of riders he led all over the Myoli."

"I like reading about lore and the Ancients."

Cain turned back to look at him. "Yes . . . I am sure." He gave a weak smile and continued reading.

Eirek picked up a book and looked through it with feigned interest. He put it back and went over and sat at the longchair next to Cain. "Cain, that man, in the labyrinth, you knew him. How?"

"It is nothing complex, Eirek. I am a prince of Epoch; because of it, I know many things about the royalty who ruled before me. Their tale is rather tragic; however, that prize changed their lives."

"Hydro picked up some sort of necklace in the labyrinth."

"He did?"

Eirek nodded. "Right before the big explosion."

Cain's gaze wandered. "I . . . I need to go." Cain shut his book and left it on the table. "I pray you find whatever you are searching for."

When Cain left, Eirek slumped and tilted back onto the longchair, wondering why Cain left so abruptly. He had been doing that ever since the first trial. Eirek wondered if Cain was still dealing with the fact that he had lost due to Eirek's unhelpfulness or if it was because Eirek saved him twice. He crossed his arms and blew air up into the tresses of his brown hair. His gaze left the mountains in the distance and went to the book that Cain had left on the table. Eirek picked it up and read the title: *Living in History*. It didn't interest him. Eirek put it back on the table and continued his search for something that could be of relevance during the second trial.

CHAPTER 24

RIDDLES

By the time the knock came to wake Hydro, he was already dressed in a boiled, mottled-gray rhinoskin breastplate strapped at the sides. A coat of chainmail hung over him, protecting any uncovered flesh. His cotton pants allowed air to circulate through the day, and the black-leather boots would be comfortable enough with the foot-length sack of down feathers placed in the bottom of each.

The necklace he seized in the first trial stared back at him from the dresser drawer he hid it in. He wanted to find out more about its history, but so far he had only uncovered what Cain told him before the first trial—that if this was the prize, then it could make denied blessed and grant Hydro the ability to use power even if the source was not physically present.

Wear me, Prince Paen. Together our bond will win this trial. The girl's voice was enthralling; since the first trial, it had caused Hydro to pick it up multiple times. But when he did so, the scales would clench down, biting his fingers and drawing little specs of blood. The trance would break then. Or others would come and knock on his door, like what happened the day before with Cain.

"May I help you?" Hydro had said. He had just started skimming *The History of Epoch.*

"You took the labyrinth's prize?"

"I do not know what you are talking about." Hydro tried to close the door.

"Eirek told me he saw you pick up a necklace. . . . Where is it?"

"I picked it up, yes, but left it there."

142

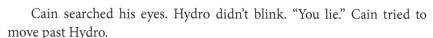

Cain searched his eyes. Hydro didn't blink. "You lie." Cain tried to move past Hydro.

"I would not think about that, Prince." Hydro grabbed the hilt of his blade.

Cain traced his arm diagonally down, then looked back at Hydro. "The prize belongs to Epoch. To my family."

"Your family will need a new prize now."

Cain's brows furrowed. Hydro unsheathed his sword a little—just enough to hear it come out from the scabbard. After that, Cain left without a word, and Hydro went back to studying his dry text—receiving no additional answers.

If you wear me, the others will not be able to steal me. Keep me for yourself.

He put a piece of clothing over it and pushed the drawer back in place. *The last thing I need in a trial of wit is my own leaving me in the form of a talking necklace.*

After Hydro sized himself up in the mirror, he made his way to the lobby and found he was the only contestant there. To the left of Guardian Eska, Senator Numos stood with his cane out in front of him, the dark-gray mockingbird sigil as poignant as ever on his overflowing silk robe. A vast majority of the lobby was illuminated by the light filtering in through the stained-glass windows on the side of the lobby's door. Above, half-circles— one red and one blue—symbolized the rising suns.

Conseleigh Luvan led the other council members as they made their way down the winding steps. He wore a buttery-yellow silk shirt with lines of black and buttons of silver. The outfit gave Luvan an albino appearance; his eyes looked more russet than usual. At the rear, a younger man in his late thirties wore an orange fleece, nearly matching the color of his hair. If Hydro remembered correctly, his name was Riagan. And Ethen wore a vest coated with leaves and a black shirt underneath that exposed his scarred upper arms. The three men sat themselves behind three wooden tables placed in the lobby. Conseleigh Tundra stood to the right of the tables near Guardian Eska—showing her seniority and, Hydro assumed, that this was her individual trial. She wore a silky blue gown and ice-clam pearls around her neck. Her left hand relaxed on the table, opened, and returned back to her hip. A pair of keys sat where her hand had been.

Hydro caught a whiff of honey perfume and turned to see Gabrielle walking into the lobby; she was trailed by Zain. Hydro assumed each of them would provide little competition, considering the amount of damage they sustained in the labyrinth.

Gabrielle was lightly armored, clad in a half-cut leather top coated with a purplish material covering past her midriff and the Gracie's embroidery on the upper right. How much protection could it provide in combat?

Zain wore a short-sleeved version of his regular outfit. It was an academy outfit, that much was obvious even without the red Gazo's embroidery on the upper left side.

At Finesse, Hydro and his classmates had also worn uniforms. His father had bought ten for him, solely to cut down on the laundry. Hydro didn't miss those days; the uniforms always choked his neck and suffocated his body, completely unsuitable for a midday event.

The others showed up shortly thereafter, at which point Tundra began her speech.

"Contestants . . . the orbs are in place; it is now your task to bring them back. You will come forth, one at a time, when we call your name. From Luvan, you will receive your riddle; from Ethen, your maps; and from Riagan, you will receive a tracking device to be placed around your ankles. The latter is a safety precaution."

Safety precaution? If it truly was a safety precaution, then why didn't they wear them in the labyrinth? No. There were places on the Core meant only for a guardian's eyes or the eyes of his apprentice. Soon Hydro would see those places for himself.

"Prince Hydro Paen," called out Tundra.

Hydro strode forward to the tables of walnut wood, where straw-woven baskets lay filled with various things. At the first table, Luvan handed him a piece of parchment, curled and tied with a red ribbon. Next, Ethen handed him a scroll. At the last, Riagan gave him a black band with a metal square on its outer side that had flashing a green light.

While the others received their things, he strapped the band to his ankle. The other two items he wouldn't open quite yet. Depending on what the riddle said, he may need to seek information in the library. But he wondered how much good that would actually do him, considering the times he was there before proved to be fruitless. If anything, though, it would allow him to read his riddle in solitude.

"Prince Cain Evber," Tundra read.

Cain walked forward wearing a leather vest with white chainmail underneath. He glanced at Hydro and then redirected his gaze back to the conseleigh. His black gloves were similar in color to Eska's; strapped over his back with a silver chain for each were two metallic black batons.

"And lastly, Eirek Mourse," finished Tundra.

Hydro grinned. *You certainly called it right; the commoner will be last, and I will be first.*

After the commoner received his things, Tundra spoke again, "Contestants, you now have all the materials you will need. The trial will end when the first contestant enters the lobby carrying his or her orb, or five hours from now—whichever occurs first. Good luck, and may the Twelve and the Ancients be with you."

Tundra exited the room, and the rest of the conseleigh followed—each carrying a woven basket. Hydro did not know where the commoner went, but Zain, Gabrielle, and the Garian were heading upstairs, leaving only Cain and him in the lobby. Hydro glanced at Cain. When the look went unreturned, Hydro ascended the stairs, noticing on the way that Tundra's keys still laid on the table. *She must have forgotten them.*

When Hydro entered the library, he settled himself on an eccote wood table in the far right corner. He rolled the map out in front of him, holding its sides down with a pen holder and coaster already on the table. He didn't examine it though. What good would that be if he had no idea what to search for? He plucked apart the ribbon and opened his riddle.

> *If water is blue, why must this one be red?*
> *It's not harmful though, just simply misread.*
> *Give yourself, let it settle, and once you do,*
> *You'll find the stain you made changes back to blue.*
> *Once you speak the words that you need to speak,*
> *You may find yourself holding what you came to seek.*

Hydro's eyes glanced from the riddle to his map. Water. He needed to focus on lakes. Seven of them were spread out across the map: Finis, Darse, Crimson, Dolob, Lufmrah, Penase, Funjhi.

How am I supposed to know which lake is red? He looked toward the scale of the map, the closest lakes—Funjhi and Lufmrah—were a league away. Funjhi was to the north and Lufmrah to the east. Darse was the farthest, but it was close to Finis, which was on the other side of the mountain range. That was four leagues though. Dolob and Crimson were on opposite sides of the Core, to the south of Guardian Eska's estate. Penase lay to the northwest. Hydro assumed it had to be one of the five northern lakes, for the southern ones were farther than the rest of them. Still, the word *crimson* lured him. *Are these the lake's actual names, or are they clues as well? Damn riddles.*

Hydro tapped his fingers on the wooden table. If he didn't leave soon, the other person with the same riddle might solve it before him. An epiphany struck him. Rising from his chair, he went to a small podium placed before the columns of books—it was a search machine that let you easily find any books by keyword, author, or title. Hydro typed "spells of power" into the search bar, and after loading, a green light shot out from the podium and wound its way around the library. Hydro followed it to a catch-all book titled *Power's Spell.* If he was going to change the water from red to blue, he would need magic. However extensive his training was at Finesse and with Professor Haruko before that, this particular spell remained foreign to him.

He took it and returned to his desk to browse through it. It was organized fairly well; once he located the spell, he memorized it, tore the page from the book, and walked over a few rows. He removed a random book, which he promptly replaced with the spell tome. *Try finding this now.*

Grabbing his things from his table, Hydro made his way downstairs to the lobby. Those keys were still on the table. *Did she forget them?* Hydro took a closer look at them—they weren't for rooms. He grinned wider. *The Twelve take me now.* He grabbed them and headed out the doors.

The hot midday air greeted him. But if these keys proved to be useful, he could be free from the suns' wrath soon enough. He looked to the right and walked down the steps. From exploring the surrounding estate during that first week, he knew where the hovercrafts were kept. *This should make traveling much easier.*

Around the estate, a large crimson tent with golden flaps had been set up next to the habitat arena. Once inside the tent, Hydro stood in the shadows of five hovercrafts, evenly spaced throughout a quarter of a mile. Now it was just a matter of finding which one matched the keys. On the fourth try, he managed to successfully start one. Dust kicked up in the air, and the smoky-gray anitron hovered in its case just as the craft did. *These trials are too easy. Adaptability is key.*

Hydro inched out of the tent and noticed someone walking in the raw heat. It was Gabrielle. *Beware of the girl with black hair.* Was she going after his same riddle? If she was, she was headed toward Penase Lake. He would have time before she got there. Hydro shifted the craft into a higher speed and drew up the roof to block out the suns. As he flew past Gabrielle, he saw her face twist in curiosity. She yelled something, but Hydro couldn't hear from inside.

"Which lake to start with first?" Hydro spoke to the steering wheel. He laughed. He couldn't believe it actually worked. Everyone else had to travel by foot—time was no issue for him now. "Might as well start with the ones farthest away." As he drove past the estate, he saw Zain vanishing toward the north into the desert.

He passed ash trees and cacti. Lizards crawled over the sandy floor; but for the most part, the ride was empty of sights. In a matter of minutes, the estate vanished behind him, and the mountain range that loomed in front became larger. It took him twenty minutes to travel—but had he been walking by foot, he wouldn't have even reached a league yet.

Hydro stared at a calm blue lake. *At least there is some challenge to this game.* He doubted that Finnis Lake on the other side of the mountains would prove any different in color, but he needed to check. He guided the hovercraft up the steeply inclined terrain, parking next to a small tree with leaves. It wasn't so dead here.

From the craft, his view of the lake was obscured. *It needs to be here though; the map says it does.* Hydro exited the hovercraft, feeling the heat again. A lizard crawled on the ground. *Use some liquid, could you?* Hydro spat and hit the lizard on the head. Another crawled on his foot, and he gave it a little kick, sending it down the inclined hill.

To his left, a mound of boulders gradually progressed up the side of the mountain range, connecting with a rocky wall that circled around the area for another mile. *I can still climb.* Even if the Garian wasn't with him, he was going to prove to himself he climbed mountains, not hills.

With ease, Hydro traversed the mound of boulders until he was able to see over the rocky wall. The water was still and calm in the mountainous basin, flowing out into a river on the far north side. But none of that mattered. It was blue. He brushed his hand through his hair and leaned against the rock. The wind hit him and cooled him with a wisp of the lake's water.

Hydro traveled back to the hovercraft and took the scroll out from the passenger seat; he laid it on the hood, bending over it to keep it from flowing away. Five other lakes remained unseen. Two were far south, and if Gabrielle was his competition, it did not seem like she was headed that direction. Zain wasn't headed that direction. No one was.

Hydro focused on the three options left then—Penase, Funjhi, and Lufmrah. *Decisions.* If it was at Lake Funjhi, Zain may be his opponent. If he went to Lake Penase, Gabrielle may be his opponent. Neither, Hydro thought, would pose much of a threat—he could always steal the orb from either of them afterwards. That left Lufmrah and perhaps a different adversary—no competition or no orb? Still, it was the best place to start. Hydro rolled up his map and got back into the craft.

The ride there was the longest ten minutes of his life. Once at the base of the lake, his heart sank. It was blue. *No, this has to be it. This has to be it.* Hydro slammed his fist into the steering wheel. Then, he saw movement. He squinted and noticed a long, white pier extending across the lake's diameter. A person's indistinct figure stood on the pier. Hydro exited the craft, sprinting toward the person. *If someone else is here, then perhaps I'm still right? But why is it blue?*

As he got closer, Hydro noticed red starting to filter throughout the lake. *The riddle's been solved.* He looked to the pier and noticed the fiery hair of Cain. Prince Evber stood up and readjusted his glasses as Hydro pounded toward him.

"Even with cheating, you are too late. The riddle has been solved already."

Hydro noticed a slight cut from Cain's hand, still dripping blood to the pier. In the middle of the pier, right in front of Cain, was a rotating blade lodged in a circular underwater flask.

"I did not cheat. I merely adapted. Tundra laid the keys on the table for everyone to see. I am the only one who took them." Hydro walked closer, his hand moving toward his hilt. "And just because you solved the riddle does not mean the orb is yours."

Cain chuckled. "Do you intend to take my orb, the same way you harbor the labyrinth's prize? You probably do not even realize why this is the lake."

What did it matter? Hydro chortled. "Amuse me."

"*Lufmrah* is *harmful* spelled backwards and misread. If you relied on skill more than carelessness, you would have figured it out too."

The motor hummed. *There is not much time left.* Hydro looked at the lake, the red dye was expanding. *I need to finish him before I take the orb, otherwise I will not be able to use power.* Turning his hip away from Cain, he gripped his sword. *Fast. I have to be fast.* He turned back and swung at Cain, catching him on leather padding, but missing flesh.

Before Hydro could even try another assault, Cain reached behind his back and attached two metal batons together. Once together, he fingered the slit in his padding. "I did not think you would strike so dishonorably. You shall pay for that . . . Prince." Cain pushed the buttons on each side of his elongated baton, and his dual-sided halberd formed, ready for use.

CHAPTER 25

DUEL OF PRINCES

Cain stared at Prince Paen, who gave him a glare that rivaled the one that Troy Pavos harbored when Cain dueled him in the labyrinth.

This battle would be different though. Cain wouldn't lose.

Cain swung his halberd. Prince Paen ducked and swung his sword, but Cain slammed it with the tail end of his weapon. Cain pushed Prince Paen's sword away and used his long leg to pummel Hydro's stomach. As Hydro lurched backwards, he mumbled, "*Vesi.*"

Cain jumped backwards as a wave of water crashed down on the pier. In retaliation, Cain focused on the earth around the lake's perimeter and said, "*Maa.*"

Like fog in the air, the sand and dirt surrounding the lake shot up. While dust blocked the light and veiled the water, Cain tapped a button on the side of his glasses. A silver film slid down the lenses, allowing him to see through the dirty fog. *Pathetic, Prince. Try using power now.* As long as Prince Paen could not see the other elements, like water from the lake or fire from the suns, he couldn't use them.

Cain tiptoed forward, wary of the creaking planks. The prince was confused; Cain could see him looking at the dome he had created. *What hope do you have battling me in power? My family has the longest rule of any family in power. The sages treat with my family, when they only visit yours.*

Farther, Cain crept. He couldn't see the lake's progress. *Is it completely red yet?* Years of training at Castle Thoth had taught him control, and he would keep hold of the spell until the battle finished. *A little closer now.* Cain jumped back from Hydro's slash. Hydro lunged, and Cain backed up more. *He is swinging blindly.* At the next strike, Cain held up his halberd to block Hydro and then pushed the middle part of his weapon into Hydro's chin. It sent the prince reeling back—only a little, to Cain's dismay.

A succession of strikes came then, as quick and hard as slaps of wind. One after the other, Cain dodged and blocked. The shorter sword was no match for the length of his halberd.

Stab. Cross. Lunge. Sweep. Lunge. Cross. Cain read Hydro's movements, as though Cain embodied Baristan Corbello, the knight from *A Dance of One Thousand Swords*, the hero who never lost a duel against thousands of empires and who wooed a planet's worth of girls. *If Gabrielle could see me now.*

"Enough!" Prince Paen slashed downward.

Cain dodged with ease. "Too—" Cain stopped in midsentence. A pain erupted from his stomach. He looked down. The sword had transformed into a lance. As he stumbled back to the pier, dust that blocked the sky also fell. The lake had become red.

"Slow," Prince Paen finished. "I think not. My steel adapts as well as I do."

Reality slowly sank into him. Corbello never had to deal with morphing steel—would the folk hero have fallen? At the moment, Cain's armor was the only thing clotting his blood.

Damn zircha steel. . . . Cain struggled to stand. *I am no Baristan Corbello. He never would have lost. . . .* Cain looked at his halberd that lay on the pier. *He never would have given up either.* Cain grabbed the weapon and got to his feet, rebounding with an onslaught of attacks on Prince Paen. Swords kissed. Wind hissed. Water licked their feet. For a spell, it seemed that Cain had the upper hand, managing to breach the prince's defenses with the butt of his halberd.

But before Cain knew it, he was sprawled out on the pier once again—with a pain in his chest from where a shield had collided into him. In midlunge, the prince had changed it. *Zircha steel . . . blasted metal.*

Before Cain could react, Prince Paen yelled, *"Vesi."*

From both sides of the lake, water rose like cobra heads about to strike. Then they did. Cain held his breath and gripped his weapon; he wouldn't want to lose it in the deluge. He did his best to raise an earth barrier but the tidal wave overtook him, throwing him around in its current and pushing him back past the pier and into a boulder. His spine erupted in pain, and his skull screamed with agony. Blood soon soaked his hair as dizziness overcame him.

"I tried. . . ." Cain coughed. His clothes were wet, his glasses were cracked. He looked with fragmented vision as the same water that had crashed onto him now swirled like a whirlpool, swallowing redness.

From the middle of the lake, an orb appeared and floated into Hydro's hands. *That should be mine.* Cain lifted his body, only to collapse. He looked around and noticed the hovercraft. There was still one way to stop Hydro.

"Maa!" Cain yelled, mustering his remaining strength.

Spires erupted all around the hovercraft. Cain struggled to maintain the spell. His arms shook as energy dissipated from his body. With a loud crash, the hovercraft split in two. A spire impaled its metallic gut. Cain smirked.

"What are you doing?" Prince Paen yelled and ran toward Cain.

"Adapting," Cain answered weakly. He released the power.

The rest was up to the Ancients.

⚜CHAPTER 26⚜

A TEST

Cliffs loomed overhead to the west. Eirek had been heading for them ever since he received his riddle:

Wind lacks emotion when air is at rest;
When not, it blows north, perhaps east, south, or west.
Capture emotion by following its path,
Leading you to a face that is now cracked,
Now scarred by the very creatures they keep.
Pass their test to receive the orb which you seek.

As soon as he stepped outside, gusts of wind told him where to go. When he noticed that he was being led to giant cliffs, he was even more confident of the answer to his riddle. The *face now cracked* suggested that Eirek should look for the face of a mountain—cracked and scarred by years of wind. Eirek changed direction with different slaps of wind, continuing to follow it southwest for another thirty paces. Then the wind stopped.

What is going on? I just felt it.

A gust caught him on the right side of the face and then the left, and then it seemed to even blow up from underneath him. He closed his eyes as dust and dirt was kicked up with the unexplainable breeze. The wind intensified and swirled around him. Before too long, Eirek twirled in its might, flailing and screaming as it carried him off the ground. *How am I flying? What's going on?* Eirek tried rolling. Little vibrations shook his body and kept him in place. Fifty feet above the ground. Seventy-five feet. One hundred. He closed his eyes.

His back slammed up against the cliff face, causing him to groan. He looked down, seeing boulders and ground and certain death if he were to fall. *Shouldn't have looked.* He twisted his head, searching for the source of his captivity. Then he saw them. Light-blue things, as small as the gnats that plagued farms in Cresica during the warmer months, stood out against his white crushed-leather tailcoat.

"What . . . what are you?" Eirek kicked and flailed his arms.

A thousand tiny, high-pitched squeals, in unison, said, "We're windies."

"What?" Eirek shook his head in distress.

"We're windies. What's your business here, human?" asked a new singular voice.

Eirek squinted and saw a fairy—twice the size of the others—land on his nose. *Is that the leader?* "I'm following the wind. I was sent by the conseleigh."

A strange buzzing of whispers followed. *Did I say something wrong?* He doubted their tiny arms could pummel him very hard—but they could drop him. That would be fatal.

"What do you want?" asked the same faint voice.

Eirek went cross-eyed, refocusing on the leader, who wore a thin strip of wire that crossed his chest like a toga and a miniature crown on his brown head. He stared at Eirek with black eyes and straddled Eirek's nose, awaiting his answer while twirling a baton half the creature's size.

"I'm here because of Eska's Trials. My task was to find the orb."

"You will need to pass our test first."

Slowly he was carried down and set on one of the huge boulders that functioned as a perimeter for a small clearing approximately fifteen paces in diameter that lead into a cavern. A gust of wind lifted him down from the rock. When on the cracked earth once again, free from the windies' hold, Eirek breathed a sigh of relief. Quickly he half-walked, and was half-shoved, into the cave.

A cool, blue-walled cavern—littered with sand and plagued with bits of fungi—swallowed his presence. It was colder here. And the air was thinner. To compensate, Eirek staggered his breathing. From within the center, he waited. In front of him, the windies gathered themselves and took the form of a large face with pale-blue skin and sullen eyes. Eirek's eyes widened. *What kind of power is this?*

"The quality of your answers determines your performance in this test." The mouth moved seamlessly, as though it was one giant blue face rather than a mixture of thousands—if not millions—of little fairies.

Despite how easy the riddle had been, now he needed to think on his feet. No amount of schooling with Jahn or advice from Angal could teach him that. He exhaled and focused.

"Our first question: Why do you seek the orb?"

The question threw him. Was there a wrong answer? *To win? Is that answer too blunt? Because I was told to find it? What do they want?* The collaged face smirked and rolled back-and-forth, hovering in midair. *Think, Eirek, think.* A faint buzzing played in his ear. They expected him to fail, but he wouldn't. He couldn't.

"I . . . I seek the orb because I want . . . I want . . ." Eirek thought back to his trip with Angal to Syf. The Clayses couldn't have expected him to get accepted. To him he was just another man under their rule. "I want to win the attention of others."

Though it swayed back and forth like a cradle, the collaged face gave nothing away. "Our second question: What do you hope to gain from the attention of others?"

"By gaining the attention of those who only see the cloth on my back . . . I will start gaining not only my own confidence . . . but theirs too. . . ." That didn't sound right. Eirek shook his head. "Let me start over. . . . Guardian Eska said that even after the Trials are finished, we will need to impress the families in power for every nation . . . by gaining their attention and then their trust. It will serve as knowledge that any person, even those of my cloth, can do something extraordinary like become guardian. . . . With that knowledge, common folk like me will try harder and . . . I believe . . . well, I believe they will try harder and rise into statuses others are born into and make this universe better because of their efforts."

There was buzzing. The collaged face merely rocked back and forth still. "You speak of knowledge. . . . Where does knowledge derive from?"

What kind of question is that? What kinds of questions are any of these? He thought back on his experiences before and throughout the Trials. Instantly something came to mind. "Each of these trials is meant to test a different strength. . . . This trial is meant to test the strength of the mind. . . . My . . . my uncle told me that strength comes from understanding. . . . He said that it comes from courage and vindication, and it's not something that can be taught. . . . It has to be realized. . . . My only strength in the Trials is my mind . . . is my knowledge. . . . So, to me, knowledge is understanding."

Silence crept into the room.

"What is your name, human?"

He gulped before answering. "Eirek."

"Eirek, your answers tell us the type of man you are. You are the type of man who can change the world if given the chance. Take the orb with our blessing."

The face broke apart. A majority of windies who had made up the face flew farther into the cave but returned seconds later with a gray orb, the shape and size of a crystal ball. Eirek stretched his arms to receive it.

"Eirek, my name is Berol." The leader of the windies fluttered before him. "We will be watching you. If you ever need us, just say my name."

Eirek nodded and exited the cave. He looked at the orb in his hands. *I did it. I passed their test. I won the trial.* A human's shadow stood at his feet. Looking up, he saw Gabrielle with her sword drawn.

"You passed zeir test? Excellent, I will take za orb off your hands." Gabrielle jumped down from on top of one of the boulders and walked toward Eirek.

"You can't have it." Eirek withdrew his sword with his right hand and pointed it toward her, halting her advance.

"I would like to see you try and stop me."

Without warning, she swung her sword, which Eirek barely avoided. He regained his footing, although the gray orb tucked underneath his left arm grew heavy. Gabrielle controlled the entire battle, and Eirek did his best to jump out of the way or block her swift strikes. *I can't keep this up.* To try and change the sway of battle, Eirek slashed overhead. She spun around the strike, moving her hand down to her leg, and by the time she came to a complete rotation, she had a dagger in her hand and drove it into his sword arm. A howl of pain erupted from Eirek, and he dropped his sword. He had never been stabbed before. Yanking the dagger from his arm, he threw it to the ground. Fresh blood painted his clothing a dark red. His stomach heaved as he was kicked. The orb went rolling, and Eirek's lips kissed the ground. *No, not the orb.*

"Berol!"

A loud buzzing echoed from the cave. Within seconds, a million little windies descended upon him and Gabrielle. They picked up Eirek's fallen sword and continued to fight Gabrielle.

"What magic is zis?" Gabrielle fought a dancing blade with no holder.

Eirek fetched his orb. Once he cradled it in his left arm again, he turned and saw Gabrielle pushed back toward the boulders. "Berol, stop!"

The sword halted in mid-air and floated back to Eirek's outstretched arm.

"Can you take me to Guardian Eska's estate?"

"How fast?"

"As fast as you can."

Before Eirek knew what was happening, thousands of tiny blue flickers surrounded him—lifting him up and whisking him through the air. The last he saw of Gabrielle, she was sprinting toward him, choler and confusion on her face.

☙CHAPTER 27☙

MIRAGE

It is essential that you use what you find,
For only it will befit the holder of time.
The suns' gazes linger when on time's quarter.
When fast do lag, the slow remain hoarders.
But if you give what's meant to be given,
The orb is yours, completing thy mission.

The riddle kept playing in Zain's mind as he paced around the sundial. After receiving it, he had gone to the library and found there was only one sundial on the Central Core, and it was located in Funjhi Desert. He was pretty confident in his observations, for the references to *time* and *the suns' gazes* couldn't mean otherwise.

His fingers caressed the rough granite pillar that sprouted from the ground. The sundial had been cut to resemble two cupped hands. The shadow pointed to two forty-five, but Zain needed to wait until three. That was time's quarter, after all.

As he paced, he looked around at the surroundings. Trees bordered a small lake near the sundial. To the north were larger sand dunes, and to the south there were only dunes, boulders, and a rusty sword, which, for whatever reason, was sticking up in the middle of nowhere, hard to miss, for it was at the bottom of a large sand dune that Zain had needed to climb. He hadn't picked it up because he already had a sword. A good one at that.

His gaze darted to and fro and then back to the sundial. It was close now. Was someone hiding behind the sand dunes or the boulders, waiting for him? Tundra mentioned there was another contestant with the same riddle. Where were they? He kept an eye on the time, but unease still rippled through him. *Don't second guess yourself.*

Zain clenched one fist. This was it. *Three o'clock.*

A loud, grinding sound erupted from the sundial. Where the shadow struck three, a slot opened. Heart pounding, Zain consulted his riddle once more.

> *But if you give what's meant to be given,*
> *The orb is yours, completing thy mission.*

"What is meant to be given?" Zain examined the slot. It was the perfect shape for a sword. *Am I to give mine?* He read through the riddle again.

> *It is essential that you use what you find.*

Images of the rusty sword danced through his mind. *The sword, the sword. Am I supposed to use the sword?* He turned and backtracked, but he only got as far as a nearby boulder before there was a grinding noise behind him. The slot was closing. *How much time is left?*

He ran back and gripped the sundial's base. *This will have to do.* He unsheathed his sword and held it to the Axiumé. Fluidly he pushed it down, forcing it into the slot. A motor inside clunked.

Stillness. Silence. Sound.

A grinding. A crack. A hiss.

Steel fell around him like rain, and Zain covered his neck and head. Broken pieces littered the ground. *My sword. It's . . . it's ruined.*

He scrambled to pick up the shards, sharp and hot to the touch. *No. No. No. This can't be happening.* Try as he might, he couldn't gather them all. He ignored the burning in his hands and the pain of poking shards. *I can still win. I need to still win. I can put this back together.*

"Another trial lost."

Zakk! His ears perked. His skin prickled. He looked around but saw no one. His friend couldn't be here. Zakk was dead. Was he hearing things? "Show yourself!" Zain gripped a piece of broken sword like a dagger. The blade bit into his hand, drawing blood. "I'm not afraid of you."

"Everything in your voice tells me you are." A cackle followed.

Steel being drawn chimed the air. Zain recognized that sound anywhere. A strike flashed toward his right. Zain closed his eyes and held up his makeshift knife to block it. It was knocked away. Zain used his own hands to shield his neck and head—the blood sticky and warm. His breathing heightened. "No. No. No. . . ." He looked at the shards still on the ground. A boot stepped in front of him. Zain blinked. He looked up. Nothing.

"You can't even face me. Pitiful."

The blood from his hands mixed in with the sand, sticky and gritty. They became heavy. Zain clenched them, thinking back to how Zakk's hands felt as he let go of them. His eyes started to blur. Shadows shimmied around him, even amid daylight. A jolt to the left side of his face; the grainy sand kissed him. He pushed himself up. Then he was knocked down to the other side. Teeth rattled inside his mouth.

"Did you enjoy killing me, Zain?"

The sound of swords slashing through air stung Zain's ears. Armor jerked violently on his back. Steel dragged up his arms toward his shoulders. He shuddered when he felt the steel on the back of his neck. "Stop! Stop! Please, stop!" Tears traveled down his cheeks, ending up on the hot, sandy floor.

Hot breath kissed his ear. "Knowledge is power. Learn it."

Then it was over. Seconds seemed like minutes. Zain just lay in the fetal position, broken and bloodied. Weakly he tore a piece of fabric from his undershirt and wrapped it around both hands, laden with slits from the shards of sword. Red soaked into white, just like the sand soaked his tears. He stared at his shattered sword. It lay there. Broken. Like Zain. *Is Zakk alive? That was his voice, I know it was.*

"Hey, you be okay?" A hand touched his back.

Zain jolted and scurried away. It was only Cadmar. "Did you see him?"

"See who?"

Zain shivered and rubbed his hands up his arms. Blood smeared them through the cloth. Zain crawled on his knees to Cadmar. "Zakk. He was here. Zakk was here!"

"Who's Zakk? No one was here. Did I miss the trial?"

Cadmar held the rusty sword in his hand. Zain returned upright to his feet, his mind speeding like a hovercraft. *Cadmar is here. Cadmar and Hydro won the last trial. If Hydro wins, two points separate us. Only Cadmar could tie him then before the fourth trial.*

Regardless of whether the prince acquired his prize or not, Zain needed to make sure he was there to stop Hydro if he had. One more trial was all he needed to win. But he had no weapon. His sword lay broken to pieces in the sand splotched with red. Cadmar held a sword though. Zain turned to see Cadmar bending over the sundial.

"You're too late," Zain said. He inched closer. His hand slid up to his chest pocket, which housed his knife.

"What do you mean?"

"I mean . . ." Zain gripped the leather handle and pulled. It came out clean. He inched closer. He threw and caught the knife in his hand, feeling its lightness.

Cadmar turned around.

"I'm sorry."

With his free hand, Zain hit Cadmar across the face and then tackled him. The giant flailed and tried to throw Zain, who put the knife to his throat. Cadmar's flailing arms went limp. He looked Zain in the eyes. After a quick glance, Zain moved his gaze toward the knife. His hand was shaking, but it was there, right underneath the neck. He thought about how Gabrielle had done the same thing to him. He looked back to Cadmar's eyes. *Were my eyes this confident?*

"If you be killing me, get it over with already."

"I just want the sword." Zain's hand shook; his breathing tightened.

Releasing the sword, Cadmar never took his gaze off Zain, who pressed the knife down on Cadmar's throat and then leaned to get the sword. Once he felt it in his grasp, Zain put it in the sheath his other sword had been in. The giant scanned him.

He's waiting for me to get up. I'll need to be fast about this. Zain tightened the grip on the knife and pulled back from Cadmar's neck. As soon as he did so, he threw an elbow to the giant's face and sheathed his knife. By the time Zain got to his feet, Cadmar had straightened his posture again. As Zain kicked sand into Cadmar's face, he strung a list of words together that Zain had never heard before. Then. He ran.

With the minor distractions Zain had caused, he could certainly outrun the man. But could he outrun time? Was Hydro already there? Somewhere past the dunes and boulders and shifting sand, Eska's estate stood, calling him back. With each shuffle of his feet, his head throbbed and ticked. Throbbed and ticked. Throbbed and ticked.

CHAPTER 28

AT THE DOORSTEP

This trial should be over by now. Hydro fumed at Cain's last act of defiance. *It wasn't enough to mock my intelligence; he had to destroy my hovercraft too.* Hydro hadn't even checked to see if the prince was still alive. Because of Cain, the past three miles were a medley of walking and running and panting and sweating and cursing the grueling gaze of both suns.

By the time Hydro arrived within five hundred feet of the estate, rancid sweat drenched his upper body. In the silver light of the afternoon, the white walls appeared sepia. The estate beckoned him to become Eska's apprentice with an auspicious gaze. He didn't run. He couldn't run, albeit he wanted to. Triumph sewn onto his face, he cradled the orb in his left arm, cherishing it as he would a trophy.

Within three hundred feet, he summoned his remaining energy to awkwardly jog. The once plush leather sole of his shoe was now beaten and extinct. Prince Evber had been more of a challenge than Hydro anticipated. Where the halberd had connected, gashes converged like tributaries of a dried river. Was anyone else here already? *No, they can't be,* Hydro reassured himself.

One hundred feet. Victory within his grasp. He paused. From the shadows of the estate's east side, a figure emerged. Zain.

Hydro scanned his opponent but saw no orb. "Could not figure yours out, I take it?" he muttered.

Another fifty feet and he would win. Hydro stepped forward. Zain blocked Hydro's advance, the tip of a rusty blade lightly poking the rhinoskin.

"Out of my way." Hydro brushed the sword aside and continued walking—until Zain reshuffled himself in front of Hydro, halting his progress.

"I can't let you pass."

"You do not want to face me, fool." Hydro tried pushing the sword away again, but Zain held it tight.

"Yes, I do."

Determination stared Hydro in the eyes, but he merely smirked. "That is a bad decision."

Hydro gripped his sword and swung it at Zain, who jumped back. For the majority of the dance, Hydro lunged and swung to his right, trying to accommodate for the orb he held in his left arm. Zain was always faster than him though. Sparks flew as the swords sang to one another a ballad of defiance. An animalistic side of Hydro enjoyed the fierce battle. His royal side did not. There was a time and a place for battle—and now, when he was exhausted and so close to victory, was not one of them. He swung his sword, managing to close the gap between Zain, and lifted his elbow into Zain's face, causing him to stumble backwards. *This needs to end.*

"Maa!" Hydro shouted and lifted his arm upwards.

Nothing happened. Hydro remembered the orb. *Stupid ball.* He wanted to drop it, but he couldn't risk Zain picking it up to claim it as his own. *How to dispose of him?* A breeze attracted his attention, and he looked to his left.

A light-blue, glowing cloud swooped in from the direction of the breeze. *What is that?* It vanished. The commoner appeared in its place. *What kind of power did he use?* Hydro spotted an orb in the commoner's hands. *How did he solve it? He's closer.*

"What are you two doing?" the commoner asked.

"Eirek, get inside. Now!" Zain yelled and then redirected his attention back to Hydro. He smirked.

That cur! This was his plan all along. Rage boiled inside him. Hydro stepped forward and threw all his weight into his stroke. Sure enough, Zain blocked it—but Hydro's slash was so powerful that the rusty sword broke in half.

As Hydro followed through with his cut, he focused his mind on changing the sword to a hard, metal shield, and within seconds, his weapon obeyed. Using the momentum of the slash, he changed his position and brought his shoulder upwards—connecting the steel with Zain's jaw. It worked even better with Zain than the tactic had with Cain. Zain was thrown back and skidded to the white porch, the steps of which the commoner walked.

"Are you okay?" The commoner turned around at the loud collision.

"Get inside!" Zain grimaced.

My chance! Hydro changed his shield back to a sword, sheathed it, and sprinted. Five steps. Four steps. Three steps. So close. And then . . .

His side thundered with pain as he was thrust to the ground—Zain's panting, broken body toppling over him. Broken gums bled their jelly onto him.

"Not today, Prince!"

Hydro kicked Zain off of him and stood up. Eirek had disappeared. *No!* Hydro bolted up the steps two at a time. His hope sank as he saw Eirek holding his orb over his head in the lobby. Hydro clenched his fist. A struggled laugh drew his attention away from indoors. Zain still lay on the ground as he laughed. Hydro bolted down the steps.

"If this was Acquava, I would have you killed." Hydro knelt by Zain.

"Too bad you aren't in Acquava." Zain laughed some more.

Hydro grabbed Zain underneath the chin, forcing him to look into cold, hazel eyes. "You will pay for my loss today."

Zain still managed a grin. "In spells or in bonds?"

Hydro bristled. *How dare he jest with me!* The orb weighed heavy in his left arm. "It is a shame you were stupid enough to botch your riddle. Seeing as I will not need my orb anymore, I shall give it to you." Hydro smirked.

Hydro took the orb in both hands, raised it over his head, and slammed it down over Zain's right hand. Orb and bone broke upon contact. A howl erupted from Zain's mouth, a note of pain Hydro only heard when his father took him to the dungeons of their castle to mock the liars and murderers and cheaters who deserved pain.

Hydro took him under the chin again. His hand felt the moistness of Zain's tear-soaked cheeks. "Try fighting now, filthy cur."

Hydro stood up and left Zain behind—broken, beaten, and bloody on the ground. As he turned around, Conseleigh Tundra glowered at him from the steps. "I heard a yell. What happened?"

The other conseleigh stepped outside as well. Hydro didn't answer.

"Hydro, did you do this?" Tundra looked toward Zain, who clutched a bloody hand.

Guardian Eska stepped forward, past the conseleigh. He looked at Hydro. And then to Zain. And then back to Hydro. He knew that look; his father gave it to him whenever Hydro rowed with his mother at supper or when he saw Hydro disinterested in council meetings and village hearings that he had been forced to attend.

"He broke my hand!" Zain yelled. He rolled on the ground and stomped while holding his limp right hand with his left.

"Hydro, did you do this?" Guardian Eska crossed his arms.

"He got in my way."

"So you be breaking 'is 'ands?" Ethen strummed his short beard.

"You are dismissed from the Trials!" Tundra yelled. "A call will be made for your departure." She stormed up the steps.

A pit formed in his stomach. No. It couldn't be. He needed to win. He had to become guardian. He didn't want to continue to receive those same looks of disappointment, as he couldn't bring himself to change his attitude toward his mother or the tedious duties. He couldn't bear hearing the snickers from all the families of power. He couldn't bear the thought of Pearl's wrath for squandering her blessing. For the first time, a cold feeling crawled over him. Disappointment. Not only his own, but his family's—and the guardian's as well.

"Tundra!"

The older woman with blue hair came back into view, summoned by Eska's voice.

"That is not your decision to make."

"Hydro broke Zain's hand out of spite!"

"He deserves a hearing," Guardian Eska said.

"Edwyrd, the trial was already over!"

"Tundra, I agree with Edwyrd; it is not your decision to make. The boy is entitled to a fair hearing," Luvan spoke.

Hydro wanted to correct Luvan, who dared to call him a boy—but the man argued on his behalf. He figured he'd let that stand. His fate hung in the balance by the elders before him.

"You are blind, Luvan! This was an act of hatred!"

"Be that as it may, every action requires a just and equal reaction," Luvan responded.

"And that is dismissal!"

"Enough! All of you," Guardian Eska spoke. "There will be a hearing. Zain, you will be required to attend. It will wait until you heal. The Trials will be postponed until any decisions are finalized. Ethen, instruct the servants to take Zain to the apothecary. Riagan, take Tundra's location device and keys to a hovercraft and retrieve the straggling contestants. Tundra, Luvan, to my chamber—now!"

The elders departed. Hydro still shook, but he looked up when footsteps echoed from above him. The commoner stood with the orb in his hands, shocked. "Why did you do it?"

"You want to have a heart-to-heart with me, Commoner?"

"No, I want to know why you're so angry."

With you? Your bourgeois blood. The fact that you stole my trial. And because you don't deserve to be here. Hydro walked up the stairs, and when he was on the same plane as Eirek, he stopped. "You might want to visit Zain in the apothecary. To thank him for your victory today. He will not be helping you out again." Hydro chuckled and scanned him over.

The commoner just looked back at him. Silence.

"No remark? Perhaps the feeling of winning is just so new to you?"

"Perhaps the feeling of losing is new to you?" Eirek walked back into the estate.

Hydro continued to glare at the commoner despite the fact that he never looked back to notice it.

❧ CHAPTER 29 ❧

VISITORS

A granite pillar looms over Zain. Suddenly he is slammed against the ground as shards of steel rain upon him. He extends his arms toward the suns, attempting to catch the falling shards. One by one, they slice into his back and arms. He writhes in pain, collapsing. His breath weakens. A hot voice whispers into his ear, "Knowledge is power. Learn it."

As he opens his eyes, boots appear in front of him. "Zakk?"

A rough hand clenches his chin. "Look at me, Zain. Look at me!"

He closes his eyes and resists and flails. His eyes become hot. One eye and then the other.

"Look at me, Zain. Look at me."

He doesn't want to be touched, so he twists his neck away. No longer is it a rough hand holding his chin not letting him resist.

"You need to look at me, Zain. Zain . . . Zain . . ."

Pounding lights greeted Zain as he opened his eyes. Stars came next, followed by blurry images of people hovering over him. Some disappeared. Some remained, merging with other blurriness. Zain tried lifting his hands. He couldn't lift his left, and his right felt heavy. *What. What happened?* Blurriness dissolved to clarity.

An older lady with red hair was next to Zain's bedside. She was tall in height and large enough so Zain could not see behind her. Her tresses were cut off at the ears, above which she wore a visor. Bracelets could hardly dangle from her large forearms as she held a vial up to her eyes. A thick, milky-white liquid ran slowly along the flask's bottom.

"You're awake. Good. Drink this, dear." She tapped one finger against the bottom of the flask twice and gave it to Zain.

"What is it?" His jaw felt heavy. He tilted his head to the right and fluttered his eyes. His hand was in a cast. "What happened to my hand?" He looked to his other hand and noticed it strapped to the bed.

"Don't speak. Just drink." His nose was pinched. Despite his efforts to squirm, he opened his mouth out of necessity, and the vial was shoved inside—all he could do was swallow a gritty substance that tasted like week-old milk and chunks of calcium and iron. "Adored Amiti will be with you shortly, dear. In the meantime, you have a visitor."

Zain coughed. And coughed.

She finished circling a few items on a clipboard and then laid it on the desk next to Zain's bedside. From the desk, she took a glass of water and put it to Zain's lips, tilting it back. He swallowed and pulled away when he had enough. She left then, allowing him to finally notice a person behind her sitting with his hands folded underneath his chin—Jamaal.

"Jamaal! How long have you been here?"

"Only since this morning. Thanks for talking to Eska for me. Upon proof of ID to the gatekeeper on Hown, I was allowed entrance. I was supposed to only have one hour, but you were still like this. . . . I have an hour now that you've woke." Jamaal looked at his telecommunicator.

An object wrapped in a gold cloth lay in his lap. It held the shape of a sword. *A new sword!* Zain looked at his brother and noticed another man of tan skin walk toward him from the back. Bracelets of various colors dangled to his gait, announcing his presence if Zain wouldn't have noticed otherwise. The brown hair that might have been present as early as seven years ago was gray and white and frizzy. His eyebrows were bushy, and his maple eyes hid behind thick, circular glasses.

"I am 'appy to see you be awake, Mr. Berrese." On the scarlet, heart-shaped pocket was a name badge that read: Adored Issac Amiti. "When your brother was admitted 'ere earlier today, I told 'im I wasn't sure 'ow much longer you'd be asleep."

"How long have I been asleep?" Zain tried to scratch his head, but his hand was still strapped. "And why am I strapped?"

Issac was at the foot of his bed now. "I see Tanya didn't undo tat." The man went to Zain's left and unfastened the brace. "For ta past few days, you been 'aving violent nightmares. So much so, we needed to strap you down."

"Days?" Zain's neck tensed.

"Two, to be exact. And for tose two days, you've been under ta influence of poppy milk so we could perform some . . . surgeries."

"Like . . . what?" Zain could no longer hold his abdomen; he fell back onto the pillows.

"It seems you be missing two teeth, so we 'ave replaced them with teeth of silver. Your jaw be dislocated, so we . . ." the man coughed, "attached a metal bracing along its base. Another injury like tat, and it may be irreparable."

"What about this?" Zain lifted his cast.

"Well tat was ta obvious ting we performed. Tat elixir you swallowed 'as been doing its job in regenerating ta fractured bones in your hand." Adored Amiti looked at the clipboard, humming as he flipped through the pages. "Ta cuts on your hand are deep, but we disinfected tem. Tey will heal, but you'll 'ave scars."

Great. As if memories weren't enough to remind me of everything my hands have done wrong. "Will I be able to continue?"

"Guardian Eska expects you to. After you are released 'ere, you are to go immediately to 'is chambers."

"No. Will I be able to continue?" Zain held up his casted hand.

"You will not regain full strength by ta next trial if tat is what you are wondering. But everyting looks decent 'ere. In two days, you will be released . . . once we've administered a few more doses of maro nectar."

Using his left hand, Zain pushed the pillows up against the back of his bed and aligned his body to a sitting position. He slunk into the pillows and looked outward, at nothing particular, just hopelessness. *Great.*

"Good day, Mr. Berrese. I will need to tell Guardian Eska of your progress." Amiti retired to the back of the apothecary, disappearing through the sliding glass door.

"Zain, who did this to you?"

Which injury? Zain looked at his left hand; it was no longer bandaged with a bloody T-shirt but a white fabric that still allowed him to flex his fingers. *Zakk can't be here. He can't. What did I see? Did the sun and heat affect me that much?* And then he looked at his right hand, remembering Hydro smashing the orb into his hand. Zain had felt the bones break and pop on impact.

When Zain didn't respond, Jamaal asked again, "Zain? Who did this to you?"

"What does it matter?" Zain sighed and looked away.

"Because they need to be reprimanded!"

"Guardian Eska is taking care of it."

"Is that why you need to see him?"

"Partially. . . . He also wants to examine what you brought me." Zain's eyes moved to the object laying on Jamaal's lap.

Jamaal grabbed it and leaned forward, putting it on Zain's lap. "Dad made this to honor all of your accomplishments at Gazo's shortly before he left for Empora. He was going to give it to you upon his return."

"Has he returned from Empora yet?" With his left hand, he unwrapped the cloth. A scabbard—the length of Zain's arm—with a half-foot hilt lay brilliantly on the bed. He gripped it with his left hand and lifted it but had to release it immediately; it would require both hands.

"No. Not yet. But you can't think on that; you have to focus on the Trials. That's what Mom and I want you to do. It's what Dad would want you to do. And it's what Zakk would have wanted too. . . ."

Zain clenched his left hand, biting back his grimace. *For Zakk. . . .* The raspy voice clung to his memory; it sounded exactly like Zakk's. *Knowledge is power. Learn it.* Cadmar hadn't seen anything though. Was guilt really this hard to get rid of? Shyly he looked at Jamaal as a heavy sigh escaped him. "Jamaal . . ." He was already tearing up; he hadn't even said anything yet. *Get a hold of yourself.*

"Yeah, Little Bear?"

That made Zain smile. "I . . . I . . . know where Zakk is. . . ."

Jamaal repositioned himself. "What? You do? Where?"

"He's . . . he's . . ." Zain looked at his hands. *I can't hold on to him forever.* "He's . . . dead . . . in Lake Kilmer."

"You said—"

"I didn't know what else to say! I was afraid. I was . . . I was . . ." Zain looked away, trying to hold back his tears.

"How do you know he's there?"

Zain didn't respond. He looked at his brother and saw Jamaal comprehend the reason for his silence..

"Zain . . . you didn't. . . . How could you?" Jamaal stood up and paced around Zain's bed with both hands on top of his head.

Zain recapped the ordeal, fidgeting his gaze throughout the whole story. For the most part, he remained strong, but then he told Jamaal about seeing Zakk on the Core.

"You killed your best friend. Your best friend!" Jamaal spoke in a raspy voice and leaned over the foot of Zain's bed, hands stationed on the railing.

"I . . . I didn't expect him to die. I just didn't want him to win the Trials. Almost every tournament, he boasts about his accomplishments. I . . . I couldn't have him ruin this opportunity for me."

"There never was any opportunity. No one can bring back the dead, Zain!"

"How do you know that?" Zain lifted his left hand to dry the wetness on his cheeks.

"Because it's only logical. You are born, you live, and you die. That's life. . . . Does Guardian Eska know?" Jamaal sat in the chair again. He rested his chin on the knuckles of his clasped hands.

Zain looked at his brother and shook his head. "I . . . I don't think so." He looked at his sword. "Do I even deserve this?" Zain took it from the scabbard and laid the sword on his lap. Four jewels were cast into the sword—a symbol of his father's love; they could be seen from both sides and added richness to the already-decorated cross guard with inlaid gold. Sprinkled red rubies made the cross-shaped pommel sparkle like the night sky.

"Zain . . ." Jamaal moved his chair closer to the bed. "You don't. I . . . I will be the first to tell you that . . . and, dammit, you make things hard . . . on me . . . on Mom . . . but we are family. . . . And although you don't deserve it, I . . . I think you can still earn this too. A person's strength doesn't come from knowledge or power. . . . I . . . I think it comes from persistence. You cannot let the obstacles you've had become setbacks. They need to be the forces that encourage you to move onward. 'To make things better,' you said that you were going to do that."

"I want to. . . . I . . . I just don't know how."

"That is something you need to figure out for yourself, Zain. But there is hope."

"Thanks, Jamaal." Zain leaned forward and gave as strong of a bear hug as he could.

"Everything will get better. Even this." Jamaal let go and pointed to Zain's cast.

Zain nodded and plugged a tear that had come to his eye. He yawned. The drowsiness came out of nowhere. Was it the medicine?

"My time is almost up. Reine expects me for a late supper with the family, still. "

Zain yawned again and stretched his left arm over his head. "Tell her I say hi."

Jamaal chuckled. "I will. Get better, Little Bear. Goodbye."

Zain nodded and twisted his head into his pillow, trying to find comfort. Exhaustion didn't allow him to watch his brother leave. For the first time in a while, Zain had no problem falling asleep. As he dozed off though, he wished he knew whether it was because of the medicine or because he let loose his secret.

• • •

Tanya hovered over Zain, shaking the flask of Maro Nectar with a flick of her wrist. Zain was ready for the treatment. Though it tasted horrible and the pain in repairing fractured bones was horrible, he could feel it work. When he would get bored before the medicine took its affect, he practiced flexing his hand beneath his cast.

"Tilt your head back, Mr. Berrese."

Zain opened his mouth to be fed the white substance. A pinch of his nose, and Zain digested the ivory goop. Afterwards he drank water and wiped his lips on his bed sheets. "Thanks, Tanya; it gets a little easier every day."

While Tanya was filing through her clipboard, Zain noticed movement from the other side of the apothecary. Eirek was being led in by Lucielle, the blonde cleric. He looked at Zain, and once Eirek realized Zain saw him, he quickened his pace, stopping behind a pillar in the middle of the room.

"I will be right back with your prescription, Mr. Mourse," Lucielle said.

"Eirek?" Zain tried to angle his neck around the larger nurse's body.

"Zain . . ." Eirek poked his head out from behind the pillar and walked over to Zain's bed.

"Well, Mr. Berrese, it seems like you will be leaving tomorrow as scheduled. We need to run one more test, and the fluid has to work its way into your system."

"Does Guardian Eska know?"

"He is expecting it." Tanya retreated behind the doors to the back of the apothecary.

"So . . . what is that meant to do?" Eirek fidgeted with his fingers.

"Regrow bone. I didn't know you were hurt."

"Still from the first trial. . . . Adored Amiti said it'll be the last dose."

"Humph." Zain looked back to the doors as Lucielle exited.

"Here is your bottle, Mr. Mourse. Take it till the week's end, and you should be fine."

"Thank you." Eirek took the bottle from her hand with a smile.

As she left, Zain watched Eirek rotate the bottle in his hands, then Eirek lowered his gaze to the sword between Zain's legs. Using his left hand, Zain tilted the sword back and forth, watching the light from above bounce off the jewels. He looked back up to Eirek. *What is he waiting for?*

"So the rumors were true," Eirek muttered, standing at the front of Zain's bed.

"What rumors?" Zain's brows furrowed as he looked toward Eirek.

"Dominic mentioned you had a visitor. Who was it?"

"Who's Dominic?"

"Our wing's servant."

"Oh . . . yeah . . . it was my brother."

"He made that sword for you?"

"My dad did. My brother brought it to me. My dad is gone on business right now."

"It's beautiful."

"Thanks . . ." Zain fingered his sword. *If only I could wield it properly. It will be a long time before then though.*

There was silence. Still, Eirek didn't leave. Zain looked at him. Was he struggling with something too? It seemed everyone was here.

"Thank you, Zain. For everything. I'm . . . I'm sorry—"

"Eirek . . . don't thank me. I didn't do it for you. I did what I had to . . . and will continue doing what I need to do . . . to . . . make things better." Zain doubted that Eirek heard the last part, as he had muttered it under his breath. Zain clenched his left hand.

Eirek must have noticed his movement, for he said, "I need to say something though. . . . If . . . if it hadn't been for me . . . then you might not be here right now. Your hand might—"

"My hand will heal. Prince Paen will pay for what he did. . . . He will not set me back."

"I hear he is to be dismissed from the Trials. You and he have a meeting with Guardian Eska."

"Whether or not he will be dismissed remains to be seen. But he will pay, that I know." Zain clenched his left hand, and for the first time, he felt nothing. Absolutely nothing.

❦ CHAPTER 30 ❦

THE THIRD LETTER

Even though Zain had been short with him, Eirek could not blame him. It was because of Eirek that he was in the apothecary. There was a sense of conviction in Zain, though, and confidence too. *He hasn't even won how can he remain so confident?* Even with winning the second trial, he would need more if he were ever to be guardian.

On his way back to the lobby, Eirek stopped to take a closer glance at two of the portraits hanging in the hall. Men, idolized in golden frame and an angel-white background. Profiled from the chest to the head. Names spelled in onyx and embossed on an ivory plaque at the base: Guardian Jorey Raule and Guardian Matthau Crevon. How peculiar that such a prestigious position did not receive a crown; instead they wore a sleek, black bandanna fitted to their heads, obscuring most of their hair. Exactly like the one Guardian Eska wore.

Will I be featured next to you eventually? What did each of you fight for? Eirek wanted to touch them, but he refrained to staring into the unwavering eyes of the past guardians.

"Wondrous, aren't they?"

Eirek turned his head to see Conseleigh Tundra approaching. Her heels enabled her to stand at eye level with Eirek. Her flowing, kimono-sleeved dress—trimmed with beads, sequins, and copper thread and highlighted with intricate cerulean designs—reached below her knees. Open slits in the sleeves allowed the loose rayon fabric to hang to her waist, exposing a silver bracelet with diamond beads that snaked up her right arm.

He didn't respond. He turned back to the portraits.

"Each guardian vows to protect Gladonus from any danger threatening to disturb it, until the Ancients see fit that they be relieved of their duty."

"What of the Twelve? I thought that was their job?"

"The Twelve never reached an agreement as to which clan would protect the Core. And after the Great War, tensions still ran high, so they gave the duty to someone not of First Blood but bestowed upon them abilities and tools and longevity to protect the Core."

"How do you know that?" The question came out before Eirek realized how stupid it was. *She's a conseleigh. Of course she knows.*

"I have been at Guardian Eska's side for thirty-five years now."

Eirek noticed the nostalgia creep into her voice, as if she remembered her own ceremony—if one had even occurred. He gulped, continuing to stare at the paintings and barely noticing Tundra pass him by. "One last question." It had nagged at him ever since seeing the portraits.

"Yes, Mr. Mourse?"

"Why does Guardian Eska wear a black bandanna over his head? Why not a crown? Isn't he the king of Gladonus?"

"The bandanna is called a reimaje. He may oversee everything that occurs in Gladonus, but that does not make him a king or a lord. He is guardian. The cap is enchanted with special magic from the Twelve. It holds all the secrets to Gladonus. It is passed down from guardian to apprentice when the time comes for the passing of power. Every incident, every thought that the guardian possesses or witnesses is transferred directly to that cap. It also blocks Guardian Eska's thoughts from outsiders . . . and . . . there are other powers. . . ."

Eirek looked back to the portraits. The guardians' faces were full of strength and knowledge.

"Why is it . . ." He looked around, and his smile turned to a thin line as he noticed Tundra had vanished, "black?" he asked the painting, as though it could answer. It didn't though.

He lingered a little longer, then adjourned to his room. Approaching his door, Eirek noticed an envelope attached to it. The next trial. *What will this one be?*

Before he could open it, Cadmar's voice called to him. He came down the hallway with axe in hand. "I be wonderin' when you'd find the letter. Where were you?"

"I visited Zain in the apothecary."

"That git! Why you be visitin' him?"

"I . . . wanted to say thanks, I guess."

"That git tackled me and put a knife to my throat. Then even after I did what he said, the git be elbowin' me and kickin' sand in me face. And then he ran off like some header."

"He helped me win the second trial."

"That he certainly did, Commoner." Hydro walked out from his own room. "He will not be helping you win any more trials, especially not this one."

"You won't be here for the next trial, Caffler," sneered Cadmar.

"We will see about that." Hydro continued down the hall.

"I can't wait for him to leave. He won't be missed."

Eirek twiddled his thumbs. Even though the man belittled him constantly—and never referred to him by name—the prince worked as hard as the rest of them to make it here. Eirek wondered if Hydro was nervous behind the stalwart façade he displayed.

"You do not feel the least bit nervous for him?" Eirek asked Cadmar, his eyebrows arched.

"No. You didn't have to spend time with him during the interview, or for a whole trial."

Eirek sighed. "Still…" He muttered, so soft he believed Cadmar didn't hear him.

"I'm going to train a little in the habitat arena. You should be doing the same."

"What do you mean by that?"

"Look at the letter. Take care." Cadmar left, disappearing into the lobby.

Eirek turned his head and raised an eyebrow. Excitedly he opened his letter on his way into his room.

Dear Contestants,

I would like to thank you for your patience in this past week. It is now time, however, to inform you that your third trial will take place in three days. Designed by Conseleigh Ethen Rorum this will test your skill with weapons against other contestants. More information will be given at tomorrow's dinner, when everyone is present.

Sincerely,
Guardian Edwyrd Eska

A tournament of weapons. Eirek gulped at the thought. His training wasn't nearly as advanced as that of his fellow competitors. It's not like he didn't train. He did. At night. When nobody else was around. He had improved by a few levels, lasting a little longer each time. Instead of awkward strokes, his swings had become more fluid and his footing more stable. He liked to think it was the reason he managed to keep his orb during the second trial. That and the windies, of course.

The excitement that Eirek held previously was now sapped. *Thinking I could actually become guardian was foolish. A guardian needs to have more than brains.* Eirek set the letter on his desk and sat on his bed. He opened the bottle he received from the apothecary and swallowed a pill with the help of a glass of water sitting on his nightstand. The only thing Eirek could think about was which contestant would receive an easy match.

❦CHAPTER 31❧

DECENCY

Hydro walked into the lobby keeping his eyes peeled for anyone of note. He had a plan for the remaining part of the Trials. In the event his hearing went sour, Hydro would make the commoner's life miserable. He had already done enough to Zain. But would she help? Past a corridor, he headed toward the other contestants' rooms. *Now, which one is hers?*

"Will you be here later?" he heard a male voice inquire.

"I zink I will visit Zain."

"Why is that?"

"It's nozing. Just somezing between us wiz concern to zis next trial."

"Bye, my flower. I will see you tonight at supper."

Hydro paused next to the golden statue of Ancient Bane. *That was Cain.* Hydro peeked around the statue; two rooms away, a door closed. He backpedaled into the bathroom behind him, pretending to emerge from it just as Cain walked down the hallway.

"Prince Paen, interesting to see you here."

"Our wing's bathroom was in use."

"Good luck at your hearing."

Cain strode past him, pausing as Hydro retorted, "I would not have one, if not for you."

"Funny. I thought it was Zain who stopped you."

"It was both of you."

"I would hardly expect you to take responsibility for your failures." Cain flounced into his room.

Hydro clicked his tongue and grunted. *Enough with you, I have business to deal with.* Hydro walked farther down the hallway, eventually

178

letting his knuckles rap against Gabrielle's door. When it opened, Gabrielle greeted him with a confused expression.

"Prince Paen? What business do you have wiz me?"

Hydro barged inside before she could shut him out. "Business you are about to find out."

Gabrielle closed the door and turned around. She wore a black blouse trimmed with red frilling near her breasts. Stitched in purple threads were the words *Gracie's Academy* near the left lapel. To the left of that stitching was another of the same color—a circle with a dagger extending down from it. The black skirt that hugged her hips was tiered with frills from the hemline up. As she extended her right arm to her lip ring, the bracelets on her arm jingled.

"I like business. Especially za unexpected kind. People are too predictable."

"You and I share a common enemy." Hydro paced the room. It was littered with clothes.

"Everyone here is my enemy, Prince. It is my apprenticeship, after all."

Hydro chortled. "Of course it is. Tell me, then, how the commoner managed to outsmart you during the second trial?"

"Zat boy won wiz Zain's help. He didn't win on his own."

"But the commoner solved a riddle that you could not."

"What is your point, Prince?"

"I hate the commoner as much as you do. He embarrassed both of us."

"Zis is true. What would you have me do zough?"

"Poison him. Incapacitate him."

"And what makes you zink zat I am capable of zat?"

Hydro approached her and took her right arm, running his fingers through her jewelry. "These bracelets give you away. You know adored arts, do you not?"

She shook her forearm free and walked away. "You're foolish, Prince Paen. Perhaps zis is just jewelry. I am a lady, after all."

"A clever lady. I know what I see; stop the innocent façade."

Gabrielle tilted her head back and laughed. "You flatter me, Prince." She turned back around and put a palm on his chest. "But, I am a decent lady. . . . Zere is no façade."

What game is she playing? "Why do you refuse to help?"

"You are correct in saying zat Eirek embarrassed boz of us. But he embarrassed you much more so, and zis next trial will embarrass him plenty by itself." She brushed back her hair and looked at Hydro.

"How do you mean?"

"Even zough Tundra defended za fact zat you used a hovercraft. I find it interesting zat you still lost. It makes me wonder if you can, in truz, win a trial by yourself?"

"I won the first trial with no one's help."

"You would have died if Zain and I had not distracted zat man."

"What are you saying?"

"I am saying zat you are not nearly as competent as you zink you are."

"You bitch, I—"

"I am trying to help you; let me finish, Prince." Gabrielle glared at him. "Alzough I am capable of making zis poison, you do not need it. What person besides me will you have trouble defeating? Cain, you have already beaten. Zain, you have already beaten. Eirek is no zreat. And—"

"The Garian is of no threat. . . ." Hydro turned away from her for a moment and then looked back at her. "You seem confident. . . ."

"I have never lost a tournament. . . . Zis one will be no different. Your focus should be on zis hearing, not sabotage. Decency before deceit."

Hydro glared at her. *What is her aim?*

"Now, I believe zat is all." Gabrielle lowered her chin and furrowed her thin eyebrows.

"I guess it is." Hydro clicked his tongue.

He walked from her room to his room. *I will remove that smirk from her face.* In the hallway leading to his room, he saw Senator Numos by his door, reaching for the door handle.

"Senator Numos," Hydro called, making himself known.

The senator's hand retreated. "Prince Paen, I was looking for you."

"Most people knock before reaching for the doorknob."

"Yes. Yes. I did. I thought I heard you. Silly me."

Hydro pursed his lips. *I am sure you did.* "What did you want to see me about?"

"I was hoping to perhaps conduct another interview? I want to get your opinions of how this past trial went."

"I would rather not discuss it. It should have been mine." Hydro clenched his fist.

"Of course. I was surprised when I had to conduct my interview with Eirek Mourse."

"Humph. If that is all, Senator Numos, I have to start preparing for tomorrow."

"Of course. Good luck with that." Senator Numos nodded and left, hobbling on his cane.

Hydro entered his room and looked around. Everything appeared normal. He went to his dresser, opened the drawer of clothes, and filtered through them until he found the necklace.

Wear me, Prince.

Hydro just looked at it.

Do you not want me to be yours, and only yours?

Does it call to others, like it does to me? Hydro wondered. Is that why the senator was here? How could Hydro find out if it called to them without seeming crazy or raising intrigue?

You lost the second trial because you did not have me with.

I lost the second trial because of Cain and Zain, not you.

You will lose this next one if you do not wear me.

Hydro stepped back from the drawer and looked around. Was he going crazy? Cautiously he moved forward and looked at it again.

I do not need your help. I am confident on my own. I have Pearl's blessing.

Yes, and what a blessing it has been. . . .

Is it being sarcastic? How dare it mock the Twelve?

The Twelve are nothing, wear me and I will show you a true blessing.

Hydro threw clothes over the necklace and closed his drawer. *How is it talking to me?* Hydro turned around and looked at his desk, not a single book had helped so far. And now, as much as he wanted to, he didn't have time to research. He needed to prepare for his hearing. He could not leave here without being apprentice; there was too much at stake.

Going over to his desk, he sat down and began writing his speech— surely there would be one; he knew that much from the time he sat on council with his father. Although everyone wished him good luck, Hydro knew it was an empty sentiment, nothing more than a hug from his mother. Little did the others know that he would be staying around for the third trial. A new piece of evidence had given him hope, and he was determined that it would sway the tides in his favor.

Hydro put the pen down and cleared his throat. "I may be a prince, son to Lord Hydro Paen of Acquava, but that still leaves me only human, fallible to the strength and impetuousness of emotions. . . ." Hydro smirked and picked up the pen, ready to continue writing.

CHAPTER 32

THE HEARING

Guardian Eska sat upon plush velvet seating in the comfort of his golden throne. Composed of leftover gold scavenged from Gladima, the city of origin, the throne predated the guardians. When the Ancients fought in the Great War, the power used was unimaginable, and it caused a dome of dirt and sand and water and mountain to tear off from the planet and form above—creating what was now the Core. The heavens split. And every planet felt each vibration from every strike. Though he couldn't see it in his reimaje, he felt and saw Jorey Raule's reaction to it as he lived on Agrost.

To his right and left were two of his conseleigh—Tundra Iycel and Luvan Katore. Eska knew Tundra waited anxiously for the hearing; she wanted to do away with the prince. In striking down Zain, the prince had caused her much grief, because she still had to defend his actions against the other competitors in using the hovercraft during the trial. Eska couldn't help but consider the grief he caused her as well in revoking her decision.

Eska stole a quick glance at her. He had seen Tundra angry before, and when she was, her words cut like the ice scimitar she wielded. Luvan was more reasonable, raised among the politicians of Mistral. Ethen and Riagan remained more unbiased than Tundra was becoming. When Tundra told him about her conversation with Eirek while he looked at the portraits of the past guardians, he began to see her feeling drawn to him. Eska assumed it was because Eirek won her trial. He digested the information, and like the other kinds he had gained, he stored it. The Trials were to test their performance, and they were far from over yet.

"So, they are on their way, my guardian?" Tundra asked.

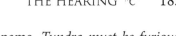

She referred to him by title, not by name. *Tundra must be furious.* Anger breeds spite—she was becoming no better than Hydro had been, but she would cool eventually. It was in her Sereyan nature.

"Yes, Ethen and Riagan are bringing them now."

"Both are with them?"

"A safety precaution Luvan and I discussed," Eska said.

"You have started making decisions without me already, my guardian?"

Until you become less biased, yes, is what Guardian Eska would've said, but Luvan spoke for him. "Lady Iycel, do not overstep your place. You forget our responsibility. It is not to make judgments; it is to give council. We are Edwyrd's conseleigh. It is up to Edwyrd to make the correct decision, and it is our duty to stand by whatever decision that is, whether we agree with it or not."

Guardian Eska exhaled. Hostility amongst his council was never a good thing. Their fealty completed him as much as it completed them. Selecting conseleigh was as rigorous a process as anointing an apprentice. At ages eighteen through twenty-five, an apprentice's mind was more developed than loyalty. This was crucial because the Core shared treaties with no nation, and the guardian had to remain candid of mind, favoring no nation—not even his or her own. Still, it was natural for lords and ladies, senators, or advisors and receivers to remain attached to their homelands. Those inducted as his conseleigh were sound of mind, thoroughly dredged through life's problems. Because there were four council members, impartiality was never an issue.

Guardian Eska, we be 'ere.

Come in, then, Ethen, Guardian Eska communicated. "They are here," he said aloud to the two in the room.

The double doors opened. Ethen led, wearing a silk vest of plaited green and white. Underneath was a long-sleeved, rough, black shirt. The golden C that marked him as a conseleigh was pinned near his left breast. His conical beard was groomed, but mainly because he stroked it often—especially when in deep thought.

Ethen turned around. "Stay 'ere." He separated Zain Berrese and Hydro Paen an arm's length apart and then positioned himself next to Tundra.

Riagan took his own position next to Luvan. The deep-red skin from his years on Pyre—prior to being chosen to fill in during Conseleigh Ariel's absence—contrasted well with his darker, long-sleeved shirt. The man let no facial hair grow, but he harbored a pierced left ear similar to Luvan's.

Eska looked to the two contestants. Only Hydro's continuance hung in the balance; Zain was here to provide testimony and for Eska to share a word with, in private, once Hydro's matter was resolved. Eska needed to examine his gift. Once the adored had cleared Zain to leave, Riagan fetched him from the apothecary and brought him straight here, to make sure no tampering could be done to the gift.

"Both of you realize why you are here today?"

"Yes, Guardian Eska," both answered in unison.

"Hydro, you are charged with breaching the rules of the Trials, established after introductions: Any contestant caught in gratuitous acts of violence outside of the scope of the Trials may face dismissal," Guardian Eska recited. "The act of fracturing Zain's hand is gratuitous in nature, and since it occurred after the second trial was already finished it is outside the scope of the Trials. How do you plead?" Eska asked.

"I admit to those charges, my guardian." Hydro bowed.

Eska scanned the prince. *At least he knows better than to lie.* Hydro kept his hands at his sides. *He must be fighting nerves.* Did he fight tears too? Hydro kept his head tilted up like he was about to sneeze.

"There you have it, Guardian; he admits to his trespasses," Tundra proclaimed. "He should be dismissed."

"And if you were in Hydro's soles, would you have said differently? Admitting to faults is a lesson in humility; there is more to this hearing than right and wrong, Lady Iycel," retorted Luvan.

"Like what?"

"Like motive!"

"Quiet, both of you. Prince Paen, Luvan is right—why did you do this to Zain?"

Hydro exhaled and spoke, "I may be a prince, son to Lord Hydro Paen of Acquava, but that still leaves me only human, fallible to the strength and impetuousness of emotions. After Cain destroyed my hovercraft during our battle for the orb, I was angry. When Zain stopped me outside of your estate, after I had already solved my riddle and collected my orb and was about to win, he prolonged me just enough so that Eirek could win. It frustrated me even more. Have any of you ever desired something? More than Gladonus itself? And then, when it was so close to you—so close you could touch it—you could not have it?"

Guardian Eska ignored his desire to glance at Tundra. Was she listening?

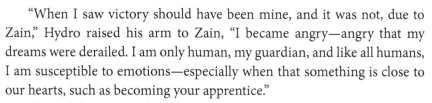

"When I saw victory should have been mine, and it was not, due to Zain," Hydro raised his arm to Zain, "I became angry—angry that my dreams were derailed. I am only human, my guardian, and like all humans, I am susceptible to emotions—especially when that something is close to our hearts, such as becoming your apprentice."

The words were spoken elegantly—like a prince should speak. *He is obviously prepared.*

"You can't tell me you're accepting that!" Zain objected. "The man broke my hand, costing me perhaps even the third trial, depending on its nature."

"It was your decision to get in my way," Hydro said.

"So you think you can just blame emotions for your loss of self-control?"

"What of you holding a knife to Cadmar's throat? Or even after he acquiesced to your demand, elbowing him and kicking sand in his face?"

Gasps. Eska straightened his posture. This was new. Zain's gaze revealed the truth in Hydro's words.

"And how did you hear of this, Prince Paen?" Tundra asked.

"I overheard Cadmar talking to Eirek in the hallway."

"Zain, is this true?" Tundra asked.

Silence. Zain blushed. "My sword broke during the second trial. I saw that he had a weapon. . . . I . . . I would need it if I wanted to stop Hydro from winning. That's why I did it."

"How did you know he was winning?" Riagan asked.

"I didn't, but in case he showed himself, I needed to stop him. I couldn't let him get another point in these trials, because . . . because becoming apprentice . . . is also my dream. Guardian Eska, you said after the first trial that we need to adapt to our situations, and I did. Conseleigh Iycel . . . you said this past trial was meant to test our ability to analyze every angle; I did that too. . . . If Hydro or Cadmar had won, it would be more difficult to catch them. And knowing that Cadmar had already failed, I was bent on stopping Hydro."

"How is that any different?" Hydro asked.

"Because I did it to stop you; I didn't do it out of spite and frustration that I had lost."

"You acted outside the scope of the trial, same as me! You held a knife to Cadmar's throat."

"Both of you, enough! Riagan, take them out, and come back. We need to discuss." With his ungloved hand, Eska strummed the little patch of hair on his chin. He waited for his youngest conseleigh to return. The arguments made were well constructed, but what would his conseleigh think?

Riagan reentered and stood before Eska. His other conseleigh stood near him as well. Together they formed a circle.

"Go around and let me hear your thoughts. Tundra, you will start. And, Luvan, we will end with you."

"The news about Zain holding a knife to Cadmar's throat is disturbing, but he did not kill. There was no violation there as I see it. In both cases, a significant difference persists: Zain did it after his particular riddle was finished, yes—but before the trial itself was complete. He needed to keep Hydro from winning. Zain was smart; he analyzed the situation. Hydro was just furious."

"If you are basing it on merit of analyzing the situation, then Hydro deserves nothing either. He was the only contestant to pick up your keys, Lady Iycel."

"That is not relevant to the matter at hand, Riagan," Tundra said.

"Then neither is telling how Zain analyzed the situation. He threatened the life of another contestant. And even after Cadmar gave into Zain's demands, Zain proceeded to hit him? I see no difference in either of their actions. How can you punish one and not the other?" Riagan spoke. "On Pyre, the heat plays with minds—but that does not mean the firesons succumb to it. When I ruled as lord, my firesons were picked for their tough bodies and tough minds. If both acted outside the scope of the Trials, then both need to be punished or not."

"Te Trials were meant to test every contestant in te face of 'ardship. It was Zain's choice to block Hydro's path. In Chaon, tere is a saying: Plant your bed of flowers, ten watch tem grow. In Zain's case, 'is flowers were vicious. Because 'e blocked Hydro's path, 'e cost Hydro te Trials and 'ad to suffer te consequences. Hydro is no different; 'e is now waiting for 'is flowers to grow. It is up to Edwyrd weter 'hose be roses or irises."

"Luvan?"

"Both acted outside the scope of the trial. If you punish one, you must punish the other. Riagan said it best."

"What do they deserve, then? Do both deserve dismissal?" Guardian Eska asked.

"That is an extreme punishment," Luvan said.

"They need to be excused from the next trial. If you do not do something, a trend will surely continue," Tundra said.

"Because your trial is finised, you tink it is all right for contestants to miss mine? Toma'awke 'imself wouldn't miss it."

Eska was glad Ethen spoke. The third trial was especially important for him because he could determine the level of training each would require. Eska strummed his stubble. He was impressed by Hydro's preparation. He was also impressed by Zain's ability to analyze the situation, even if he hadn't solved his riddle; it showed a certain sense of intelligence. The conseleigh returned to their positions by his side; they didn't speak, allowing him to concentrate. *How to make my decision?*

Eska stole a glance at Tundra. She looked off across the room, probably at the portrait of her homeland and Peril's Path—a mile-long, icy, narrow road surrounded by two seas. His chest sunk. He knew what he needed to do.

"Riagan, bring them in."

Once they were brought in and separated, Eska stared at both of them. Before he spoke next, he looked at his conseleigh—all stood rigid and stoic; they would be numb to whatever decision he posed.

"Prince Paen, Zain Berrese, both of you conducted yourselves in ways unbefitting to the Trials. However, dismissal from the Trials is too harsh of a punishment. Also, to punish one but not the other would be unfair. It has been suggested that you miss the third trial, but that is not possible. You will compete in the trial, you will retain all of your privileges, and this hearing itself is a lesson in your own humility. Think before you act. Your mind can be your largest weakness but also your greatest strength. Are there any questions?"

Silence.

"Riagan, lead Prince Paen out. Mr. Berrese still has business with us."

Once the prince was gone, Eska continued, "Mr. Berrese, General Satorus informs me that your brother has since visited you while you were being treated. Is this true?"

"It is, my guardian."

"And the gift that he left you with?"

"Here." Zain shrugged and allowed the scabbard that hung from his back to slide in front of him. He unsheathed the weapon and let it sparkle, catching the rays that filtered in from the wall of glass windows and doors behind Eska.

"A sword?" Ethen said.

"My father made it for me before he left for Empora. It was meant to be a birthday gift."

"How fortunate that you receive a new sword just when your old one breaks. Perhaps the Ancients are looking after you?" Luvan said.

Zain didn't respond. He looked down at his sword and back up again, stoic as stone.

"Bring it here," Eska demanded.

Zain stepped forward and held it out to him. Eska took the blade and slid his gloved hand down the steel. It was true steel. Four gems, finely-cut, were spaced throughout. The blue topaz, for strengthening courage and overcoming obstacles. The opal, bringer of emotions. The garnet, the embodiment of devotion. And finally, the peridot, said to strengthen life's ambition. *Too many aggressive stones—and too fueled by emotion and passion.* If Zain embodied the qualities of his jewels, there wasn't room for reasoning or serenity—but that is what his conseleigh provided. The sword lusted for battle, even though it had never seen a single day. Did Zain see more than just the colors of the gems?

"Your father made this for you?"

"Yes, my guardian."

"The sword is a beauty. Do you have a name for it yet?"

Zain shook his head.

"All weapons deserve a name. In time, you will think of one for it. Adonis, here, has only been in the hands of guardians after the Great War. It is one of the eleven ether forged weapons." Guardian Eska withdrew the blade he kept near his throne. It was slightly longer than the length of Zain's, with steel a smoky-gray like swirling clouds. "Adonis was created by the Smiths before they were banished from Gladima. It is a beauty, is it not?"

"It is, my guardian." Zain's eyes scanned the blade up and down.

"Your sword is well crafted and designed; perhaps your father is a Smith reincarnate?" Eska chuckled a little. "It's good; there are no spells or enchantments on it. You are free to use it. Like Luvan said, perhaps the Ancients themselves want you to succeed in this next trial."

"Gabrielle mentioned something of a weapons tournament?"

"Yes. Ethen will be providing information at tonight's supper. I suggest you come with questions."

"Thank you, Guardian Eska."

Guardian Eska nodded. "Riagan."

Upon mention of his name, his conseleigh led Zain out the door.

"Tundra, I am sorry things did not go your way today," Eska said.

"I hope you made the right decision. . . ."

Eska strummed the stubble on his chin with his ungloved hand while he stroked Adonis with his gloved hand. *The guardian's blade. Steel forged from the ether of the universe. Steel that can never break. Steel sharp enough to cut through stone and earth.* Eska looked into the smoky-gray metal. Sometimes he got lost in its enchantment as he tried to find his reflection. Today he saw it clearer than other days. It showed his muse. He hoped that he made the right decision. And wondered what would happen if he hadn't.

❧ CHAPTER 33 ❧

SHADOW SPARRING

A crimson letter hung on Zain's door. Although he knew what the trial was about, thanks to Gabrielle visiting him the day before, he took it off, broke the seal, and read it all the same.

He went inside his room. He clenched and unclenched his right and left hands experimentally. *The trial is too soon.* His hands were still sore—the right one more than the left. He knew how to use both sides; most Gazo's students did. In fact, use of the left side was one thing that all beginning students needed to show promise in before advancing to weapon knowledge. Instructor Klum always preached, "Know yourself right to left and left to right before you focus on winning the fight." And although it was tested early on, it wasn't tested for later in training, under the assumption that utilizing both sides would be a part of your daily regimen. Zain hadn't done this as much as he would have liked. *If only I had more time.*

He tossed the letter on the hardwood desk and unstrapped the longsword on his back, setting it down next to the letter. He walked back to his bed and sat with his forearms to him so that he could look at the wounds on his hands. *Strength comes from persistence. You cannot let the obstacles you've had become setbacks. They need to be the forces that encourage you to move onward. . . .* His brother's advice spoke to him while he looked at his hands. The wounds would make gripping the longsword tougher. But not impossible. Only Zain could determine what that was. *I'm possible.* He clenched his hands.

The door creaked. "I zought I heard you return."

It was Gabrielle. A cinnabar strapless bodice—patterned in damask roses and strapped in sable around the sides of her small frame—pushed up her breasts. Strapped any tighter and Zain feared that her breasts might reveal themselves. A darker shade of red silk dropped to below her knees. Four-inch, black heels elevated her height to match his. Her silk-like, black hair was parted to the left; she had exchanged her once-purple lip ring for a scarlet one. *She's beautiful.*

"Zain, are you all right?" She closed the door.

He corrected his slouched posture and refocused on her eyes, trying to prevent them from drifting any lower. There was a certain redness on her skin and cheeks that he had noticed the day before when she visited him in the apothecary. It had faded into a slight pink today, enhancing her allure.

"Yeah, I . . . I just got back from the hearing."

"What has been decided?"

"Hydro is getting away with what he did to me."

She stepped closer. Zain's groin tightened. Fantasies danced through his mind.

Gabrielle smiled. "It isn't him who you should be worried about."

"Who, then?"

Gabrielle closed the door and then turned her head toward Zain. "Me." She gave a little laugh and bent her hand toward herself. "Zis trial is a tournament of weapons. Za perfect zird trial." She walked over to him and put her hand on his chest. The aroma of her cherry fingernail polish invaded his nostrils. "I expect we still have a deal?"

Zain remembered her coming to the apothecary. At first he thought it was because she wanted to see how he was doing. But it wasn't. She merely posed for him the situation to finally see which school was better: Gazo's or Gracie's. A challenge Zain would have relished if not for the current condition of his hand. If he could beat Gabrielle, it would prove his worth to Gazo's—and to Zakk.

"As long as we do not face each other in the first round, yes."

Even with his condition, Zain couldn't back out of a challenge. Not from Gracie's. He was not the type to make excuses. *Do not let obstacles become setbacks.* His brother always had advice for Zain; he had always been the father figure that his own dad, Laron, couldn't be, because he was away on business all the time. Unfortunately that left the role of brother unfulfilled—until Zakk. But Zakk was gone . . . and dead. . . .

"Pray whatever prayer you do zat we don't. I look forward to seeing your skills."

He only prayed to his steel. "I will."

"Shall we go to dinner, zen?"

"No. I have to shower first." Zain hung his head. "Gabrielle?"

"Yes, Zain?"

"I . . . I . . . the other day . . . I . . . overheard you and Cain. . . ."

"What did you hear?"

"About your dad. . . . I'm . . . I'm sorry. I still feel awful about not acting faster."

Gabrielle sniffled and held up her head. "Za past is just zat—past. . . . We all have somezing we try and forget."

"Thank you for not telling anyone about what happened . . . before . . . before the Trials."

"It is not my story to tell . . . just like mine isn't yours to. . . . I would appreciate it if you didn't tell anyone." She blushed. She retreated before Zain could say more.

Zain hung his head again. Although it was delayed, he was glad he apologized. If he was to be in the proper state for this next trial, he needed to forget everything else. He needed focus, and that was not something he could obtain by having underlying guilt. There was already too much of that.

Zain undressed, proceeding to shower for the first time in days. In the mirror, he displayed his newly-silver teeth. Two of them. When he talked, his jaw felt heavier—but not enough to affect him. Staring at his reflection, Zain clenched and unclenched his right hand. *Hydro will pay. Only blade can hush nobility, and now I have the perfect one.* Even Guardian Eska seemed to admire his sword. But time was short, and although he knew the longsword, it would take a little while getting reacquainted with its grip, feel, and stance.

Zain entered the dining hall—the last contestant to arrive. Gabrielle engaged in deep conversation with Cain. The prince's glasses looked different (having wider lenses), but similar to the frameless pair that Zain saw him wearing earlier. But even these couldn't hide the fact that his eyes devoured her dress, continually sinking lower. Eirek and Cadmar were busy talking as well. That left Hydro to look at him—the last person Zain wanted to see. *You will lose. I will make sure of that.* Zain took his regular seat, focusing on Guardian Eska instead of Hydro.

Eska faced the contestants. "My apologies for the delay of this third trial. Zain Berrese and Prince Paen met with me and my conseleigh today. The decision has been made that the Trials will continue as normal. There will be no dismissal or additional sanctions."

"Slimy caffler," Cadmar muttered, just audible enough for Zain to hear.

Zain glared at Hydro, who smirked while sucking wine between his lips. *You'll learn your place soon enough.*

"Contestants, as guardian, I hope the day will never come that you need to pick up your blade. But such ideals are rarely possible. That is why it is essential to be trained in combat. Ethen will explain the trial and how this tournament shall function."

The man with darker skin (but lighter than Zain's) stood, still in the green vest from earlier that day. Before he spoke, he strummed his conical beard. "Contestants, before I became Guardian Eska's conseleigh, I was an advisor for current Lord Zalos Kapache's father, te late Lord Zaron Kapache. During tat time, I learned much about tournaments, 'aving conducted plenty for te Kapache family. Tat is why your next trial will be a tournament of weapons. And only weapons of steel. You will fight on te notion tat te first strike wins."

When Ethen spoke, his vocals resembled those of Adored Amiti in the apothecary. Both had southern accents—obviously from Myoli, deep in the south past the Thieving Isles, where the Krine Sea spilled to the Bernine Sea and where laid Chaon, the nation of jungles and exotic animals. Klaff Mountain towered there, a spire to all who wished to become something greater. All they needed to do was conquer the mountain that had never been conquered.

"Tomorrow evening, an 'our after dinner, you will meet in te lobby and receive your first opponent's name. Now, are tere any questions?"

Guardian Eska stood, and all hands up in the air went down. "Before questions, I will add a few more details Ethen failed to mention. I, myself, will perform two spells on your weapons. First I will make it so that your weapon can neither tarnish nor break during this trial. The second spell will make any contact leave a black mark upon your bodies. This will help in determining the first strike. Ethen will now take your questions." Eska sat and sipped his wine.

Next to Zain, Cadmar raised his hand. "Are we allowed to use more than one weapon? For example, my axe and my heater shield—may I use both?"

"Excellent question! Yes, bot are considered weapons and may be used. If you come prepared before te trial wit bot, ten you may have bot be blessed. Prince Evber, a question?"

Zain saw that the prince no longer had his glasses on; he dangled them in mid-air between his fingers. During the middle of his question, he put them back on. "How are the brackets to be arranged for the tournament?"

"You will receive te name of your opponent te same way you received te name of your partner during te first trial. So tere will be te first round consisting of tree bouts; te winners of tat round advance to a final round, where tere will be a tree-way duel. Is tat understood?"

Zain looked to Gabrielle, who only slyly smirked at him. If they were not paired against each other in the first round, the trial would be theirs. At least, one of theirs. And Zain didn't doubt it would be his.

Gabrielle raised her toned arm. "What happens at za end of zis zird trial? Earlier you mentioned zat not everyone will be competing in za forz." She directed her question toward Guardian Eska.

Eska stood, prompting Ethen to sit. "The fourth trial will test the performance of each remaining contestant. Only those individuals who have managed to win a trial already will be allowed to compete. Any more questions?"

Zain raised his hand. "And what will happen to the people who do not have a point?"

"You will be allowed to stay here until the conclusion of the Trials, but you may compete no further. Any other questions?"

No one raised a hand. Before sitting, Eska snapped his fingers. Servants carried platters of food through the double doors in the back of the dining hall. Zain ate fast; cutting and chewing the tender pork was nothing but a chore. He plucked a few loaves of bread from straw baskets, but he did not butter them; instead he tore them off in his mouth. He gobbled it down like a sophisticated barbarian, having the decency to at least wipe his face after every few morsels of food.

He excused himself from the table much sooner than the others; training took precedence over gluttony. Sleep would come when he won. However, the training arena would no longer be appropriate—it would be too crowded. Before he headed there, he wanted to familiarize himself with footing and strokes.

His wing servant, Heather, the same servant who had failed to take his bags on his arrival, was on the first floor in the hallway before the three-way split. She dusted a portrait of a large comet. It looked like dragon's breath falling through an indigo sky. She stood on her toetips, reaching for the top of the golden frame, when he approached her. Zain whiffed the faint stench of sweat coming from her black blouse.

"Heather."

"Mr. Berrese." She wiped her forehead. "How may I assist you?"

"Is it possible to turn on the lights for the sparring court outside?"

"Why, yes, I can help you with that. Let me fetch a light first." She turned around and rummaged through a storage compartment. Zain had noticed it once before—extremely narrow, holding the bare essentials. Once she held a light in her hands, along with a remote of some sort, she proceeded to the lobby. "If you will follow me."

Zain trailed her through the lobby doors into the blackness of night. The air was hotter than he expected. She led him around the estate on a cobblestone walkway—past the small stone steps, floored in shallow water, to a circular stone court. Four pillars were erected that resembled swords thrust into the ground, their pommels shining yellow in the air. Golden benches outlined the perimeter of the court. A circle of golden bricks highlighted the scarlet bricks within and, even farther, the silhouette of a dragon. These four beacons illuminated the dark.

"The lights will shut off after a period of inactivity, so make sure you do not rest too long. If you do need to restart the lights, push the button located on the northernmost sword pole, located on the . . ." She made an L-shape with her left thumb and index finger. She pointed with her right hand at the spot where the two came together.

"The cross guard," Zain offered, chuckling at her lack of knowledge.

"That term sounds fine to me. Goodnight, Mr. Berrese. Colin is on duty tonight. Contact him if there are any problems."

"Thank you, Heather."

"It is my pleasure. Good luck."

He watched as the deathly-thin woman walked away, a slight limp to her left side. If he wanted to win this trial, he would need more than luck— he needed skill. He pulled his sword from the scabbard and set the sheath down on one of the benches. He turned and stepped onto the stone court, the sole of his foot swallowed by the dragon's open mouth. Focusing, Zain envisioned the opponent he would face and took his first swing—slow and steady into the air.

Lunge. Sweep. Stab. Shuffle. Slice. Block. Zain mixed the different approaches every fifteen minutes. One session focused on evasive maneuvers like shuffling backwards while parrying or twirling and blocking. Other sessions focused on aggressive combinations with the intent to throw his eventual opponent off-balance. Yet at other times he focused on footwork, bouncing left and right and front and back on the balls of his feet. After a few hours, he began to feel himself get acquainted with the weapon and how he would need to hold it with both hands due to its weight. A few times he needed to rest and stretch his hands so that he could properly grip the sword again. He never let his rest last longer than five minutes. Time was of the essence.

Zain sliced through the air and then shuffled his feet forward. He lifted his elbow up, making sure to practice all combat techniques, not just those of steel. He unfurled a barrage of assaults that ultimately ended with his ankle giving out and him collapsing to one knee. *Damnit.*

"Your balance is off."

Zain stood and looked around. "Who's there? Zakk, is that you?"

"You're going to lose."

A flash of steel came to his right. Zain raised his sword. Before metal collided, the sword disappeared. Zain blinked and shook his head. *Am I going crazy?* "How . . . how can you do that? Where are you?" There was a quiver in his voice that he didn't like to admit.

"Ask yourself that question. You already know the answer."

"I saw you. I know you're here."

"How can I be here when I'm at the bottom of a lake?"

Another flash of steel. Another block. Another vacancy in the air. *Is he here? He can't be.* Zain never saw the aftermath of the fall. Just the choler in Zakk's eyes. *Zere are zings worse zan deaz. . . .*Gabrielle's words infiltrated his mind. *Pain . . . hopelessness . . . and futility. . . . Is that what Zakk was feeling on the way to the lake below?* Zain crumbled to his knees, letting go of his sword. It clanged and clattered. And then, silence.

"I . . . I . . . never meant to . . ."

"To kill me?"

Zain felt something drag across his shoulders. It felt like a knife. The sharp tip prickled his skin and sent a chill through his body. His chest heaved. He put an arm to his eyes to block the tears. "All . . . all I wanted . . . was to see Ava again." Zain sobbed.

"We all wanted something, Zain. Death was never one of them. . . .How can you even compete in the Trials?"

Zain touched his head to the golden brick. Tears slid down to water the court. He rolled over to his side, and with blurry vision, he looked at his sword. He reached for it, but it was out of range. He shook his head while it lay on his arm. Tears slid down his cheek. As he wiggled his fingers toward his sword—the only companion he had—he felt phantom fingers crawling between his fingertips.

Zain didn't know how long he reached for his sword. Or how long he lay there after he had given up. But the lights of the court shut off eventually, leaving him in the dark, hopeless and alone

❧CHAPTER 34❧

LADY'S CHARM

Gabrielle hardly touched her meat. She only ate it to fit in with the men, but in truth, she preferred the texture of leafy greens and the warm, soothing feeling of soup. This dinner was rather dull. Nothing like when Cadmar and Hydro got into a small fight. That was exciting. And she loved excitement. Cain—next to her, pinching and massaging her thigh underneath the table—was hardly that. She smiled and fluttered her eyes, but that was to keep him bound to her. In truth, the only thing of interest at this dinner was Zain excusing himself before the others could finish even half of their plates.

"Your friend left," Cain pointed out to her.

"I see zat."

"Where do you think he went?"

"I don't know." Gabrielle tore off a piece of bread and placed it in her mouth. In truth, she figured he went to train, such was the Gazo's mentality. She needed to as well; but first there were other things that needed tending to. Things only she could do.

"Probably didn't feel good." Hydro leaned over the table and looked at her.

Gabrielle feigned a smile. "What makes you zink zat?"

"After every trial, Zain's been in the apothecary. Only so much one can take."

"You forget that I have as well, Prince." Cain sipped his wine.

"And that is why you haven't won yet." Hydro snickered in Cain's face.

Gabrielle shuddered. Ever since the second trial, the two of them hadn't exchanged pleasantries—merely glares or rude comments. It wasn't decent, but could princes truly be expected to act as decently as her? Still, she needed her princes to cooperate. She would deal with them later.

"It doesn't matter if you've won or not; zis next trial is mine, and so is za one after zat." She laughed.

The princes chortled. Perfect. *Stubborn princes. The only thing you've seen of women is flowing dresses, braided hair, and fancy titles.*

She fluttered her eyelashes, softening her tone. "Did I say somezing amusing?"

Neither of them spoke.

Figures. You men can talk, but you can hardly act. Gabrielle straightened her posture and dabbed her lips with the linen.

The rest of the dinner passed smoothly; she had acted her part in breaking the hostility. Gabrielle excused herself from the table after everyone finished eating—aside from Senator Numos, who still helped himself to a few ladles of soup while in deep conversation with Ethen Rorum. She would acquaint herself with him during their interview after she won the trial. Before then, only knowing the contestants who posed a threat mattered—their wants, needs, and motivations. Knowing them would allow her to manipulate them. *Decency before deceit.*

She didn't have time to waste. Cain lusted for her, based on his pinches and massages. She wouldn't let him have all of her tonight though—just a kiss, to quench his thirst.

Stashed underneath a pile of clothes she hid a small box and a trunk filled with herbs and draughts brought for the sole purpose of keeping her healthy. In truth, she didn't like having her clothes sprawled all over, but she did it to make herself seem reckless instead of calculating, forgetful instead of attentive, barbaric versus decent. Life was a play, and although she knew the script, she preferred to live one act at a time, always giving her best performance. Men never understood how many weapons one actually had.

You have to be decent, but deceitful, before you can show form, yet, also be formidable. Her head instructor, Carla Sonetta, constantly reminded her of this.

She grabbed a tube from the smaller box and unscrewed its cap. There was a small brush for lip application. She swirled the brush around in the liquid for a second and applied it to her lips. *Just enough Lady's Charm.* Perhaps she would be able to give every contestant a kiss; once they kissed her, they'd want another—and she would surely grant that wish. In time, the liquid would work its way into their systems, doing nothing other than slowing their reaction times just enough. She applied another layer, taking care not to ingest any herself.

A knock at the door.

She put the vial away and straightened her cinnabar dress; it was drifting a little too low. She tucked her hair behind her ears and opened the door. "Prince Evber, I knew you would come."

He stepped in, and she closed the door. "You looked too stunning tonight. I needed to see you. I wish to extract my flower's nectar."

Cain placed his hands on her shoulders, working his way down to her breasts. Gabrielle tilted her head back; his fingers were already well-acquainted with her body. If only he would go even lower than her breasts. Most nights they would. His hands pulled down the left side of her bodice, revealing her own excitement. He was of soft hands, something she had never experienced in her father's rough hands—the hands of a mechanic who treated his wife and daughter like tools after those of his own occupation were whisked from his grasp.

Gabrielle reminded herself that even a temptress could be tempted. She yearned for him to kiss her breast and swallow her nipple. She wanted his glasses to fog again due to their body heat and for him to need to take them off. But not tonight. Tonight she must focus.

"Stop zat, Prince," Gabrielle whispered as Cain's forefinger stroked her nipple.

He pulled back and readjusted his glasses. His green eyes stared into hers. Gabrielle readjusted her bodice, concealing herself again.

"Is something wrong?" Cain asked.

"Nozing, really—but why don't we start wiz a kiss first?"

Cain smirked. So did she. They kissed—she grabbed his shoulder blades, and he grabbed her waist. Normally she would battle tongues with him, but not tonight. Tonight she let him amply use his tongue to lick the inside of her mouth and her lips. When it intensified too greatly, Gabrielle pulled back and cleaned her lips with her fingers.

"You did not fight tonight, my rose." Cain moved forward.

That was close enough. She put a hand on his chest. "I'll save my fighting for tomorrow, my prince."

"Pray to not fight me. It would be hard to see such a woman as you removed from the tournament in the first round."

"And what makes you certain you would win?"

"My family has held the longest ruling of all of the current families in power. We have lived and fought and studied in Castle Thoth since the late reign of Guardian Jorey Raule."

"A long history doesn't make you a great fighter."

"We would not have had such a long reign if we were not."

"Well, I have never lost a match in a tournament."

"Never?" Cain moved closer, holding her chin with his left hand.

"Not once."

"Ah, but you never faced men before at an academy only for women."

"And perhaps you've never fought a woman."

Cain chuckled. "You are my flower, my rose, and even in our gardens, they are delicate."

"Every rose has its zorn, Prince."

"And every stem can be clipped."

"Goodnight, Prince."

"Did I put you in a sour mood? Just let me . . ." Cain tugged on her earlobe. He leaned in; she stopped him.

"No, you didn't. It's not you; it's just tradition."

"Very well. Good luck tomorrow, Gabrielle."

"And you too."

Cain exited, and Gabrielle relaxed. She never had sex the night before a tournament. Her body needed cleansing from all outside sources if her prayer was to be heard. The Ancients were pure—so she, too, needed to be.

Gabrielle walked back over to her chest and reapplied the lip liner. She would try to tempt Prince Paen to kiss her. He was the only other one who might prove difficult. Cadmar's size may be difficult to compromise for, but he was heavy and slow compared to her lightness and agility, a mammoth to her lioness. Still, if she could give Cadmar a kiss, she would. Even without Lady's Charm, Eirek would be an easy task. Zain she wouldn't try to seduce— Gracie's would beat Gazo's on a fair playing field. It was only decent.

She applied a thick coat, humming all the while. *All men think alike, in steel and power. True strength comes from utilizing all of your weapons, even flesh when needed. By doing this, you will shatter the defense of men every time.* Another lesson Sonetta drilled into their heads. Sonetta took a personal interest in Gabrielle one summer and took her to the first capital of Empora, Rydel, along the Krine Sea. There, Carla showed her how to lure men, enthrall them, and then rob them. The money they collected went to fund women's shelters in Empora, a cause Gabrielle could rob for.

She locked up her smaller chest and put some clothes back over it. *Cain should be in his room by now.* She left her room and looked toward Cain's room to the left. The door was closed. She didn't want to raise any suspicion. If the others found out that they weren't the only ones kissed, it would divulge her purpose.

Only maids were in the lobby. Gabrielle smiled at them and proceeded to the other hallway. She didn't know which rooms belonged to which contestant, so she guessed.

She knocked at a door to the left, past a golden statue of Ancient Lyoen. Hydro opened it. "What do you want?"

"Nozing. I am glad you listened to my advice." She walked forward, letting herself in. Once inside, she closed the door. She looked around; his room was organized, much more so than hers. On his desk was an assortment of books laid open to varying pages. *Interesting. I never took him for a reader.* His drawer in his dresser was open, and when she noticed it, Hydro moved in front of her.

"If you want nothing, then you can leave."

"Well, zen I lied." She laughed and flipped back her hair. It was a subtle tactic to make herself more desirable by exposing more neck. "I suppose I do want somezing."

"What is that?"

"I came to give you a kiss and wish you luck tomorrow." She placed her hand on his shoulder and tugged on his earlobe. She pursed her lips but did not lean into him. He would come to her; they always did.

"I do not need your kiss."

"Just like you did not need my advice?" Gabrielle stared into his hazel eyes, never faltering her gaze. Good eye contact hid anything.

Hydro didn't answer. He looked at her lips though.

"Without me, you may not be here."

"Be quick with your point."

"Well, you owe me a kiss. It's only decent." Gabrielle crawled her hand up his neck and then to his lips.

"Yes . . .it. . .is," Hydro muttered.

She almost had him. She stood on her toetips and tugged his ears. "Zen kiss me."

She didn't expect her line to work as well as it did. Within seconds, Hydro was shoving his tongue down her mouth. She held onto his shoulders and let him kiss, putting up no resistance. After a little while, she battled his tongue back with hers and then pulled away from him. *Not a bad kisser for being so prude.*

"There, we are even now you have your kiss."

"Yes, we are. I look forward to seeing you in za final tomorrow."

"What makes you so certain you will see me there?"

"As long as you do not face me, you will see me zere. I told you zat before." She smirked and left.

Outside Hydro's room, she looked at the next couple of doors. There were multiple doors, but Gabrielle assumed the arrangement was similar to their wing's arrangement—two contestants on one side, and one contestant on the other side. She decided to go left and knocked on the door.

"Who it be?"

She didn't answer. If she could get him to open the door, then she could easily enter. She rapped again. The doorknob turned, and Cadmar stood inside his room. He didn't say anything, just merely looked at her. With his shirt off, his stocky chest was exposed. Although it wasn't chiseled, it was hairy.

Certainly is a mammoth. Gabrielle's eyes looked up to him and smiled. "Cadmar, may I come in?"

She didn't wait for the man to say yes or no; she pushed him back by putting her palm to his hairy chest. With her other hand, she closed the door behind her.

"What be it you want?"

"I just wanted to wish you luck in tomorrow's event."

Cadmar eyed her up and down. "I'll be fine. Thanks."

"Alzough you won't win, you deserve luck same as za ozers."

"And what luck that be?"

"Lady's luck. Za kind you get wiz a kiss." She wrapped her hands around his broad shoulders.

"You be all over Cain all the time. I've never even talked with you."

"Cain is all over me, Cadmar. But you are strong like him. Tall like him. Why, you even have za same color hair as him . . . almost." She giggled and then slid her left hand up his strong neck and tugged on his chin.

"I can't. . . . I need to train."

Gabrielle put her right hand behind Cadmar's head, not letting him pull away from her trance. "Your fazer is an elite. Don't you want to make him proud and win at least one round tomorrow?"

"What does a kiss have to do with that?"

"Your fazer protects your lady's honor. It's only chivalrous. . . . I zought you were zat type of man. . . ." She slid her hand down his chest. A part of her wanted to go lower than his midline to see if everything was proportional, but she stopped herself. "Are you like your fazer? I guess not." Gabrielle turned around, but his large hands spun her back.

His eyes searched hers. She bit her lips and smiled. The next thing she knew, his lips were on hers. The kiss was rough and unpracticed, but she did the best she could with it. She helped to guide his movements by tilting his head with her hands placed around his cropped hair. After a few minutes of kissing, Gabrielle pulled away.

"You battle lips as fiercely as I'm sure you will tomorrow," she teased. She wiped her lips clean.

Cadmar chuckled. "Aye, I will. There be a lot of matches that be mine to win."

"Yes, I'm sure zere are. Just not za one wiz me." Gabrielle smiled, dissolving the tension she built. "Goodnight, Cadmar."

She left without hearing him say anymore and disappeared back into her hallway, not even halting at Eirek's room. The man was no threat to her, and if she did face him, she wanted to humiliate him for the second trial.

In her room, Gabrielle closed the door and then unzipped the back of her dress with efficiency, allowing the red bodice to fall to the ground. Her breasts looked smaller now—about the size of Cadmar's fist. She walked over to the window and looked at the purple sky, letting the millions of stars gaze at her nakedness while she gazed up at theirs. They were the life and light of so many hopes. They bore themselves to all; in return, she would bear all too. She removed her lace underwear but kept her garter on. She never removed that. Ever.

"Ancients, hear my prayer. My mind is yours, free to zink as you zought. My body is naked and pure, free to fight even za darkness of night. Take my soul, uncovered and untainted, free to bind. Never let us forget zat you give za air we breaze; never let it grow stale. Never let us forget zat you drench us in za flames of Freyr and Lugh to keep us warm, even when zings seem cold. Never let us forget zat you make solid za water, which helps us stand. Never let us forget zat you feed us, spiritually and physically, wiz your words and grains zat you give us."

The first part was always recited, adopted from the First Prayers even before the Great War. Gracie's expected students to memorize it. Sonetta said this is where power came from—as well as how the founder of the academy, Grace, had been able to overcome her abusive husband, Gazo—the man who had led Pelop Swander to victory over Empor Rydel. Gabrielle thought long and hard about the next part; this was her chance to make her own prayer.

"Ancients, let my charm work as mysteriously as you do. Ancients, let me maintain my streak tomorrow. Ancients, no matter who I face, please let me win. Ancients, to zis, I pray."

CHAPTER 35

THE FIRST ROUND

It was still an hour before supper and even longer until the trial. Eirek wished it would just finish already. He had tried his hand at sparring harder opponents the night before in the habitat arena, but he did not last very long with them. Tonight the only thing Eirek wished for was to put up a mediocre fight. He didn't want to look completely inept in front of Guardian Eska. As he looked from where he sat on his bed to Cadmar sitting on his chair, he sighed.

"What be the matter?"

"I wish this trial was over already. I already know I'm going to lose."

"Everyone has their own strength, Eirek."

"And mine is not sword fighting."

"Mine not be partnership, but somehow I managed to get a point. . . . What I be trying to say be don't count yourself out. . . . Maybe lady luck will be on your side as well."

"I don't believe in luck . . . not for fighting anyways."

"Well, Gabrielle seems to."

"What do you mean?"

"Gabrielle didn't visit you to wish you luck?"

Eirek shook his head. "When?"

"Last night. She forced her way into my room and kissed me and wished me luck. It be odd."

That is odd. Why didn't she talk to me? Is she still mad at me for the second trial? Am I that insignificant?

"She be no elitetess, but she seems nimble," Cadmar continued. "More nimble than they be. In this type of match, that might be all the difference."

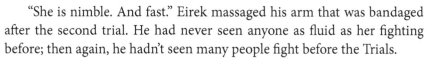

"She is nimble. And fast." Eirek massaged his arm that was bandaged after the second trial. He had never seen anyone as fluid as her fighting before; then again, he hadn't seen many people fight before the Trials.

"We Garians, my aul man 'specially as an elite, were built for endurance, not some single stroke."

"What is an elite even?" Eirek asked.

"An elite be a person in Lady Aprah's armed militia. To be an elite, you be climbing mountains without harnesses, you be running six days of every week, you be spending as much time training as you do sleeping, you be protecting your lady's honor at all costs." Cadmar looked to the window, settling his chin on his forearms.

"What did you have to do to become one?" There was no response. *What is he looking at?* "Cadmar?"

"Sorry. I . . . I be . . . What be the question?"

"What did you have to do to become an elite?"

"The Passage, it be called. The same as my grandfather Caerul Briggs completed."

"What be it?"

"It be a week-long journey to the nation of Sereya. Once there, you need to pass the Dunes of White, go around the major city of Eurardor, and arrive at the capital, Iberene. In Iberene there is a flower with crystal petals and blue nectar. My aul man told me it's been called the lady's flower. You need to pluck one of those, travel all the way back to Gar, and give it to Lady Aprah. It was her mother's favorite flower before she died in the revolt. . . . That be what my grandfather told my aul man, who told me."

Eirek didn't know how long the journey was, but it seemed perilous. "Everyone has to complete that?"

"If they be wanting to serve as an elite for Lady Aprah, they do." Cadmar chuckled.

Eirek's shoulders slunk. He looked over to his blade leaning against his closet door. The blood was long gone from it, and the pain had dissipated from the first trial, but the memories still hadn't. Cain had been such a strong warrior, so had Hydro and Zain. What chance did he have competing against any of them? "I suppose it's almost supper, huh?"

"I think it be." Cadmar stood from the chair and walked over to the door. "You coming?"

"I'll . . . I'll meet you there."

"Take care."

When Cadmar left, Eirek went over to his sword and picked up the amethyst sheath. He withdrew the blade and watched the different hues of grey on the sword mingle with one another. Eirek didn't know how it worked, and he didn't expect Angal to know either, even if it was his blade. His eyes drifted to the pommel—a black ball with two silver rings; it floated above the hilt but was not actually connected. He let his thumb bounce it up and down, feeling the tingle in whatever energy made it stay in place. *Please help me win. Let me be noticed. For once.*

. . .

Supper finished in no time. Compared to the other evenings, there was very little talking. Perhaps because for at least three of the contestants, their continuance in the Trials rested on their performance after dining. Eirek was glad he already had a point, but he did not want to already lose any intrigue he might have gained with Guardian Eska by winning the second trial.

Once in his room, he changed into his tailcoat and threw on loose-fitting, brown linen trousers. He strapped the sword to his belt and walked out of his room. *This is it.*

In the lobby, he took a place next to Cadmar and clasped his hands in front of his body. *Who will I face?* Out of everyone, he did not want Gabrielle or Hydro—those two, he felt, would do their best to show his lack of skills.

Guardian Eska stood in front of his conseleigh and raised his arms. "Contestants, you stand on the cusp of the third trial. Just as you received your partners outside Zas Labyrinth, you will also receive your opponents for the first round of this trial. Eirek, if you will start, it will progress to the right until we reach Gabrielle."

Once Eska finished chanting a foreign-sounding spell, Eirek opened his eyes. In front of Eska was a jeweled holographic box. Seconds later, a green hand waited to enter his mouth to extract his name.

"Eirek Mourse," he half shouted.

Something tugged at the back of his throat. Eirek shut his eyes and cowered, but the flitty sensation persisted. When he opened his eyes again, a green line encoded with his name glided toward the box. *I'll never get used to that.*

When the others finished, Eirek looked toward the box. It started to shake, gently rocking until it exploded into violent spasms and dissipated altogether. A name floated in front of him: Gabrielle Ravwey.

He gulped. Before he could wallow in his predicament, Eska spoke, "Eirek, come and receive a blessing for your weapon."

While he walked forward, he glanced toward Gabrielle. She smirked at him and played with her lipring. *Great . . .*

In front of Eska, Eirek stood still and let him speak in foreign words he couldn't comprehend. When the spell finished, threads of green power weaved a web around his body.

"Hold out any weapons you wish to be protected."

Eirek unsheathed his sword and held it out to Eska. When Eska saw it, his eyes seemed to waiver, but then they refocused, and he chanted another foreign spell. The same type of green web wrapped around the cloudy steel. Once it was finished, Eirek sheathed the sword and stepped back into line.

The conseleigh stepped forward and strolled behind each contestant. Eirek felt a hand scrape his scalp and then a piece of cloth wrap around his head as he was blindfolded. There was a grinding noise as his feet left the familiar surface of the ground. He flailed, caught offguard by the power. Seconds passed, then minutes. Eirek had no idea what was going on. Did any of them?

Soon his feet touched the floor again; blindless was lifted. He looked around, forcing his eyes to make out whatever they could. Flames crackled around a circular room with rows of bleachers. And there, in the center of the bleachers, was a throne made of polished mahogany. Mosaic blue-and-gray tiles, faded and worn from years of use, covered the floor. *Where are we?*

Guardian Eska wasted no time in speaking. Beside him were his conseleigh, and a few rows ahead of him, near a white railing, sat Senator Numos. "Contestants, I will oversee the battles from my position here. Ethen will direct the matches at your ready."

"Contestants, te first match will be between Eirek Mourse and Gabrielle Ravwey. Touch te tips of your blades togeter, take ten paces back, and let te match be underway. If you are not competing yet, please join us in te bleachers."

Eirek stayed in the circular arena, his shoulder slunk as he looked toward Gabrielle, whose face betrayed nothing. He drew his steel and approached her. *Here we go. Everyone here is my equal.* Eirek remembered Angal's words,

hoping to find some sort of confidence in them. *We are equals. I can beat her. I know I can. I can't let Eska see me fail.*

When they touched the tips of their swords together, Gabrielle put her hand on Eirek's shoulder and pulled him close. "Za fairies won't be helping you out zis time," she whispered, then she turned and retreated.

Eirek gulped and walked away, taking time to look at the bleachers. Eska sat forward in his seat, and the conseleigh sat beside him, sans Conseleigh Rorum, who stood, arms behind his back, near the white railing. Once back ten paces, Eirek turned around and noticed Gabrielle bouncing up and down on the balls of her feet.

Is she going to—

He didn't have time to finish his thought, for she lashed out with her rapier. Eirek turned his wrist awkwardly to block the blow. Then he twisted his arm to block another strike, needing to hold his sword with both hands to prevent it from slipping from his clumsy grip.

Although the strikes were fast, they never came in more than a succession of two. In-between her assaults, she would flick the hair out of her eyes and walk around Eirek, always keeping him moving. *She's toying with me.*

Eirek lunged toward her, but she sidestepped and batted the sword away with her own. Even though it was already out of her way, Gabrielle twirled and brought the sword down on Eirek's with ferocity and momentum. The sword clanked to the ground, as Eirek's hands couldn't hold on to it. The blow caused him to lurch forward and stumble to the mosaic floor. He looked to the bleachers; Eska had settled back into his throne, and Hydro chortled by himself.

When he looked back, Gabrielle stood in front of him, sword tip pressed against his chest. She dragged it across him in the form of a circle and a line down to his midsection. Eirek looked on his chest and saw a black mark begin to trace the sword's outline.

"Gabrielle Ravwey, congratulations. You will be advancing to te final round. If you will bot exit, we can begin te next match."

Eirek hung his head low as he heard Gabrielle leave his proximity. Although he didn't expect to win the trial, he wished he could have had a better performance. *What does everyone think of me now?* As he walked to the bleachers, he couldn't look at anyone, even Cadmar. He sat by himself, hoping to avoid the gazes he once sought.

CHAPTER 36

HEATED RIVALRY

That match did not take very long. Mine won't either.

Hydro looked to his opponent, a few rows down from his own spot on the bleachers. The Garian sharpened his silver dual-bladed axe. It looked different than the one he had seen in the labyrinth. That didn't matter though. *Why is the Garian wasting his time sharpening it? We have wards on us. Stupid Garians.* Hydro saw only the crown of his russet hair, for the large heater shield outlined in silver and bronze strapped to his back covered almost all of him. Repoussé in the center of the shield was an eye, fused of lead and antimony.

"Te next match will take place between Prince Hydro Paen and Cadmar Briggs," Conseleigh Rorum announced.

Let us get this match done with. Hydro stood. Dizziness rushed to him. He massaged his head. *I must have stood up too fast.* His senses returned quickly, and he walked down the steps to the arena—the Garian was already on his way to the arena floor. On his way down the bleachers, Hydro looked at the others and noticed his processing was slow. *That is interesting.* He shook his head and continued, hoping his ailment would cease by the time he reached the final match—Gabrielle was too fast for any decrease in his reaction time. She put up a good show for everyone and humiliated the commoner much more than poison would have. He bypassed the commoner, who could only look at the floor.

When on the arena floor, Hydro traversed to the center, wiggling his left hand's fingers through the air, trying to remember the axe's weight from when he held it during the first trial. He was sure it was the same one from before, but the color of the steel did look off.

When he arrived at the center of the floor, he noticed the look of determination in the Garian's eyes. Also, his wardrobe—he had dressed light, wearing nothing more than puffy trousers stuffed into black boots and a shirt, slashed at the sleeves. *One display of intelligence.* With Eska's protection, there was no need for armor, so even Hydro found himself wearing his lightest-fitting silk outfit.

Before him, the Garian slung the giant shield off his back and attached it to his left forearm. Hydro clicked his teeth. Maneuvering around the shield would prove difficult.

"Contestants, tap your weapons and retreat ten paces. Good luck."

Hydro unsheathed his sword. Until later, he would keep it as is. He swaggered toward the Garian, even though the man towered over him by more than a foot.

"Do you remember your saying, Caffler?"

"Yes." *Fear not what blade can slice or magic can touch.*

"Are you afraid?"

"No."

"You should be."

"And why is that?"

"Sword cannot slice through me. Power cannot touch me." The Garian chortled.

Hydro grunted and clicked his tongue. With Eska's protection, he was an equal to Hydro—everyone was. *No, no they aren't.* No one was his equal. The Garian may fight for his family's honor, but he was not the same as Hydro. The Garian had no duties to uphold; he did not have a whole nation relying on him to win or a goddess who had put her stock into him with a blessing.

"I may not be able to slice through you. But I will break you."

"Mountains never break." The Garian furrowed his brows and straightened his lips.

"Everything crumbles, in time," Hydro retorted. The words seemed slow to him. Hydro looked toward the Garian's eyes and noticed a slight glaze to them, not their usual russet color.

"But when mountains crumble, the men climbing them do as well."

Hydro sneered and retreated. He bounced on the balls of his feet, hoping that if he kept active he wouldn't feel as slow. The loose grip he held with his metal hilt tightened as the attacks began. Shock vibrations radiated through his hands as he parried the Garian's heavy swings. He held his sword tightly to repel the blows. Even though the Garian wasn't faster than him, Hydro still had trouble maneuvering around him due to his size. When he did try, either the shield or axe blocked his route, and he was redirected in front of the giant. *Normally this would not be difficult. Why am I slow?* Hydro wasn't sure if the Garian seemed slower than what he had seen during the first trial or not. He was inherently going to be slower due to his size, but Hydro couldn't help but notice altered movements in his attacks.

Hydro blinked and noticed the Garian raise his shield and pound it with his axe. After letting him have a few moments of glory, Hydro retreated. *This isn't working. How am I to strike him when his entire body is defended with that shield?* He didn't have more time to think, for the giant thundered over to him. He brought his axe down, swung his shield like a backfist, and then brought the axe upwards. Hydro could recognize each strike well enough, but reacting to them was different. Normally he would not need to parry them, preferring to avoid them altogether, but he was not fast enough for that tactic. And afterwards, the Garian kept with him, as if the seventy pounds of steel combined in both hands was like just three pounds to someone of Hydro's stature.

"Are you getting tired yet, Caffler?"

"Tired of you." Hydro slashed and retreated once more. *How much endurance does the man have?* If Hydro wanted to best the Garian, he needed to think quickly.

"Are you breaking yet, Caffler?" the Garian mocked through swings of his axe.

It didn't affect him though. The more the Garian talked, the less focused he was. *Perhaps it's time to change weapons.* Hydro smirked; he would use the same tactic he had used on Zain to throw the giant off balance. First, though, he needed to push him back—and that meant starting an offensive.

Lunging and slashing, never slowing his pace, he used his momentum to counteract the giant's fierce swings and blocks. One step, two steps. Soon the wall behind the Garian was approaching. Hydro kept dancing on the tiled floor, displaying agility like a spider sliding on water. *Just a little closer now.* The Garian swung overhead, and Hydro managed to block with both hands on his sword. While his sword struggled with the axe in a stalemate, the Garian pushed forward with his shield. *No!* He couldn't get away. The axe held him in place. Hydro needed another option. *I didn't want to do it this early.*

Seeing no other choice, Hydro tilted his opponent's axe and focused on changing his sword to a lance. The weapon extended downward in length and blocking the incoming shield.

The Garian stepped back. "Zircha steel. Interesting. Me too."

Hydro's eyes widened as the axe in the Garian's hand also switched to a lance. The Garian jabbed at him, and Hydro batted it away. *How does he have one?* He thought the axe looked different. *This may be more difficult now.* He glanced toward the bleachers; although his eyes saw everyone on their feet, his mind did not process their excitement.

Hydro sneered. His movements needed to count. The lance was his worst weapon. He jabbed for three counts, switched to his sword, and swung for another few. The Garian switched with him to an axe. *At least the Garian is slower too.* Hydro was sure of his opponent's condition now. If the Garian was of normal speed, the fight would be finished now because of how fast zircha steel could change. But if Hydro was managing to stay with him, then it was obvious he was affected by the same spell. *Was it something I ate?*

Hydro readjusted his grip and swung over the top, stealing only air. The Garian swung toward Hydro's midsection, but Hydro blocked it by switching back to his lance. He shoved with his shoulders, managing to push the giant back a few steps. *That's all I need.* Hydro then started a steady succession of strikes, as if paddling a canoe.

Push him back a little more. Hydro swung faster. *Yes, there he is.* Once the Garian was in position, he changed his lance into a large heater shield and swung upwards using the continuing momentum. The Garian moved forward with his shield.

Boom.

The tactic worked horribly. Even with his momentum, the giant's size and the steel's thickness dominated Hydro's shield, pushing him to the ground. Now on his back, Hydro watched as the Garian snickered and brought his axe overhead. It came down. Closer. And closer. Hydro pushed his shield up with his shoulders, sending the axe back slightly. The Garian then lowered himself to one knee and dropped his shield to the floor. Hydro rolled, avoiding the massive steel, which rang against tile. *This is it.* Hydro switched shield to lance, and as he crunched his abdomen, he swung toward the Garian's exposed body, hitting his right side. A black streak soon formed.

Upon seeing the mark, Hydro collapsed. *That was too close.* In and out, his stomach heaved. The Garian fought well—however little Hydro liked to admit it.

Hydro turned his lance back into a sword and sheathed it, all the while lying on the ground. He blinked and turned his head toward the bleachers. The commoner tilted his head and looked towards Guardian Eska. He noticed Guardian Eska rise and start to clap his hands. The others soon followed. Hydro smiled. *If Mother could see me now.*

Hydro stood and looked at the Garian, who met him with a venomous stare. "Good match . . . Cadmar." Hydro extended his hand. It stayed unaccepted in the air for a few seconds before finally being eclipsed by a rough, massive hand.

"Aye . . . that it be." The giant walked away.

Hydro felt too nice. His name wasn't *Cadmar,* it was *the Garian.* Scratching his irritation, he continued. "Gari . . . an," Hydro panted, still tired from the match. "You lasted longer . . . than . . . I expected."

The Garian snorted and steered away.

"Prince Paen, congratulations," Conseleigh Rorum paused, "you have earned a spot wit Gabrielle in te final match."

Hydro looked at Gabrielle, who only smirked. *She is dangerous.*

"Zain Berrese and Prince Cain Evber, your match will begin now. Please make your way to te arena."

Hydro returned to the bleachers and sat a row behind Gabrielle. The next match didn't concern him; he had beaten both of them before. What concerned Hydro was the slowing of his senses and the woman who sat in front of him: Gabrielle.

❧CHAPTER 37❧

A PRINCE'S BANE

"Contestants, touch your weapons and retreat ten paces."

Zain itched for the opportunity, despite what his body said. To help hide his exhaustion, he twisted his body and stretched his arms, subtly yawning into the crimson long-sleeved undershirt of his Gazo's uniform. Over that shirt was a black vest with gold buttons and a knife holder on the chest pocket.

Unlike other times, he was exhausted. His eyes weren't watery; there was no water left in them after he broke down early in his sparring session. Zakk had been there. At least, he thought Zakk was. The voice seemed real enough. The steel dragging along his shoulders felt real enough. But it wasn't real. How could it be?

He must have laid in the dark for an hour in silence and recluse before trying to practice again. His mom wasn't there to help him through it like she had been for Ava. No one was.

When dawn's breath had touched the court, Zain went inside to start training in the habitat arenas, trying to test for each environment. Others had come in, though, and kicked him out, but he still managed to get five hours of training in. At that point, after refueling his body with a quick lunch, he went outside and practiced wherever he could find lingering shadows from the estate.

As the tips of their swords touched, Zain looked toward Hydro, hoping to get his attention. The prince was in conversation with Gabrielle. *What are they talking about?*

"You will not be joining them next round."

Zain refocused on Cain. "I have unfinished business with the prince—"

216

"That makes two of us."

"And with Gabrielle."

"What business do you have with her?"

"You won't be joining next round; don't worry," Zain said.

Zain stepped back, tapped the tip of his sword to his shoe, and studied his opponent, who wore a flowing, golden, silk undershirt with a black wool vest. An owl perched on a tree branch in the colors of purple and grey displayed his family's sigil.

Upon his first approach, Zain tested the prince's reaction time. Lunge. Slash. Pierce. Cain blocked each by teetering the sides of his double-bladed halberd. *Decent.* Zain expected no less. The steel song died soon enough; they circled each other once again. Zain shuffled to his left, always keeping his chest up and his eyes on Cain. His sword would be able to swing faster than his halberd due to the kayak-like grip the weapon required. His sword was just as long too. But Cain's height and lengthy arms gave him an advantage when it came to shuffling forward or back and lunging. It was something Zain would need to keep conscious of.

Slash. Swing. Strike. Lunge. On the tile he was as graceful as a dancer onstage. Zain kept an offensive going as much as possible, wanting to throw the prince's balance off kilter and to stave his exhaustion. He blocked when needed, but as his combinations became more elaborate, he noticed the prince's blocks and movements wavering. It wasn't likely that he was exhausted already. *Is he tricking me?*

Despite his fluidity, Zain still had difficulty breaching Cain's defenses. Because of the grip, the halberd could block faster than the longsword. He needed to switch tactics. Zain lunged and swung and ducked underneath a swipe. *Perhaps if I switch postures.* It was a subtle movement; not many people ever caught it. He had used it to win three of his five tournaments for Gazo's. Here it would be helpful because it could counteract the reach advantage Cain had.

Zain charged forward. Lunge. Slash. Strike. He switched his feet, now leading with the left. Lunge. Slash. Shuffle backwards. Cain managed a solid defense of all the attacks, using each side of his halberd fluidly. But he didn't catch the switch. That, Zain was sure of, for the prince still held his feet in the same position.

I need you to swing at me horizontally. Zain bounced light on his heels. With his left leg in front, and holding his sword with his left hand, he could reach farther. The extra inches would possibly be enough to tap Cain. At least Zain hoped.

Zain saw fury in Cain's eyes. *Does Cain know something is wrong with him?* Zain wished he knew why the prince seemed lethargic. Cain swung horizontally as if to slice Zain in two. *My chance.* Zain ducked underneath and swung at the prince's midsection. Cain jumped backwards. Did it hit him? Seconds passed. A black streak clouded the prince's silk-and-wool attire. The fighting halted.

"Excellent display, bot of you. I am sorry, Prince Evber, but you will not be advancing. Zain Berrese, congratulations—you 'ave earned your spot in te finals."

When Conseleigh Rorum finished, Zain looked at the prince. His glare could kill, but he extended a hand anyways. Probably out of duty, not out of want.

"Congratulations." Cain nearly spat out the words.

"Are you okay?"

"I do not make excuses for losing."

Zain looked at him, held high by honor and pride. Cain pulled him closer, then whispered upon his ear, "Do not lose to Prince Paen."

"The prince will fall."

"Good." Cain pushed a button on his halberd, and it shrunk into a baton.

"Te next match will begin in fifteen minutes. Take tis time to rest. Cain, you may return to your seat. Zain, you may as well, or you can stay out tere too. Te choice is yours."

Zain stretched his legs and loosened his back, both of which were sore from exhaustion. He sat on the floor and looked toward Gabrielle. The exchange of dialogue with the prince had stopped. She stretched her wrists, and Hydro massaged his head. *Was he suffering the same as Cain?* His gaze wandered to Guardian Eska, who sat relaxed in his throne. Zain could feel Eska's eyes on him. When Zain glanced back, Eska turned his gaze on Gabrielle, Hydro, and then to his conseleigh. *What is he observing?*

Stretching more, Zain let his eyes rest. Memories flooded back to him— studies at Gazo's, lessons from past tournaments, anything that might give him an advantage. Gabrielle used a rapier, light and quick; if landing the first strike meant a win, she would have the advantage. Zircha steel was, as well, a lighter metal. That left Zain with the heaviest weapon, but also the weapon with the longest reach—so long as Hydro didn't shift to a lance.

Fifteen minutes later, the others made their way to the middle of the arena. Zain had finished his stretches and now looked between Gabrielle and Hydro. Unlike usual, Hydro did not seem his arrogant self, for even he had yet to smirk or try to belittle them. Zain looked at Gabrielle, who smiled back at him and flipped her hair. *Was that her doing?* Did she do it out of fear? Or so that they could settle the debate of their schools without worry?

Conseleigh Rorum spoke, "Te tree of you will form a triangle, touch tips wit each oter, and retreat ten paces. Tis battle will be a melee where te last one without a black streak is declared te winner. Good luck, all of you. You may begin."

Zain's sword was already unsheathed. He found his grip again and flashed Gabrielle a glance. She tucked her long bangs back behind her ears. Zain inched forward and touched tips with the other contestants, then retreated ten paces. Hydro eyed both of them. Zain looked toward Gabrielle, and she, too, looked back and forth.

"Gabrielle," Zain said. "Keep out of this."

Gabrielle raised her thin eyebrows but backed away, keeping her sword at the ready.

"You want to lose again?" Hydro snickered.

"Losing isn't an option."

Zain ran toward Hydro. Clanging swords echoed repeals of one another. During that time, Zain focused more on the weapon than Hydro's stance. If the steel were to change, he needed to react. Despite the prince's arrogance, he was good—much better than Zain expected. But, like Cain, his movements seemed off and slow. *What happened to everyone?*

It was surprising Hydro and Cain still managed to block as well as they did. When Hydro tried to lead an offensive barrage though, Zain easily batted away each of the strikes, always keeping his eye on the steel. Strike. Pivot. Lunge. Steel changed to a lance. Zain batted the lance away and then ducked as it went over top of him. Zain shuffled back. *That was too close.* There wasn't a good enough opening to hit Hydro yet. He looked at Gabrielle, who shuffled with them, bouncing on her feet all the while.

Directing his attention back to Hydro, Zain said, "Do I represent my academy now, Prince?"

Hydro didn't answer.

Blades hush nobility, nothing else. Even princes fall humble to the blade. Zain lurched forward, swinging upwards. While Hydro swung with his lance, it changed to a shield. Zain's eyes widened. The collision broke his grip. Even for a lighter metal, the shield held well. Zain watched the sword fall from his hand, and another smirk appeared on Hydro's face. Hydro changed the shield to a sword and swung down. Zain rolled out of the way, managing to grab his sword. He turned around to see Hydro on the ground.

What happened?

Behind him Gabrielle stood with the rapier in her hand. Zain looked toward Hydro—a black streak scoured his midsection. Zain's face hardened. She had saved him, yes; but he wanted to be the one to best Hydro.

"Prince Paen, I am sorry tat you have lost, but if you please, gater your sword and retreat to te bleachers, so as not to disturb the oter contestants."

Hydro sheathed his weapon. On his way out, he paused next to Zain. "Royalty does not need help fighting. You will never fight like me." Hydro glared from him to Gabrielle but said no more.

"You are not letting zis opportunity escape us, Zain."

"I was fine."

"You're tired. And sloppy. I hate to challenge you like zis, but Gracie's must know zat zey are za better school." Gabrielle moved toward him.

Zain shuffled back. "Gazo Sabore is who taught you ladies to fight."

"No. He gave us a purpose to fight. Supplication and practicing in solitude is how we learned to fight."

"Humph." Zain held his sword in front of him, keeping her a safe distance away. "Then I hope Gracie's Academy has taught you well."

"As I hope yours has."

"Whatever the outcome, it's an honor." He twirled his blade and lashed out, which was parried in haste.

"It is. . . . Whatever za outcome."

Gabrielle advanced two paces. Too close for Zain's taste. After blocking a few blows, he stepped back, creating space. *She's faster on her feet. Her sword is lighter. I'll need to keep her at bay.* Maintaining a slight bend in his arms, he extended his sword again.

A furious and steady succession of strikes and blocks followed each other's movements back and forth on the lobby floor. Lunge. Block. Swing. Parry. Slash. Duck. Zain fought for control of the battle, but Gabrielle forced him to block just as much as he attacked. Never did he blink, needing to focus on suggestions in her body movements of future attacks. When he saw her crouch, he shuffled back, knowing she would lunge. When he saw a twist in her shoulders, he blocked overhead. Constantly Zain kept aware of his feet and hand positions—for any mistake would cause him to fail.

She had been trained to exploit any flaws. He had been trained to cover his weaknesses—and that he would do.

Continuous movement and bobbing of his heels kept him from getting cornered. Although the rapier was fragile, it wouldn't break, no matter how hard he batted it. Eska's blessing prevented that. *However, maybe I can knock it out of her hand.* Compared to his grip, it wasn't as strong.

He commenced a steady barrage of swings, staying out of the blade's radius. Soon Gabrielle appeared overwhelmed. Twisting his back and bending his knees, he jumped and unwound his body. Using his momentum, he spun and swung at Gabrielle. She barely managed to put up her sword, but the force ripped it out of her hand like a tornado would pluck houses from the ground. Not halting his momentum, he continued into another spin. His midsection rustled. He lurched again toward her and connected blade to body, propelling her to the ground. A black streak appeared seconds later.

I won; I actually won. He extended his sword in the air, triumphant, and looked down at her body. Her gloved hand gripped her dagger.

Zain's eyes bulged. He lowered his sword, patting down his belly. A streak had formed on the black vest of his academy uniform. He looked back toward her. She smirked. Had he won?

He looked toward Eska, who had left his throne and walked down the steps to stand near the railing. The guardian engaged in deep conversation with the tanner, conical-bearded man. *The answer. What is the answer?* Every person in the room looked to them for some sort of conclusion.

"Dynamic finish. I 'ave not seen tis close of a sword match in all my years on Chaon. It is my overwhelming pleasure to extend my congratulations to our newest winner . . ."

Conseleigh Rorum paused. The minute seemed like eternity. Had he won?

"Gabrielle Ravwey."

Zain buckled to his knees. His sword clanged in defeat. The dagger. He forgot about the dagger. How could he have forgotten when it played such a crucial role in her victories?

His eyes watered. His vision blurred. He pounded the floor. He looked up. In the shadowed section of the wall, slightly to the left of where Eska stood, a familiar smirk slid against a dark face. *Zakk!* He wiped the tears out of his eyes. The man had vanished. *Am I going crazy?*

A hand, nails painted in cherry, came into view. He looked up to see Gabrielle's smile.

"A good match."

After Zain wiped the wet remnants from his cheek and sniffled he took the hand and pulled himself up. "It . . . it was a pleasure. Gracie's Academy has taught you well. I can see why you have never lost a tournament." It was so hard keeping his head up.

"Gabrielle, you have won and will advance with Cadmar, Prince Paen, and Eirek to the fourth trial. Zain and Prince Evber, I am deeply honored you have attended my trials, but neither of you will compete directly in the fourth trial, although you may remain here until they are finished. As for the rest of you, take this opportunity to slumber; instructions will come on the morrow. Line up and we will replace the blindfolds on you and lead you out," said Guardian Eska.

Zain's hand slid over his steel, stopping at each jewel. Before the blindfold eclipsed his sight, Zain sheathed his sword and slung the scabbard over his back.

⚚CHAPTER 38⚚

MOTIVATIONS

The night sky was purple with stars of copper and gold. Some shined brighter than others, but most were dim and uneventful. *My star is probably dim. I've achieved nothing great but embarrassment.* The sword being ripped from his hand, him falling to the floor chasing it, and the laughter he saw Hydro display afterwards reeled in Eirek's mind. *Maybe if I found my star, I could wish to be skilled with weapons.* Until that day, Eirek would need to reserve himself to practicing.

"Don't be too down on yourself . . . at least you have a point. That be one more than Cain or Zain. You still be in this."

Eirek looked toward Cadmar. He had followed Eirek back into his room after the trial. He meant good, but words were only words. Although the next letter wouldn't come out for a little while, Eirek was sure that the next trial would be difficult. It needed to be to separate the last of the contestants.

Eirek sighed.

"And be thinkin' of it this way: You lost to the champion. You be not losing to some slimy, watery caffler."

Eirek chuckled at how much Cadmar hated losing to Hydro. "Thanks, Cadmar. I'm sorry you lost to Hydro."

"That fight be odd anyways."

Eirek dismissed the stars for a little and looked at Cadmar, eyebrows raised. "What do you mean?"

"I felt . . . slower than usual. When I moved my head, it took . . . it took my mind a second to catch what I be seeing. . . . It be odd."

"I . . . I thought you looked slower. Something felt off."

"I tried being aggressive, hoping it be temporary . . . but I was slow. . . . The caffler be too. Otherwise I be never able to last against zircha steel that long."

"I never experienced any of that. . . . Just humiliation. . . ."

There was a silence then. Cadmar seemed to be staring off at his dresser.

"Cadmar, what . . . what if it was Gabrielle?"

"How could it be?"

"Well, I ate the same as you that night. It couldn't have been the food. Gabrielle saw you though; she didn't even talk to me."

Cadmar's head perked up. "That catty vixen . . ." Cadmar stood up.

Eirek stood up too. "Where you going?"

"She sabotaged us with that kiss. . . . That hoor's melt!"

Eirek bolted around Cadmar to stand in front of his door. "Wait . . . what? She kissed you? And what's a hoor's melt?"

"The kiss be for luck, she told me. Get out my way."

"Let it go. If Hydro didn't get dismissed for fracturing Zain's hand, I doubt she will get dismissed."

Cadmar's rigid shoulders relaxed, and he backed off into his chair. "You be right. . . ."

That was close. "What is a hoor's melt?"

"Offspring of a hoor." Cadmar straightened his posture and crossed his arms.

"Why do you think Hydro was involved?"

"Who be knowing anything a hoor's melt does besides splitting both sets of her lips?"

Eirek sighed and slunk his shoulders even more. Did anyone find him important? The Mourses did. Angal did—at times anyways. But they were all a planet away, and it was Guardian Eska here he needed to impress, not them. And after him, the families in power, who would vote on his apprenticeship. *How do I impress them all?*

When he tired of looking for Agrost, he returned his gaze back to Cadmar. "So what do you think the fourth trial will be?"

CHAPTER 39

THE LAST CRIMSON ENVELOPE

Two days after the conclusion of the third trial, Hydro sat on his bed thinking of Gabrielle and listening to the sound of his cracking knuckles. *That bitch will pay.* A single knuckle popped.

Perhaps I should have listened to that monster in the labyrinth. "Beware of the girl with black hair." Rather vague, Hydro thought, but who else could he have been talking about? The man had incapacitated Gabrielle; had he been able to see into her soul?

Hydro looked to his dresser. *Maybe she knows something about the necklace. Something I don't.* He moved over to the bureau, pulled open the drawer, and removed the layers of clothing until he found it.

You should have worn me. You would have won then.

Hydro grabbed the shirt it sat on and wrapped it like a makeshift present to avoid the biting. He stuffed it in his pocket, not caring how awkward the bulge looked. He had no time for its mental jousts now. He had been listening to them enough for the past two days, ever since losing the trial.

Hydro soon found himself traveling to the other side of the estate. Once he arrived at Gabrielle's door, he knocked. The moment she answered, her smile turned to a thin line. Hydro barged in and slammed the door behind him.

Gabrielle pulled a dagger from the garter that hid beneath her black skirt that extended to her knees. Hydro caught her forearm before it reached his neck. With his other hand, he grabbed her left arm and locked it behind her back. A necklace of alexandrites hung loosely around her neck, and she smelt of myrrh.

"What do you want?" She struggled against his grip.

"To talk."

"Zen talk."

Hydro released his hold. Cautiously he eyed her, making sure she wouldn't retaliate. She wore a long-sleeved, low-cut, silver shirt. He put his hand in his pocket and took out a white shirt that he usually wore underneath his tunics. Like a platter, he held it out in one hand and removed the folds of cloth with his other. When the necklace was revealed, he looked at her eyes. They widened, but it wasn't the reaction he had expected. *The bitch can act; her eyes give nothing. She knows. She must know.* "What do you know about this?"

She leaned in close, tucking a loose strand of hair behind her ear.

"Do not touch."

She stopped and glared up at him. "Nozing. Should I?"

"You are lying."

"Where is zat from?"

"The labyrinth." Hydro kept making sure it was out of range of her grasp. "Is it calling to you?"

Gabrielle's jaw dropped slightly. Then she closed it. "How did you know?"

She's seen enough. He wrapped up the necklace and pulled it away from her. "What is it saying?"

"Nozing . . . nozing at all."

"You lie."

"It is nozing zat concerns you, Prince."

Bitch. "So you know nothing about the necklace?" He stuffed the necklace in his pants pocket again.

"Nozing." She crossed her arms. "What makes you zink I do?" She raised her eyebrow.

"Nothing. Goodbye."

Was it her? What other girl could it be? There were bound to be millions of females with black hair in the whole of Gladonus, and he was to be weary of one. Did she even have anything to do with the necklace? *The monster told me about her; the necklace never mentioned anything about a girl with black hair. Perhaps I have been searching for the wrong information.* . . . He had been researching in books related to Epoch and found references to the necklace, but never any information concerning it. *Perhaps I should search people in connection with the necklace. Maybe this black-haired girl will be there.*

As he entered the lobby and approached the staircase, Colin, the senile, hunched servant, attracted his eye. Or, rather, what the butler carried—one crimson envelope. *The next trial.*

He maneuvered past the old man without even a gesture of acknowledgement and went to his room. Sure enough, their wing had already received letters signifying what the last trial would include. He took the envelope off his door and rushed into his room, closing himself off from the rest of the estate.

Dear Contestants,

If you have received this letter, then that means you have advanced to the fourth trial. The previous trials have tested your partnership skills, your intelligence, and your ability in fighting with blade alone. Each trial has been difficult in its own way.

If you have noticed the absence of my youngest conseleigh, Riagan Inferno, it is because he has left to put things in order. More information will be given at tonight's dinner, as I speak on his behalf while preparations finish. Dinner will be at seven. I hope to see all of you there.

Sincerely,
Guardian Edwyrd Eska

Hydro stood in front of the mirror attached to his dresser. *Rather vague. I wonder what this trial tests?* Hydro set the letter down and pulled out the shirt his necklace was wrapped in. He laid it out next to the letter.

This trial will demand great strength, Hydro Paen. I can give you that.

I do not need your help.

Do you ever wonder why it is you won the first trial and have lost both since?

I did not need to wear you to win the first trial.

You had me with you though.

Well, then, I will simply have you again, Hydro rebutted the necklaces argument.

You will need more strength than that. You will need the strength I can

provide by wearing me.

How do you know?

Do you think Eska would make a last trial easy?

Hydro broke the stare with the necklace by turning around. The tactic didn't work.

This is your last chance to make your family proud. To make Acquava proud.

His ears perked. He looked back at the necklace, at the equilateral triangle in the middle of the pendant. *What power will you give me?*

Power Pearl could only imagine blessing you with. Power that will make you win, like it did the first trial. Power that will not fail you.

Will you hurt me if I wear you?

There is always pain before pleasure. But you will grow used to it in time.

The voice was enthralling. He slid his fingers around the equilateral triangle; it felt like obsidian with gold bands. The scales were larger than his thumbs, but they were polished and perfect. There was power to them—that Hydro could feel.

He looked below his blue tunic to the golden-chained necklace that dangled his sapphire ring—a ring only given to the heirs of the Acquavan throne. *I do not want to take it off.*

You do not need to. But what has it given you so far but strife and duty? It has never won you anything besides your mother's scorn and your father's expectations.

But it's who I am.

Wear me, and I can show you who you can be.

Hydro looked back to the necklace on the dresser and slid his hands over the scales. He unlatched the back of it and turned it around. As it approached his neck, he could see the scales gravitate toward his flesh.

Do not be afraid. I will show you truth and give you power.

Hydro latched the necklace behind his neck and let the scales touch his skin. The pendant felt warm. For a second, nothing. Then Hydro yelled as his flesh was bitten into by the necklace. He collapsed to the floor, tightened his neck, and closed his eyes—doing anything he could to get through the pain. *Pleasure will come. Pleasure will come.*

His head throbbed. His vision became blurry. But when his senses returned after a minute's time, he stood and looked at himself in the mirror. The hair on his body prickled, and his senses were heightened. His vision seemed clearer, more focused. There was energy flowing through his veins, the likes of which he had never felt. He felt swift, powerful, and hungry. It was adrenaline, and natural to him, as if he were a shark prowling through the ocean.

This is just a taste of what my necklace offers, Hydro Paen. Do you not already feel the power course through your veins?

When will I receive all of it?

Someday. . . . When you are free of the man you are and know and embrace the truth of the man you may become.

🕷 CHAPTER 40 🕷

AMENDS

Zain didn't know how long he lay on his bed. It had been two days since the conclusion of the third trial. He thought that there couldn't be any more tears to cry, but he was wrong. Although they had tapered off, they came in the form of amends he would never get to make, of people he would never get to see again, and of reputations he failed to uphold. *Why did I ever choose to compete? Are these scars going to form for nothing?* Zain inspected the deep wounds on his hands.

A knock came to his door, prohibiting him to inspect further. "Who is it?"

"Gabrielle. May I come in?"

What does she want? "Just a second." Zain went over to his mirror and wiped his hands over his cheeks, trying to mask any wetness that may have accumulated. Since the last trial, he had refused to wear a Gazo's uniform, knowing that he didn't deserve to wear it. Instead he wore training shirts with the sleeves cut off at the shoulder. His eyes were red, but there was not much he could do about that. *What does it matter? I have no one left to impress here. . . .*

He turned around and opened up the door for her. From her blue eyes to her ebony lip ring to the necklace of alexandrites that hung loosely around her neck, his gaze drifted lower until he noticed she held a crimson envelope in her hand. "Is that . . ?"

She raised her hand and nodded. "Za details for za last trial just came."

"Why does that matter for me? You won the last trial, remember?"

"I do. . . ." Gabrielle bit her nails and then looked back to Zain. "And zat's why I'm here. I . . . I wanted to say zank you for a good match."

"Gracie's will be proud. . . ." Zain turned his head away and looked far off into the mirror on his dresser. His eyes were sullen from lack of sleep.

"Zey will be. I'm sorry zat we didn't face each ozer under proper circumstances. . . ."

"What do you mean?"

"Your hand. I know it must have been difficult to adjust after what zat prince did . . . but listen. . . . Zain, I don't zink za ozers know zat you are za reason zis fourz trial is even happening."

"What do you mean?" he asked again.

"You and Cain slowing down Hydro in za second trial, just enough to let zat Eirek win. Without eizer of you, Hydro would be ahead."

Zain smiled in the recognition but remained silent. He didn't know what to say.

"You haven't realized all zat you've done, but you have done a lot. For everyone. It's hard not being in za last trial, but . . . I . . . I just want you to know zat . . ."

A slight sensation came to his cheek. Myrrh invaded his nostrils. He looked back to her as she shrunk from her toetips. She smiled, a hint of blush in her cheeks. Then she left before Zain could say anything. He wanted to chase her, but a faint beeping emanated from his nightstand. *Who's calling?* He closed his door and proceeded to retain his position on his bed. He reached over for the watch and checked the identity of his incoming call. Mom. Zain accepted the call. "Mom? Why are you calling?"

"Zain . . . oh . . . oh, I had to. It's been too long since I've talked to you, and Jamaal told me everything that's happened with Zakk."

Zain's neck tightened. "What did he say?" Zain gulped.

"I'm . . . I'm sorry about Zakk. . . .He was a good kid . . . with good intentions. I know you two were close."

Zain did his best to hold back his tears. Still, he felt a wetness come to his eyes that he plugged with his thumb. *What about my intentions? They were good too. They were. . . .* "It's . . . it's fine. I . . . I've learned to accept it. . . . It's . . . hard not to think about it, you know?"

"I do, Zain. I do. I think about your father every day. Still nothing since the last letter . . . not even a call."

Zain shook his head. Another thing wrong in his life. "I wish everything would just be back to normal again."

"It will be, Zain. Soon enough. . . . How are the Trials going?"

Zain shook his head.

His mom nodded. After a brief silence, she said, "Listen, Zain?"

A beep and a flash blinked in front of his mom's face. He had another incoming call. From Jamaal. *What does he want?* "Mom, Jamaal is calling. I'll need to put you on hold. . . . "

"I'll be here when you get done. . . ."

Zain pushed the crown of his telecommunicator twice to switch the call to his brother. "Jamaal?"

"Zain, I'm glad I caught you. How is everything going?"

Zain shook his head. "I lost another trial. . . . I am not competing in the fourth trial."

"What kind of trial was it?"

"A weapons tournament . . . the one thing Gazo's trained me to do. Gracie's beat me. I let down our school . . . Instructor Barrata . . . Zakk . . ."

"Listen, Zain, about that—"

"I . . . I'm talking to Mom now. You told her about him?"

"Nothing that you and I discussed while I was there. Listen, Zain—"

"I still feel him. . . . I thought I saw him while I trained . . . just like I thought I saw him during the second trial. Why can't this guilt—"

"Zain! Zakk may still be alive."

Zain shook his head, trying to sort out what he just heard. "What?"

"Zakk may still be alive. After I left the Core, I let Gazo's know where you said they would be able to find him . . . so that they could make proper arrangements for a funeral if need be. . . . The search team couldn't find a body."

"They checked all of Lake Kilmer?"

"They looked underwater best they could with a diving team. But there was nothing. They checked a mile radius around the lake. . . . Nothing."

How is that possible? Zain's brain couldn't process thoughts. He stared forward, past the hologram of his brother, to his closet, completely dumbfounded. "I . . . I . . . Are you sure?"

"No . . . not at all. But I . . . thought you may like the news."

Zain was too confounded to process his brother's words. "I . . . Mom is on the other line. I need to go."

"Bye, Little Bear. Good luck in the remaining trials, if there are any. . . ."

He didn't bother telling Jamaal that the Trials were over for him. He let the call fade away, and after a little while, his telecommunicator automatically switched back to his mom.

"Zain . . ."

Zain tilted his head back up to look at her miniature hologram. "Yeah, Mom?"

"Are you okay? What did Jamaal have to say?"

"I . . . He . . . he just called to wish me luck."

"Are you okay? You seem distant."

"It's nothing. . . ." He shook his head. "What did you want to tell me?"

"If you want to move back home once you return . . . if staying in that apartment by yourself is too hard. . . . There's always room for you here."

Zain smiled. "I will, thank you."

"Bye, Zain."

"Bye, Mom."

The connection ended, and Zain slunk into his bed as much as possible. *Is Zakk alive? Could he be here on the Core? That's impossible. He missed the transport. He can't be here.* Zain remembered the hot, raspy voice on his ear. He could feel the steel drag up his arm. And over his shoulders. His hair rising. He looked at his hands, at the wounds of deep red. A feeling crept over them then—not a phantom feeling, but a real one. One so very real that it brought a tear to Zain's eye that he failed to stop.

❧CHAPTER 41❧

QUESTIONS

Eirek sat in the dining hall next to Cadmar. Zain had yet to show. Just hours before, the last letter had been delivered, and Eirek found himself pacing his room and constantly checking the silver sky as it faded into a dark purple.

There had been no allusion to what this next trial would be. Because of that, ideas and possibilities ran through his mind. Some he expressed to Cadmar when he came in for a little talk immediately after receiving the letter, the others he kept in his mind. *Could it be to climb Mount Klaff?* Eirek had never climbed before; if it was that, he would surely lose. *What if it is a battle of power?* He would fail that too. At one point, the futility of possible outcomes overwhelmed him so much that he stopped thinking about it.

The too-large blue tunic that Eirek found himself wearing allowed him to hide amongst the others who stood out. Cain and Hydro both donned rich silk in the colors of their house, and Gabrielle dressed for the occasion as well with a silvery long-sleeved shirt and a necklace of alexandrites hanging loosely around her neck. Cadmar wore a sleek, dark-blue shirt that suffocated his body, accentuating his thick chest and his arms corded in muscle. Even though he was no longer in the trials, when Zain sat down next to Eirek, he was dressed in the usual academy uniform of red stitching and black vest with a long-sleeved undershirt.

Guardian Eska stood, claiming the room's attention. "Before we commence with questions, I would like to congratulate Gabrielle Ravwey on winning the third trial. She will join the finalists from the previous trials: Cadmar Briggs, Prince Hydro Paen, and Eirek Mourse. The four of you have

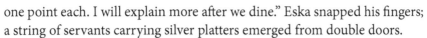

one point each. I will explain more after we dine." Eska snapped his fingers; a string of servants carrying silver platters emerged from double doors.

No more than two feet apart, along the table of more than twenty feet, platters were laid out from Eska to Senator Numos, who wore dove-white silk with a mockingbird sigil sewn below the left lapel. Turkey marinated in honey, smoked ham, grilled steak, tossed and mixed greens, and an assortment of fruits sweetened the air.

Eirek filled his plate and unfolded the scarlet linen shaped like a tower. He picked at the food but after a while set the silverware down on the linen. He wasn't hungry—for food anyways. *What is this last trial?*

In a matter of minutes, the lights dimmed. From Eska's gloved hand, a white light—resembling a flashlight—shot across the room and gathered above the middle of the table, displaying a tall, rotating holographic volcano.

"A few nights ago, after the third trial concluded, I spoke with Riagan. We discussed at length what your final trial should be. He wanted a test of power and your control of it. . . ."

Eirek looked down at his hands. *Great . . . another trial failed.*

"But such a task would be too easy."

Eirek's ears perked and he looked at Eska. The conseleigh shifted in their seats, apparently unaware of what he was about to say.

Eska took a breath. "The fourth trial will be held on Pyre. Riagan is in the nation of Therus at present finishing arrangements with Lord Requart. The trial will take place two days from now, but we will leave for Pyre tomorrow after lunch."

Eirek turned to Cadmar. "Isn't that the fire planet?"

Cadmar nodded.

Eska wasted no time in continuing, "Your task will be to climb to the summit of Vatu Volcano by dusk. The trial will start at dawn, at one of Pyre's first colonized towns, Blen, approximately ten miles from the base of the volcano. "

Eirek looked on in amazement. He had only heard of volcanoes; from a distance, they looked more menacing than the Spera Mountains. If he correctly remembered what he learned about universal geography from teachings in school, there were lakes of lava instead of water. The holographic image changed to a small village the size of Creim.

"Lord Requart will provide stallions for all of you. Their feet will be coated with special horseshoes to shield their hooves from the hot ground."

The holograph switched back to the volcano, still rotating.

"A ship will be waiting at the summit to transport you from the planet. During the trial, each of you will be required to wear the bands given to you during the second trial."

Eirek stared as the holograph zoomed in to magnify rocky cliffs of the volcano. There seemed to be a path that curled around it. But it looked narrow. *Does Eska mean to kill us? How is that even possible?*

"Are there any questions as to what's expected?"

Eirek raised his hand as soon the question was asked—in time with the other three contestants.

"We will start with Cadmar and proceed around the table, finishing with Gabrielle."

"My guardian, if we be fallin' and touchin' the ground, will our exposed flesh be burnin' from this heat?" Cadmar tapped his fingers on the table as though he was playing a piano.

"Imagine the area around you to be a stove. Yes, you will suffer burns if you fall or touch the ground. That is why we have coated the horses' hooves. There will be no protection for any of you, however—aside from the protection of your clothing. Eirek?"

Eirek took a sip of water to collect his thoughts and steady his lips. "The trial starts exactly at dawn and ends at dusk?"

"Yes. It starts at dawn. And will end when the orange skies start to fade, and the volcano becomes completely shaded."

"Surely you don't expect all of us to make it there if this is the last trial? What if someone does not get to the ship in time? What happens then?" Eirek asked.

Eska paused, letting silence gather in the room—a cold silence that matched the severity of his words. "Then you will die."

Eirek shook his head, hoping he misheard. Behind Eska, the conseleigh looked at Guardian Eska in shock. After a moment of stillness, their eyes glowed, and they looked toward one another. *What kind of power are they using?*

Numos gasped, almost as though he choked on a mouthful of food. Hydro sat silent. Cain and Gabrielle muttered rapidly with one another. Eirek noticed Zain slink in his chair.

Cadmar tapped Eirek on the shoulder. "Did he be saying that?"

"Yeah . . . yeah . . . he did," Eirek whispered back to Cadmar.

"Beg me pardon, Guardian, but my people have a saying: Walk the path, climb the cliff, conquer the mountain, but—"

"Do not die for the crown. . . ." Guardian Eska paused and turned his attention to Cadmar. "I am aware of the various sayings on Onkh, Mr. Briggs. There is also a saying that goes: When a man is pushed against a mountain, he climbs it. It is my belief, and the belief of the guardians before me, that the toughest trials test you truest. Out of the candidates left, how else am I to separate the strong from the strongest? I outlined in my letter that the Trials were to push you past your limitations. My conseleigh have tested for qualities, but their trials have not pushed you in the ways I endured under my own master, Guardian Matthau Crevon. So I ask: Is this something you would die for? If not, I suggest you not participate," Eska finished.

Silence sunk in and so did the weight of the statement. *What would Angal do?* Eirek looked up from his linen and tried seeing out the windows, but the glare wouldn't allow him to survey the night sky.

"Next question, Prince Paen."

"You mentioned we are to ride ten miles from Blen to the base of the volcano on steeds. Just to make sure, all steeds given will be of equal caliber, right? I wish not to receive a stallion with a fractured hip."

"All stallions have been well cared for and have equally exercised every day. But it would be folly to think all of them could run at the same speed. That is impossible. It is the luck of the pick, one that might prove of the essence, that determines who gets an early lead. When you arrive at Blen tomorrow, all of you will have equal opportunity to select your stallion. Miss Ravwey, what is your question?"

"How is za winner determined for zis match? What if more zan one makes it to za ship?"

"The first person who reaches the ship will win the trial."

As if anticipating the answer, she retorted, "How is zat fair?"

"By what do you mean, Miss Ravwey?"

"You say zat zis trial is determined to test our fear . . . and our willingness to survive. If we compete in zis trial and go zrough all of it to get to your ship, and za only benefit in it is to keep our lives . . . zen . . . zen where is za justice in zat? Za person who is zere first isn't necessarily za best apprentice. Why . . . in a trial like zis, za first one might have been reckless in his climb up za volcano, and recklessness in a position such as za apprentice is not a good trait. Why not advance furzer if you make it to za ship in za allotted time? Za trial is still difficult . . . but at least we do not rush recklessly into deaz's grasp. We plan and strategize and take za most careful route in such times—qualities of a true apprentice and leader."

Eirek could hardly understand her. He had never been able to adjust to her accent. Whatever she said, though, must have struck some chord in Eska, for he remained silent in contemplation—deep contemplation.

"Miss Ravwey, you make a valid point. You are correct; recklessness is not something I wish to award the winner by making him or her my apprentice. . . . I will come up with a fifth test if need be. A test determined strictly by me." Guardian Eska clenched his gloved hand and looked back to his conseleigh, whose eyes had stopped glowing and now looked up to their guardian, jaws gaped. "Are there any more questions?"

Silence settled.

When Eska sat back down, the conseleigh leaned over their plates and started moving their lips, smothering him in words.

Eirek looked across the table—Hydro ate his food like nothing grave had been said; Cain and Gabrielle spoke in whispers. Next to him, Zain sat with his forehead resting on his clasped hands. *Is even he thinking about whether or not he would partake?*

Eirek remembered what Angal told him when he had discovered him in the forest: "I missed the most important adventure of my life, and because of it, the woman I loved I will never get to see again in this lifetime." Unlike Angal's situation, there was no woman in his life. There was no contentment in dealing with families of power, unless he considered going unnoticed by them beneficial. To show those above him that a man from his cloth could do extraordinary things, he would need to compete. Or die trying. There wasn't any other option. Eirek stabbed the meat with his fork and placed it in his mouth, letting his teeth drag on the utensil as he pulled it out.

❧CHAPTER 42❧

BLEN

Eirek stepped off the ship he had boarded five hours earlier. The past half-hour even the air-conditioned chamber of the ship couldn't ward off the heat trap rising from the atmosphere. Pyre was the last place Eirek wanted to visit—with the exception of Sereya, the ice nation north of Gar.

Conseleigh Inferno was waiting for them on the outskirts of Blen—a village with black cobblestoned roads, harsh and cracked, that led to crude shops and homes made of red clay and black straw. "Where is Conseleigh Iycel?"

"She has Sereyan blood, Riagan. She cannot stand the heat. Arrangements are made?"

"Lord Requart plans to send the horses on the morrow. He, too, will be present."

"I look forward to treating with him."

"The others may not." Riagan peeked around Guardian Eska, Senator Numos, and the other two conseleigh at the contestants. His brows furrowed, and his gaze lingered on each of them. He reestablished proper posture, looked at Guardian Eska, and turned around. "Follow me."

Pounding from a blacksmith's shop reminded Eirek of the Mourses. The air felt like a furnace. He could only imagine how it felt in the forging room. Every few feet, he took his loose, white linen shirt and wiped the sweat from his brow. He glimpsed barter shops, a herb broker and, rather than a fruit vender as in Creim, a meat vendor stood present with a multitude of lizards hanging from a clay awning. From the butcher's enclave, a sulfuric scent of roasted lizard shot into his nostrils so abruptly he could taste it.

The villagers strode around, clad in white togas—men and women alike. Eirek realized how alien their group must seem dressed in what he considered normal clothes. Every villager had dark-red skin—including a few babies Eirek saw stealing their mother's milk from an exposed left or right breast. Each man had a forest of chest hair that escaped the top of his toga to breathe in the humid air. Larger men and women donned two togas to obscure their would-be exposed flesh. Those were few, though; here, almost everyone was fit, as though their lives depended on it. Perhaps the most intriguing thing about these villagers was that, save a portion of children who had not even seen ten years, each adult walked this black expanse of cobblestone barefoot, apparently with no discomfort.

The quick quarter-mile jaunt through town led Eirek to a massive building. With nearly fifty windows, it dwarfed the other shops and homes in town. As with the other shops and homes, the same brick-red clay material was used in its formation. It reigned as a mountain with a capped peak of black hay in lieu of snow. A redwood sign read: *The Dormant Volcano* in charcoal lettering. It certainly did mimic a volcano, starting with a large base and winding up to the top.

Eirek maneuvered past Cadmar and Cain, neither of whom had begun to sweat. Riagan wore magnificent orange silk, reminiscent of the clouds that drifted above Eirek. A black badge embroidered with a sewn red phoenix marked the left lapel of his charcoal-colored overcoat. *How can he wear so many clothes and not sweat?*

A chirp caught his attention. Eirek looked at the sky. A flaming arrow sped toward him. Eirek ducked. Screamed. And cowered. It was only when laughter became audible that Eirek removed his hands from his head. On Riagan's shoulder was a fiery bird with a black beak and ash that constantly fell from each flap of its wings.

"Eirek, you never be near a phoenix before?" Cadmar asked.

Riagan chortled. "Eirek, my apologies that Nii gave you a scare."

"It's . . . it's all right." The heat had already blushed his cheeks, hiding his embarrassment.

"It's all right, there, boy." A thick, sweaty hand—jeweled in a rainbow of colors—touched his already-soaking white shirt. Although he had started near Eska in front, he trailed to the end by the walk. The silk white robe—with a gray mockingbird on a white badge—was drenched worse than Eirek's shirt.

"Thanks." Eirek made brief eye contact with Numos before noticing that the others had entered the inn.

Eirek followed them into a stuffy lobby, worsened by the multitude of bodies awaiting service. A chubby man, even larger than Senator Numos, sat behind a desk. He wore two ebony togas threaded with fire-red strands. A row of piercings sat underneath his bottom lip, right above his chin. Eirek counted four; they were all the same red color. When the man saw Guardian Eska, he quickly put away his book and smiled with yellow-stained teeth.

"Gu . . . Guar . . . Guardian Eska? Is it you? I have only seen pictures. Never . . . never . . ." The man couldn't seem to finish his thought. He seemed exhausted, like he just ran a marathon.

"Yes, it is me. And you are?"

"Narum, if it pleases you. If not, I change it."

Eirek chuckled at the response. Although he had grown accustomed to Eska's presence, he wondered if the villagers of Creim would react the same way to Eska's appearance. Angal always said how Eska seldom left the Core.

"No need, Narum. Give me eleven rooms for tonight."

"Eleven rooms. Of . . . of course. I have that." The man turned around; using his chubby fingers—some of them only stubs—he fumbled for eleven different keys, all made of bronze. They landed on the clay desk with successive thuds. Ethen grabbed the keys and divvyed them to each person there.

"Narum, is there a dining hall in this establishment?" Eska gripped the red-clay surface while surveying the lobby.

"For a party this size?"

"Yes."

"There is . . . but other guests . . ." The man didn't finish his statement. "I . . . I did not know this be . . . be part of Trials. . . ."

"It was just decided, Narum. Now, about that dining hall?"

"I make special reservations for your party . . . for dining quarters."

"Excellent. Thank you, Narum. You've been most helpful. Riagan, if you could. . . ."

His conseleigh reached into a brown deerskin sack attached to the belt at his hip.

"I . . . I pos'bly take no money from Guardian Eska. Rare enough to see Riagan here. New lord does not come at all. Sight of Guardian Eska and last lord of Therus only payment I need."

"Narum, we insist. When can the food be ready?"

Narum gulped. "By time you make comfy in rooms."

"Thank you."

Eska led the way up the clay staircase spiraling up the edge of the wall. It was narrow, so Eirek waited for the others to go in front of him. By the time he started up the stairs, Riagan had finished counting out five stacks of gold bonds. Eirek had never seen so much gold in his life. Neither had the innkeeper.

"I cannot take this. Too much. Too much."

"You will take. Eska insists."

"Bonds come in two, though; not five."

"Then here is six; three bonds of two."

That is the last Eirek heard before the sound died in the stairwell. His room was on the floor with all the others who had succeeded in past trials. The remaining two, Prince Evber and Zain, were assigned to the second floor with Senator Numos and perhaps another random family; he heard sounds coming from one of the closed doors.

"Yes, I will pick him up. We should be back by in two week's time."

The man's voice seemed older. The accent was slight, but it reminded him of Tundra's. It seemed like his vacation was ending. Why anyone would vacation here, Eirek couldn't fathom.

The heat made Eirek want to leave, but he couldn't yet. There were still people he had to prove wrong, and a trial he had to complete.

Compared to his room on the Core, Eirek's lodging was half the size, consisting of a clay floor hidden beneath a carpet of straw. If nerves would not allow him to sleep, then a hard, scratchy straw bed covered with woolen sheets would fulfill that duty. *Do these people think I'm going to freeze at night here?*

As soon as he stashed his stuff in a corner by a dresser, he approached the window. His room faced the opposite side of town. The village's crude—although established—way of life ended at a post that welcomed travelers and bid others luck on the frontier.

Gradually the colonized area of shops and clay houses turned into a landscape of obsidian and felsic diverged into massive gorges and arroyos on the sides of the black cobblestone road. Withered trees with blackened leaves sat scarce on the cracked ground with white magma spewing up from where their roots soaked in the nutrients of the planet's volcanic underbelly. Gases climbed the stuffy air to oddly organic orange clouds, which blocked the last of the light. Dusk had fallen; by this time tomorrow Eirek would need to be at the summit of a volcano—or die.

Phoenixes weren't the only creatures that claimed the air as home. Rock squids floated stealthily as they stalked their prey, which scurried on the ground below. Eirek saw one dive down like a hawk, picking up its prize with rocky tentacles. Another squid spat magma from its bowels as a larger predator of stone charcoal attacked from above. Each was the size of Cadmar, albeit made of stone. He could only imagine what monstrosities he might see tomorrow.

At dinner, Eirek took a spot next to Cadmar on a mound of red clay. He wondered what the clay material was and why they used it for everything. Their table was black, made from a type of wood Eirek didn't recognize and less than one-fourth the size of Eska's grand table in the dining hall. Despite the lack of assigned seating, they positioned themselves where their regular spots would've been in the estate. Everyone's cheeks were flushed red, and sweat beaded their faces, except Conseleigh Inferno, Guardian Eska, and, surprisingly, Cain.

Eska raised a cup of the wine. "I am glad you have all found this position something worth dying for. But as the adage goes: Words are water, rarely ice. I hope you compete tomorrow, for dawn's breath may be the last time I see you. Or tomorrow may mark one of many more days I will share with you as my future apprentice. The best advice I can offer is to trust in yourself and your abilities. Out there tomorrow, the barren plain awaits you—as does the opportunity of a lifetime."

Eska took another gulp of the wine.

Riagan rose with his own glass of dark-red wine. It sloshed in the movement, becoming a stain on the black tablecloth. The phoenix hopped from the left side of his shoulder to the right side and nuzzled against his head. "Contestants, I agree wholeheartedly with Guardian Eska. Tomorrow, past the plains of Vatu, atop Pyre's largest volcano, lies an opportunity. I hope you seize it. Remember that as you ride out tomorrow. Remember that as you think about the bonds you've forged. Remember that when you think of the man or woman you are now and the one this trial will force you to become."

Eirek gulped down the words. What at one point he would have considered an impossibility, he now looked to with a certain numbness of someone who had nothing to gain by going back to the inequality of Creim life, but everything to gain and show by winning the trial. *This place may be my crematory—and this is my last meal?* Eirek examined each piece of food with his fork.

"Eirek, you be okay?" Cadmar asked through a mouthful of roasted lizard.

"Just a little uneasy about this food. I want to at least live to see tomorrow," he joked.

Cadmar laughed.

Eirek's plate was full of black leaves that looked rotten and had an ashy scent to them. Below the leaves was a red pudding, and to the right there were chopped bits of red meat—charred to black on top and coated with red powder. Eirek's jaw soon became sore after chewing the meat so thoroughly. And the pudding was almost too thick to swallow—stinging his throat on the way down, although leaving the pleasant aftertaste of cinnamon.

Zain remained silent. Eirek noticed him occasionally sparing glances at Gabrielle. His lips bled from being bit so hard—and so many times.

"Zain, you okay?" Eirek asked.

"What . . . what was that? Sorry?" Zain lowered his head and picked at his piece of meat.

"Are you okay?"

"Yeah . . . yeah. I'm fine. . . . I'm just thinking."

"About what?"

Zain shrunk away and looked at him. "Nothing . . . nothing."

Eirek found that odd, but he didn't press further. Zain wasn't even competing; what did he have to worry about? Eirek turned back to his meal and continued eating everything on his plate. But even the food could not fill the canyon of anxiety he experienced—anxiety that hid itself in the form of reality and necessity, but anxiety nevertheless.

Supper finished, and everyone returned to their rooms. Orange clouds became dark blue amid the lack of light. They were spread thin, like ghastly dead fingers. Stars shined, but Eirek didn't bother glancing for his tonight. It was no time to place hopes in wishes. He settled for a prayer instead. "God Fueco, please protect me from your fires . . . and if you don't, Anemie, please let me into the heavens of Axiumé; spare me from the pits of Abaddon. Come dusk tomorrow, let me have the opportunity to see those who have made me who I am today: Jahn Mourse, Jerald Mourse, Sheryin Mourse, and even Angal. And . . . and even Linn Clayse. . . . Let my victory give her parents and families like hers new lenses to see through. The Twelve, to this, I pray."

He climbed into his bed, not bothering to cloak himself with covers. Even at night, he sweated. Lying there, he continued thinking about anyone who had ever been a part of his life—and who may discontinue to, come dusk tomorrow.

❧ CHAPTER 43 ❧

A HORSE RACE

Hydro rose from bed only to stare out his window. Unlike two nights previous, he had been able to sleep. No nightmares of a large black serpent with wings swallowing him whole plagued him—only squawks and yelps and grating stone that tapered off as he tired. Dark-green gases mingled with the yellow clouds of dawn that were thick enough to block Freyr and Lugh from showing. Perspiration already accompanied him.

Normally Hydro would know how to dress for a trial; on this planet, however, the unbearable humidity might crush his stamina if he donned thick armor. But if he wore nothing, the harsh animals of the plains would tear him apart. Then an idea came to him. *Let's really test out this necklace.*

Hydro put his hand in front of him. *"Vesi."* Water sloshed around his hand and traveled down his arm, cooling him. *Perfect.*

Minutes later he decided upon steel shoulder pads that hooked to a suit of chainmail covering his rhinoskin armor. Deerskin hides were used for his breeches; a belt of leather kept them in place while providing him with a place to attach his sword. Lastly he stuffed the ends of his breeches into thick, black boots; if he needed to walk, no harm would come to his feet. Before he finished dressing, he could already feel the sweat line his back.

"Prince Paen, it's time!" Riagan commanded from behind the bedroom door.

Hydro snuck his hand underneath his chainmail and felt the outline of the necklaces strapped to his neck. *Let's win this. For the sake of Acquava.* He could feel a slight tingle filter through his fingertips, and it traveled up his arms and to his elbows.

In the hallway, the other contestants made their way outside too. Gabrielle wore a ballistic nylon one-piece suit of armor, her long hair tied back in a ponytail. Her blue eyes resembled sapphires—exuding confidence and fearlessness. The Garian wore chainmail over boiled leather, which Hydro could already tell was cracking from the arid heat. This sartorial choice would surely boil him alive. *This last trial is for winners. You shouldn't even be here.*

As Hydro prepared to descend the staircase, the commoner exited his room. A quick glance revealed a white crushed-leather jacket—the same he had worn for the first trial. *Neither should you, Commoner. You probably cannot even saddle a horse, much less ride one.*

Outside, gaseous fumes still clung to the air of night—a tainted stench, nothing like the fresh pines and the briny air on Acquava. As Eska led the procession of contestants down a black cobblestone road, Hydro noticed villagers poking their heads out of their doors and windows. Just like his departure from the castle grounds, these people were here to see him off in this trial. They were not here for the others. Babies yelped for milk from their looking mothers, only to be hushed by fingers.

He envisioned his family and the other families of power all ready to see him win. He would see his father and Aiton again at Coronation. Perhaps then things would be better with his mother, and if not, well, he never had to see her again. He could not wait for that day. He never thought about failure. Like *equal*, the word *failure* soured his mind and tongue.

At the outskirts of the village, four horses stood two feet apart of one another. Riagan was deep in conversation with a shorter man, whose rosy cheeks flamed with freckles. Trimmed brown hair revealed a stub of onyx in the man's left ear; he sported a brown cloak (similar to those worn by magician) and a badge of an ear—the standard for advisors to any lord. On the left breast of the cloak was a sigil of a five-tailed sitting creature stitched in black on a field of orange.

Riagan addressed the group, "Contestants, these are the four horses loaned to us by Lord Requart. His advisor, Stuant, has helped me set up this trial."

Stuant began to speak but was cut off by the vibration of heavy thuds. As the sound increased, Hydro's eyes widened. Not even the rotund Senator Numos could eclipse the massive animal that strode toward them.

Hydro had only ever read about and seen pictures of Lord Requart. Now, as the lord rode the animal forth, Hydro felt a new level of respect for the noble.

The beast chauffeured Requart closer to them; its face and body resembled that of a dog, but much larger—barely smaller than a full-grown male elephant. Large fangs protruded from its mouth and hung past its chin. Tufts of fur dangled, as would a beard. Gold chains clung to each of its four legs, right above the paws. Splotches of black fur that were shaped like flames covered the beast's body. Its five long, slender tails floated in the air; at the end of each sat a flame, burning brightly. The beast's red eyes idled on Hydro for a few seconds, then proceeded taking in the rest of its surroundings.

Do not be alarmed. Now that you wear me, Prince Paen, animals will notice you more.

Why is that?

Because knowledge is feeling. It comes from intuition. They feel the knowledge you now possess.

What knowledge is that?

The necklace wouldn't answer.

The lord dismounted; he handed his reins—attached somewhere beneath the beast's chin—to a guard who shadowed them.

Why are guards even here? Surely no one would even think of attack if they needed to contend with that beast.

"Edwyrd, where are these contestants of yours? Your future apprentice?" The man's voice was deep and confident.

Lord Requart was as tall as the belly of the beast, so when the animal sat, Lord Requart stood eye level with it, stroking its mane. Requart was bald, and etched under roan eyes was an inch-long scar. On his chin was a thick goatee of brown hair. The lord had wrapped himself in a black, knee-length cloak buttoned in the front but split at the bottom. The same sigil as Stuant's was on the upper left breast of the cloak, and Hydro knew now that it was meant to be a silhouette of the animal.

What is that beast's name?

It is an enkine, Prince Paen. They are bonded, and because of it, they have great power.

There is also great risk and sacrifice.

Hydro waited for the necklace to say something, but it didn't.

"Lord Requart, it is my pleasure. Contestants, if you will please step forward and introduce yourselves so that the lord and his enkine can have a clear look at you."

How did Lord Requart manage to bond with one of those? From what Hydro had read in text about rare species, the enkine remained one of the rarest, only existing on Pyre; fewer than two dozen remained. During the time of unsettlement in the collapse of the Ancients, hunters stalked them for their hides; it took masses of people to bring down a single beast.

While the others uttered their names, Hydro continued to stare at the beast. Its red eyes moved from contestant to contestant as each one spoke. *It must understand.* Suddenly the eyes of fire were on him once again.

Without a hint of hesitation, Hydro declared, "Lord Requart, my name is Prince Hydro Áylan Paen II from Acquava; my father, Lord Hydro Paen, rules there."

"Yes, I know who your father is very well, boy."

Hydro's eyes flared. *Boy? How dare he!* Such disrespect from a lord to a prince! His father would hear of this. But then he reconsidered; if a war were to occur, his father would have to face . . . that. He gaped at the enkine again, wondering how the beasts ever managed to become endangered.

The bald man covered his mouth with a fist, clearing his throat. "Contestants, I am pleased to have met all of you. Today, one of you will become the apprentice to our guardian. Thus far, you have proven yourselves as fighters; however, these plains, this volcano, and this trial will determine the final outcome. If you wish to earn the title of apprentice to Guardian Eska, then conquer what lies before you. I will not be at the top of the volcano waiting for you; for the moment, my work and duties force me elsewhere. I will see one of you at Coronation however. May the god Fueoco protect you on this day, aiding you in defeating the fire and heat of Pyre." The lord nodded and stepped back. Three additional guards revealed themselves from behind the enkine. "These gentlemen will help you mount your horses. Good day to you all."

Lord Requart climbed back onto his enkine and tugged on its golden chains. Heavy thuds broke the crowd's murmur as the beast retreated with its master. Together they stood as tall as the houses and shops of the small town.

"Contestants, behind you are your stallions." Riagan extended his right arm. "Choose now the one for you. Once done, stand by it, reins in hand, and one of Lord Requart's guards will come assist you."

Hydro noticed the commoner dash over to the horses; as tempting as that felt, he first wanted to examine each one. In total, there were four: one white, one brown, and two black. As Eska had assured them, each of the horses seemed of equal stature. Now it was a matter of position. Eirek had already claimed the white horse on the left side, leaving one black and one brown in the middle, with the second black horse on the outside. Because of its location, Hydro rushed to the black horse on the end, knowing that he wouldn't want to be crowded by the horses around him.

"Garian, that one is mine."

"It's mine, Caffler." The Garian puffed up his chest and pushed into Hydro.

Compared to the enkine, not even the Garian appeared large. Hydro held the Garian's stare for a while. Fighting here would hardly be worth it. Besides, the Garian would need all the advantages he could get, with that thick armor on him.

"Fine, take it."

Gabrielle claimed the brown horse and already sat in her saddle; that left the other black horse, which stood idle next to the commoner.

A guard waited to assist Hydro. "Off with you! I can saddle my own horse!"

The guard, dressed in sheets of armor and a steel halfhelm, retreated at Hydro's bark.

How can they wear such heavy protection? He looked toward the commoner, who had been the first to mount his own horse. "Try not to slow mine down, Commoner."

A pocket in the clouds—now turning orange and yellow with the air of day—allowed Freyr and Lugh both to cast their light among the cracked, black floor of felsic. Deep scars of white magma boiled over the surface. Every few minutes, a geyser of magma erupted in the distance. Even farther a black spiral rose, disappearing above the yellow clouds. Flames darted to and fro in the sky; whether they were peaceful phoenixes or other creatures that waited for their carcasses remained to be seen.

Hydro remembered the families of power, who all expected him to win; Pearl, who expected him to win; and his father, who had told all of them that he would win. "For Acquava." His whisper crackled upon the humid wind, dying as soon as it left his lips.

"Contestants, may the Ancients bless you today in your travels. I will be at the summit of the volcano. I hope to see at least one of you by dusk." Eska's eyes glowed. A line of fire sprouted three paces in front of the horses. The sudden power caused them to neigh, but they stayed in place. "Now go!" The fire died, releasing them into the care of the Vatu Plains.

The sound of hooves clattering upon the barren surface filled Hydro's ears. His horse jetted more than ten feet ahead of the others. Kicking the horse's thigh, he sped up and pulled farther away from the others.

Heat dragged and clawed at his skin. Within minutes, it already dripped with sweat. The armor caused an irritating itch that he couldn't scratch while at a gallop. On Acquava, he had never experienced such unforgiving temperatures; the surrounding sea didn't allow it. Here, there was no cool sea air to relieve him. There was water though. For Hydro anyways. At such a fast pace, however, he focused solely on maneuvering his horse. Once he got farther ahead he would cool off.

His hand brushed his horse, congratulating it for the good work it put out. "It seems this trial will—"

A loud thump drowned his words. He looked to his right just as a giant boulder hurtled toward him. Ducking, he noticed short, red stubs of skin as something flew over him. *What was that?*

His horse neighed, then reared. Another boulder arched over his horse's head, struck Hydro in the stomach, and knocked him off the horse. While in midair, he realized that the red stubs were arms and legs, like those of a tortoise. When he hit the ground, he wasted no time in using his arms and feet to push the creature off of him and stand. In front of him he saw his horse fall to its side and another identical creature dig into his horse's stomach with talons. The horse whinnied for help in its own tongue.

The creature stared at Hydro through yellow eyes. Hooves clattered upon the cracked ground. Hydro looked up and saw the others approaching—the commoner with a look of worry, the Garian with a smug look, and Gabrielle with a disinterested look. Once they moved on, he turned and stared at the creature that attacked him.

He withdrew his blade as he looked toward the stench of dead meat. *Fear not what blade can slice or power can touch.*

Behind the creature, the horse was dead, the innards completely cleaned. The creature wore blood across its black face. It climbed over the remnants, a low growl escaping its mouth as it exposed rows of fierce-looking teeth.

The ground trembled. To Hydro's left, two more creatures appeared. He was surrounded.

They pose no threat to you, Hydro Paen. I attract them, but they are nothing to us.

Hydro sneered. "What pit of Abaddon did you crawl out from?"

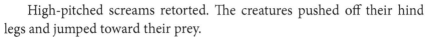

High-pitched screams retorted. The creatures pushed off their hind legs and jumped toward their prey.

Hydro shuffled back, allowing the first one to crash on the ground in front of him. As soon as it landed, he rushed to its boulder-like body and swung toward the strong, black neck. The head retreated into the boulder before steel connected with flesh.

Shit. He ducked as the other two creatures lunged for him. They collided in midair, and in order to escape being crushed by their weight, Hydro jumped and rolled on the felsic floor, immediately regretting that decision. His skin was on fire, and he noticed his hand was coated in black.

There is no time to waste.

Hydro turned around to see all three beasts exposing their razor-sharp teeth. Their talons scratched the felsic floor, and they moved away from one another, intending to surround him again. Each movement was another thud, and their tongues licked the air. One after the other, the creatures hissed and jumped, each at a different height and trajectory—their goal to catch Hydro off balance. *Clever creatures; too bad it won't work.* "Vesi!"

As each creature was on its way down, a sphere of water caught them in midair. They now let out gurgles instead of hisses. Their short talons clawed the air. Hydro kept his focus on controlling the water. *Abaddon drown all of you.* Hydro smirked and walked around the three spheres, savoring the struggle each one gave. They clawed for no longer than a minute, but Hydro did not release the sphere of water until minutes afterwards, as he continued to make his way around each limp body to admire his work.

His knees buckled as the heavy creatures fell to the ground. The natural curve of their bodies caused them to roll slightly until the limp ligaments stopped the cycle. Hydro walked over to them and stepped on their bellies.

"What interesting little creatures you were." He parted their purple lips with his blade, exposing rows of teeth. Lifeless sulfur-yellow eyes stared at him.

He looked back to the white frame of his horse in disgust. Charcoal flies hovered around it. *This makes things more difficult.*

He sheathed his sword and glanced down at his hands; they were still black from rolling on the felsic floor. "Vesi." Water formed around them, cleaning the mar. He let the water filter up his arms and to the back of his neck and hair, drenching him in its coolness.

The feeling was a momentary relief, for he was without a horse. There were leagues upon leagues before the volcano, and even then, he needed to climb it. *What do I do now?* He ran a hand through his jet-black hair and tapped his foot. Biting on his lip, he paced around the dead boulder creatures.

Knowledge is feeling. Look around; you will see the answer you need.

Above, black hawks with striped red wings spotted the sky. Caws of battle rang through the air; hawks faced off against phoenixes for territory. The cawing ceased when stony-scaled manatees disrupted them, swallowing whole the few that lingered. Squids of red and black rock kicked their legs in the air, having swallowed jets of fire that erupted from a distance. When the fire expired, they landed on the ground again, looking for more magma to ingest. *Interesting . . .*

Do you see what you must do? If you attract it, it will come, and it will obey you.

Hydro looked to his hands, recalling the winter he lost his sister. He couldn't cast fire then—there was no source for him to draw it from. Ever since that day, he never liked trying the spell.

"Palo . . ." Hydro muttered, expecting it not to work.

Fire drenched his hands. He waved them in front of his eyes. *I can do the spell! Do you see this, Mother?*

"Palo!" Hydro roared.

The fire from his hands shot upwards, forming a large geyser. *Where are you, squids?* He focused harder; the geyser expanded. Soon he caught the attention of a squid that hovered above him. *Come swallow this fire.* When the squid rolled up its tentacles, it cued Hydro that it was getting ready to inhale, so he squelched the fire bit by bit. The squid gravitated to him, baited in, as blood to a shark. Closer it came. And closer.

❦ CHAPTER 44 ❦

THE SUMMIT

Ten minutes after the start of the trial, Guardian Eska tossed four black spheres, each one as large as a fist, into the air. They hovered, beeping for a spell before following the horses.

"What are those?" Zain asked.

"They are trackers. They allow us to see every movement of the trial on the screens they are synced to," Luvan spoke. His blond hair, streaked with silver, looked greasy with sweat.

"Are both of you ready?" Guardian Eska asked Prince Evber and Zain.

Zain nodded and looked at Prince Evber, who nodded as well.

Zain followed Eska half a mile to the west of the city, where three ships were docked. There was one ship that was shaped like a phoenix; streaks of black lined its belly. The second ship was a tank-like ship similar to the one that extracted Zain from Lake Kilmer. And finally there was a purple vessel, shaped like a massive bubble and with a large front glass window, next to the phoenix-shaped ship; attached to its sides were stiff wings with engine blasters pointed downward.

The large group of soldiers with ash-black armor started to move past the ships.

"The firesons will not be accompanying us to the summit," Stuant said, looking back toward the soldiers marching away from the village.

"Where will they head then?" Senator Numos asked.

"Once outside of Blen, they run back to the castle as part of their training," Stuant explained.

"In that steel?"

"It is not true steel . . ." Stuant waited for Senator Numos to fill in the pause.

"Nyom Numos is my name. I'm a senator from Mistral."

"Yes, well, it is not true steel, Senator Numos. The zircha metal is farmed from Lurid, beneath the surface of Pyre, and shipped to here and Nova, and then we sell it to other nations."

"Armor that can change shape. . . . Interesting."

"Most indeed. It allows us to combat the terrain and the wildlife of Pyre much more easily."

Zain watched the soldiers fade from site, then he turned back to the ships.

"Conseleigh, take Riagan's ship to the summit. Stuant, Prince Evber, and Zain, you may ride with me in the other," Guardian Eska said.

The ramp lowered and Zain ascended it. In the cargo area, he took a seat to the left side, just as he had before, and Cain took a spot close to where Gabrielle had been positioned. Through the blaring of the engines, Zain continued to look at the ramp and replay the image in his mind. *Zakk could still be alive.* He rubbed his hands together and fingered each wound. *How can he be alive?*

When thinking became too much, Zain reserved himself to looking at the monitor in the back hull. Flocks of phoenixes flew; they stayed clear of the rock squids and charcoal-black birds shaped like manatees, which glided through the air to claim their territory. Yellow clouds momentarily blocked any view, but once they were breached, Zain noticed the summit of the volcano lay still even higher. White light flashed sporadically in the sky near the summit.

A large thud knocked Zain to the ground. *What the . . . ?* He looked to the monitor and saw nothing but green vapors. Then he looked to Cain, who was strapped in his spot and flicked his eyes back and forth between the door leading to the pilot chamber and the screen. The prince had yet to sweat, and Zain wondered how that was even possible.

"The wyvern will be gone shortly," Guardian Eska's voice filtered through the speaker boxes in the hull.

Wyvern. The types of creatures he had seen in his short time on Pyre made him wonder how anyone survived. Zain stayed on all fours while the knocking continued rocking the ship. Then the green fumes were gone, and the summit came into clear view. Zain got up and reclaimed his seat.

At the summit, the ship made a circle three times. Tongues of fire reached out and licked the open air.

"Contestants, do not worry. The volcano is dormant; it has been since the destruction of Vatu Village," Stuant's voice filtered in through the speakerboxes.

It doesn't look like that. The tongues of fire continued licking the air.

"Starting our descent. Brace yourselves," Guardian Eska said.

Despite the small flames, it was a smooth descent, with only minor rocking as the ship touched down.

"We're here," Zain said.

"Yes. . . . That I am thankful for." Cain unbuckled himself but was slow to stand.

The ship's entrance opened. Heinous heat flooded them. Sulfur bit at Zain's nose, and humidity scratched his skin. He stood and walked out of the ship and onto the felsic floor. Even through the soles of his shoes, the hot felsic bothered him. Above, more clouds gathered—but not creatures.

There was an alcove around the mouth of volcano that was large enough for boulders to sit and for the other ship to land as well.

When the other one landed, Luvan and Ethen strode out first, followed by Senator Numos. Their combined perspiration countered that which Guardian Eska, Riagan, Stuant, and, surprisingly, Prince Evber, lacked.

"I do say, it's quite hot here." Numos fanned himself with his portly hand and readjusted his eyeglass every few waves. He made his way to the small gathering that took place near Eska and Stuant. The conseleigh peered over Eska's shoulder at a small flat-screened device he held in his hand.

What are they looking at? Zain redirected his attention to Cain, who sat alone on a rock and gazed down into what he could see of the volcano's mouth. Not wanting to interrupt whatever the others were reviewing, Zain strolled toward Cain and stood five paces back from the mouth of the volcano. *How is it so hot here? And why doesn't he sweat?* He looked at the prince, who returned his gaze.

"Zain, it is a shame we could not partake in the finals, yes?"

"Would you have?"

"I ask myself that question too. In the books you read, they tell tales of men who fight hordes of enemies without fearing death. But life isn't like those stories. The Trials have made me realize this."

"So your answer is no?"

"My family needs me alive to carry on our reign of Epoch. Nothing is worth leaving them defenseless." Cain fingered a necklace of warm-colored feathers.

"What necklace is that?" Zain had noticed the necklace before, but he never cared to talk with Prince Cain.

"My mother's. She says it keeps our heritage alive. But we, too, have rings of authority. I wear mine at all times." Cain held up his right hand; one finger sported an emerald—cut like a perched owl and as green as his eyes—attached to a gold band. "These trinkets remind me of my duties as a prince . . . duties that have gone unfulfilled these past several weeks."

"I'm sorry to hear that." Zain used his forearm to wipe beads of sweat from his brow. *How does this prince not sweat?*

"You have done nothing wrong."

Maybe not to you. But I've done more wrong than I'd like to admit. The belly of the volcano rumbled, interrupting his guilt. "I think it's going to erupt."

"You heard what Stuant said while on the ride up. It is dormant. It has not erupted since Vatu Village was destroyed."

"He could be wrong. . . ." Zain peered at the chasm as magma rumbled below. Through the throat of the volcano, he saw its yellow-and-red bile. Every so often, large, yellow eyes seemed to stare up at him, as though a serpent hid beneath the lava. But the magma was like staring into Freyr itself, so Zain looked away before too long. Cain still had yet to sweat—even here next to the volcano's mouth.

"Why aren't you sweating?"

"I do not know." Cain sat and stared ahead, stoic as stone.

"What do you mean you don't know?"

"I do not know a lot of things anymore. This is one of them."

"And the others?"

"The reason for my slowness these past several weeks. My movements seem . . . altered."

"Like during the third trial?"

Cain looked at him. "I am not one to make excuses. You did your part, and Gabrielle did hers."

"Do you think she'll—"

"Edwyrd, another horse is down!" Riagan's voice yelled.

Zain turned around and saw that Eska was not with the group anymore but near the summit's cliff, which jutted out and overlooked the terrain below.

Guardian Eska responded, disappointment evident in his voice, "Whose is it this time?"

Zain abandoned the prince and moved closer to the others.

"Gabrielle's."

Zain's eyes widened. He maneuvered in between Luvan and Ethen, watching the screen that Riagan held. Red dots crawled over a horse's carcass, but Gabrielle was nowhere in sight.

"Gabrielle?" Eska stared off into the sky near the summit's circumference.

"She isn't on screen," replied Riagan.

"Aren't you going to help?" Zain asked.

Guardian Eska turned around and walked toward them, hands still clasped behind his back. "That is strictly forbidden. They all knew the gravity of this trial. I withheld nothing." Harsh as heat, Eska stared at him—brow furrowed.

"So that's it? How is she to make it to the top?"

"That is her problem to solve, Mr. Berrese. Just as it is Prince Paen's."

Zain looked to the conseleigh; their faces were tense. "None of you are going to help?"

"Every contestant knew how arduous this trial would be," Luvan stated.

"Guardian Eska is right," Ethen agreed.

"You watch them suffer but don't send aid?"

"Rules are rules, Mr. Berrese. We have never given aid to any trial; this one is no different," Guardian Eska said.

"Why do those who have power to help people never use it?"

The question went unanswered. Zain stormed off, returning to Cain's side. "Did you hear?"

"Yes."

"And Gabrielle? Didn't you say that you would protect her?"

"When did you hear that?" Cain's eyes flashed toward him.

"I overheard you and Gabrielle after the first trial."

"I . . . I . . ."

"Never meant it? Are words really just water?"

Cain's eyes dropped to the felsic floor. "I cannot."

"Why not?"

"My family needs me."

"She needs you!"

The statement went unanswered. *The prince is nothing more than a coward.* He could finally see what the Trials made people—heartless. All of them. *I would do anything for the ones I care about. I would've done anything for Ava.* Zain clenched his hands tighter. His side ached. Tears slid down his cheek. *I wasn't able to help her. But, Gabrielle, I can save her. . . . I can still protect the people who need protecting . . . just like Zakk would have done. . . . I can still be a true warrior . . . even if I lost the tournament.* Zain looked to the throat of the volcano. Magma bubbled below. *I'm possible.*

"Fine. I'll help her," Zain said.

Cain looked up to meet his challenging gaze. Irritated, scared eyes hid behind frameless glasses. He stared down a moment later, unmoved by Zain's words.

Pathetic, Prince. Zain walked over to the group staring at the monitors. "If none of you are going to help, then I am."

"You cannot do that," Guardian Eska said. He had reclaimed his spot on the cliff and looked out over the eastern terrain.

"The Trials are already over for me," Zain retorted.

"The choice is not yours to make."

"We make our own choices. You just choose not to."

He started to leave, but Eska's voice halted him. "If you leave, you may die here as well."

Zain turned around; Eska's back still faced him. The guardian stared out at the sky, a ruthless renegade to humanity. He kept his hands together behind his back—his crimson cape ruffled, distorting the image of the sun and dragon silhouette.

"There are things worse than death. . . ." Zain walked away from the group. None of them followed—not that he expected them to. If he needed to rescue her by himself, he would. His walk turned into a jog and then a sprint as he traveled the path spiraling down the sides of the volcano.

CHAPTER 45

SCALING THE CLIFFS

Eirek continued to steer his stallion for another mile past Hydro. After working with saddles for three years at his shop, he knew how to adjust for the different speeds of the horses, so he stayed with the contestants much better than they probably expected. Now, after Hydro's incident, Gabrielle took the lead, and Cadmar was gaining ground on Eirek.

Though the prince had belittled him, even he didn't deserve this planet as a tomb. With a quick flick of his wrist, he yanked his horse's reins to the right, veering directly in front Cadmar. The black horse neighed and reared back, nearly causing Cadmar to topple.

"What in Orekus's name you be doing, Eirek?"

"We have to go back. This isn't right; no one should die because of a trial."

"Don't worry 'bout the caffler. He deserves it." Cadmar readjusted his grip on the reins, but Eirek blocked the path of his horse.

"We can't just leave him!" Eirek protested.

"Eirek, Eska be making it clear this trial might be our lives. Hydro took the risk."

"We all took the risk . . . but . . . but we all have an obligation to save those in need."

"Gabrielle's getting farther ahead! We have to go."

"Let her!" Eirek kicked his horse forward, pushing Cadmar's horse back.

"Eirek, I be sorry. I be your friend. But we be needin' all the time offered to arrive at the summit." Cadmar kicked his horse forward, backing up Eirek's horse.

"But . . ."

"Hydro be capable of takin' care of himself and only himself." Cadmar maneuvered his horse past Eirek's. He paused to look Eirek in the eyes before continuing, "Ask yourself this question: Would he do the same for you?"

Cadmar trotted ahead as Eirek digested those words. He hung his head and looked toward the volcano and then back to the village that had become a faint speck on the horizon. Tightening his hands on the reins, he pulled to the right, kicked his stallion, and headed toward the volcano. A knot stuck with him through the whole journey as he did his best to stay behind Cadmar's horse.

By the time the volcano's shadow was in front of him, he had caught up with Cadmar. A stench of burnt, rotten eggs blasted his nose. His armor encapsulated hot fumes, telling him to collapse from exhaustion. But he wouldn't. He couldn't. Before him, the volcano loomed, its face hidden behind a beard of yellow and orange.

"Listen," Eirek's horse trotted alongside Cadmar, "I am sorry for stopping you."

Cadmar didn't answer. He put one finger to Eirek's lips, pointing with his other to the area around the volcano.

Black rocks—dipped in an orange paste—protruded skyward, arching sideways over fields of volcanic flora and between black gorges. Geysers of fire erupted, attracting hovering rock squids, as nectar did bees. Whenever a squid landed, it did so over a geyser, arching its legs, lowering its body, and swallowing up the fire—only to burst into the air again, renewed. Other fire-eating, shale-scaled monstrosities that were the size of Eska's estate stalked the broken, shapeless landscape. They had eyes of fire, claret skin with vertebrae covered in black fur, and hands that could squeeze around any human. Boulders as large as Lord Requart's beast jarred the volcano's base.

"Where's Gabrielle?" Eirek asked. Ever since she pulled ahead when Hydro's horse got tackled, they had not been able to catch up to her.

"The hoor's melt be dead for all I care. Be quiet and be movin' quick. . . ."

Eirek couldn't agree more. If any of these beasts perceived them as a threat, it would be the end of them. Black frogs striped with red—and as large in size as Eirek—hopped across the land, clearly relishing the chance for geysers of red to erupt under them. He rode closer and saw one of the frogs get picked out of the air by a giant rock-scaled manatee.

Eirek gulped. A fulsome smell that he couldn't quite place bit his nose. "Do you think she's safe?"

Cadmar didn't get a chance to respond. Geysers of fire erupted, silencing the buzzing and flapping of wings. Magma streamed out from the cracks, and Eirek carefully guided his stallion opposite the lines of orange fire. The smell remained, and now Eirek recognized it—spoiled meat.

Twenty paces ahead, he saw a large ribcage picked nearly clean; a piece of brown skin still clung to the rear. *Gabrielle's horse.* Charcoal flies—each an inch in diameter—swarmed the slab of ribs. They resembled a black cloud in front of them. A hint of red manifested in its center. Quickly Eirek steered rightward to avoid it.

"Do you think she . . ?" Eirek whispered.

"Eirek, I dunno. Don't be worryin' bout her. The hoor's melt deserves it," Cadmar replied.

Eirek sighed and continued following his friend. So far, the rock squids appeared ignorant to their presence. Eirek noticed Cadmar's russet hair fill with black dots that were like ash. Overhead, a group of phoenixes speckled the orange sky, ash raining from their wings like volcanic snow. Even his white jacket was now sprinkled with it; he tried to wipe it off, but it only sunk into the soaked armor. The thought of the coolness of one less layer tempted him, but removing it would only render him vulnerable.

Eirek scanned the steep cliffs in front of him. Farther down—between two large boulders covered in red moss—was a pathway. He recalled seeing a path when the trial was first explained to them. Still, there was no Gabrielle. Could she already be climbing the volcano by foot? Was she safe?

"This way," Eirek said.

Clacking against the misshapen floor of felsic, they cautiously approached. The path was narrow—allowing just enough width for their horses to travel side by side—but it circled up the volcano and provided the only navigable course. Certain times, Eirek's leg brushed against the harsh volcanic side. Sometimes the path shrunk, allowing only a single horse to pass; at other points, it transformed into a large platform, able to fit a party of ten horses easily. It was at the first of these platforms where they found Gabrielle.

"Eirek! Cadmar! My horse, my horse!" Gabrielle rushed toward them; the skin on her arm was slashed with red and black. Her eyes were red, and her hair appeared greasy.

Cadmar ignored her and continued up the path.

"Cadmar, what are you doing?"

"For her? Nothing."

"How can you say that?" Eirek kicked his horse to trot and stop before Cadmar could get to the narrow path.

"She just be tricking you."

"She needs help." Eirek looked at Gabrielle, who stayed back and rubbed her arms.

"Then you take her . . . but don't let the hoor's melt kiss you." Cadmar announced his decision loudly and moved his horse around Eirek's and up the path.

Eirek looked toward Gabrielle, who looked to Eirek and then to the ground. He moved his horse over to her. "Get on."

Gabrielle smiled and tucked her hair back behind her ear. A tear Eirek saw start to slide down her cheek was brushed away in the process. After she climbed on, she put her arms around his midsection. "Zank you, Eirek."

He looked down at her hands, noticing that they were charred and rippled with boils. "What happened?" He kicked his horse and steered the horse to the path.

"One . . . one of zose . . . zose . . . monsters attacked my horse. It . . . pushed it on its side, and I was, well . . . my horse almost trapped me. I just barely managed to get out before . . ."

"Before what?"

"Zese ants swarmed my horse and . . . and . . . dug into it. . . ."

"What do you mean dug into it?"

"Zey killed it from za inside."

Eirek shuddered. "How did you—"

"Be quiet," Cadmar's voice called.

Eirek rounded the bend and saw Cadmar stopped on the path where it approached a small opening, only large enough for five horses. But horses were not joining them; instead, a gigantic lizard with green scales was curled asleep in the middle of the path, and a second identical lizard licked the air with a tongue split at the tip. A single nostril the size of Eirek's eye was located above the purple lips. Instead of ears, the lizards possessed short, round recessed holes where red facial skin narrowed into green scales. Approaching its newest meal, the reptile echoed a hiss of delight. Eirek gulped at the sight of the huge tails—bulbed at the end like a club— dragging across the felsic.

"Quiet, quiet," Cadmar demanded.

The one that was awake turned its head toward the noise. Eirek studied its eyes, glazed with white that folded back. *They're blind.*

Eirek bumped his arm into Cadmar's, pointing at the very narrow opening they had to move around the creatures. Cadmar nodded and kicked his horse forward. Eirek followed, holding his breath and watching as the lizard licked the air no more than two arm's lengths away. Because he watched the lizards, his steering became sloppy, and the horse came too close to the cliff. Rocks crumbled underneath the back hooves, creating an avalanche down the volcano's side. His horse whinnied, rearing back.

The sound caused the other lizard to wake, and it joined its kin in jerking its neck toward the noise. Both shot out their tongues—a long hiss slithering on the air. The parted lips exposed four large, pointy front teeth columned by smaller daggers.

"Move it!" Cadmar yelled.

Eirek kicked his horse's side as hard as he could and trotted after Cadmar. Gabrielle's nails dug into the sides of his skin in spots where the armor was not as thick. Eirek heard thuds behind him, but he never looked back. Gabrielle constantly commanded, "Faster!" and that was all Eirek needed to hear. He kicked his horse constantly; in an attempt to get it to gallop rather than a trot, but the winding path made that impossible. Still, the thudding behind them eventually stopped. Eirek relaxed the tension in his shoulders, and he felt the pinching in his sides dissipate, but that wouldn't help the numbness growing in his legs, as well as the chafing.

Farther and farther up Eirek and Gabrielle followed Cadmar, nearing the crown of clouds. Eirek noticed a smaller dragon with only two legs; it swooped down, spitting a jet of green acid. It pounced on a manatee, which squawked before falling, defenseless, and crashing into the side of the volcano. Falling pumice caused Eirek to lurch off the path at multiple times during the ascent. What else awaited them above the crown of clouds?

Eventually the path spread out into another plateau, leaving enough room for a small party. Eirek took the opportunity to dismount and stretch and massage his legs.

"We lost zem?" Gabrielle asked as Eirek helped her dismount.

"I hope so. What do you think, Cadmar?"

Cadmar circled his horse like a cat finding a resting place, then he dismounted. "I can't say. I'm still shocked at that large wyvern that attacked in the sky. Did you see it?"

"How could anyone miss it?" Eirek walked to the back wall; but as he leaned into a stretch, he immediately pulled back.

"It burns, doesn't it?" Gabrielle showed him her hands and then pulled back her hard nylon to reveal her left leg, severely reddened. "I . . . I try my best to ignore it . . . but . . ."

"Eh, wrap it up. We haven't even broken the clouds yet." Cadmar sweated more than the others.

Eirek walked around, hoping to loosen his numb legs. As he plodded along, his leather tailcoat cracked where he bent to stretch. Something on the ground caught his attention—a mound of red rock, no taller than half a foot and shaped like a miniature volcano. Red ants crawled in and out carrying bits of felsic with them. *How do the ants survive here?*

"Eirek, get away from zere."

Eirek bent closer and looked at the small creatures. "They're only ants."

"Eirek's right. I can squash those," Cadmar agreed.

"No, no! . . . Before, Eirek, zose are za ants. . . . Zose things, my horse . . . stumbled onto. Zey . . . zey . . ."

Eirek shot up and jerked away from the ants.

"Gabrielle, be calm!"

"No, Cadmar, if Gabrielle's right—"

"Zose ants crawled inside my horse wiz zeir pincers and devoured it from za inside and broke zrough its flesh . . . and—" Gabrielle spoke fast and harsh but stopped when rocks crumbled to the left from the steep mountain cliff.

From below the plateau, a purple tongue waved in the air, then two thick arms, then a head. Rocks to the right crumbled, and Eirek looked up to see a platform, which was home to another lizard. Rocks hit the floor, creating a scurry amongst the ants and horses alike. *We're trapped.* The horses neighed and whinnied. Gabrielle yanked at their reins, but they pulled away from her and trotted up the path. *What are we going to do now?*

Eirek looked at the others and walked toward them. They could retreat, but where would that get them? Ants scurried over their broken hill near the wall, and the lizards were now on the plateau, licking the air as they searched for their prey.

Gabrielle withdrew her rapier, then Cadmar withdrew his axe. Eirek gulped and withdrew his sword; he worried about how much of a help he would be against the creatures twice his size. His eyes darted between the lizards, the ants, and the rocky bluff.

"On three," Cadmar whispered, shaking his axe in the air. "One . . ."

A charge wouldn't work. Each lizard, protected by scales and armed with a clubbed tail, was at least one-and-a-half times the size of Cadmar. How could they win? Eirek searched frantically; next to him, Gabrielle panted.

"Two . . ."

Eirek put a finger to his friend's lips. He looked between Gabrielle and Cadmar. They both stared, waiting for him to speak.

"Well . . ?" Gabrielle whispered.

Eirek turned his gaze to the lizards, then the ants, and then the bluff and repeated the process. The bluff was just high enough to climb, with a little help.

With the tip of his sword, Eirek pointed to the bluff. "Follow me."

CHAPTER 46

AN ALTERNATE ASCENT

The fingers on Hydro's left hand had grown accustomed to the wet and stringy nerves attached behind the rock squid's eyeball. Hydro had drawn it in with fire and jumped on top of it when it was close enough, keeping his hold by squeezing his legs and grabbing onto its eye socket. His right hand led it to the volcano with a path of fire, which had caused the creature to seemingly forget about Hydro's presence.

The clouds were close now. The large pillar of fire that raged underneath him pushed the squid upwards and consumed much more energy than the short separate patches of fire he had enticed the creature with on the way to the volcano. The overwhelming proximity of fire and the necklace had helped him not to tire thus far. But now his fingers began to shake, and sweat from his hair slid into his eyes.

You need to reach deeper, Hydro Paen. When you bond, you will become stronger.

Hydro ignored the necklace's statement. A rock squid would not be the first creature he would bond with if he had his choice. Hydro pushed his shoulder down more, straightened his right arm, and grunted. "For Acquava!" A surge of fire escaped from his hand; the rock squid shot up higher. Almost there.

In front of him, stationary boulders sprang to life with familiar yellow eyes. Sulfur stung his nose, and the dry air burnt his eyes. He grunted to ignore the irregular beating of his heart. His skin throbbed with each beat, and the tingle that at one point had soothed each of Hydro's fingers now panged like they were being slowly cut at each knuckle joint.

Something wailed behind him. Hydro looked around and saw a stone-scaled manatee flying toward him, its mouth open. *Shit.*

"Aaahhhh!" Hydro yelled and leaned into the spell. Fatigue tempted him to give in like a broken promise.

His eyes became blurry from exhaustion, but a shadow approached him. Then a larger shadow shot down from the orange clouds hundreds of feet above. *What?* Hydro blinked and noticed a wyvern dig into the manatee using talons as large as Hydro's own body. The trajectory of the strike pushed the manatee into the side of the volcano. In the attack, the large beast clipped his smaller squid on one of the tentacles, throwing it into the wall. Hydro tried to hold on for life, but his hand was ripped from its grip, and he was tossed against the volcano's side.

Jagged rocks scratched his back and arms. As he fell, Hydro looked up and saw green plumes of gas swallow the squid. A guttural shriek escaped from the creature. Still, he fell, his arms brushing against the volcano wall the whole way down. *For Acquava, I need to—*

He suddenly landed. Boulders thudded around him from the impact. But he didn't have enough energy to care. Upon opening his eyes, he noticed his clothes were black with felsic. Irritation crawled over his neck and arms. Cuts and bruises flared with pain as slivers of felsic managed their way into his open wounds.

Use my power, Hydro Paen. Cleanse yourself.

I'm trying to find it! Hydro tried lifting his palm, but he could only manage twitching his finger.

Find some or fail your nation. It is your choice.

Hydro looked around him. He had fallen on a path slightly below where his squid was attacked. He looked up and noticed the crown of clouds above him. His crown. Hydro tried to lift his hand toward them, but he couldn't manage it. He coughed, and in his exertion of energy, blood splattered his lips. *Where are you now with your ard leaves, Elias?*

For minutes, he rested. Some of the time with his eyes closed; other times he looked around. Nothing surrounded him but fallen pumice. Both necklaces clung to his neck, choking him. The heavy breathing eventually staggered, and he regained functionality in his joints.

You have rested enough; you need to win.

Scenarios of his family's disappointment played for him. Jeers and whispers from other families of power made his ear twitch. Pearl scratching her nails into his skin—drawing blood like she did with the mermaids—for his failure became vivid. *I need to win.* Ignoring the burns on his hand, he used the wall behind him for support and managed to stand.

"*Ve . . . vesi.*" Hydro held out his hands and watched as water cleaned his wounds, removing the black felsic. The heat that had irritated his skin subsided.

After the spell was done, he collapsed to his knees. He panted. And as he stayed there, he heard yelling. *That sounds like the others.*

He pushed up from his thigh and cautiously descended the path. The voices attracted him like the fire that lured the squid. Is it them? He turned the bend, and to his surprise, he saw two horses kneading the felsic floor. They neighed and shook their manes as they returned his gaze. Hydro couldn't help but smile at his luck. He was about to approach the horses when a voice captured his attention.

It was the Garian's. "We have to get to the top of this cliff. That creature will kill us if we be goin' back."

"Okay, how do you suppose we do zat?" Gabrielle's voice retorted.

Interesting. It seems the voices are coming from . . .

Hydro limped closer to the edge and looked down the cliff. Below, two large lizards climbed over fallen rubble on a lower path, nearing the three opponents who were stationed on a small ledge halfway up the cliff. They were unaware of Hydro's presence. Tiny little black orbs hovered around all three contestants. Hydro glanced over his shoulder and spotted one stalking him ten paces back in the air above. *What are those?*

"Just push me up. Don't worry, I'll help you out." The Garian motioned for the other two to push him up the cliff.

"Well, I am za lightest. Why not me?" Gabrielle crossed her arms.

"The strongest person has to pull the others up from the top. Now, push!" the Garian commanded.

The lizards were starting to climb the cliff toward the jutting rock. Purple lips parted, and a split tongue licked the air. Farther up they climbed, using the fallen pumice as their path.

"How can I trust you?" Gabrielle swatted away one of the lizard's claws with her sword. "For all I know, you will leave me here again."

"Gabrielle, I trust Cadmar," the commoner answered her, poking his head around the Garian's body. "We did save you before, you know."

Gabrielle let out a sigh. "You saved me . . . not za mammoz."

Hydro watched as the two heaved the Garian upwards. Still, they hadn't noticed him. *This is too perfect.* Hydro stepped a few inches back, waiting until the Garian grabbed the path. Once Hydro saw those rough fingers, he moved forward.

The look of astonishment on the Garian's face gave Hydro a renewed sense of energy. It was as priceless as the Hall of the Lords was to Hydro's family. "A stupid Garian told me something once: When mountains crumble, the men climbing them do as well." Hydro pushed his black boots down, cracking fingers and edges both.

"I . . . can't . . . hold on," the Garian huffed.

Kneeling down to increase the pressure on the Garian's knuckles, Hydro looked past his face to the others below. They stared at him in shock. He turned his back to the russet eyes that darted back and forth into Hydro's own hazel ones. He whispered so that only the Garian heard, "That is the point."

Taking his foot off the chubby hand, he kicked loose the Garian's grip.

Hydro watched the Garian fall past the small jutted cliff to the path below. After that, he turned his gaze on Gabrielle and the commoner. They looked up at him with disgust hot on their faces.

Before he could open his mouth to gloat, Hydro unexpectedly felt himself knocked sideways. Fists pounded against his face. Teeth rattled in his mouth. He put his forearms in front of his face, giving him time to identify the person on top of him—Zain. *That cur.* Hydro shot a knifehand straight to Zain's throat, and the man backed off of him.

The blow only allowed him enough time to get to his feet. Zain stood as well, massaging his throat. Hydro tucked in his elbows, protecting himself as best as he could. When Zain threw a left hook, Hydro caught it with his forearm and punched Zain across the face. His knuckles cracked, and Zain reeled back. He rebounded, and in a matter of seconds, they exchanged blows again, using only their fists and feet. Duck. Weave. Jab. Bob. Uppercut. Kick. *All I need is one well-placed punch.*

A series of kicks and punches followed, and Hydro did his part to block them. Soon enough, he began his offensive. Jab. Shuffle forward. Jab. Shuffle forward. Kick. Backfist. Uppercut. Not every move hit Zain, but Hydro relished every time he connected with Zain's jaw.

Back and back, Hydro pushed Zain until he was near the cliff's ledge. *Finally.* Hydro grabbed Zain's shoulders and drove a knee into him. Holding him, Hydro whispered one last final taunt, "Congratulations."

"For what?"

"For somehow managing to lose a trial even after being eliminated from the competition." Hydro drew back his shoulder and punched Zain in the stomach, muttering, *"Voima!"* upon contact. That word multiplied his power but drew upon his own energy as being part of telekinetic power. Zain lurched backwards. Hydro didn't bother watching his fall; he couldn't care less.

"Zain!"

Hydro smirked and stepped forward coolly, fully in control. Below, the Garian hovered over Zain's body, attempting to scare off giant lizards with his axe. *A shame the fall couldn't have killed both of them.*

"What did you do?" Gabrielle looked up, sobbing.

Hydro didn't respond. Instead he said, "Quite the predicament all of you are in. You see, after I take this horse, there will only be one left. Your Garian friend is down there, holding off the lizards—but for how much longer? One thing for certain is that three of you will be left without a horse." Hydro glared at the commoner and Gabrielle on the jutting cliff and then down to the other two on the lower path. "A pity." Hydro clicked his tongue and turned around.

He ignored the pleas for mercy that scratched the air. He looked back toward the horses; they seemed to eye him with caution. Had they enough sense to know what he had done?

Walking up to the black horse, he petted its mane. "You were supposed to be mine from the beginning," Hydro said to it. He looked at the other one, disgusted. That one had been the commoner's horse. Hydro was tempted to snuff its life, just to ensure the others would be permanently stranded; but he decided against it. It was unbefitting of royalty. Also, he didn't want to have to answer to Lord Requart and his giant beast if the lord should ask what happened.

Stepping into the saddle, he tugged on the reins, impelling the black horse to shake its head. "Now, let us get to that summit, shall we?" Kicking its sides, he galloped off, wearing a triumphant grin

CHAPTER 47

SACRIFICE

"Hydro, you can't just leave us here!" Eirek yelled.

Silence.

"Zain!" Gabrielle bent over the ledge and looked down. "Zain! What are you doing here?"

A medley of growling and hissing and cursing was the response from down below.

When he was sure that Hydro was gone, Eirek turned around and looked below. Cadmar had managed to drag Zain's body from the wall to the path that descended back. But the two lizards were closing in on them. Eirek knew the shouting wasn't helping, but their instincts and the heat played with their senses.

"You need to leave." Gabrielle grabbed him by the shoulders and pulled him back toward the wall.

Eirek shook his head and backed away. "We need to go down there and help."

"You know zat you won't be a help for zis. You need to win zis trial and stop anozer horrible ruler from reigning."

"But . . ." Eirek lowered his head and peeked over the cliff.

"But nozing. Your brain has gotten you zis far, but zis here," Gabrielle pointed down below, "zis doesn't require zat." She touched the side of his head. "A guardian needs zat."

"You are committing suicide if you go down there though." Tears flooded Eirek's eyes.

"No, I am returning a favor. You helped me back zere; you are za reason I am zis far."

271

"But . . ." Eirek tried to find some reason why he needed to be down with the others. But Gabrielle was right. What help would he be? He snuffed the tears from his eyes.

"But nozing. Now here." Gabrielle crouched. "Climb on my shoulders."

Screams and roars boomed from below. Eirek couldn't focus. His head was dizzy.

"Hurry."

Eirek shook his head and awkwardly climbed on Gabrielle's shoulders. He supported himself with the wall, ignoring the sweltering heat emanating from the rocks best he could. He felt himself lifted, but he was still a little too far from the next level.

"I can't reach it." He was just inches short.

"Jump from my shoulders."

Eirek braced himself and then jumped, managing to grab onto the ledge. The rock burned, but he wouldn't give in. He couldn't fall back down. Gabrielle needed to go help the both of them survive. They needed to survive. They needed to.

Eirek pushed one forearm over the ledge. And then the other one. He grunted to escape the heated felsic. Once he pulled himself up, he turned back around and looked at Gabrielle. "Gabrielle, thank you. Don't die. Don't let them die!" Tears slid down his flushed cheeks.

"Zere are zings worse zan deaz . . ." Gabrielle paused, "like letting anozer Victor Zigarda rule over za universe."

Eirek didn't understand what she meant. But he didn't have time to ask, for she hopped down below with her rapier drawn. Regardless, he needed to survive and win for the people who had given him everything to see him this far. He needed to show royalty that a man like him was equal, no matter the task. He needed to show himself that he was worthy.

Eirek got to his feet and ran to the horse behind him. He jumped on the saddle and kicked its side, hoping to make it to the ships before dusk. Clouds still crowded the air, but the once-yellow ones were now turning blue, like they had been the night before.

By the time he reached the volcano's summit, the blue dyed to a darker hue. A low rumbling noise reverberated through the air, but Eirek wasn't sure if it came from the volcano's throat or from the two ships that had ramps extended, waiting to depart. Riagan led a black horse into the back of the tank-like ship. Senator Numos conversed with Hydro, who upon seeing Eirek curled his lips.

"Eirek, I see you have just barely made it. Congratulations." Eska offered his gloved hand to Eirek. "Dismount from your horse so Riagan can get it into the ship."

"No. We need to go back for the others." Eirek held tight his reins but moved closer to the group of people.

"Eirek, it was Zain's decision to go back, just as it can be yours. I will not interfere in any of this trial. There is still half an hour until takeoff."

"But you can. You have the ability to. You're Guardian of the Core!" Eirek stiffened his upper lip to keep from crying.

"Rules are rules. Help them if you want, but I cannot guarantee you that the ships will still be here if you are lucky to return."

Eirek looked back and knew how far they still were down the path. What would one horse do anyway? It couldn't carry all of them, and there wasn't enough time for multiple trips. He hung his head low, let go of the reins, and dismounted his horse. If he was to show royalty that he was an equal, that people like him could do extraordinary things, he needed to live. *I can't let the sacrifice of others go to waste.* He clenched his fists and looked toward Hydro, who seemed untroubled about it all.

"Riagan, the horse," Eska said.

When he dismounted, Riagan gave him a canteen of water and demanded that he drink. Eirek did out of necessity, but his stomach tightened afterwards. He looked at the others acting like nothing was wrong, like three individuals weren't about to lose their lives.

Eirek didn't bother joining the others. The conseleigh and Stuant looked at the device that Luvan held in his hands. Hydro and Senator Numos continued conversing. And Guardian Eska looked out over a cliff to the terrain below. *What does he look for?* Every so often he would turn and flick his gaze back and forth between the remaining people, but the guardian said no more.

Eirek paced and scratched his arms and rubbed his hands. The irritation had caught up to his skin. As he walked, he hoped that he would see the others come around the bend, but he never did. Cain came to him at one point from where he had been sitting near the mouth of the volcano.

"Eirek . . . you made it."

Eirek nodded.

"Is . . . is Gabrielle . . ?"

Eirek shook his head. "She . . . she boosted me up to help the others."

Cain hung his head low and twirled the feather necklace with his index and thumb. "I should have saved her. I . . . I . . ." A tear slid down the long face of Cain. He swiped it before it fell.

"Guardian Eska, it is almost time," Luvan said.

Rumbles came from the volcano. Fire licked the air from the volcano's throat.

"You say this volcano hasn't erupted?" Senator Numos asked Stuant. Numos took his eyeglass piece and rubbed it on his sweaty silk.

"Not since Vatu Village. This is most peculiar. We need to leave . . . now."

The volcano shook, and Eirek nearly lost his balance. *They really are doomed now.*

"Senator Numos, Prince Evber, Prince Paen, and Eirek, you will ride with the conseleigh. Luvan, I will meet the ship at the Core once I finish delivering Stuant and the remaining horses back to Castle Tynd."

"Yes, my guardian. Everyone, into the ship."

Eirek glanced at the path once more and walked with Cain to the phoenix-shaped ship. The ramp extended from its middle, and unlike the tank ship, this one had windows instead of just a monitor.

He took a spot next to Cain, across from Senator Numos and Hydro. Luvan entered the cockpit, and Riagan and Ethen were in a compartment next to them that was separated by a glass door and windows.

"Strap in and prepare for takeoff," Luvan's voice filtered in through speakers placed near the ceiling.

The engines blared. The ship shook. Eirek strapped in and steadied his hand on his leg. The harsh heat slowly became swallowed by a faint breeze of coolness as the doors started to close. The door came closer. And closer. And finally it closed. A chill crept over Eirek, but it wasn't from the cool air coming from the fans of the compartment. It was a chill as he realized the mistakes he made.

❦ CHAPTER 48 ❦

TEAM OF THREE

Unable to open his eyes, Zain heard things. Queer things. Roars of protest shouted by Gabrielle and Cadmar. Steel striking scale sung a familiarity to Zain like he was back training in Gazo's. Seconds passed. Then minutes. Still blind to the world, still in the new pain and the old, he watched as Ava appeared to him—her smile as catty as a thief, her eyes a pair of prehnite gems. *"You need to get up."*

"I'm trying . . ." Zain reached for her. He yearned to hold her hand again, to interlock it with his, the way they used to when they walked together up the path to the Anga Mountains.

"They need you, Zain. Hold onto them like you did me."

"But I let you fall!" Zain cried. "I let everyone fall." He didn't look down at his hands. He couldn't look away from Ava. She was here. Really here. Her familiar black hair, streaked with blue and red as magnificent as the suns, fell past her shoulders.

"Fate felled me. Not you. . . . It was never you."

The image slowly faded. Light ravished his eyes again.

There was only one lizard now. Cadmar was on top of it, and Gabrielle had no sword. He swung his axe on the monster's back, but the strikes did no damage. He was soon thrown off to the volcano side. Gabrielle dodged a swipe of a claw, and as she tried to climb the lizard's back, the club-like tail hit her off into the volcano's wall, daggers of felsic dropping all around her.

"No!" Zain scrambled to stand.

Redness swelled from near the collision. *What is that?* The lizard turned to face Cadmar and Gabrielle. *I need to act fast.*

Zain ran to the steep volcano wall and used his legs to springboard himself onto the scaly, red back of the lizard. The tail swung at him. Zain gripped the scales harder, slicing open his hands (holding the scales was like clutching sword blades). The tail went overhead, and a rush of hot air passed him. The lizard growled and trampled the ground, creating short tremors. Zain noticed the redness double in size. *Are those ants?*

He shifted his position to face the front instead of the tail. As best as he could, he crawled forward on the lizard's back. When his hands wrapped around the thick neck of the lizard, it moaned and roared up on its stubby hind legs. Zain looked down and noticed he was nearly ten feet from the ground. The redness now pooled in between the lizard's legs. Then it started to climb.

A throaty yelp escaped the lizard's mouth. It clawed the air. The tail swung violently below, making a crater of the path. Cadmar was standing again, while Gabrielle still lay, sheeted in felsic. The large man limped over to the lizard but stopped a few feet away at the cusp of the red pool. *Why isn't he going farther? The belly is exposed?*

Zain looked down and noticed the red overtaking the lizard's legs and continuing to climb. A longer yelp slid from the lizard's mouth. Then it started to topple backwards. Right before the fall, Zain pushed off, using the scales as support for his feet; he grabbed under the beast's jaw and threw it down. The motion only lasted seconds, although it seemed to last an eternity. The beast collapsed, landing hard on its scaly back. Zain was now on its stomach, and he could feel it rumbling and pulsating. Redness poked through the underbelly. *What is going on?*

He jumped off and ran toward Cadmar. "What . . . what is happening?"

"Those ants be eating it from the inside out. Gabrielle warned us about them."

Zain looked over to Gabrielle, who still lay amongst the sheets of felsic. He walked to her, brushed the felsic off of her, and shook her. Blackness marred her skin. "Gabrielle . . ." Zain wrapped his arms around her and started to lift her.

"I'm . . . fine. . . ." Gabrielle muttered. She opened her eyes.

Zain pulled her up and helped her walk toward Cadmar, who looked on as the ants still cleaned the carcass of the lizard. "What happened to the other one?"

"Gabrielle surprised it from above, which allowed me to use my axe. She stabbed its head with her sword. Then it be stumbling back and off the cliff." Cadmar pointed to a part of the path that was partly collapsed.

"You lost your sword?" Zain asked.

"I couldn't wizdraw it in time." Gabrielle scratched at her face and her arms.

"Don't scratch. I know it burns, but your skin will be raw by the time we reach the top," Zain said.

Gabrielle smiled and pulled back her nails. "We need to leave to get zere in time."

Cadmar holstered his axe and limped forward, starting to lead. "We best be movin', then."

Zain nodded and followed with his hand on his side. The endorphins had exited his body as the battle ended. Heat plagued and bothered him once again. Irritation crawled up his arms and his neck, and he wanted to scratch, but he resisted.

Slowly they ascended the path at Cadmar's pace. Gabrielle was to his side, arms crossed over her chest. She looked down, silent and stoic.

What is she thinking about? Zain looked up and noticed the clouds fading from orange to a bluish color. The volcano shook. "Cadmar, we need to go faster."

"You try walkin' with a bad ankle. That caffler threw me down the cliff. He better not win."

"Eirek will win. I told him he needed to," Gabrielle said.

"Do you think he'll make it in time?" Zain asked.

"Of course he be . . . while . . . while we're here to die," Cadmar said. "You two need to leave; I'm slowing you down." He tried pushing himself off of Zain.

Zain tightened his hold. "Without you, we would have died back there."

Cadmar looked at him and then down to the floor. "At least we die honorable, then. . . ."

"Honorable? You think this is honorable? Eska has the ability to save us, but he won't. Do you see these small black orbs following us?" Zain extended his finger to one of them. They were hard to see in the darkening sky. The clouds were bluer now, and a purple color crept through the atmosphere, replacing any trace of orange. Dusk had come.

Cadmar squinted. "I never noticed those before."

"What are you talking about, Zain?" Gabrielle asked.

"Eska is observing us from there. He has been this whole time. He watched your horse die, Gabrielle. He watched you get thrown from the cliff, Cadmar. But he doesn't do anything. He is watching us die. Being guardian is nothing more than being stone." Zain steamed. *If I was guardian, I would save them. If I had the power, I would use it.*

The volcano shook again; Zain lost his balance, stumbling back and throwing a heavy elbow across Gabrielle. Cadmar buckled under the tremor. Engines blared. Zain looked up to see two ships gliding across the massive expanse of purple sky. *They left. They really left.*

Zain was on all fours, panting heavily. Now he understood what Gabrielle told him in the first trial. The futility and hopelessness of their situation was worse than any death. Even through the heat, chills crept up his arms. *At least I tried to make things better.* He snuffed a tear from his eye and pounded the felsic with his fist. He didn't care about the pain anymore—what would it matter in a couple of minutes?

Stones traveled between the pillars of his arms. Footsteps reverberated. And a voice came, raspy and familiar, "You weren't even allowed to participate in this trial, yet you manage to lose . . . again. Funny how you keep losing everything—your friend, your trial, your life."

Zain didn't want to look up. He knew the voice too well; it had haunted him throughout the Trials. "How are you here? You're . . . you're . . ."

"Dead? I'm not dead, Zain."

Zain opened his eyes and noticed Zakk wearing the Gazo's uniform. *Did he wear it to taunt me?*

"I saw Zain let you go. You can't be here," Gabrielle said.

Zain looked towards her. She was on her hands and knees. Her hand slowly crept down her thigh.

"You reach any more for that dagger and I'll slit Zain's throat." Zakk's hand reached for the knife strapped to the chest of his Gazo's uniform. He refocused his attention on Cadmar and said, "Same goes for you and that axe, Giant." Zakk spit on the felsic floor and looked back to Zain.

Zain closed his eyes. He didn't want to see the dirt-brown eyes that he had looked into so many times before. His head jerked back. He cried as he felt the hot breath on his face. A sharp pain erupted from his jaw, like something was being forced into his skin. Warm blood dribbled down his throat. Hands clenched his cheeks.

"Look at me, Zain. Look at me."

Zain shook his head, trying to deny reality. He screamed as his left eyelid was forced open. He tried blinking it shut, but the rough fingers kept him from doing so.

Dirt-brown eyes stared at him. "Look at me, Zain. See how real I am?"

"Ho . . . ho . . . how . . ."

"Because . . . I'm possible. . . . Isn't that right? Isn't that what we say to ourselves when we are at our lowest? Isn't that what I continued telling myself after my best friend let me fall!"

Zain opened his eyes and cried. "I . . . I . . . just wanted . . ."

"And it's always been what you wanted. . . . Fight for others . . . then fight for yourself. Gazo's would be ashamed of you. . . . So would your parents. . . . Too bad the lord never told your dad . . ."

An engine blared. Zain looked past Zakk. Lights poked from the clouds. Then the bubble-shaped ship appeared. Its window was tinted, obscuring the pilot's face completely. A metal bridge extended from the side of the ship, and a side opened.

A sharp pain ruptured from his stomach, and Zain collapsed. His cheek burned on the felsic floor.

Zakk walked away, dragging his feet. But then he stopped before the ramp. "Don't worry about your mom. . . . She'll be cared for. Very well." Zakk cackled and then disappeared into the ship, which then flew off into the clouds.

"Who that be?" Cadmar asked.

"How is Zakk here?" Gabrielle asked.

He ignored them and rolled over. Dark-blue clouds swarmed the air. A hot wind blew. The volcano shook. And it continued to shake. It roared. A humming occurred, and Zain noticed the black balls that had been following them come closer. They seemed larger now. *Are you going to enjoy watching me die, Eska?*

Red paste shot up into the air, catching his attention. It traveled high. And then fell. Coming closer. And closer. And closer. Zain closed his eyes and clenched his hands and waited.

⚜CHAPTER 49⚜

REVELATION

When hard metal clamped around Zain's body, he opened his eyes. And he saw darkness. Coolness overwhelmed him. Humming made him dizzy. And as best he could, he put his hands to his head to stop jerking. He was someplace. But he didn't know where. All around him was steel. It was tight—no wider than an arm span.

Where am I? Where are the others? Where's the volcano? How am I not dead? Am I dead? I don't feel dead.

Darkness supplied him nothing but humming. Then it stopped. A horizontal slit opened before his eyes. And it grew larger. Whatever he was inside tilted downward, and he fell out on the hard floor below.

Darkness once again. But fainter. Gabrielle and Cadmar were on all fours, looking around. There were benches. And a monitor on top of the wall. Speakers were located in the corners. *Is this the ship?*

Zain flopped on his back. The black ball hovered and shrank in size behind him, then floated over him. Zain changed his posture to see where it went. A door opened, swallowed the three orbs, and closed again.

"I'm alive. . . . Gabrielle . . . Cadmar . . . is . . . is this real?"

Gabrielle looked at him. "How is zis possible?"

Cadmar stood. "We be alive."

Engines blared. The floor shook. Once the ship stabilized, Zain got to his feet and helped Gabrielle up. "We're alive." The shock was slowly replaced by joy. He grabbed her and hugged her. Zain turned to Cadmar. "We're alive." And he hugged him too, slapping his back as well. "We're alive!" Zain shouted and raised his hands. "Where . . . where are we?"

"It looks like za ship Eska used to retrieve us."

"This be the ship all right." Cadmar walked around the perimeter, dragging his fingers across the wall. "Those . . . those . . . black balls ate us." Cadmar stopped by the door and tried to peer through the glass.

"Is that what happened?" Zain scratched his head. "Do you see anything?"

"Nothing." Cadmar turned around. "Who be that guy on the summit?"

Zakk! So I wasn't seeing things again. Zain felt his chin and then the crusty paste of dried blood on his face. *What went into my chin?* "He . . . he—"

"His name is Zakk. He trains wiz Zain at Gazo's academy. He is one of zeir star students . . . but . . . but he fell. . . . I saw him not get on za ship. How was he zere?"

"How he be appearing out of nowhere? And what be that ship?" Cadmar asked.

"What did he want?" Gabrielle asked.

Zain spun around and massaged his skull as questions continued to drown him. "Stop!" He turned around again. "I don't know . . . anything . . ."

Zain took a seat and massaged his head. No more questions followed, which allowed him to think. *Jamaal was right. How did you get on that volcano? Were you on the Core too? How can you become invisible? Who are you with? Why are you here? Why did you show yourself? What did you put in me?* He scratched his chin. It didn't feel any different—besides the blood and scabs. His head throbbed. Words reeled in his mind. It was almost as if he could feel Zakk's breath upon his ear.

Don't worry about your mom. She'll be well cared for.

What is he planning? Who is planning something? Why are they dragging my family into it? He clenched his fists and looked up, noticing that the other two sat in silence as they looked at him to see if answers were going to come to him. He didn't have any. He wouldn't have any until he went home. But where was he even headed now?

Zain looked to the monitor, but it was black. The ship hummed, offsetting their silence for a while.

"Why were you even zere? You weren't in zis trial."

Zain looked from the ground to Gabrielle. She tucked a black bang behind her ear, then proceeded to play with her lip ring. Her blue eyes stared at Zain, never blinking. He couldn't answer.

"Why was it you zat came down zat volcano?" Her eyes started tearing. She put her forearm to her them.

Zain looked toward Cadmar, who had straightened his posture at the question. His arms were crossed. "It was the only decent thing to do." Zain smiled at Gabrielle, who returned the gesture. "And, well, because no one should have to die for their dreams. . . . No one," Zain answered. He clenched his fists and remembered how he had sabotaged Zakk for trying to obtain his dreams. A knot tightened his stomach. *He's not dead. I can still make things better.*

"Dreams are funny zings."

Zain smiled and interlocked his fingers. "Why is that?"

"Because zey are your unconscious prayers. Za ones zat go unanswered by za Ancients."

"The Ancients don't answer anything," Zain muttered.

"Yes, zey do. You just have yet to see it." Gabrielle smiled and then looked down.

Silence spanned the cargo area and claimed hold for the rest of the trip.

• • •

Zain stepped out of the ship into the grave of night. Compared to the felsic and hot grounds of Pyre, the dirt was welcomed. Two silver bands lined the purple sky, splitting the stars into quadrants. On the pillars of the estate that held up the multiple second floor balconies, lights painted the mansion in a golden glow. *The Core!*

Maneuvering around the ship, Zain saw Eska. The white glow that came from his left hand identified him easily, but the darkness obscured most everything else. There was no one else. The ship had landed next to the phoenix-shaped ship, but it seemed that ship was already unoccupied. Eska turned to them and said, "Follow me."

As if pulled along in a dream, Zain followed. Gabrielle was to his right, and Cadmar was to his left. No one said anything. *Is this really happening?* Zain still couldn't believe he was back on the Core, the mansion in front of him. *I should be dead. Why aren't I?*

At the stoop, Eska waited for them before the double doors. His gaze darted back to all three of them, but it landed on Zain and stood there the longest. His lips curved into a smile. "Come."

"How . . . how . . . is zis possible?" Gabrielle asked.

"I will explain everything in the lobby," Guardian Eska said. He held the door open and ushered them in with his gloved hand.

The lobby was bright and filled with eight other bodies: Eska's conseleigh, the three other contestants, and Senator Numos. Upon entering, each person blinked, shook his or her head, and stared again. Eyebrows arched.

Cain's gaze lingered on Zain and then to Gabrielle and down to the floor.

Hydro's upper lip curled; he crossed his arms and looked away.

Eirek's gaze wandered among the three of them, and a smile overtook his face. "You're alive!"

Senator Numos furrowed his eyebrows and blinked twice before readjusting his eyepiece and tapping his cane. "Most interesting indeed."

"Edwyrd, how is this possible?" Luvan asked.

Zain turned around, wanting to know the exact same thing. Eska maneuvered around the three of them and stood in the middle of the lobby. Everyone waited for him to speak. And when he did, attention was held captive. "There was never any intention in letting them die. For the good of this trial, I could not let anyone know, because as I was taught: The toughest trials test you truest." Eska turned to face all of the contestants. "I told you during introductions that it would be your performance during the Trials that would ultimately determine who was selected as my apprentice. And only when you are not seen can you show who you truly are." He paused, giving gravity to his statement.

Guardian Eska's gaze wandered to every person in the room, lingering on the contestants: first Cain, then Cadmar, then Gabrielle, Hydro, Eirek, and finally Zain.

"Unbeknownst to even my conseleigh," Guardian Eska glanced at them. The four turned their heads at the statement. "The Trials were in part a test of partnership and intelligence and, of course, even fortitude and weapons prowess, but it aimed to test even more than that. It aimed to test the core of your character. For, as guardian, your life will not consist of trials; it will be a test of trust, integrity, and service to the people of Gladonus, whom you serve. That is a lesson that you cannot learn; it must be instilled in you through the morals and values you carry."

Zain looked around and saw all eyes linger on Eska, even the conseleigh.

"The person who will be my apprentice showed compassion, helping carry his partner in the first trial. In the second trial, he analyzed the situation and, through his intelligence, made the appropriate course of action for what he thought was right. In the third trial, he lost, but he showed great swordsmanship nonetheless. And in the fourth trial, after hearing of the mishaps of the others, he questioned my refusal to help—not knowing that help would already be provided."

Chills crawled up Zain's skin. *He's . . . he's talking about me.*

"He risked his life to try and save those in need and those whom he cared about, knowing that if he were to leave, it would more than likely be his death. And although he won no trial, it was never winning I was concerned about; it was performance, for words are water. During these trials, Mr. Berrese, you showed that words can be more than just water; they can be ice. And it is because of that, that I offer you apprenticeship, to train under me and my conseleigh for fifteen years until my term expires."

Zain saw everyone turn to look at him. Senator Numos dabbed his face with a towel and readjusted his eyepiece. The jaws of most everyone else were opened. Hydro's lips snarled. He quickly looked to the ground.

"Here is the Twelve's Decree, as I heard it from my mentor, Matthau Crevon. . . ."

Zain couldn't concentrate on what else Eska said. He clenched his hands and opened them. Wounds still marred his black skin. Remembrance snuck into him, and he started to tear. *Fight for others . . . then you can fight for yourself. Gazo's would be ashamed of you. . . .* Zakk's voice lingered in his mind. *If words are water. . . .* Zain opened and closed his hands once more, remembering how they pried apart his best friend's grip and let him slip to the lake below.

". . . To all this I—"

Zain looked up. "I . . . I . . . can't be your apprentice." Zain watched Eska's beam dissolve into a line of confusion and then he looked down to avoid the other gazes sure to follow.

"Are you certain, Zain?"

"Yes, my guardian. . . ." Zain looked back to Guardian Eska, who pulled back his hand and put it under his chin.

Guardian Eska cleared his throat. "That . . . that is most . . . most unfortunate. . . . Everyone, return to your rooms. Further instructions will be given on the morrow. . . . Con . . ." Eska shook his head, "Conseleigh . . . follow me." Eska walked past the others and up the stairs, not stopping to check if his conseleigh was following him or not. On the second floor, Zain noticed him pause and give one final glance toward him and down before he walked away.

Zain looked at everyone else in the lobby still staring at him. "I don't wanna talk about it." He stormed off to his room, not waiting for them to interrogate him.

In his room, Zain didn't even make it to his bed. As soon as he closed his door, he sank to the floor and cried into his hands. Everything he thought he wanted he had just turned down. "I'm not ice . . . if only Eska knew," Zain muttered and knocked his head back against his door. He flexed his hands.

From where he sat, he looked out the window into the night sky. *Zakk is out there . . . somewhere. Before the rest of my family gets hurt, I'm going to find him, and when I do . . . I'll make things better . . . somehow.*

CHAPTER 50

EQUALS

Dear Contestants,

Please meet in the lobby at three hours past noon today.

Sincerely,
Guardian Edwyrd Eska

It was the shortest letter Eirek had ever read. And it was placed on his door after lunch. *What is going on?*

Ever since the day before, everything seemed surreal. For the contestants to still be alive after the fourth trial, for Eska to reveal the true aim of the Trials, and for Zain to be offered apprenticeship and then deny it—it was too much. No matter what Eirek did, he continued to wonder why Zain turned down the offer. How much strength did it take to refuse an offer from the Guardian of the Core?

Zain still talked with no one at lunch. In truth, Eirek hadn't tried talking to Zain, but he had seen Cadmar try and Cain and even Gabrielle, but Zain wouldn't open his lips. So instead the others talked about it amongst themselves.

"Can you be believing Zain said no to Eska? He be refusing the most powerful person in Gladonus." Cadmar waved his hands in the air and paced Eirek's room. "Where does that be leavin' us?" He shook the same letter in his hand.

"I don't know. I . . . I just don't know about anything. . . ." Eirek sat on his bed, hands underneath his legs, and looked out the window to the

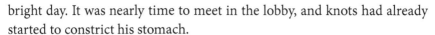

bright day. It was nearly time to meet in the lobby, and knots had already started to constrict his stomach.

"I bet it be something that black man told him at the summit. He be appearing out of thin air, after all."

"Who is that?" Eirek looked at Cadmar, eyebrows arched.

"I don't know who it be. Zakk be all I know. . . ."

"And then what happened?" Eirek turned on his bed to face Cadmar.

"He left . . . in another ship that came from the clouds . . . before that volcano be erupting."

"How did you manage to escape anyways?"

"Those black balls that were following us swallowed us whole, and next thing I know, I be getting jerked around in a cramped area and spit out on the floor of a ship."

"The black balls ate you? How?"

"Once they be opened, metal hands be grabbin' us and crammin' us inside. It be rather uncomfortable."

"Less uncomfortable than guilt," Eirek muttered. He hung his head.

"Don't be sad. . . . You didn't know. No one did. Not even Eska's conseleigh. You be playin' it safe."

Safe never gets you anywhere in life though. If I truly wanted to show that I cared about those people the same as me, I would have gone. I needed to go. . . . Why didn't I?

"Never mind any of that. Let's be headin' to the lobby."

When Cadmar shook Eirek's shoulder, Eirek looked up and smiled. A little wetness had come to his eyes, but he wiped it away. "Yeah . . ."

In the lobby, Eska stood near the stairwell. His four conseleigh stood behind him on the steps. Senator Numos took a spot near the wall close to where the hallway extended to the western rooms. Hydro and Cain were already present. And after a few minutes of anticipation, Zain walked into the lobby with Gabrielle behind him. Guardian Eska looked at Zain and then let his gaze linger over all of them.

"Contestants, I have assembled you here today to witness the final trial. This is a trial of my own design and is meant to currently break the tie that was established in the fourth trial. Eirek Mourse and Prince Hydro Paen, please step forward. . . ."

"I zought zat points did not matter? Why do zey only get to compete and none of us do? You sent zat last letter to all of us?"

"Ms. Ravwey, I sent the letter to all of you so that you could be here in witness of the final trial. You are correct in saying that points were never the true thing that mattered. It was character. Each remaining contestant here, however, does not meet the standards of character I would find applicable for Guardian of the Core, which is why I must now base my decision off of points earned and this final trial."

Gabrielle slunk her shoulders and stepped backwards, lining up between Zain and Cain. Eirek looked toward Cadmar, who hung his head low. Senator Numos grinned as he leaned on his cane. Hydro had already stepped forward. Eirek followed, leaving five paces between him and Guardian Eska.

Eirek looked at Prince Paen, who stared at Guardian Eska. Hydro's shoulders were stiff, his back was straight, and he was stoic as stone. Eirek tried to imitate his confidence in light of his scattered mind. *This is it.*

"Contestants, each trial before, you had a purpose. This trial's purpose is to test your understanding, because while some think that knowledge is power or knowledge is feeling, I believe that knowledge is understanding. As Guardian of the Core, the wealth of knowledge you gain access to is priceless, and it is being able to use this knowledge to better the universe you govern that will make you a successful guardian. So your last trial will be a riddle. You will be allotted five minutes for contemplation, at which point, Prince Paen, I will ask you to give your answer first, and, Eirek Mourse, you shall give your answer second. Understood?"

A riddle. Eirek piqued his ears and tapped his fingers on his legs. He nodded and tightened his neck.

"Contestants, here is your riddle: What is it that the Ancients never saw, that the Twelve seldom see, but that humans see every day?"

The riddle—one of the last things Angal had said to him. Angal never told him the answer though. Now that he looked back, it didn't matter. Eirek knew the answer. He smiled. Angal had told him. Not directly. Never directly. He was raised with the thought. Since youth, it had been born and bred in his mind. The prince would never understand it; his arrogance wouldn't let him. Hydro's answer might sound pretty in the air, but it wouldn't be true.

"Peace," Hydro sang, a triumphant grin on his face.

Pretty, but wrong. Eirek looked up toward Guardian Eska, staring into the auspicious eyes. "An equal," Eirek said.

Eska exchanged glances with both of them. "Both are good answers. But only one is right. Eirek Mourse, congratulations." Eska clapped his hands; the conseleigh soon followed along. Cadmar slapped him on the back. Eirek lurched forward and noticed Senator Numos giving a faint clap. He stood up again and noticed Zain and Gabrielle clapping along with Cain.

Angal would be proud right now. Everyone would. Eirek watched Hydro's puffed chest deflate—pain, contempt, and disbelief, all painted in various colors on the palette of his face.

Hydro extended his hand. Eirek eyed it as though it was some sort of trap.

"Will you take it?"

Eirek took the hand, struggling to show no pain as the grip clamped down. He wouldn't give Hydro satisfaction.

Hydro leaned in close and whispered in his ear, "You have nothing to give this position."

"I have my mind."

"If that is all you have, then you will die . . . faster than the rest." Hydro stormed off down the hallway, pushing his shoulder into Eirek before doing so.

Eirek stood in a stupor, trying to comprehend Hydro's last words.

Eska stepped forward. "Everyone, please stand back and form a circle around Eirek Mourse and me. Eirek, if you will kneel in the center of the lobby."

Eirek gulped, gazing around the established perimeter. All eyes fought over hills of shoulders to see what was to happen. In expectation, he knelt.

"Eirek, hear the Twelve's Decree now, as I heard it from my mentor, Guardian Matthau Crevon, two hundred years ago. It is with the Twelve's Decree that, upon obtaining this position, you may use our power for two hundred years. As Guardian of the Core, you may neither marry nor have any children, for that may pass on powers that are not yours to pass. Your body will age only slightly, but it shall return to its normal state during the passing ceremony. If you accept these standards, tell me so at Coronation, a mere five days from now, in front of the lords and ladies of Gladonus, from whom you must still gain approval. You may rise.

"Dinner will be at six. Contestants, use this time to pack your bags. Arrange rides for tomorrow as well. Colin will hand you a piece of paper, and on it, you will write the name of the person retrieving you so I may pass it along to General Satoris on Hown. If you feel sore, make use of the apothecary before tomorrow."

Eska turned on his heels, and with a wave of his gloved hand, he motioned for the conseleigh to follow. They disappeared behind the glass doors at the end of the hallway.

Before Eirek knew what was happening, Cadmar wrapped an arm around his shoulder. "Congrats, Eirek. You showed that caffler a lesson."

Gabrielle walked up to him with her hand extended. "Zank you for not letting him win. You will make a great apprentice."

When she stepped back, Zain stepped forward. "Congratulations, Eirek."

Eirek gripped Zain's extended hand for seconds. He wanted to ask why Zain turned down the position, but he couldn't bring himself to do it. Not here. Maybe he would alone. Before Zain left. His attention then shifted as each of the contestants approached to shake his hand.

"Thank you . . . Zain."

Cadmar, Zain, and Gabrielle headed up the stairs. Eirek assumed they were going to the apothecary to visit the adored before they left. Soon only Eirek and Cain remained in the lobby.

Cain tilted his head to those who left. When he looked back to Eirek, there was a tear in his eye. Perhaps it was naïve, but Eirek hadn't imagined princes to cry. Cain wiped away that single tear sliding down his long cheeks, pinched his eyes, and then looked at Eirek. "Congratulations." Cain extended his hand.

Eirek eyed it with less caution than he had Hydro's and took it. "Thank you."

"I would have never thought it would be you to win."

"Is that your thinking or your family's?"

Cain released his hand. "The latter." He smiled. "I am not sure what I think anymore."

"Are you all right?"

Cain broke his stare with the ground. "I am not sure what I am." His fingers slipped around his feather necklace, visible through the cut of his shirt. "I need to pack. Although I leave tomorrow, I will see you for Coronation."

Cain exited abruptly, leaving no chance for Eirek to say his goodbyes. For the first time since he'd arrived at the Trials, Eirek looked up to the picture-painted cupola. Ancients Lyoen and Bane gazed down upon him. *You may not see equals, but there were never any for you to see. And although I see them, I want to prove to all of them that I am. For everyone like me, I need to.*

☙ CHAPTER 51 ☙

IN THE NIGHT

A riddle! A damned riddle is how the next guardian is chosen? Hydro paced in his room, lips snarled. *An equal? Prince Evber is the only other prince here. What rubbish.* His breathing intensified as he gazed at himself in the mirror. "An equal!" Hydro's fist pummeled the dresser as a judge would his bench. His eyes flashed black. He blinked. Normality returned. *What sort of power is that? I must be seeing things.*

A knock at the door pulled him from further examination. He walked over and pulled the door open; an old man stood there, his hairline receding and glasses hugging the tip of his curved, beak-shaped nose. The man had gray eyes with dormant vitality.

"Yes?" Hydro's S carried for seconds after the word should have ended.

"Guardian Eska requires you to fill this out." The man extended an ivory card with gold backing.

"What is this?"

"An information card for the envoy responsible for retrieving you, due by tonight's supper. These will help Guardian Eska notify Hown of who has permission to access the Central Core."

"Fine." Hydro swiped the card from the butler's grasp.

He shut the door and walked over to the desk, atop which sat his telecommunicator. After scrolling through his watch's library of contacts, he found the person who would pick him up—advisor to his father, Len Posair. It rang for seconds until an eye-patched man appeared.

"Prince Paen, what a surprise. I had to steal myself away from your father."

"What is Father doing right now?"

"Hearing complaints from numerous villagers. In three months' time, the suns will converge, and because of it, days are longer, and there is quite a hot spell here. Droughts are bad for crops. No crops equals no payment on their lands."

"As if my father can control that."

"Hardly. Dear boy, why did you call?"

"You must first swear on your life that not a hint of this conversation befalls my father's ears."

"I will keep it in confidence."

"Nor my mother's. This is for your ears alone. Understood?" Hydro watched Len nod his head and massage his forehead with his fingertips.

"Yes, yes. Now, what is it?"

"You must pick me up from the Central Core tonight. Get here as soon as possible. We are destined to leave tomorrow, but I cannot spend another moment on this planet."

"Things did not favor you, then?"

"I wish not to speak of it. Just come."

"I need Guardian Eska's permission to land on the Core and your father's permission for use of the spacecrafts. How do you suppose I do that?"

"Figure it out with Father. I will make sure you are cleared to land on the Core." Hydro flushed in annoyance. "Do not forget proper identification. Notify me once you are here."

"Yes, Prince Paen."

The connection ended. Len would keep silent. The advisor valued his half-life. Hydro called it that because his right eye had been gouged during an unruly protest. Anyone with deformities lived a half-life, according to Hydro. If Len disobeyed, he would lose the other eye.

When finished packing, Hydro found that dinnertime had arrived. His stomach ached and gurgled at the thought of sitting across from the commoner through the meal. He would have to endure the triumphant look that filth was sure to wear. He walked alone to dinner, like he had so many times before, not being able to relate to people. The vermeil-silver halls felt like cold steel to him now. It cut deeper than skin; it cut his pride. Soon he would be rid of this place.

In the jungle-green room, Hydro sat in his normal spot between Senator Numos and Gabrielle. Cain already sat beside Gabrielle. Since the beginning of the Trials, Cain's fiery hair had grown to cover his eyebrows, resting neatly on top of his frameless glasses. A blue tunic—outlined

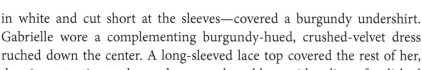

in white and cut short at the sleeves—covered a burgundy undershirt. Gabrielle wore a complementing burgundy-hued, crushed-velvet dress ruched down the center. A long-sleeved lace top covered the rest of her, drawing attention to her red sea-coral necklace with a line of polished black onyx in the front and back.

In spite of his mood, Hydro had also made an effort to wear suitable clothes for a last dinner. A cotton, white, long-sleeved shirt, slashed at the sides, lay slightly unbuttoned to show both necklaces. A silk sea-blue vest was drawn over and laced together with black threads in the front. The badge of his house sat upon the upper right of the vest, reminding everyone—even the commoner—that he was still royalty despite his loss.

Hydro noticed the extravagance of Eska's jeweled, armored shoulder pads at the end of the table. A brooch, shaped in the form of a golden dragon, connected a lavender cape to a chain dangling in front of the pads. Behind the chain, stuffed into a black dress shirt, was a necklace of Eska's own.

The conseleigh sat adorned in various dressy clothes; Tundra Iycel wore a layered, lacy dress, while Riagan Inferno donned a white dress shirt, partially hidden beneath a ruby-red scarf studded with diamonds that was across his right shoulder and wrapped around his neck.

When everyone was present, Guardian Eska spoke, "Contestants, it weighs upon my heart that this is our last dinner together. All of you deserved to be here. . . ."

Some more than others. Hydro glared at the commoner, who seemed too entranced by Eska's voice to even notice. Then he stared at Zain, who looked down at his plate and to Gabrielle every so often—but avoiding eye contact with Guardian Eska. *How do you even have the audacity to say no to Guardian of the Core?*

"And as you leave here and go your separate paths, none of you should view yourselves as failures. All of you have done something many only dream of—enduring the most grueling competition in the universe. I wish all of you luck in your future endeavors. May the Ancients and the Twelve, both, continue to fulfill your aspirations."

With yet another snap of his fingers, copious silver platters of food arrived. Delicate strips of beef and lamb, fresh fruits, and tossed green salads came out. The commonality of it all sickened Hydro. In his return to Acquava, there would be food similar to this, and there would be other nobles like Prince Evber; Hydro would need to treat with politicians like

Senator Numos, and no doubt there would be a marriage, created only with duty and authority in mind, to some other Gabrielle. There would be songs sung about the commoner's triumphs, and it would serve as false hope that their class could aspire to anything more than what their birth provided them. Hydro stabbed his salad greens and let the fork drag against his clenched teeth.

"So, Prince Paen, I assume I shall see you again at Eirek's Coronation in a few weeks?" Cain stated through a mouthful of lamb.

"My family will be there." In truth, Hydro hadn't planned on attending. But what other options were there? *Abaddon's flames swallow me if I'm forced to attend that filth's Coronation. And Acquava's seas drown me if I don't return home from the Core.*

"I am excited."

What was wrong with Prince Evber? Where was his propriety? Why did he respect this filth so suddenly? It seemed that the commoner had won over everyone. But he wouldn't win Hydro over. Ever. The day he earned his mother's respect is the day he would accept the commoner as his guardian.

"And what of your family's scorn?" Hydro asked him.

"Disappointment fades. Surely that has been the case in your family."

"My family is different."

"Our families are both pure of blood; mine has only been ruling longer."

If only our blood was pure. She tainted it. . . . "And your loss of freedom, does that not bother you? Do not all the duties you have overwhelm you?"

"Do you believe being guardian would have been any different?" Cain chuckled and pushed up his glasses.

I could go anywhere as guardian. Answer to no one. Hydro didn't answer for a little while. He cut his strip of beef, grinded it down in his mouth, and washed it down with purple wine. "What will you do now, then?" Hydro swirled the glass of wine in his hand.

"I will find another way to become history, more than just a name in my family's lineage. Do you want to know why my family has the longest reign?"

Hydro swigged his wine. "Why is that?"

"We never see anything considered failures by others as that. There is a saying my grandfather's great-great-grandfather said: Even if you fall on your face, you are moving forward. Learning to stride is a journey of self-discovery like none other."

Hydro grunted. He picked up his fork and stabbed what remained of his food and put it in his mouth. Teeth crunched. *How do I move forward now?* Wine swished around his mouth. *Where do I stride?* Swallow. *What do I do now?*

Guardian Eska stood, halting the movement of knives and forks and spoons alike. "As dinner draws to a close, so does our time together. If you pass your information cards toward me, I will notify General Satoris immediately following our meal."

Hydro passed the card that sat underneath his crimson linen. The last thing he heard before he departed was Guardian Eska calling over the commoner to talk with him. Words that should have been his. Hydro tried holding his head high, like that of a lord, but the saunter stopped shortly after crossing into his room. He closed the door and collapsed to the ground. Swelled eyes allowed tears to drizzle and collide with his cupped hands.

"I'm still a Paen. Lose or win." A clenched fist slammed against the carpet. "These tears will never touch the ground." Hydro repositioned himself on the floor, his back upright against the foot of his bed. "I am Hydro Áylan Paen II. Prince of Acquava." He spoke it aloud as though decreeing a new law. He practiced his father's voice, but it sounded unnatural. He was never meant to rule Acquava. He was meant for something more. Something greater. He was meant for apprenticeship. But now that had been stolen from him by the tip of one's tongue. He needed something different—anything to keep him from the monotony of palace life. To keep him from a slow death at the hands of duty.

In the contemplation of palace life, his cheeks dried and his clenched fists relaxed, leaving only numbness. He rubbed his neck and felt the strands underneath his shirt. He pulled his shirt forward to stare at both necklaces below. "You lied to me," Hydro said. "You said I would win. . . ."

You did win. You were first to the ship. You failed the fifth trial.

But why didn't I win that as well? I did not hear you help me.

I have no equal. The riddle lies.

What do I do now?

You could go back home. . . .

Hydro pulled the other necklace, which had a sapphire ring to show his authority and power and duty. The jewel felt cold.

But what has home ever gotten you? There is nothing for you there. You do not need those reminders.

Hydro twirled the necklace between his fingers. It represented the life he hoped to escape. *There is no need for you anymore.* He tugged and snapped the thread, stood, and put it next to the mirror on top of the dresser. The necklace he still wore intrigued him. His grandfather had told him that every piece of jewelry shared a story—his mother's necklace of a metallic-blue water droplet attached to a gold chain reminded her of her daughter's death and Hydro's failure.

But what was this necklace's story? He had yet to find anything definite, but he had time to research now before Len came to retrieve him. *Perhaps I will find something by searching for those in connection with the necklace like I was going to before the fourth trial.*

Hydro walked to the library on the second floor. On the computer screen, he typed in "Zas Labyrinth" and followed the green light that led to the book's barcode. *There must be some significant history to it. The man seemed adamant to protect it.* Hydro grabbed a book entitled *People of Power.* The cover was made of animal skin, and the pages were dry and hard. It weighed a considerable amount for a book, and this particular one was handwritten.

He plopped down at a table and set to reading, first opening up the table of contents and scrolling through the names. The faded cursive slowed Hydro only little. He had studied enough hand traces at Finesse that he was no stranger to different types of penmanship. The contents listed people he'd heard of, some he hadn't, and some that rang a note of familiarity but whose particular deeds escaped him. He turned until he found a man by the name of Zas Banegul. *Is he who the labyrinth is named after?*

He started learning about a man with First Blood who hailed from the Evolic tribe under Ancient Bane and was the first human to cast power. He was tasked to create equality, to construct something that would give even denied the ability to use power. A necklace mixed with the blood of the only black dragon ever created, Desmós, and powered by scales taken from the dragon's body could give that ability. This necklace had started the Great War.

Hydro looked up from the book and stared blankly at the bookshelf in front of him. Outside, darkness reigned. He was alone. After a moment's pause, he continued reading.

"The person to first wear the necklace was a man by the name of Beno Begare—the only denied ever born in the holy lands of Gladima. This necklace gave him the ability to use power, and with it, he killed families from the other tribes. Ancient Lyoen, leader of the Heavolic tribe, brought him to justice and tore the necklace from him. He then created the labyrinth now referred to as Zas Labyrinth, never allowing for his escape and compelling him to serve as guardian to the necklace. As punishment for creating it, Lyoen banished Zas from Gladima and imprisoned his daughter inside the necklace. Bane, seeing the injustice in Lyoen presiding over people of his tribe, initiated what would become known as the Great War.

"Being of First Blood, Zas Banegul is surely still alive, immune to time's cruelty. Although his whereabouts cannot be traced, rumors spread that he lives on the Lost Island somewhere in the Sinking Sea on Myoli. Although the location is a mystery, Chaon seems the most logical choice for his location, as it houses Mount Klaff, a towering structure that gives denied the chance to climb to the very heavens of Axiumé and ask for anything their hearts desire, whether that be wealth or power or immortality—a characteristic similar to the necklace's ability. The current record holder for climbing the massive structure is Edwyrd Eska, who I examine further on page 127. . . ."

The more he read, the heavier his eyelids became. Soon he closed them to the copious amounts of text and the world. . . .

Hydro stands in an alcove. Trees tower above him, blocking the light of Lugh and Freyr. A brisk breeze brushes against his cheeks. He can just barely make out a white outline farther amongst the trees. He sprinted here with others, but now he finds himself alone. He moves toward it, but stops.

Scales rub against his ankles. A large serpent—with wings on multiple spots of the reptilian muscle—coils a black, sinuous body around him. Hydro sweats. His hands clench.

"Stop it. Stop it," Hydro pleads.

The serpent retracts. Hydro looks into its black eyes, then at the dark-red tongue that licks his neck. It sticks its head down his shirt—and bites him.

Hydro screams in agony. Leaves erupt around him—only to flutter down like fall. The serpent yanks the necklace off the prince's neck and tosses it into the sky, then opens its mouth wide and swallows it. Reptilian eyes glow. Hydro jerks his head back. Faint throbbing and beeping filters into his mind. Soon it overtakes his senses. Throbbing and beeping. Throbbing and beeping. Throbbing and beeping . . .

Hydro awoke to the beeps of his telecommunicator. His head throbbed, and his face was moist with sweat. *Why did I dream that again? But, it went further this time.* Hydro looked around. No one. He didn't know how much time had passed, but night's grave was fully dug. The throbbing in his head subsided slower than usual. The call died. Giving only a moment's breath, it started beeping again. *Len must be here.*

Hydro pushed the side of his telecommunicator to accept the call. A holographic head of his father's advisor appeared in front of him. "Why did you not answer the first time? Did you not hear me?"

"You woke me. Are you here?"

"Yes, by the cliffs to the west of the estate."

"Excellent, I will be there in the next hour. I have to gather my things."

"Aye, Prince Paen. I await your arrival."

The advisor's holographic head faded, and his watch beeped once more, signaling the conversation's end. Hydro closed the book, letting it lay on the table. It wasn't his responsibility to shelve it.

At the threshold to the library, he heard voices. They were fast and hushed, hisses in the night—the only sign that life was present in the seemingly empty estate.

"The suns draw closer, Edwyrd. What do you suppose it will be this time?"

"Only the Ancients know that. It will cause trouble though; it is a good thing an apprentice was chosen. He will need to learn how to deal with Pirini Lilapa."

"The boy will need much work before then; I am disappointed Zain did not accept the offer."

"That is why you are my conseleigh. The boy will grow into his role in time. He shows promise and understanding. But I cannot help but think that Zain's refusal stems from him seeing Zakk Shiren during the end of the fourth trial."

"When you showed me the image, I admit, my curiosity grew. But why would that cause him to deny the position?"

"That is a prerogative all his own. But it raises other questions. . . . How was Zakk there? How was he able to conceal himself? Who picked him up?"

"A thought comes to mind . . . but . . . I will need to make arrangements to visit Sereya."

Hydro crawled forward on his belly like a snake. Even in the darkness, he saw both of them clear as crystal. *Have my eyes adjusted to the darkness this fast?*

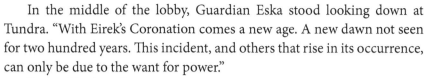

In the middle of the lobby, Guardian Eska stood looking down at Tundra. "With Eirek's Coronation comes a new age. A new dawn not seen for two hundred years. This incident, and others that rise in its occurrence, can only be due to the want for power."

"A terrible thing."

"Not all is terrible."

Hydro's mouth dropped as Guardian Eska held Tundra's chin gently and moved his lips to hers. Light, which speckled in from outside through the glass windows, bathed them. Once their lips separated, the light departed, as if nature itself longed to see the love.

"May I come up tonight?"

"Not tonight. Soon . . . I promise." Eska's voice was stern with oath but tender with respect. Hydro didn't hear them exchange goodbyes. He was still in shock. *Why such secrecy?* When he noticed that Tundra was turning to ascend the stairs, he slid back into the library.

He waited for minutes, until the distinct grinding of the lobby floor hoisting Eska to his room ended and the clacking of Tundra's heels subsided. In his room, he grabbed his duffel bag, stuffed it full of clothes from his closet, and laid it on his bed. He looked to the dresser and still saw his ring. He wouldn't need it where he was going. It reminded him of the past—a past he would outrun.

When he exited the estate, cool night air welcomed him with new adventure. An adventure he was eager to begin. The weight of the bags slowed him, making his trek to reach the mountain cliffs longer than expected.

Len stepped out from the ship's entrance and walked toward Hydro. An eye patch covered his right eye, his hands shone in jewels, and his gold teeth sparkled, illuminated by the light of the ship. A puffy undershirt spread out past his trunk-brown traveler's coat like white chest hair. On the left lapel of his coat he wore a badge shaped like an ear, his advisor's badge.

"Len, take my bag." Hydro bent down and removed the strap from his shoulder.

He followed Len to the triangular-shaped spaceship. Underneath its belly, Hydro stepped onto a triangular metal platform, and with a click of one button, he and Len were lifted off the ground and hoisted into the ship. Once the compartment closed, he walked forward and took his seat next to the pilot's chair. Len joined him as the pilot.

"Where to, my prince?"

Where am I headed? Hydro stared at the mountains that loomed before them. They stood amid the freckled cheeks of the purple sky. Beneath his tunic, the necklace itched, reminding him of his journey and the story that waited to be told. Perhaps he would be the one to find Zas Banegul. He would succeed where others failed.

With a wry grin, he turned to his family's advisor. "You will head for Chaon."

"What is there, my prince?" Len asked.

"Adventure."

Hydro closed his eyes, letting exhaustion take its toll once again. The engines blared, and the ship's music sifted through the air, lulling him to sleep. As his thoughts drifted, the vessel soared off into the night—only guided by the lights of the stars and fueled by the ambition of Hydro's dreams.

✤ CHAPTER 52 ✤

FAREWELLS

"Does anyone know where Prince Paen is?" Eska called out across the table to all in the midst of lunch.

Zain had no idea. And no longer could he care. He massaged his temples, trying to remember all the details of the past forty-eight hours. *How did he get to the summit? Who was piloting the ship? Where is he now? Will I be too late to save Mom?* He wanted to let out a scream, but instead he plunged the fork through his last piece of ham and shoved it in his mouth.

He looked up from his finished plate, tapped his feet, and teetered the fork between his thumb and index finger. Guardian Eska sat at the table's head, engrossed in conversation with two of the butlers, Colin and Dominic, the latter of whom held a necklace in his hand. *What are you talking about?* The necklace's prominent sapphire sparkled in the light from the chandeliers above and the glare from the windows. Guardian Eska grabbed it, examined it, and set it down on the table, standing up moments later.

"It appears Prince Paen left early this morning. But I will consult with General Satoris to make certain. Regardless, I shall take a few moments here to express my final thoughts.

"All of you are great warriors, eclipsing my hopes. I encourage all who leave here today to show your strength in tournaments; let the families of power in each of your respective nations know there are talented fighters still in their midst. May the luck of the Twelve and the Ancients be with you as you reestablish your lives. I hope our meals here have made you full, but I hope your pride and confidence leave even fuller. Tens of thousands applied, but I only sent out eight invitations. Each of you can cherish that accomplishment for the rest of your lives."

Eska raised his glass, compelling the others to do the same. "Let us toast to your good fortune in the days to follow, and to history—her eyes are widened by you all."

Zain swallowed the rest of the honey-sweet mead in his glass. Before he took the glass from his lips, he gazed upon Gabrielle for a second; she exchanged words with Prince Evber, her finger circling the rim of her glass. What was it about Gabrielle that kept drawing Zain back? He needed to leave. He brought the glass down as she flicked a glance toward him, smiling and biting her lower lip at the same time. *That's why.*

He didn't acknowledge the smile. He left and headed back to his room. There would be time to talk with her on the way back to Myoli. He had talked with Gabrielle after the announcement of rides, and after Zakk's words, he thought it better for his mom not to pick him up, and Jamaal was probably too busy. Empora was only across the Krine Sea, a two-hour side trip, maximum, depending on the model of ship used.

Once in the lobby, he migrated toward the eastern wing. His things were already packed; he had done that the night before after his visit to the apothecary, where they treated his burns with nectar from the katarh flowers, which Adored Amiti explained were only found in the frozen northern plains of Onkh. Once applied, the burns dissipated, and a gelid feeling crept over his entire body, prickling his skin at every application.

Even though he had packed his nicer clothes, the ones he wore for dining, he had yet to receive from Heather his academy uniform that he had worn during the fourth trial. The felsic hadn't splotched it horribly, due to the black coloring, but Zain knew it would tarnish the others that it touched. He thought the knock he heard at the door would be her.

"Hea—Eirek?" Zain blinked. "What are you doing here?"

"When I saw you leave the dining hall, I left. I . . ." Eirek looked down to the ground. He turned around and shut the door. "I need to know . . . why didn't you choose to become apprentice?"

Zain kicked the floor and looked out the window, hoping Gabrielle's mom would land. "What does it matter?"

"It matters to me. I won with your help during the second trial. And I won with Gabrielle's sacrifice during the fourth trial. I . . . even though I won, I don't deserve to be apprentice. Eska was right—all along he was. You deserve it."

"Eirek . . . Eirek . . ." Zain looked at him, and wetness started to form underneath his eye. "I don't deserve it. . . ."

"But why!"

"I killed my best friend . . . or at least I thought I killed my best friend . . . before . . . before the Trials even began. . . . For my own selfishness. For my own dreams. . . . He's been haunting me ever since then. . . . If I want to make things right with him, I . . . I can't be here."

"Is that who you saw on the summit?"

"How . . ?" Zain arched his eyebrows and tightened his neck.

"Cadmar told me someone appeared out of thin air and taunted you."

Zain lowered his gaze to the floor. "Yeah . . . it was. . . . He told me that you need to fight for others before you fight for yourself. . . . That . . . that's why I am glad you won." Zain looked toward Eirek and smiled.

"I . . . what do you mean?"

"It's not hard to see, Eirek. You fight for others. . . . I saw it when Hydro and I were dueling during the second trial. Instead of finishing the trial, you wanted to help me. On the way to the apothecary, Gabrielle told me that you let her ride on your horse during the fourth trial. . . . But now it's time you start fighting for yourself."

Eirek looked down and then up again. "What will you do now?"

Zain smirked. "Fight for others so that I can fight for myself, and it starts with fixing things with Zakk . . . somehow."

A knock occurred at the door. "Mr. Berrese?" It was Heather's voice.

"You'll be a fine apprentice. Good luck at Coronation." Zain walked forward and extended his hand to Eirek.

Eirek took it. "Thanks. . . . Good luck with Zakk. I hope you find him and make things better."

"I hope so too." Zain smiled, released his grip, and went to the door. He opened it and ushered Eirek out. Even before he left, Zain redirected his attention to Heather. She was a twig of a servant with bangs hooked to the left. No makeup graced her face, and no earrings polished her ears. Her black outfit made her look rather deathly, and he could not help but think that she looked twice the age she actually was.

"I have your clothes. Cleaned, washed, and dried exactly as you have specified."

"Thank you, Heather." He held out his arms, accepted the small pile of clothes, and turned around to pack them.

"Are you finished, then, sir?"

"Yes, Heather."

"I will have other servants carry them to the lobby for you."

"Thank you," Zain said.

"It is my pleasure and duty," she answered and left as abruptly as she had come.

A few minutes later, Zain made his way out to the lobby and saw Senator Numos and Cadmar standing beside Eirek; Gabrielle was near Cain. A middle-aged lady was deep in conversation with Eirek, Cain, and Guardian Eska. Behind Eska stood his four conseleigh, all garbed in different colors of blue, orange, yellow, or green.

Russet curls extended down the front of the lady's light-green dress, stopping before her breasts. A light-yellow shrug covered the low-cut dress, which extended to her knees. Black, high-heeled sandals made her almost as tall as her Cain. Upon Zain's arrival, she looked at him through forest-green eyes. She had a polished face and a short and slightly-curved nose that pointed upward. Dark-red lips added to her charming complexion.

"It was a pleasure meeting the future guardian. I will see you in the weeks to come. Bye, Ms. Ravwey, Sir Briggs." She nodded to each. "Come, Cain, let us leave."

The woman retreated from the lobby—a few of Eska's servants trailing behind her, arms loaded with her son's things.

"I hope to see you again, Gabrielle." Cain wrapped his arms around Gabrielle.

Zain clenched his fist, but he let it relax when Cain released the hold.

"We will. I'm certain of it."

"Bye, Eirek, Guardian Eska . . ." Cain looked at Zain and nodded but remained silent. He said goodbyes to everyone else and then left into the bright rays of midday.

Gabrielle's mother arrived a half-hour later. She was garbed in a red tube top, with a dark-orange fox-fur scarf covering her bare shoulders. Black gloves waved in the air like a politician as she made her way toward Gabrielle.

"*La maman.*" Gabrielle rushed forward to hug her. If it weren't for Gabrielle's black heels, she would have been shorter than her mother.

"Gabrielle. *Mon bebe.*" Lady Ravwey kissed her daughter twice, leaving a faint red to shade Gabrielle's soft skin. The older woman pushed wide glasses up her slender nose and looked toward Guardian Eska. "Are you za famous Guardian Eska?"

"I am," Guardian Eska said with a slight bow. "Alexa, you have a talented daughter."

Zain chuckled as he saw Gabrielle's mother wave her hands like an actress on stage.

"Vell, I'm very pleased you say zat." Alexa beamed. She turned her attention over to him. "You are Zain, correct?"

Zain nodded.

"Are your zings ready?"

Zain nodded again.

"Ve are off, zen." Just as she twirled the fox-fur scarf around her hand, she turned and retreated toward the door.

Her Emporian accent was much thicker than Gabrielle's. After exchanging farewells with everyone, the ladies left. Zain glanced toward Eska. "I'm . . . I'm sorry things did not work out."

"May you have success in whatever path you go down," Guardian Eska said. His hands were clasped behind his back.

"Thank you." Zain nodded. "Bye, Cadmar."

"Bye," Cadmar said.

"And, Eirek, remember what I said to you earlier."

"I will." Eirek smiled.

"Goodbye, then. I hope to see you again. Sometime."

"As do I, Zain." Eirek offered his hand.

Zain took it and smiled. He turned around and walked out of the lobby. The servants had finished loading the luggage into the cargo area of the cobalt, medium-sized ship. The glossy, dark paint and the polished windows reflected the silver skies overhead. The nose of the ship was hooked like an eagle's beak. Right underneath the wing is where Zain boarded a metal ramp and took his place in the company of Gabrielle and her mother.

"Thank you for agreeing to take me home, Mrs. Ravwey."

"Such a zing is nozing. Ve are happy to help."

Zain made out half the sentence, assuming the best based on her inflection.

The engine blared. Instinct told Zain to hold something. That something found him though—Gabrielle's hand. Her mother was one row ahead of them, by herself, flipping through pages of a document. Through the side windows in the lounge area, Eska's estate became smaller. The rings around the planet stretched out before the front windshield. Eventually a dark vortex appeared amidst the blackness of space.

"Now entering Wormhole One. Please buckle up," a man's voice flowed through two audio boxes placed in the passenger area of the ship.

Zain squeezed Gabrielle's hand tight. Her mother was still engrossed in her documents. Even if she had been paying attention, or cared to look back, Zain still would've held on. At least, he would like to think so. Now that he had something to hold on to.

Somewhere out there, Zakk was confused and hurt. That pain made Zain scared. He didn't know what Zakk was capable of anymore; surely he never thought he was capable of taunting him throughout the Trials. And although Gabrielle's hand supported him, he couldn't help but wonder if she would get dragged into this, or if there was even enough time to save the ones he cared for most.

✤CHAPTER 53✤

ANXIETY AND ANTICIPATION

Eirek stirred as the light burned his eyelids. Freyr and Lugh lay in the middle of the silver sky like red and blue eyeballs surveying the barren desert below and the mountains that loomed in the distance. One out of the two bands of dark silver haloing the planet was lower than usual, nearly touching the peak of a distant mountain.

Eirek yawned and stretched in the red leather library longchair. The leather-bound, five-pound book shifted from his chest to his lap. He had been studying each nation's family in power for the past three days. There was nothing else to do—an emptiness now roamed the estate hallways, an emptiness he managed to get away from in the library. But this wasn't the type of reading he enjoyed. He flipped the book over and looked at his progress. Lord Victor Zigarda stared at him from the page. Zigarda's face was marred with burns, and his eyes were as gray as granite. No heirs. No wife. His younger brother had passed away a century ago, leaving a few nephews and nieces. But if the text was correct, he was currently two hundred and five years old. How had Victor lived so long? Had he found the secret to immortality? Eirek fingered the yellow pages in awe.

A faint whistling mixed with a patter of footsteps distracted Eirek. He slapped shut the burden he had been sleeping with and twisted his back into a long stretch to see who it was.

It was Dina, the same maid who helped carry his bags to his room on the first night.

"Dear? Dear . . . oh, here you are." Her gray curls bounced for a brief moment after finding him. Her bushy eyebrows needed combing. "Is that your outfit from yesterday?"

Eirek nodded. He combed the wrinkles in his brown tunic, which was a little too large for him, that the Clayses gave him before he departed for the Core. It was from Lord Clayse's glory days as a prince when wine and woman were plentiful and he was still fit. As if needing to vindicate himself, Eirek said, "I fell asleep. . . ."

"Well it's no wonder; look at what you're reading, dear." Dina chuckled.

"Eska told me I needed to for Coronation."

"We all must do something. I'll be happy once the whole ceremony is done with. My old body can't handle stress well anymore. But we'll get through it together, dear. Now, get cleaned up. Lunch is on the table. Guardian Eska had me fetch you."

"He knew where I was?"

"He knows everything. . . ."

Eirek should've figured. Guardian of the Core wasn't just a fancy title. Knowing where Eirek was in the estate was probably like finding sand in a desert for Eska.

Eirek maneuvered past Dina and heard her continue her statement in the faintest whisper, "Well . . . almost."

Eirek paused, intrigued. What did she know about Eska's power? Were there limitations?

Before Eirek could ask, she continued speaking, "Hurry! Change and dress for lunch. Do not keep Guardian Eska and his guests waiting." She shoved the air with her hands, gesturing him out.

Eirek assumed the guests she referred to were the conseleigh, but when he finally made it to the dining hall a half hour later, he found that to be wrong. The conseleigh were there, yes, but so were four older men dressed in white robes. They sat together on Eska's left while the conseleigh sat to Eska's right. When he entered, the heads turned to him. He felt awkward and examined, like he had just been caught stealing.

"Eirek, glad of you to join us," Guardian Eska said. "Come, sit down here."

Eirek blushed from the stares but walked to the end of the table and sat next to Ethen. A plate full of food already sat in his spot. Before Eirek could pick up his fork, Eska introduced the four older men. "Eirek, to my left are the four sages of Gladonus."

The four older men stared at him in long silence. Their faces were hard and worn and wrinkled.

"Who are they?"

Snickers escaped from the conseleigh to his left. The men's faces flushed red.

Ethen put his arm around Eirek and whispered into his ear, "Te sages be First Blood who since te disappearance of te Ancients now regulate te flux of power amongst families of power."

Eirek cowered back from their glares.

The man with different color eyes—one a dark blue and the other amber—stood up clutching a staff of cloudy gray that had been leaning against the chair. "Eska, how did some ignorant boy become chosen for apprenticeship?" The man shook his staff toward Eska, the top of it shaped in the form of a C with blades sticking up and out like a porcupine's back. In the center of the C was a metal eye. The cloudy steel reminded Eirek of his own sword.

Oh no. Eirek flushed with embarrassment and looked toward Eska.

"He competed in the Trials, Cronos. Same as the others," Tundra defended.

"The Trials have not done their part, then." Cronos glared at Eirek.

Eska stood and raised his gloved hand. "Cronos, I assure you the Trials have done their job. Eirek is competent; his mind, I'm sure, is elsewhere right now, with Coronation fast approaching." Once Cronos sat, Eska did as well. "Eirek, the sages will be training you in the art of power." Eska looked toward Eirek, brows furrowed.

"Boy, you look familiar, but that is an evident mistake. Where do you come from, boy, if you have not managed to know of us?"

"Creim . . ." Eirek paused, then added, "it's a small town in the nation of Cresica."

"Is it, now? So you will manage to secure the Clayse's vote easily, then?"

"I believe so, yes. And more than that as well."

Cronos chuckled. "A majority is what you need, and if you are as uneducated about the families in power as you are of us, it seems likely you will fail."

Eirek dropped his chin, but when Guardian Eska spoke, he looked up again. "Eirek knows that he will need to impress the families in power. He has been living in the library for the past few days."

"Knowledge will impress some, that is true. As some would say, knowledge is power, but it is also confidence, and a new wardrobe will help secure the boy's vote."

"Confidence, Eirek has gained through completion of the Trials. As far as knowledge is concerned, it is understanding, not power. Eirek is of a sharp mind; I have no worries of him." Eska turned to Eirek and then lingered his gaze over his conseleigh.

"No rudeness to you, boy, but I take no stock in many things after seeing Ancients fight and Gladima torn asunder and replaced with . . . with this . . . after the Great War." Cronos licked his lips and raised his arms at all around him. Afterwards, he stared at Eirek.

"And what is so wrong with this?" Eirek tightened at the gaze. He couldn't let the bi-color eyes intimidate him. The way they gazed through Eirek, were they determining his worth?

"A boy like you couldn't understand." Cronos massaged his hands together.

"Then help me understand."

"It's not even certain you will be Eska's apprentice yet. And with the outfit you wear now, I see no hope."

The others sages stared, stoic as stone, like puppets to Cronos the puppeteer.

"Cronos, he is scheduled for a fitting before dinner," Guardian Eska said.

Eirek cocked his head. Hoping to change the subject he asked, "My fitting?"

"Yes. All apprentices are donned with their own unique gear. Also, their symbol appears during Coronation," Cronos advised.

"Symbol?"

"Yes. It is what your seal becomes." Eska twisted his arm so that he could show the silver pattern on his glove—it was an exact replica of the sigil on his cape—a silhouette of a dragon breathing fire as a sun vanished on the horizon. "It's said that the Ancients themselves pick it. Although I'm sure Cronos would know more about that than I as well."

"Divine power, a guardian's power, is used. It looks into your soul— every fiber of your being, your very morality—and determines who you are, what symbol is your own. It's almost like another name. Although I cannot speak for the Ancients anymore, as they are lost to the confines of time after the end of the Great War, perhaps they play a part."

Eirek's ears perked at the mentioning of Ancients but dropped upon the realization that power was needed. And power, he didn't have. At least, he had never been able to cast. Eirek looked at his hands. *Will Coronation just be a farce?*

"Anything else you would like to know, Eirek?" Eska took a sip from his stemmed glass full of purple wine.

"It seems the boy is rather uneducated about the ceremony. When were you planning on going through this with him?" The old man rubbed his hands together and looked back toward Eirek.

"Edwyrd planned to have him help us assemble the stage tomorrow," Tundra said. Her hands slipped around the stem of her glass as she took a sip of the mead within.

"Like Tundra mentioned, my plan was to tell him tomorrow, but perhaps a brief synopsis would be educational if you say so, Cronos."

"It may help the boy." Cronos raised an eyebrow at Eirek.

"Well to appease Cronos, then." Eska looked toward Eirek and continued, "On the day of Coronation, you will be asked questions by each family in power. They will be open-ended questions that require you to divulge your manner of thinking and character to them. If they find you true and worthy, they will cast a vote for you. Upon receiving a majority, you will be asked to take my vow as apprentice and future guardian."

"What if I don't receive a majority?" Eirek asked.

"This is who has gained apprenticeship?" Cronos eyed Eirek.

"Confidence can be gained through training, Cronos. It is simply nerves," Eska rebutted.

Eirek felt worthless. He was glad that Guardian Eska supported him, but he shouldn't need supporting. Not anymore. Not if he wanted royalty to see that he was equal to them. If he were Hydro, the thought of not being accepted would never have crossed his mind. But he was Eirek, a boy confined to the hopeless city of Creim, whose greatest adventure was taking a trek through the Amon Forest.

"If this boy should fail, do you have seconds and thirds ready?"

"There is a second, yes."

Cronos glared at him, but Eirek did his best not to falter. Why did it seem like they were against him? Were they truly? Or was it because he hadn't proven himself yet? What made Eirek more nervous is how the other ones remained mute. Their eyes bounced back and forth to the dialogue. Eirek hadn't even touched his food, but looking toward his plate, he wasn't hungry anymore. Disappointment filled him well enough.

"Come over here, boy. Let me test you for power."

"Let the boy go, Cronos," Luvan spoke this time. "You have already intimidated him enough. The power Edwyrd has is different than the power used by families in power."

"Your point is valid. But how is one supposed to deal with higher power if he cannot even control a lower tier?"

"That is what your training is for, is it not?" Luvan asked.

"Enough." Guardian Eska raised his hands. "There will be time for testing and training later. The next two days will be busy, rest assured on that. Eirek needs time strictly dedicated to learning about the families in power."

"I . . . I do need to study." Eirek smiled weakly at all of them. He pushed up from the table and started to leave.

"Eirek, you 'ardly ate anyting on te plate," Ethen said.

"I'm not hungry. Sorry. Good day, all of you." Eirek glanced at the conseleigh, then to Guardian Eska and then to the sages.

"I will come get you when it's time for you fitting," Guardian Eska said.

Eirek nodded and left. He took the familiar route to the library, dragging his feet on the carpeted floor leading toward the lobby and the tiled floor once in the lobby. Even though he did not know who those men were, he knew one thing: They weren't royalty. And if he was to impress the families in power at Coronation, he needed to put on a better performance. The fitting may help with that. He hoped to wear something regal, something to make a lasting first impression so that they did not see him as a commoner when he took the stage. He wanted something more. Something that shouted, "Apprentice!" But even if he had that something, he would need to impress them with his knowledge, something he had not done before.

He navigated his way back to his longchair that overlooked the land outside the estate. The book still lay on the table, ready for him. For the first few pages, he remained focused and interested, learning about Lord Garrett Omyon of Nova. At least the text changed—something that could not be said about the scenery. He didn't know how much more of the planet there was to see, but he wanted to see more than just the westward cliffs. More than just the dunes of sand sprawled out over miles. He wanted more interaction with people. In all, Eirek wanted something that wouldn't come in haste but in time.

CORONATION

"We do not ascend until Eska tells us to," Ethen advised. He turned around, creating slight creases in his flowing greenish-jade doublet and chest piece.

"How will he do that?"

"Trough te mind. In time you shall grow tired of using your lips too." Ethen tapped his skull and turned back to face the cliff as he clasped his hands behind his back.

To his right and left were Luvan and Tundra, respectively. Luvan wore the same outfit as Ethen, except that the dull amber color of his was dotted with black onyx to make it shine more. Tundra wore no doublet but instead wore a dress of baby blue encrusted with diamonds. Her wrist lace of crystals covered her right forearm, curling around it like her hair. Short scars near her blue lips marred her face more than the others, but Eirek still sensed a beauty to her, although surely forgotten to time. And Riagan stood behind him wearing a chest piece and doublet of fiery-red threads. He, too, had his hands clasped behind his back and looked up to the cliff's edge.

Are they waiting for Eska to speak to them? Eirek never spoke to anyone but himself in his mind. To talk to others was absurd, especially for one who couldn't use power.

Eirek looked up. Cliffs shadowed him. Atop the cliffs, crowds of royalty awaited him. And even higher up, brilliant silver crowned the sky, along with two dark-silver bands and two suns. He tightened the white glove on his left hand. Out of anxiety, he smoothed the outfit Eska had given him for Coronation. A royal-blue dress shirt had cuffs crusted with rubies and the middle dotted with golden buttons. There was a ruby-red sun flaring brilliantly from the center of the shirt to the shoulders, where a brooch in the shape of a dragon held onto a cape of silk—pearl white underneath and royal blue on the back. With it on, Eirek felt regal, like he belonged among the rich and powerful who were waiting in eager anticipation of his character.

A breeze fluttered by him then, flowing through his hair and the folds of his clothing. It cooled him and, in doing so, spoke words of encouragement in the faintest whispers. *Berol.* It had been a month's time since he had seen any of the windies, but with the breeze came the recognition that he could win over the favor of families in power just like he had won the second trial. Eirek squinted, hoping to catch some sign of them, but he saw nothing.

"Now it is time."

Eirek stepped on the platform, encouraged to do so by Riagan pushing him forward. Metal hummed and clunked. Gears cranked. And like the sapphire circle in the lobby of Eska's estate, it lifted them up.

At the top of the cliff, a giant metal arc stood as the threshold before a red carpet with golden borders. The carpet would guide him to the stage. Royalty filled the benches. At the edge of each row, armored knights held long, slender pikes. He progressed as slowly as Ethen led. Eyes evaluated Eirek. He only tried to find comfort in familiarity. And he found it. The Mourses and Angal sat next to Lady Lynda and her husband, Rybert Clayse of Cresica, and . . . Linn. She wore a metallic turquoise dress laden with black flowers and a jade necklace. Linn's curved, thin, red lips exposed two dimples on her cheeks, red with blush. Brown bangs stopped at her pencil-thin eyebrows. He could not look any longer without longing.

So he looked to the front and saw the carpet snake its way up the steps to a raised section on the rectangular steel foundation shaped like a dodecagon. At each vertex stood a black pillar with gold lettering that displayed the nation to be represented. Below the golden lettering, their sigils showed in the mandated colors black and gold. A glass window like a windshield sat atop each pillar. Placed directly underneath was a white dot as large as a dish with a black point protruding from it. Another pillar that towered over the others was erected at each of the four corners. Eirek knew from helping to set the stage the day before that each of them contained one of the four elements, and upon the taking of the vow, they would activate.

He ascended the metal steps of the rectangular foundation, passing the curious bi-color eyes of Cronos. Eirek stood at the center of the dodecagon on a circular carpet made of a crimson silk with golden threads woven around the circumference. In the center of the carpet was a large dragon, wings outstretched and breathing fire, stitched in golden silk.

The conseleigh maneuvered around the perimeter to face him and the imposing audience. Luvan offered up a tome like a sacrifice to the wind. He had received it from Cronos upon ascending the stairs. The wind accepted the offer, and it hovered before the old man with gold hair and silver strands. A once-golden pyramid covered the front. Pages flipped, but no hands guided it. Besides Luvan, the other conseleigh stood with hands folded behind their backs, stoic as the wind that had died, as if even it held its breath to witness the event.

The ceremony was about to begin.

"Please state your full name," Luvan commanded.

"Eirek Mourse." Eirek tried to read Luvan's face, but he kept it glued to the pages.

"As you stand before us here today, you do so in the humble witness of the sages from Gladima and the families in power who bring order to each of our nations. Eirek Mourse, do you accede to speaking in complete veracity to any question posed? Knowing that if you lie, your lies are direct aspersions to the venerable Ancients Lyoen and Bane?"

"This I realize. Every answer from my lips will be thought from my own mind and spoken with my own tongue."

"May the Ancients protect you and guide you today. Eirek, please kneel."

The tome traveled back into Luvan's hands, snapped shut, and was bound. The conseleigh left him then. Behind him, Luvan preached with priest-like authenticity. "Today marks a monumental event. One that has not happened for two hundred years. Contestants were picked, trials were fought, and a man worthy of the title 'Apprentice' waits for your vote.

"All of you here today are testament to the will of Gladonus, the universe the Ancients of old breathed life into. All of you have witnessed Eirek Mourse swear his oaths to be truthful on the day. Yes . . . Yes . . . trials have been endured, oaths have been sworn, but votes still need to be cast upon this man who waits to be called apprentice.

"As you ask questions, do so with outmost vigor. He will sway the vitality of your kingdoms one day, fifteen years from now. If he fails in his duties, it is you, your first, second, third, and even the fourth of your name who will suffer his failures. If he is successful, it is you who have tested him and put your faith in him. As you come to the stage today, forget the ties you hold, and remember this: Today is for the future of Gladonus, a future that can sway like leaves of a tree, a future as malleable as clay, a future that is simply ours. . . ." Luvan paused, letting his message sink in like rain to soil. "Cronos, if you will. . . ."

"Lord Garrett Omyon, come to the stage. Ask the first question and cast the first vote."

Eirek recalled any information he studied about the man. He had been Eska's mentor before apprenticeship. He was one of the few left with First Blood in him, which is the reason he lived so long. Eirek wanted to see him, but his pillar must have been behind him. A loud clicking noise echoed, and gears turned. The first questioned lingered in the grasp of time.

"As apprentice, and as guardian soon after, how will you strive to bring our universe back to the golden days of old? Back to the times when the Ancients ruled?"

"Excuse me, Lord Omyon . . . but . . . but I believe you are asking the wrong question for finding nirvana. . . ."

"Is that so? Explain, then, Eirek Mourse, what question should I be asking?"

"When . . . when you lived on the holy lands of Gladima, lost since the Great War, there were only the Ancients to pray to. Now . . . now . . . in our world . . . I believe the real question should be asked: How do we create a solid belief like that of olden days you lived in? I, myself, am caught between the two beliefs of Ancients and the Twelve, and . . . and I know that there are others like me, from my same cloth, in the same situation. To . . . to have our universe back to your days, there . . . there needs to be some implementation of standards and education on . . . on what really happened before and after the Great War. Otherwise . . . confusion will only deepen as time continues to crawl."

"An interesting observation you make. A true one as well. Eirek Mourse, you have Nova's vote."

All the reading he had ever done had paid off. Relief flooded him. Above him a white light hovered. The first of many. He hoped. There would need to be six more.

"Lady Olivia Aprah, if you will please, ask the second question and cast your vote."

In time, a woman who looked no older than thirty walked along the stage's border. A flowing gown of purple silk laced with black was held from dusting the floor by slender arms, golden bracelets chiming in royalty's song. A slit on the back of the gown revealed a tattoo of two bladed tanfas on her shoulder bones, a permanent reminder to some long sung song. She appeared at the top of the pillar a minute later, behind the windshield, looking down at him. Wrapped in a bun, her brown hair avoided bushy, arched eyebrows. Polished with purple gloss, her large lips looked a speckled bruise. "Can power and technology exist harmoniously?"

Good question. Can they? Eirek thought about the different technologies he knew about: spaceships, telecommunicators, and habitat arenas. Then he thought about the different types of power he had seen: wormholes, telepathy, and Eska's spells of power that warded them during the third trial. In every way, it seemed like they complemented each other.

"Yes," Eirek answered.

"Why do you believe in such things?" she prodded further.

Eirek had to choose his words carefully. Everyone here could use power. "Because neither is superior to one another. They rely on one another. . . . Travel in space would take decades if not for the power of wormholes . . . and . . . and the power of wormholes would be a lost power if spaceships were never created. . . . Telecommunicators would not have been invented if the power of telepathy wasn't so appealing. . . . Habitat arenas would cease to exist if those unable to cast power . . . if those unable to cast . . . never wanted a safer and more advanced way to train.

"A majority of people in Gladonus cannot use power, so if it wasn't for these inventions, the dichotomy between the strong and weak would be even more evident. It is still like this . . . even now, for each of these technologies are priced high enough so that poor folk have trouble obtaining them. . . . So, yes, they can exist harmoniously, Lady Aprah, but . . . I also think that they can benefit our society so much more than they are doing so now. . . ."

"You speak true. My parents knew what it was like to be the poor folk you describe." Lady Aprah looked at him with sky-blue eyes. "You have Gar's vote, Eirek Mourse."

Eirek grinned. Another beam of light shot out overhead. It combined with the other and waited for more to join. Lord Astor Grime was called next. The name thickened the air. It was as stiff as the man's crystal cane that supported his seventy-year-old body. From what he read when he studied, the man was as cold as the icy plains of Sereya he came from. For good reason too. It was shortly after he took office, after Conseleigh Tundra abdicated her throne to pledge fealty to Guardian Eska, that present-day Gar revolted. Under his reign, he lost control of Gar, and they successfully seceded.

Dark-blue eyes stared at him from above the tall pillar. "What motivated you to become Guardian of the Core?"

That will be touchy with this crowd. But I cannot lie. I took an oath. Eirek furrowed his brows. "I . . . I originally applied for the Trials under the advice of my uncle . . . an uncle who was more concerned with pleasing nobility. . . ." Eirek looked up to see the skin between the faint white eyebrows wrinkle, "and . . . for him . . . who is not anything of nobility himself, it meant he needed to try that much harder to impress them, and . . . just like him, I've had to try that much harder during the Trials to impress those above me. . . . I think . . . I know that in becoming guardian I will show others like me that they can be something too. . . ."

"Inspiration, the kind you suggest, leads to revolts and uprisings. . . . Do you plan on bringing chaos to our universe?"

"I bring nothing but the truth. . . . If . . . if my success brings with it uprisings, then . . . then it falls upon your shoulders as a leader to handle them. . . . No support would come from the Core."

"I see. . . . I will remember those words just as you said them, but the motivations you represent . . . and the tale I know are just too similar for my taste. . . . I am sorry; Sereya cannot lend you support."

Eirek fought the urge to shake his head. Hundreds of eyes were on him. If they saw his confidence falter, then more may join Astor Grime in denying him apprenticeship. He had not seen the correlation between his success and Grime's failure, but Eirek answered truthfully. Eska told him that lending loyalty is something never done. *There are still nine nations left. All I need is support from five of them.*

Lady Clayse, who still adorned herself in a flowing dress of celadon marked with antique threads of gold, was next. Her presence was well accepted. The approval vote he received after the question bolstered his confidence from the recent setback.

After, the next to test him was Lord Rhagoh Requart of Pyre. As the lord circled the stage in his tailcoat strapped with black belts and silver buttons, Eirek couldn't help but remember the fourth trial. Trailing the man was his pet. The enkine dwarfed Eirek's kneeled figure. Paws pummeled the steel, and chains chattered amongst themselves. During the questioning, Eirek stared at the beast, not its master. He still trembled at the beast's power. Despite the jarring effect, he got approval.

He continued to receive approval from Lady Liliana Voux of Mistral. But afterwards, the Lady of Lurid, Farah Scule, and Lord Zalos Kapache of Chaon chose not to support him. This made his current count five in his favor and three against. He needed two more in order to achieve majority and become apprentice.

"Lord Victor Zigarda from Empora, if you will please, come to the stage and ask your question and cast your vote," Cronos read.

Eirek gritted his teeth. He knew he would not receive Zigarda's vote. Eska had told him so when they were setting up the stage the day before, since it was Eska who Zigarda had lost to when he competed in his own Trials two hundred years ago.

Age and hatred made his voice raspy. "It is said that you learn through mistakes, what mistakes are you glad to have made?"

Eirek knew the question aimed to show his flaws. He did not need to roam his mind for long before an answer came. "For the longest time during the Trials, I had trouble not recognizing my confidence. Confidence that should have been instilled in me when I got accepted to partake in them. Because of it, I . . . I did not perform as well as I could have. But now I am confident as I kneel here before you today that I am a capable guardian."

"Not as capable as you may believe. . . . I see a tremble as you kneel, and there is a quiver in your voice. You do not have the amount of confidence required for this position. How can I give you my vote? You must have confidence at all times, not just when you need it. Empora cannot lend support."

The rejection from Zigarda did not faze Eirek, but the slump of three rejections in a row caused him to bite his lip. *Five to four. I need two of these next three.*

Cronos called Lord Abraham Vangle to question him next. Although the lord's pillar was located behind him, Eirek knew from studying that he was darker skinned, like Zain. He was known for his love of jewelry. Eirek tried to clear his mind through the sounds of chains clattering among the chorus of cogs. He needed to receive a vote after his streak of failures.

"What is something you wish to accomplish before the end of the year as apprentice?"

The possibilities flooded Eirek's mind. There were so many choices in front of him. But he needed something that could be easily done and show enough of his character to gain a vote. He found his answer while he stared out to the horizon. From this vantage point, he could see a different side of the mountain peaks; from this spot, he thought he saw a speck of green.

Eirek cleared his throat and answered, "I . . . I do not mean to speak ill of one of my supporters, but . . . during the fourth trial . . . when we stayed in Blen, the innkeeper there mentioned that Lord Requart did not visit often. In fact . . . I do not believe the Clayses visit my home of Creim, now that I think of it, but . . . but what I want to say is this: Because of it, people like me there . . . they do not understand what the family in power is doing for them. It is not that they are ignorant; it is that the royalty is not as transparent as they should be. Even in getting accepted to attend the Trials, I . . . I did not have any clue what Guardian Eska did. I just knew that he governed Gladonus . . . and that stories were told of his abilities. But, answering your question, I will make it a personal goal of mine to stop by and spend time with the families of power individually. And not only them, but the civilians, too, to find out how I can best help each nation . . . and what changes need to be made within the structure of the civilization. I want to not be solely an acquaintance . . . but . . . a personal contact for anyone."

"You speak a truth I do not like to admit. But I am glad you say it. And I hope to see you, then, in the years to come. Eirek Mourse, your words are exactly what Gladonus needs now. You have my vote and that of Ka'che's as well."

A sigh of relief escaped Eirek as the vote saved him from his current slump of rejections. *Six to four. One more vote to obtain.*

"Lord Hydro Paen of Acquava, if you will please, come to the stage and ask your question and cast your vote," Cronos called.

Great. He believed this man would not be the vote he needed. If anything like Hydro, Lord Paen was surely to despise him. Hydro probably mentioned Eirek when he returned home. He did not get the pleasure of seeing Hydro's father, for his pillar was behind him.

Soon enough, there came a voice. "What makes you different than the other contestants who tried out to become apprentice?"

Eirek stumbled over his hurdled thoughts. He needed to evaluate himself compared to others. But he also needed to consider how the lord would react to his answer. Would Lord Hydro act like a lord or a father who believed his son should be in Eirek's spot? He needed a way that made him look confident but not boastful. He needed the impossible.

Getting his thoughts aligned, he answered, "My ways in dealing with situations and predicaments." Eirek gulped.

"How are they different than others though? Give me an example. Use my son," the lord boomed back.

This was a trap; he could feel it. Nevertheless he had to answer. "Your son, Prince Paen, would look at things and see no possibility for failure. I look at things and realize the possibility for failure. This makes my decisions not rash but planned out."

"Are you calling my son rash, Eirek Mourse? Acquava cannot lend support." Lord Paen didn't give him time to rebut the question.

"No . . ." Eirek sighed. *There goes that.* So slightly that only he could see it, he clenched his hand into a fist, lifted it, and pounded it on the crimson and gold carpet. He bit his lower lip as Lord Paen left the stage. *One left to go. Who hasn't asked me yet?*

"Lord Davin Evber of Epoch, if you will please, come to the stage and ask your question and cast your vote," Cronos called.

Eirek tensed. *Cain's father. Will he react with the same prejudice as Hydro's father?* He gulped again and tapped his fingers on the carpet before him. *I . . . I can't lose it here. I will make him see my point of view. I need to.*

Eirek looked up and saw a tall man stroll around to the front and rise to the top of his station. His brown hair was short and slightly curled. A small goatee hung from his chin, and thick-framed glasses hugged his long nose. Unlike Prince Evber, Cain's father had no freckles and a rather pudgy cheek and shorter frame than the longer and slender frame Cain had. An apple-green vest, much too tight to his chest, held the family sigil of the owl on an apple tree. Gloves of white leather similar to Eirek's covered both hands. A long scar that ran up along his left arm to where a short-sleeved, angel-white silk shirt lay under the vest could be seen even from Eirek's position.

Lord Davin Evber readjusted the green tie that slid underneath the vest before speaking. "What does it take to be a leader?"

Considering Eirek had never been one, the question gave him pause. He tried to think back though. The only thing that came to mind was Cadmar's saying. Not wanting to hesitate too long, he answered, "I heard once from a friend that a man who is good at chess leads the best."

Eirek paused long enough for the lord to think that it was his answer. "And what insight am I supposed to receive from that?"

Eirek ran through his thoughts. "When you play chess, sir, you must examine the whole field before making any moves. . . . As you stand there . . . as the last vote to determine whether I become apprentice or not, you have had the chance to examine the whole field. . . . If . . . if you have my vote, then as guardian, in order to benefit Gladonus as a whole, I must . . . examine everything as well . . . not just focus on one planet or nation in particular.

"And also as guardian, when I assign my conseleigh, I . . . must realize that I need people who have different viewpoints. If I simply had four other bishops . . . well . . . my line of thinking could only be diagonal. I must make sure I elect rooks and horses and even a most trustworthy lady who not only serve me under fealty but also truthfully and respectfully as well."

"Eirek Mourse . . . you are correct in saying I have the final vote . . . and the last move in this game."

Eirek looked up to see Lord Evber push up his glasses.

"And as I examine the field, I notice that your answers have already aligned you for success. You have me in checkmate. Eirek Mourse, you have Epoch's vote."

A huge wave of relief washed over Eirek as he saw the white beam of light travel to the halo above.

"And Mr. Mourse, tell your friend he is extremely clever."

Eirek smiled and nodded. *Thank you, Cadmar.*

The air now breathed again as if the acceptance of Eirek's apprenticeship determined if it would live. Eirek smiled to the ground, hidden to everyone but himself. He had done it. Now it was time to take his oath. But where was Eska? He continued to kneel, ready to be elevated to the status of apprentice when he next rose.

As he stared down at the red, circular carpet below him, a giant thud caused him to lose balance and topple over. It was the least graceful thing he had done all day, and he gathered himself quickly, hoping none of the lords or ladies saw his blunder. Scaly feet with long talons and thick, scaly calves of muscle were now in his line of view. He looked up to see a silver dragon no more than an arm's length away. It was so large that it made the enkine of Lord Requart look inconsequential. Boisterous gasps escaped the audience behind Eirek.

Eirek saw the soft mythril-silver underbelly pulse in and out in exaggerated rhythms. Scales as large as Eirek's hand, and as thick, covered the

beast's stubby arms. Curtains of webby, translucent silver closed and folded, allowing Eska to unsaddle from atop the dragon's back. Standing, the
dragon eclipsed Eska in height by at least ten feet. The beast looked toward
Eska, snorted smoke, and then looked toward Eirek. Dark-red eyes pierced
into him. Silver flames spewed from the dragon's lips as it flew off the stage
and landed on the ground close by.

"Eirek Mourse, you have won enough votes to be accepted as my
apprentice."

Eirek tore his gaze from Eska's eyes and admired his attire, more regal
than his own or any he had seen today. White belts were strapped diagonally to the middle and overlapped a white vest with bright ruby-red buttons. He wore a white long-sleeved shirt made of the same material as the
vest. A red belt, buckled by a silver dragon, slashed his mid-section, and a
dragon brooch clasped a flowing cape adorned with ruby red on the inside
and a pearl-white outside. Eirek saw strands of a necklace that hid in his
shirt. It seemed that Axiumé itself sent Eska.

"You must now acquire my vote. Are you ready to make your vows?"

Eirek nodded weakly.

Eska smiled as he looked at Eirek and then tightened his lips and walked
around the perimeter to address the crowd, "Families of power spanning
the system of Gladonus, you have met Eirek with questions, and he has
responded with answers. For some of you, these answers were wrong; for
most of you, they were right. Now he must answer one more question before he can state his claim as my apprentice. In witness of you all, he states
his oath to me and the gods whose power he will inherit in time."

Eirek tightened his grip on his knee as he brooded over the question
to come. If he wanted to say no, he should have done it when Zain rejected
his apprenticeship. Now, after he had earned the favor and confidence of
a majority of families in power, he needed to accept this oath, and with
it, show the people over Gladonus that even ordinary people could do
extraordinary things.

Eska stopped in front. "As apprentice and future Guardian of the Core,
do you accept the standards and regulations set in place by the Twelve? If
so, say, I do."

"I do."

"Then, Eirek Mourse, repeat after me: I, (state your full name) . . ."

"I, Eirek Mourse . . ."

"Hereby declare that I will serve Gladonus to my fullest potential . . ." Eska waited for Eirek to repeat.

"That I will remain impartial to the needs of any one particular nation . . ." Eska paused again.

"And that the power bestowed to me on the day of passing . . ." Eska waited.

"By the Twelve, of who have First Blood . . . will remain mine and mine alone . . . through the abstinence of love and marriage and heirs. . . .To all of this, I swear . . . in the presence of the Ancients, the Twelve, and the families in power."

Eirek finished with a certain gut rot in his stomach—one that only formed when in the presence of a guilty conscience.

"Eirek Mourse, I now dub you my apprentice." Eska let the fingertips of his gloved hand map Eirek's forehead. As the fingers made their way to each of his shoulders, a white light traveled behind like a comet's tail.

With one hand, Eska withdrew a blade one and a half times the length of a longsword. He held it up to the sky and let the light that shot from each of the nation's pillars condense at the tip and slowly sheath the sword. From around the perimeter, he heard animals bark or growl or roar or hiss, talking to each other in foreign tongues. *Are they closer to power than humans?* The dragon's roar overpowered all others. The pillars at the four corners of the stage shot out lights of red, yellow, blue, and brown—one for each element. It combined with the light from above and sharpened the glow from Eska's blade.

Eska held up his gloved hand to let his power mix with the power of the elements. Blue overtook red; brown sodded them out, and the mixture of elements looked like nothing Eirek had ever seen. It surpassed the ocean he had seen before the Trials or the sights he saw in Pyre. The miniature cloud of power coruscated a cylindrical wall encompassing Eska and Eirek, keeping them privy to the secrets of Coronation. The light rotated. Eirek heard languages he did not understand.

"Eirek, rise." The familiar voice caused Eirek to look up. Eska extended his hand and Eirek took the help. Blood rushed through him. Awe numbed him. The cylindrical wall that circled around glowed in a light of purple and pink and blue. Eska sheathed his sword and then directed, "Hold out your hands."

The faint outline of an object started to appear. Two circling rings stood atop a long, slender object. *My sword?* Eirek shot a glance to his sword and saw that his pommel glowed. Faces pushed against the cylinder like a person pushing his face against a bed sheet. Eirek blinked. *Does Eska see them?* The guardian did not seem affected.

Two voices collided, one's strong and proud, and the other booming and overpowering. In perfect unison, they said, "Eirek, you have been chosen."

Who was that? The glove on his right hand became embedded with his sword's image. He turned his hand over and caught the fully formed object in his hands. *How was this made?* It fell into Eirek's hands, and he could feel its warmth. It was a brooch in the shape of his sword. He twirled it through his fingers.

"The Ancients have spoken. Wear it and keep it close to your heart. It symbolizes something important to you, something you would be lost without."

The cylindrical wall of energy died and the noise with it. Turned by Eska's hand, Eirek saw the audience standing. A clap rang out. Then another. And soon a thunder of applause roared throughout the hundreds of people present. Not everyone applauded, but a majority did.

"The ceremony has finished. I understand if you must leave at this moment, but all of you are welcome to dine with us tonight."

Eirek followed Eska down the steps. A crowd of people awaited their presence. First among them were the Paens. Hydro was absent. They pulled Eska away.

Eirek tried to sort out the other families as best he could. Names, memories, and details fought for his attention like the voices in the air. He didn't realize how to deal with such attention and found himself continually glancing at Eska, hoping for his strength and confidence. But Eska was busy with the Paens. Was it Hydro they talked about? Hands on his shoulder stopped him from worrying more. He looked and saw the conseleigh standing by his side.

"Congratulations, Eirek," Luvan said.

"Yes, congratulations," Tundra said.

Eirek smiled and focused on the families of power ahead of him. The Clayses talked with him more than the others, but all congratulated him or feigned their acceptance of his apprenticeship. After the line of royalty ended, Eirek heard a voice he had not expected to hear ever again.

"*Hóigh*! Eirek!"

Eirek watched Cadmar walk from a row of chairs to his position. He wore a brown long-sleeved shirt with silver squares on the sleeves. "Cadmar, what are you doing here? I thought only families of power could attend this ceremony."

"Did you notice the armored guards who held the long pikes while you walked down the aisle?"

Eirek flicked his gaze to a knight striding behind Cadmar carrying a long pike and sheeted in earthy armor. He was as tall as Cadmar but stockier. On the sides of the helmet the sigil of Gar was crafted—an eye with steel eyelashes that looked like pincers around it.

Once Cadmar made it past the congestion of families mingling in the middle of the aisle, he stepped to his right to allow the knight to stand beside him. "Lady Aprah never travels without her elites. Since my aul man is one, I chose to come as well."

Eirek had wondered who the men in the earthy armor were.

"*Hóigh!*" Cadmar's father, Corrigan, removed his helmet, revealing his amber eyes. Prominent scars covered his face, showing his age and experience. Corrigan set down his helmet, retrieved the shield from his back, and banged his axe against it, just like the formal greeting Cadmar had extended Eska.

Eirek blushed and looked around. The ruckus caused families of power, like the Scules and the Evbers, engaged in conversation near them, to look their way. Shortly after the display, they returned to their talk.

"Don't be so shy now, lad." Corrigan stepped forward and slapped Eirek on the back with a gauntlet. "You be havin' good answers today. I be glad Lady Aprah showed her support. After the questionin', Cadmar here told me he told you that last sayin."

"He did." Eirek turned his gaze to Cadmar. "Thank you, Cadmar."

"I be surprised when you used our sayin'. But I be glad when it all worked out."

Eirek beamed. "As am I. Are you both staying for supper?"

"No, Lady Aprah has to leave soon. Word amongst the castle is that a new breakthrough in technology has been found."

"What is that?" Eirek asked.

"Force shields that appear on command. If we don't have to carry these around anymore," Corrigan raised his shield, "and still can be protected, the possibilities be huge."

"I am glad to see Gar is thriving since your seceding," Tundra said from Eirek's right.

"I am glad as well, Conseleigh Iycel. I hope you do not think Gar ill for uprising."

"It matters not what I think. Lady Aprah has grown to be a capable leader in Gar's twenty-five years of independence."

"A young leader for a young nation. Our energy knows no bounds, and Grime be, well, my father says he be harsh."

"Sereyans typically are. But Grime is certainly more so."

Eirek noticed Tundra smile. He did not know whether Tundra was truly happy or if it was an act like so many other courtesies he experienced today. It seemed Cadmar and his father were just as suspicious based on the arches in their bushy eyebrows. But they left with smiles on their faces all the same and shook Eirek's hand and each of the hands of the conseleigh as well.

Eirek sighed, disappointed at the too-short reunion. He turned his head and saw that Eska had finished talking with the Paens and now talked with Lord Requart, their bonded animals at their sides, at the stage's perimeter. Hydro's parents now talked to Victor Zigarda, who hid beneath a brown cloak. Victor and Lord Paen shook hands and then Lord Paen handed Victor a flask and continued talking. That raised Eirek's curiosity, but he was pulled away from the view by Luvan's voice. "Who are you looking for?"

"I was looking for—"

"Me?"

Eirek spun around to see Angal and, to his side, Lord Garrett Omyon—a man with amber eyes that hid behind narrow-framed glasses, a shaved pate but a long beard that extended to his stomach, and more bracelets on his forearm than Adored Amiti. For being of First Blood, Eirek was surprised to see his face tight, not loose with wrinkles. He wore loose, flowing garbs of golden silk, slashed with red, and tied in a red sash. On either side of Angal and Garrett were the Clayses and the Mourses.

He looked from Angal's blue eyes that held a hint of purple to the salad-green eyes Sheryin had, and he couldn't stop the tears from swelling in his own. He stepped up and hugged Angal. "Thank you for pushing me to do this."

Angal tore back from Eirek's grip. "You did this for yourself, Eirek."

Eirek wiped his cheeks with his ungloved hand and then stepped to the Mourses. He opened his arms and gave a hug large enough for three people. He squeezed as hard as he could, not knowing when he would see them again—Eska hadn't explained training to him yet. Tears came to his eyes again.

"Easy, Eirek," Jahn said.

Eirek pulled back and wiped his tears with his thumb. He looked into the steel eyes of Jahn and Jerald.

"Are you the Mourses?" Tundra asked.

Jerald stepped forward. "We are."

"Your son has a mind like I have never seen and a determination to match," Tundra said.

Eirek blushed and looked at the Mourses. Jerald and Sheryin beamed at him. Jahn was about to say something, but Sheryin spoke before he could. "Yes, he certainly does. He certainly does."

Eirek smiled and looked to Angal, who was looking down, then looked up and smiled.

"And, this is my uncle, Angal." Eirek pointed to his uncle and looked back to the conseleigh.

"It is a pleasure to meet you as well, Angal," Tundra said while the rest of them nodded. "If you please, I need to have a word with Guardian Eska."

"I as well," the other conseleigh said in unison.

They left then, walking toward Guardian Eska, who was in conversation with the Evbers. Cain occasionally glanced back to Eirek, and when he did so, he smiled. *The abruptness is kind of rude.* His brows furrowed as he noticed the conseleigh in conversation amongst the group. *What do they talk about?*

"Eirek . . ." Angal waited until Eirek focused in again, "I want you to meet Lord Garrett Omyon."

"It is a pleasure."

Eirek extended his hand in courtesy but was lost for words, so all he did was nod. From what he read, this man had actually seen the Ancients.

"This is who I mentioned to you seasons ago," Angal said, directing his speech toward Garrett.

Seasons ago? How long have they known each other? How do they know each other?

"Yes, I do see the resemblance. He does too though." Garrett motioned with his eyes, but Eirek couldn't follow.

"Resemblance to whom?" Eirek butted in.

"Nothing. Ga—Angal, can I have a word please?"

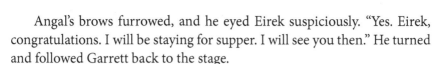

Angal's brows furrowed, and he eyed Eirek suspiciously. "Yes. Eirek, congratulations. I will be staying for supper. I will see you then." He turned and followed Garrett back to the stage.

"As are we," Jahn said.

"Does that mean . . ?"

"Of course we are staying, Eirek," Lynda said. "We are their transportation back home."

Eirek blushed and looked at the Clayses. Linn smiled and brushed back her bangs. Eirek stepped forward to shake each of their hands, and while doing so, he smelled the jasmine and white rose that lingered in the air.

"Thank you for your support. Without it, I would not be here right now," he said.

"Eirek, thank you for proving us wrong and winning the Trials. Your answers were brilliant. You did a great thing for Cresica today," Lynda said.

It shouldn't have taken me winning for you to acknowledge me, but I am glad you finally do.

"Eirek, it is dinner. Bring yourself and come." Eska's voice pulled him away from his thoughts.

Eirek nodded and turned his gaze back to the Mourses and Clayses. "I will see you all at supper."

"Of course. Go," Sheryin said with a smile.

Eirek left and caught up with Guardian Eska. None of the conseleigh were with Eska this time; instead Eirek noticed that they were ushering the families of power to the platform that would take them down from the cliff. A majority of the families had stayed—all wanting to eat supper with the Guardian of the Core more than his apprentice, Eirek supposed. At the cliff's edge, Eirek waited until the other families who were staying boarded the platform and departed.

And then it was just he and Eska. When the platform arrived at the top, Eirek noticed Eska's gaze locked on the sky, looking ahead to the stars that would eventually shine.

"What do you look for in the sky?" Eirek asked.

"Guidance. The suns draw near, and the stars seem to shine less."

"My uncle Angal told me that everyone has a star and that if you find it, you can make a wish, and the Ancients will grant it no matter what. Is that true?"

"The Ancients can do a matter of mysterious things, Eirek. Did you hear them today?"

Eirek tightened. A breeze hit his cheek. "Yes."

"As did I. I cannot wait to see them, once I leave this place."

"You still have years left though."

"I have seen empires rise and fall. I have seen loves live and die. To me, years have been like days. It will go fast enough, and especially now that I have your training to concern myself with." Eska turned his gaze toward Eirek and put his arm around his shoulder. "You answered every question well today. I am proud of you, Eirek."

Eska tried moving forward, but Eirek didn't budge. He needed to ask Eska something. "Would you have been more proud with Zain?"

Eska tilted his chin down. His brown eyes searched Eirek. "No, Eirek. You have something that he did not have."

"What is that?"

"Understanding. I saw it during Coronation. That is how you were able to procure the votes needed."

"Did Zain really not have that?"

"To an extent he did." Eska walked forward on his own, hands clasped behind his back, keeping his cape from picking up in the sudden breeze. "He had the understanding to fight for what meant most to him. But he lacked to understand others, and that is why it seemed like he rushed into things." Eska turned around, three paces away from Eirek now.

Eirek looked down to the ground and then back up again. "He . . . he said something to me before he left. He said that you need to fight for others before you fight for yourself."

"He is right. With those votes, you showed you can fight for others, and now you have the vindication to fight for yourself. With it, your star will shine brighter, and in no time, you will figure out which one is yours, like I have mine. It will call to you, and all it asks is for you to call back."

"Have you called to it yet?"

"No. There is nothing I need yet. But perhaps someday I will." Eska looked back into the sky for only a brief second. He turned his gaze back to Eirek and extended his gloved hand. "Let us go, the families of power are waiting for us."

"All right." Eirek smiled and stepped aboard the platform next to Guardian Eska. On the ride down, he asked, "How close was your vote?"

"At the time of my vote, there were only ten nations. Lurid and Gar ceased to exist. I received eight; it seems that Victor's father did not want to vote for the person who ruined his son."

Eirek wanted to ask what he meant, but he reserved the question for his thoughts. "Do you still remember your trials?"

"Every one of them . . ." Eska's voice trailed off, and his gaze looked distant once again.

What were they like? Eirek wanted to ask, but he stayed silent. There would be time to learn more about his mentor during the next fifteen years.

A hovercraft operated by one of the servants was already waiting for them by the time their feet touched dirt. Eska and Eirek sat in the back seat and said nothing as the wind hit their faces. The hovercraft landed outside the estate, and Eska led Eirek inside to the dining room, allowing him to sit by the Clayses, the Mourses, and Angal. Eirek noticed that Cain's family had stayed for dinner as well and sat across from him and between Lord Grime of Sereya and Lord Paen of Acquava.

In time, the families left. He exchanged goodbyes and blessings with each lord and lady still present. Some were feigned and some were genuine, but afterwards, each was guided out of the estate by pairs of servants at the doors. Off in the distance, engines blared.

Past the drapes he imagined the beautiful sky that Eska had looked upon earlier. It could offer him no guidance here due to the reflection of chandeliers. He still looked at the windows and imagined trying to find his star amongst the rest of them. One wish. Whatever he wanted. How does one even choose? How had Eska actually found his?

"Eirek, come sit up here," Eska said.

It broke Eirek's concentration. He took Eska's advice and sat with the remaining conseleigh and the sages at a spot to Eska's left, near Cronos.

"Do you know what event is fast approaching?" Eska asked.

Eirek stopped to think but then shook his head.

"The Meeting of the Twelve happens annually. This year it coincides with your acceptance."

"Where is it?"

Cronos explained, "At the brink before Axiumé. Just as Chaon hosts Mount Klaff, which extends to the heavens, Gar, too, hosts Mount Volan. It is not as well-known as Mount Klaff because it is not as publicly viewable. To get there, you have to cross the Sacred Passage." Cronos let his hand slide back to reveal lines of wisdom with strands of hair left and forgotten by the others. The two eyes bore into Eirek.

"How do I get through?"

"You need power," Cronos muttered before Eska replaced his answer.

"Power will get you through, yes. But a few of my conseleigh and Cronos will accompany you through the Sacred Passage as well."

It seemed that the desire to travel would be granted soon enough. But did it even matter? If what Cronos said was true, and he needed power, he may not even be able to go. He never casted a spell before, of the times he tried. Eirek looked down at his hands and noticed they had become sweaty. "I . . . I thought that I receive power . . . special power by being guardian?"

"Yes, upon the passing ceremony, you will receive the power of my guardianship, but you are not guardian now; you are my apprentice," Eska explained.

"So it seems now is the perfect time to test you," Cronos said.

"Now?" Eirek's voice quivered.

"Yes," Cronos answered. "Hold out your hands."

Eirek froze. What would happen to him once they found out he couldn't cast? A knot tightened in his stomach, and he was reluctant to extend his hand. Cronos pulled it from him regardless.

"Fire is an easier element to control. Say *palo*."

"*Palo*," Eirek said.

Nothing happened.

"You said it wrong. See the fire you want to control; obtain it's essence from the chandeliers or from the candelabra. Feel the fire that you want to create inside you. This comes from your confidence; the elements do not give their abilities away to those not worthy. Once you do, let your confidence in controlling it spread its way from your mind. . ." Cronos put a long finger on his head and dragged it across his skin to his chest, "to your heart. At that very moment, when you feel a burning in your chest, and it's about to overcome you, say its true name, *palo*, and its power will be yours," Cronos advised.

Eirek glanced nervously to the side. The council watched him intensely. Guardian Eska had his jaw cupped by his thumb and index finger, waiting on his newly appointed apprentice. This was it. *Will he still accept me even if I can't cast? No, I will cast. I can cast.*

Eirek focused on the fire flickering off the wicks of the candelabra farther down. *I will control you.* He reached with his fingertips, hoping to obtain some implausible ambition. A part of him felt its warmth, even though it was a body's length away. Then he closed his eyes and let the vision he had in his mind of controlling fire sink its way down his body.

His chest singed, and he tightened his lips, trying to ward the sensation. Then his chest flared, beating with the same intensity he experienced in the fourth trial while he outran the lizard. His fingers started to itch. His eyes watered, breaking through the dam of his eyelids. Eirek inhaled. Slowly he rotated his palm so that it faced upwards.

"*Palo*," Eirek whispered.

The beating of his heart receded. Eirek opened his eyes. A small orange glow grew from his palm. It wrapped itself around his wrist, warming him and owning him. It confided in him the secret of confidence, kindling his threaded qualms.

❦ EPILOGUE ❦

Zakk looked at the scenery from the inside of a caracraft. To the west was the Krine Sea and beyond that was Ka'Che, a place he could never go back to, not after Zain's betrayal. The first capital of Empora, Rydel, was slowly coming into view from their position on the Great Bridge. On the horizon Zakk could see the Red Cloud.

"He is surely back from Coronation at this point."

"I don't see why we needed to land in Chaon when we could have been there already," Zakk said.

"Dear boy, you should know why. Knowledge is power. The best element isn't fire or water or earth—it's surprise. If Eska has no more knowledge of us than what you blundered on the summit of Vatu, then he has no power."

Zakk rubbed his neck, trying to quell his prickled skin. He could still feel the electric jolts crawl down his neck to his spine that the doctor reprimanded him with after failing to remain concealed on Vatu Volcano. Still, Zakk should have known better. He let his want to haunt Zain cloud his mission.

He looked toward Doctor Cere, the man who had saved his life after Zain's betrayal. He knew the old man was right; Doctor Cere's knowledge proved that. Zakk had never seen so many ingenious inventions. To survive the cold, the doctor gave him warmth in the form of a ruby ring. To sneak onto the ship in Epoch and to conceal himself on the Core, Zakk was given another ring that, when in function, would expand into a halo that hovered above his head and bent the light around him, distorting the wearer's image.

334

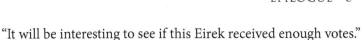

"It will be interesting to see if this Eirek received enough votes."

"Yes."

"Do you think Zain would have received votes?"

Zakk remembered the first time he was told that Zain had been chosen as apprentice after not even winning a single trial. His brows had furrowed and he had punched his leg. He remembered all the questions he posed himself: *Why didn't Zain accept it? How did he win?*

"No. He has never been good with words."

"It is lucky for us that he turned down the position. He has quite the gall to say no to Guardian of the Core. . . ." Doctor Cere looked at him.

A receding hairline circled the doctor's head, and glasses hugged his large nose, shielding his dark-gray eyes. The man wore a white lab coat with the sigil of a black spider located on the left chest. Underneath the lab coat was a black turtleneck that swallowed his neck. Frail cheeks and bony fingers made him seem weaker than he was, and perhaps if it wasn't for the rings adorning his fingers, he would be. Now, though, each of those rings served a purpose: One was used to warm him when he was cold, another to cool him when he was warm, and yet another served to make him invisible whenever he saw fit. The others, Zakk didn't know.

A beeping sound broke the silence that had filtered in. It seemed they had a call coming. Doctor Cere touched a button on the dashboard of his caracraft, accepting the call.

"Are you back to Empora yet?"

Zakk looked at the hologram of Senator Nyom Numos's face. His chins bounced as he talked. When Zakk had stayed with him on the Core, the man had never seemed to be able to open his eyes fully, which surprised Zakk, for he thought the eyeglass he wore would help that.

"No. Coronation would have just ended. We have been traveling from Chaon."

"I do not understand why you go to such lengths."

"To avoid suspicion. And I do not understand how you managed to not obtain the blood and fingerprints of every contestant." There was a rise to Doctor Cere's voice.

"I told you. I received the ones that matter: those who won. Why would I possibly raise suspicion by interviewing those who lost?"

"Because Cain Evber is among those who lost. His prints would have been valuable." The doctor let silence settle in its nest before continuing, "I suppose the damage will be done regardless."

"As long as Zakk managed to implant the device to track Zain's position, everything should go as planned."

"I did," Zakk said.

"You have your shifters in place?" Senator Numos asked.

"They have been in place for years now. We've only needed access to the Core." Doctor Cere smirked.

The first time Zakk had seen shifters was on the night he met Doctor Cere after his plunge into Lake Kilmer. He witnessed rats change into humans armed with knives and swords. From his education at Gazo's, he thought shifters were extinct, being hunted after the Great War for their ability to shape form for hours after a physical touch with humans, or days if they drank their blood.

"Yes, well, I am glad we could arrange some sort of deal." Senator Numos grinned, making his large cheeks look like those of a chipmunk. "I suppose I will see you all in four months, then . . . to avoid suspicion." Senator Numos exaggerated the last part in an obvious attempt to infuriate the doctor.

The connection ended.

"Worthless swine." Doctor Cere snorted.

The Red Cloud that had been just a speck grew larger as they crept closer.

"We will be back home to your new family soon enough." Doctor Cere smirked. He looked at Zakk and readjusted his glasses. "One that won't kill you. One that recognizes your potential. When we take over Ka'Che, Zain's will die. It's only equal."

Zakk looked away to the vastness of greens and mountains to the east. He found his fingers tapping the glass like a piano. "And after that?" he asked. He looked toward the man who found him and saved him at the base of Lake Kilmer after Zain released him.

Doctor Cere didn't answer; all he did was grin, like he held the fate of Gladonus in his hands.

❦ABOUT THE AUTHOR ❦

Michael Thies graduated from the University of Wisconsin-Eau Claire with a Bachelor of Arts degree, double majoring in Creative Writing and Advertising. Only twenty-three himself, he has taken a leap forward in his career as an author with the release of his debut novel, *The Trials of the Core*. When he is not writing he maintains an active and social lifestyle and works as a social media and sales manager at a marketing firm in his hometown of Slinger, Wisconsin. To stay in touch with Michael and receive updates, a monthly newsletter, and exclusive content not featured elsewhere, signup at www.guardianofthecore.com. Don't forget to follow him on Twitter at www.twitter.com/michaelethies.